Jean Rhys

The Collected Short Stories

Jean Rhys

The Collected Short Stories

Introduction by DIANA ATHILL

c. 1

W · W · NORTON & COMPANY

NEW YORK · LONDON

SS

RHYS

First Edition

The text of this book is set in Primer. Display type is Benguiat Book Condensed. Composition and manufacturing are by the Maple-Vail Book Manufacturing Group. Book design by Marjorie J. Flock.

ISBN 0-393-02375-3

W. W. Norton & Company, Inc., 500 Fifth Avenue, New York, N. Y. 10110
W. W. Norton & Company Ltd., 37 Great Russell Street, London WC1B 3NU

1 2 3 4 5 6 7 8 9 0

Contents

Introduction by DIANA ATHILL	vii
Illusion	I
A Spiritualist	6
From a French Prison	10
In a Café	13
Tout Montparnasse and a Lady	16
Mannequin	20
In the Luxemburg Gardens	27
Tea with an Artist	29
Trio	34
Mixing Cocktails	36
Again the Antilles	39
Hunger	42
Discourse of a Lady Standing a Dinner to a Down–and–Out Friend	45
A Night	47
In the Rue de l'Arrivée	50
Learning to Be a Mother	55
The Blue Bird	60
The Grey Day	66
The Sidi	68
At the Villa d'Or	73
La Grosse Fifi	79

Vienne	94
Till September Petronella	125
The Day They Burned the Books	151
Let Them Call It Jazz	158
Tigers Are Better-Looking	176
Outside the Machine	189
The Lotus	210
A Solid House	221
The Sound of the River	236
I Spy a Stranger	242
Temps Perdi	256
Pioneers, Oh, Pioneers	275
Good-bye Marcus, Good-bye Rose	285
The Bishop's Feast	291
Heat	295
Fishy Waters	298
Overture and Beginners Please	312
Before the Deluge	323
On Not Shooting Sitting Birds	328
Kikimora	331
Night Out 1925	335
The Chevalier of the Place Blanche	341
The Insect World	350
Rapunzel, Rapunzel	361
Who Knows What's Up in the Attic?	366
Sleep It Off Lady	375
I Used to Live Here Once	387
Kismet	389
The Whistling Bird	396
Invitation to the Dance	401

Introduction

THESE STORIES fall into three groups: up to page
124, early work, written before Jean Rhys's first novel; from page
125 to page 275, stories written, or completed, in the sixties (some
of them were probably begun a good deal earlier); from page 275
to the end, stories written, or completed, when she was an old
woman.

She published the first group in 1927 under the title *The Left
Bank*. Like all her work, these stories relate closely to her own
experience: she was teaching herself, as she wrote them, how to
turn personal experience into something of value to other people.
They contain touches of self-consciousness (the last line of
"Hunger," for example) which she never allowed herself in her
later work, and an occasional cuteness (like calling Miss Dufreyne, in "In the Rue de l'Arrivée," "the Lady," which is the sort
of thing she came to detest). But this does not prevent Miss Dufreyne's being an accurate self-portrait. What Jean Rhys had to
say and how she said it had not yet blended into the clarity and
simplicity of her mature style, but the process was on its way.

She had lived in the Caribbean until she was sixteen; in
England (which disappointed and frightened her) until she was
twenty-nine; and then in 1919 had married a Dutchman called
Jean Lenglet and had gone with him to Paris. At first she was
happy there. She had escaped from the cold-eyed English and
her sense of herself as despised by them for being an ignorant
"colonial," and the relief was intoxicating. She was able to look

out at what surrounded her and take little "snapshots" of it with a light heart. But only too soon things began to go wrong. The Lenglets never had enough money; her first child died when he was about three weeks old (although her story about his birth leaves this unsaid); and Lenglet's too-good-to-be-true job in Vienna really was too good to be true—it took him into a French prison, and how it did so is recorded in the marvellous story "Vienne." Fear, loneliness, cruelty—these became her subjects. She struggled to treat them defiantly, even jauntily, and learnt as she did so that this was a mistake. The essential thing was to treat them truthfully: to write in a "voice" as near that of natural speech as possible, and to tell how things really were. Which meant, of course, how things were for her: *a* truth, not *the* truth—the latter being something which no honest person can claim to tell.

Jean Rhys's truth was that of a woman who was no good at managing life—so inept in practical matters that circumstances which would have been difficult for anyone were crushing for her—and who suffered from a tendency to be paranoid. She was well aware of this tendency, but used to say "When people are paranoid you can bet your life they have something to be paranoid *about.*" Which is true—but then, so has everyone. The difference is that the robust psyche confronted with—say—a touch of suspicion or dislike on the part of a new acquaintance, will either disregard it because this new person is unimportant in her or his life, or will take it for granted that it will change to friendliness as the acquaintance deepens. The "person who is paranoid," on the other hand, will see only the suspicion or dislike—will magnify it—and will very often, in consequence, behave in such a way that the hostile feelings are confirmed and increased. This unhappy condition was one into which Jean could easily slip, and it colours many of the substantial stories of her middle period.

Yet these are, without question, her best stories. There are times when she allows her paranoia to colour what she writes too luridly (in "Outside the Machine," for example, the crude beast-

liness of the women who turn on the patient who attempts sui-
cide is portrayed with a kind of fierce relish, while the narrator is
curiously remote in describing the unexpected kindness of old
Madame Tavernier). But usually Jean Rhys is seeing the character who represents herself as impartially as everything else in
the story, and therefore persuades us that the whole thing did,
indeed, happen just like that. Reading her, we understand that
we deceive ourselves when we hope that the powerless are not
despised and pushed aside; we understand the devices by which
they manage to survive (which include humour—witness "Tigers
are Better-Looking": there is more humour in Jean Rhys's observation of life than is usually recognised). And these sad stories
are told—here is where the spell they cast comes in—in a voice
of great charm. Jean *was* charming. I knew her only for the last
fifteen years of her life, but even as an old woman her voice, her
look, her manner, her way of laughing until the tears ran down
her face, made her unusually attractive. Because she had learnt
to pare everything extraneous away from her prose, it expressed
the essence of how she saw things—and therefore, the essence
of how she was. Which makes it quite mysteriously charming,
given the melancholy nature of what is being described.

Some of the late stories are very small, because she was too
old and weary to take on anything bigger. She would attempt
only what she knew she could do—but what she could do, she
still did right. And there are two stories in this group which are
extraordinary: "Who Knows What's Up in the Attic" and "Sleep
It Off, Lady." Who else has reported back from the frontier of old
age with such clarity, speaking truthfully about being old in the
voice of the young person who continues to inhabit all of us for
so long as we hold onto full awareness?

Of the three hitherto uncollected stories, "Kismet" is a welcome retrieval from Jean's "chorus line" days, but the other two
make me feel sad. These two little fragments from her last years
mark the point at which her strength began to fail, and she could
no longer quite bring off what she was trying to do. But to end

Jean Rhys

The Collected Short Stories

Illusion

MISS BRUCE was quite an old inhabitant of the Quarter. For seven years she had lived there, in a little studio up five flights of stairs. She had painted portraits, exhibited occasionally at the Salon. She had even sold a picture sometimes – a remarkable achievement for Montparnasse, but possible, for I believe she was just clever enough and not too clever, though I am no judge of these matters.

She was a tall, thin woman, with large bones and hands and feet. One thought of her as a shining example of what character and training – British character and training – can do. After seven years in Paris she appeared utterly untouched, utterly unaffected, by anything hectic, slightly exotic or unwholesome. Going on all the time all round her were the cult of beauty and the worship of physical love: she just looked at her surroundings in her healthy, sensible way, and then dismissed them from her thoughts . . . rather like some sturdy rock with impotent blue waves washing round it.

When pretty women passed her in the streets or sat near her in restaurants she would look appraisingly with the artist's eye, and make a suitably critical remark. She exhibited no tinge of curiosity or envy. As for the others, the petites femmes, anxiously consulting the mirrors of their bags, anxiously and searchingly looking round with darkened eyelids: 'Those unfortunate people!' would say Miss Bruce. Not in a hard way, but broadmindedly, breezily: indeed with a thoroughly gentlemanly intonation. . . . Those unfortunate little people!

She always wore a neat serge dress in the summer and a neat tweed costume in the winter, brown shoes with low heels and cotton stockings. When she was going to parties she put on a black gown of *crêpe de chine,* just well enough cut, not extravagantly pretty.

In fact Miss Bruce was an exceedingly nice woman.

She powdered her nose as a concession to Paris; the rest of her face shone, beautifully washed, in the sunlight or the electric light as the case might be, with here and there a few rather lovable freckles.

She had, of course, like most of the English and American artists in Paris, a private income – a respectably large one, I believe. She knew most people and was intimate with nobody. We had been dining and lunching together, now and then, for two years, yet I only knew the outside of Miss Bruce – the cool sensible, tidy English outside.

Well, we had an appointment on a hot, sunny afternoon, and I arrived to see her about three o'clock. I was met by a very perturbed concierge.

Mademoiselle had been in bed just one day, and, suddenly, last night about eight o'clock the pain had become terrible. The *femme de ménage,* 'Mame' Pichon who had stayed all day and she, the concierge, had consulted anxiously, had fetched a doctor and, at his recommendation, had had her conveyed to the English Hospital in an ambulance.

'She took nothing with her,' said the *femme de ménage,* a thin and voluble woman. 'Nothing at all, *pauvre* Mademoiselle.' If Madame – that was me – would give herself the trouble to come up to the studio, here were the keys. I followed Madame Pichon up the stairs. I must go at once to Miss Bruce and take her some things. She must at least have nightgowns and a comb and brush.

'The keys of the wardrobe of Mademoiselle,' said Madame Pichon insinuatingly, and with rather a queer sidelong look at me, 'are in this small drawer. Ah, *les voilà!'*

I thanked her with a dismissing manner. Madame Pichon was not a favourite of mine, and with firmness I watched her walk slowly to the door, try to start a conversation, and then, very reluctantly, disappear. Then I turned to the wardrobe – a big, square solid piece of old, dark furniture, suited for the square and solid coats and skirts of Miss Bruce. Indeed, most of her furniture was big and square. Some strain in her made her value solidity and worth more than grace or fantasies. It was difficult to turn the large key, but I managed it at last.

'Good Lord!' I remarked out loud. Then, being very much surprised I sat down on a chair and said: 'Well, what a funny girl!'

For Miss Bruce's wardrobe when one opened it was a glow of colour, a riot of soft silks . . . everything that one did not expect.

In the middle, hanging in the place of honour, was an evening dress of a very beautiful shade of old gold: near it another of flame colour: of two black dresses the one was touched with silver, the other with a jaunty embroidery of emerald and blue. There were a black and white check with a jaunty belt, a flowered *crêpe de chine* – positively flowered! – then a carnival costume complete with mask, then a huddle, a positive huddle of all colours, of all stuffs.

For one instant I thought of kleptomania, and dismissed the idea. Dresses for models, then? Absurd! Who would spend thousands of francs on dresses for models. . . . No nightgowns here, in any case.

As I looked, hesitating, I saw in the corner a box without a lid. It contained a neat little range of smaller boxes: Rouge Fascination; Rouge Manadarine; Rouge Andalouse; several powders; kohl for the eyelids and paint for the eyelashes – an outfit for a budding Manon Lescaut. Nothing was missing: there were scents too.

I shut the door hastily. I had no business to look or to guess. But I guessed. I knew. Whilst I opened the other half of the wardrobe and searched the shelves for nightgowns I knew it all: Miss Bruce, passing by a shop, with the perpetual hunger to be beautiful and that thirst to be loved which is the real curse of Eve, well hidden under her neat dress, more or less stifled, more or less unrecognized.

Miss Bruce had seen a dress and had suddenly thought: in that dress perhaps. . . . And, immediately afterwards: why not? And had entered the shop, and, blushing slightly, had asked the price. That had been the first time: an accident, an impulse.

The dress must have been disappointing, yet beautiful enough, becoming enough to lure her on. Then must have begun the search for *the* dress, the perfect Dress, beautiful, beautifying, possible to be worn. And lastly, the search for illusion – a craving, almost a vice, the stolen waters and the bread eaten in secret of Miss Bruce's life.

Wonderful moment! When the new dress would arrive and would emerge smiling and graceful from its tissue paper.

'Wear me, give me life,' it would seem to say to her, 'and I will do my damnedest for you!' And first, not unskilfully, for was she not a portrait painter? Miss Bruce would put on the powder, the Rouge Fascination, the rouge for her lips, lastly the dress – and she would gaze into the glass at a transformed self. She would sleep that night with a warm glow at her heart. No impossible thing, beauty and all that beauty brings. There close at hand, to be clutched if one dared. Somehow she never dared, next morning.

I thankfully seized a pile of nightgowns and sat down, rather miserably undecided. I knew she would hate me to have seen those dresses: 'Mame' Pichon would tell her that I had been to the armoire. But she must have her nightgowns. I went to lock the wardrobe doors and felt a sudden, irrational pity for the beautiful things inside. I imagined them, shrugging their silken shoulders, rustling, whispering about the *anglaise* who had dared to buy them in order to condemn them to life in the dark. . . . And I opened the door again.

The yellow dress appeared malevolent, slouching on its hanger; the black ones were mournful, only the little chintz frock smiled gaily, waiting for the supple body and limbs that should breathe life into it.

When I was allowed to see Miss Bruce a week afterwards I found her lying, clean, calm and sensible in the big ward – an appendicitis patient. They patched her up and two or three weeks later we dined together at our restaurant. At the coffee stage she said suddenly: 'I suppose you noticed my collection of frocks. Why should I not collect frocks? They fascinate me. The colour and all that. Exquisite sometimes!'

Of course, she added, carefully staring over my head at what appeared to me to be a very bad picture, 'I should never make such a fool of myself as to wear them. . . . They ought to be worn, I suppose.'

A plump, dark girl, near us, gazed into the eyes of her dark, plump escort, and lit a cigarette with the slightly affected movements of a non-smoker.

'Not bad hands and arms, that girl,' said Miss Bruce in her gentlemanly manner.

A Spiritualist

I ASSURE YOU,' said the Commandant, 'that I adore women – that without a woman in my life I cannot exist.'

'But one must admit that one has deceptions. They are frankly disappointing, or else they exact so much that the day comes when, inevitably, one asks oneself: Is it worth while?'

'In any case it cracks. It always cracks.'

He fixed his monocle more firmly into his eye to look at a passing lady, with an expression like that of an amiable and cynical old fox.

'And it is my opinion, Madame, that that is the fault of the woman. All the misunderstandings, all the quarrels! It is astonishing how gentle, how easily fooled most men are. Even an old Parisian like myself, Madame. . . . I assure you that of all men the Parisians are the most sentimental. And it is astonishing how lacking in calm and balance is the most clever woman, how prone to weep at a wrong moment – in a word, how exhausting!'

'For instance: A few months ago I was obliged to break with a most charming little friend whom I passionately adored. Because she exaggerated her eccentricity. One must be in the movement, even though one may regret in one's heart the more agreeable epoch that has vanished. A little eccentricity is permissible. It is indeed *chic*. Yes, it is now chic to be eccentric. But when it came to taking me to a chemist and forcing me to buy her ether, which she took at once in the restaurant where we dined: and then hanging her legs out of the taxi window in the middle of the

Boulevard: you will understand that I was *gêné:* that I found that she exaggerated. In the middle of the Boulevard!'

'Most unfortunately one can count no longer on women, even Frenchwomen, to be dignified, to have a certain *tenue.* I remember the time when things were different. And more agreeable, I think.'

The Commandant gazed into the distance, and his expression became sentimental. His eyes were light blue. He even blushed.

'Once I was happy with a woman. Only once. I will tell you about it. Her name was Madeleine, and she was a little dancer whom some *sale individu* had deserted when she was without money and ill. She was the most sweet and gentle woman I have ever met. I knew her for two years, and we never quarrelled once or even argued. Never. For Madeleine gave way in everything. . . . And to think that my wife so often accused me of having a *sale caractère.* . . .'

He mused for a while.

'A *sale caractère.* . . . Perhaps I have. But Madeleine was of a sweetness . . . ah, well, she died suddenly after two years. She was only twenty-eight.'

'When she died I was sad as never in my life before. The poor little one. . . . Only twenty-eight!'

'Three days after the funeral her mother, who was a very good woman, wrote to me saying that she wished to have the clothes and the effects, you understand, of her daughter. So in the afternoon I went to her little flat, Place de L'Odéon, fourth floor. I took my housekeeper with me, for a woman can be useful with her advice on these occasions.'

'I went straight into the bedroom and I began to open the cupboards and arrange her dresses. I wished to do that myself. I had the tears in my eyes, I assure you, for it is sad to see and to touch the dresses of a dead woman that one has loved. My housekeeper, Gertrude, she went into the kitchen to arrange the household utensils.'

'Well, suddenly, there came from the closed sitting-room a

very loud, a terrible crash. The floor shook.'

'Gertrude and I both called out at the same time: What is that? And she ran to me from the kitchen saying that the noise had come from the salon. I said: Something has fallen down, and I opened quickly the sitting-room door.'

'You must understand that it was a flat on the fourth floor; all the windows of the sitting-room were tightly shut, naturally, and the blinds were drawn as I had left them on the day of the funeral. The door into the hall was locked, the other led into the bedroom where I was.'

'And, there, lying right in the middle of the floor was a block of white marble, perhaps fifty centimeters square.'

'Gertrude said: *Mon Dieu*, Monsieur, look at that. How did that get here? – Her face was pale as death. – It was not there, she said, when we came.'

'As for me, I just looked at the thing, stupefied.'

'Gertrude crossed herself and said: I am going. Not for anything: for nothing in the world would I stay here longer. There is something strange about this flat.'

'She ran. I – well, I did not run. I walked out, but very quickly. You understand, I have been a soldier for twenty-five years, and, God knows, I had nothing to reproach myself with with regard to the poor little one. But it shakes the nerves – something like that.'

The Commandant lowered his voice.

'The fact was, I understood. I knew what she meant.'

'I had promised her a beautiful, white marble tombstone, and I had not yet ordered it. Not because I had not thought of it. Oh, no – but because I was too sad, too tired. But the little one doubtless thought that I had forgotten. It was her way of reminding me.'

I looked hard at the Commandant. His eyes were clear and as naïve as a child's: a little dim with emotion. . . . Silence. . . . He lit a cigarette.

'Well, to show how strange women are: I recounted this to a-lady I knew, not long ago. And she laughed. Laughed! You

understand. . . . *Un fou rire.* . . . And do you know what she said:
    'She said: How furious that poor Madeleine must have been
that she missed you!'
    'Now can you imagine the droll ideas that women can have!'

From a French Prison

THE OLD MAN and the little boy were the last of the queue of people waiting to show their permits and to be admitted to the *parloir* – a row of little boxes where on certain days prisoners may speak to their friends through a grating for a quarter of an hour.

The old man elbowed his way weakly, but with persistence, to the front, and when the warder shouted at him brutally to go back to his place he still advanced.

The warder yelled: 'Go back, I tell you. Don't you understand me? You are not French?' The old man shook his head. 'One sees that,' the warder said sarcastically. He gave him a push and the old man, puzzled, backed a few steps and leaned against the wall, waiting.

He had gentle, regular features, and a grey cropped moustache. He was miserably clothed, hatless, with a red scarf knotted round his neck. His eyes were clouded with a white film, the film one sees over the eyes of those threatened with blindness.

The little boy was very little; his arms and legs matchlike. He held tightly on to the old man's hand and looked up at the warder with enormous brown eyes. There were several children in the queue.

One woman had brought two – a baby in her arms and another hanging on to her skirt. All the crowd was silent and overawed. The women stood with bent heads, glancing furtively at each other, not with the antagonism usual in women, but as if at companions.

From the foot of the staircase leading down from the room in which they waited, ran a very long whitewashed corridor, incredibly grim, and dark in spite of the whitewash. Here and there a warder sat close against the wall looking in its shadow like a huge spider – a bloated, hairy insect born of the darkness and of the dank smell.

There were very few men waiting, and nearly all the women were of the sort that trouble has whipped into a becoming meekness, but two girls near the staircase were painted and dressed smartly in bright colours. They laughed and talked, their eyes dark and defiant. One of them muttered: *'Sale flic, va'* – as who should say: 'Let him be, you dirty cop!' when the warder had pushed the old man.

The queue looked frightened but pleased: an old woman like a rat huddled against the wall and chuckled. The warder balanced himself backwards and forwards from heel to toe, important and full of authority, like some petty god. There he was, the representative of honesty, of the law, of the stern forces of Good that punishes Evil. His forehead was low and barred by a perpetual frown, his jaw was heavy and protruding. A tall man, well set up. He looked with interest at the girl who had spoken, twirled his moustache and stuck his chest out. The queue waited patiently.

The *parloir* was like a row of telephone boxes without tops.

Along the platform overhead one saw the legs of yet another warder, marching backwards and forwards, listening to the conversations beneath him. The voices all sounded on one note – a monotonous and never-ending buzz.

The first warder looked at his watch and began to fling all the doors open with ferocious bangs. A stream of rather startled-looking people poured out, their visits over. He beckoned to the queue for others to come forward and take their places. He called the dark-eyed girl who had spoken, staring hard at her as she passed, but she was busy, looking into her mirror, powdering her face, preparing for her interview.

To the opposite door of each box came a prisoner, gripping on to the bars, straining forward to see his visitor and starting at every sound. For the quarter of an hour would seem terribly short to him and always he listened for the shout of the warder to summon him away and always he feared not being on the alert to answer it.

The monotonous buzz of conversation began again. The warder on the roof sighed and then yawned; the warder outside twirled his moustache and stared at the wall. Then a fresh stream with permits came up the stairs and he tramped forward weightily to marshal them into line.

When the quarter of an hour was over the doors were flung open again.

As the dark-eyed girl passed out the warder stared hard at her and she stared back, not giving an inch, defiant and provocative. He half smiled and actually drew back to let her pass.

The old man came last, shuffling along, more bewildered than ever. At the gate of the prison all the permits must be given up, but he trailed out unheeding. The important person who was taking those documents shouted: 'Hé! your permit!' and added: 'Monsieur,' with cynicism. The old man looked frightened, his eyes filled with tears, and when his permit was snatched from him he burst into a flood of words, waving his arms.

A woman stopped to explain to him that if he asked for it next visiting day it would be given back to him, but he did not understand.

'*Allons, Allons*,' said the warder at the gate authoritatively. 'Get along. Get along.'

Outside the people hurried to catch the tram back to Paris.

The two girls stepped out jauntily, with animated gestures and voices, but the old man walked sadly, his head bent, muttering to himself. By his side the little boy took tiny little trotting steps – three to the old man's one. His mouth drooped, his huge brown eyes stared solemnly at an incomprehensible world.

In a Café

THE FIVE MUSICIANS played every evening in the café from nine to twelve. 'Concert! The best music in the Quarter,' the placard outside announced. They sat near the door, and at every woman who came in the violinist, who was small and sentimental, would glance quickly and as it were hopefully. A comprehensive glance, running from the ankles upwards. But the pianist usually spent the intervals turning over his music morosely or sounding melancholy chords. When he played all the life seemed to leave his white indifferent face and find its home in his flying hands. The cellist was a fat, jolly, fair person who took life as it came; the remaining two were nondescripts, or perhaps merely seemed so, because they sat in the background. The five played everything from 'La Belotte' upwards and onwards into the serene classic heights of Beethoven and Massenet! Competent musicians; middle-aged, staid; they went wonderfully well with the café.

It was respectably full that evening. Stout business men drank beer and were accompanied by neat women in neat hats; temperamental gentlemen in shabby hats drank *fines à l'eau* beside temperamental ladies who wore turbans and drank *menthes* of striking emerald. There were as many foreigners as is usual. The peaceful atmosphere of the room conduced to quiet and philosophic conversations, the atmosphere of a place that always had been and always would be, the dark leather benches symbols of something perpetual and unchanging, the waiters, who were all old, ambling round with drinks or blotters, as if they had done nothing else since the beginnings of time and would be content so to do till the day of Judgment. The only vividnesses in the café, the only spots of unrest, were the pictures exposed for sale, and the rows of liqueur bottles in tiers above the counter of the bar, traditional bottles of bright colours and disturbingly graceful shapes.

Into the midst of this peace stepped suddenly a dark-haired, stoutish gentleman in evening dress. He announced that the Management had engaged him to sing. He stood smiling mechanically, waiting for silence, gracefully poised on one foot like the flying Hermes. His chest well out, his stomach well in, one hand raised with the thumb and middle finger meeting, he looked self-confident, eager and extraordinarily vulgar.

Silence was long in coming; when it did he cleared his throat and announced: *'Chanson: Les Grues de Paris!'* in a high tenor voice, *'Les Grues!'* The pianist began the accompaniment with its banal, moving imitation of passion.

The *grues* are the sellers of illusion of Paris the frail and sometimes pretty ladies, and Paris is sentimental and indulgent towards them. That, in the mass and theoretically of course, not always practically or to individuals. The song had three verses. The first told the pathetic story of the making of a *grue;* the second told of her virtues, her charity, her warm-heartedness, her practical sympathy; the third, of the abominable ingratitude that was her requital. The hero of the song, having married and begun to found a family, passes the heroine, reduced to the uttermost misery and, turning his head aside, remarks virtuously to his wife: 'What matter, it is only a gru . . . u . . . er!'

The canaille, as the third verse points out, to forget the numberless times on which she had ministered to his necessities!

All the women there looked into their mirrors during the progress of the song: most of them rouged their lips. The men stopped reading their newspapers, drank up their beers thirstily and looked sideways. There was a subtle change in the café, and when the song finished the applause was tumultuous.

The singer came forward with his dancing, tiptoe step to sell copies of his song. . . . *'Les Grue. . . . Les grues de Paris! . . .* One franc!'

'Give me two,' she said with calm self-assurance.

The pianist chalked on a little black-board and hung up for all the world to see the next number of the orchestra.

'Mommer loves Popper. Popper loves Mommer. *Chanson Américaine. Demandé.*'

Peace descended again on the café.

Tout Montparnasse
and a Lady

AT TEN O'CLOCK of a Saturday evening the ordinary clients of the little Bal Musette in the rue St. Jacques – the men in caps and the hatless girls – begin to drift out one by one. Those who are inclined to linger are tactfully pressed to leave by the proprietor, a thin anxious little man with a stout placid wife. The place is now hired and reserved, for every Saturday evening the Anglo-Saxon section of Tout Montparnasse comes to dance here.

In half an hour's time the fenced-off dancing floor is filled by couples dancing with the slightly strained expressions characteristic of the Anglo-Saxon who, though wishing to enjoy himself, is not yet sufficiently primed to let himself become animated. So even the best dancers look tense and grim though they sway and glide with great skill and have the concentrated air of people engaged in some difficult but extremely important gymnastic exercise.

Most of the men are young, thin, willowy; carefully picturesque and temperamental, they wear jerseys or shirts open at the neck. Most of the women are not so young, with that tendency to be thick about the ankles and incongruous about the shoes, which is nearly always to be found in the really intelligent woman.

For they are very intelligent, all these people. They paint, they write, they express themselves in innumerable ways. It is Chelsea, London, with a large dash of Greenwich Village, New York, to liven it, and a slight sprinkling of Moscow, Christiania and even of Paris to give incongruous local colourings. The musicians are in a tiny gallery, a concertina, a banjo and a violin – the concertina, a gay soul who winks and smiles violently at every woman whose eye he can catch. At the door sit watchfully two little French policemen with enormous moustaches. After each dance *tout Montparnasse* sits at the little tables in the body of the hall or stands at the pewter covered bar and drinks *fine à l'eau* – a surprisingly weak *fine*. Nevertheless, as the evening progresses they grow gayer and gayer. . . . And more outspoken. . . .

Thus one evening a very romantic lady, an American fashion artist, who was there to be thrilled, after having read the *Trilby* of du Maurier, and the novels of Francis Carco, which tell of the lives of the apaches of to-day, expressed her candid opinion of a supposed Dope Fiend who sat in a corner, glassy eyed, his head against the wall, his face of an extreme pallor. He was as a matter of fact a very hard-working and on the whole abstemious portrait-painter, who, having been struck with an inspiration for his next picture, was merely gazing into infinity with the happy intenseness of one about to grasp a beautiful vision.

'*Why* bring people like that?' she inquired hotly. 'Why?' She went on to explain how easy it is to be broad-minded and perfectly respectable, to combine art, passion, cleanliness, efficiency and an eye to the main chance. 'But one must know where to draw the line. *That* is an instance of how not to do it!'

Sipping her third artificial lemonade she gazed with an intense reproof at the pallid gentleman. Suddenly he glared back. He was suspecting her of taking mental notes of him for journalistic purposes or perhaps, oh horror, of having designs upon his peace of mind. He rose, shook himself, and thus disturbed in his musings, lamented:

'Oh, God! How I hate women who write! How I *hate* them!' in an agreeable voice.

Someone now enlightened the romantic lady as to the distinction and sobriety of her late victim, and thus robbed of her thrill, over her fourth lemonade she began to yearn for the free life of

the Apache and to wish that some of the original clients of the
Bal Musette had stayed. . . . There had been a dark man in a red
muffler, his cap well down over his eyes. . . . Or a girl in a check
dress with something about the way her hair grew. And the air
with which she wore her shabby frock and walked had been
graceful . . . exciting. . . . Provocative! . . . The brain groped vaguely
for the word. Melancholy descended upon that romantic fashion
artist, and discontent with her *milieu*. In her youth she had considered herself meant for higher things! . . . Artificial lemonade
of the sort supplied at the Bal Musette is greatly conducive to
melancholy.

'I don't get any *kick* out of Anglo-Saxons,' she said out loud.
'They don't. . . . They *don't* . . . stimulate my imagination!'

Nobody listened to her and upon her the infinite sadness of
the world descended.

At a quarter to one the music stopped and *tout Montparnasse*
by this time very lively indeed ordered its last drink at the bar
preparatory to drifting on elsewhere.

The romantic lady finished her sixth lemonade and then per-
ceived her *ci-devant Dope Fiend*.

Solitary at the end of the room he sat, one long thin arm clasp-
ing his pallid head, his body drooping complicatedly over a little
table top, his face expressive of the uttermost dejection, the
uttermost remorse.

Inspiration came to the romantic lady. She had been told that
this was a successful and respectable portrait-painter as she was
a successful and respectable fashion artist. . . . He like herself
must now despise his success and must mourn for the higher
ideals of his youth. . . . Though he was very young!

Then . . . Here was a kindred spirit. Here was someone else
who, at one o'clock in the morning at a Bal Musette in Montparnasse, saw the empty grimness of life. Saw it! Knew he would
never express it – and despaired. It is thus that, fortified by artificial lemonade, the romantic mind moves.

She drifted across the room, put a hand on his melancholy
shoulder and murmured:

'You are sad! I am so sorry! I understand!'

The young man lifted a heavy head and blinked several times. Smiling in a vaguely happy way, for although normally abstemious, on a Saturday night he could condescend like others, he looked at the lady. Then, recognizing her, panic came into his eyes and he looked wildly round as if for help.

'I!' he exclaimed indignantly. 'I'm happy as a sandboy!'

From a little distance a friend swooped on him, heaved him up, said in a bored and patient voice: '*Come on*, Guy!' and marched him efficiently away. From the back he looked like a helpless, lovable child being led away by its nurse. The tragic lady sighed and made ready to depart. The proprietor served a last Porto to the remaining few. The Saturday dance of Tout Montparnasse was over.

Mannequin

TWELVE O'CLOCK. *Déjuener chez* Jeanne Veron, Place Vendôme.

Anna, dressed in the black cotton, chemise-like garment of the mannequin off duty was trying to find her way along dark passages and down complicated flights of stairs to the underground from where lunch was served.

She was shivering, for she had forgotten her coat, and the garment that she wore was very short, sleeveless, displaying her rose-coloured stockings to the knee. Her hair was flamingly and honestly red; her eyes, which were very gentle in expression, brown and heavily shadowed with kohl, her face small and pale under its professional rouge. She was fragile, like a delicate child, her arms pathetically thin. It was to her legs that she owed this dazzling, this incredible opportunity.

Madame Veron, white-haired with black eyes, incredibly distinguished, who had given them one sweeping glance, the glance of the connoisseur, smiled imperiously and engaged her at an exceedingly small salary. As a beginner, Madame explained, Anna could not expect more. She was to wear the *jeune fille* dresses. Another smile, another sharp glance.

Anne was conducted from the Presence by an underling who helped her to take off the frock she had worn temporarily for the interview. Aspirants for an engagement are always dressed in a model of the house.

She had spent yesterday afternoon in a delirium tempered by a feeling of exaggerated reality, and in buying the necessary make up. It had been such a forlorn hope, answering the advertisement.

The morning had been dreamlike. At the back of the wonderful decorated salons she had found an unexpected sombreness; the place, empty, would have been dingy and melancholy, countless puzzling corridors and staircases, a rabbit warren and a labyrinth. She despaired of ever finding her way.

In the mannequins' dressing-room she spent a shy hour making up her face – in an extraordinary and distinctive atmosphere of slimness and beauty; white arms and faces vivid with rouge; raucous voices and the smell of cosmetics; silken lingerie. Coldly critical glances were bestowed upon Anna's reflection in the glass. None of them looked at her directly. . . . A depressing room, taken by itself, bare and cold, a very inadequate conservatory for these human flowers. Saleswomen in black rushed in and out, talking in sharp voices; a very old woman hovered, helpful and shapeless, showing Anna where to hang her clothes, presenting to her the black garment that Anna was wearing, going to lunch. She smiled with professional motherliness, her little, sharp, black eyes travelling rapidly from *la nouvelle*'s hair to her ankles and back again.

She was Madame Pecard, the dresser.

Before Anna had spoken a word she was called away by a small boy in buttons to her destination in one of the salons: there, under the eye of a *vendeuse*, she had to learn the way to wear the innocent and springlike air and garb of the *juene fille*. Behind a yellow, silken screen she was hustled into a leather coat and paraded under the cold eyes of an American buyer. This was the week when the spring models are shown to important people from big shops all over Europe and America: the most critical week of the season. . . . The American buyer said that he would have that, but with an inch on to the collar and larger cuffs. In vain the saleswoman, in her best English with its odd Chicago accent, protested that that would completely ruin the chic of the model. The American buyer knew what he wanted and saw that he got it.

The *vendeuse* sighed, but there was a note of admiration in her voice. She respected Americans: they were not like the English, who, under a surface of annoying moroseness of manner, were notoriously timid and easy to turn round your finger.

'Was that all right?' Behind the screen one of the saleswomen smiled encouragingly and nodded. The other shrugged her shoulders. She had small, close-set eyes, a long thin nose and tight lips of the regulation puce colour. Behind her silken screen Anna sat on a high white stool. She felt that she appeared charming and troubled. The white and gold of the salon suited her red hair.

A short morning. For the mannequin's day begins at ten and the process of making up lasts an hour. The friendly saleswoman volunteered the information that her name was Jeannine, that she was in the lingerie, that she considered Anna *rudement jolie*, that noon was Anna's lunch hour. She must go down the corridor and up those stairs, through the big salon then. . . . Anyone would tell her. But Anna, lost in the labyrinth, was too shy to ask her way. Besides, she was not sorry to have time to brace herself for the ordeal. She had reached the regions of utility and oilcloth: the decorative salons were far overhead. Then the smell of food – almost visible, it was so cloud-like and heavy – came to her nostrils, and high-noted, and sibilant, a buzz of conversation made her draw a deep breath. She pushed a door open.

She was in a big, very low-ceilinged room, all the floor space occupied by long wooden tables with no cloths. . . . She was sitting at the mannequin's table, gazing at a thick and hideous white china plate, a twisted tin fork, a wooden-handled stained knife, a tumbler so thick it seemed unbreakable.

There were twelve mannequins at Jeanne Veron's: six of them were lunching, the others still paraded, goddess-like, till their turn came for test and refreshment. Each of the twelve was a distinct and separate type: each of the twelve knew her type and kept to it, practising rigidly in clothing, manner, voice and conversation.

Round the austere table were now seated Babette, the *gamine*, the traditional blonde *enfant;* Mona, tall and darkly beautiful, the *femme fatale,* the wearer of sumptuous evening gowns. Georgette was the *garçonne;* Simone with green eyes Anna knew instantly for a cat whom men would and did adore, a sleek, white, purring, long-lashed creature. . . . Eliane was the star of the collection.

Eliane was frankly ugly and it did not matter: no doubt Lilith, from whom she was obviously descended, had been ugly too. Her hair was henna-tinted, her eyes small and black, her complexion bad under her thick make-up. Her hips were extraordinarily slim, her hands and feet exquisite, every movement she made was as graceful as a flower's in the wind. Her walk. . . . But it was her walk which made her the star there and earned her a salary quite fabulous for Madame Veron's, where large salaries were not the rule. . . . Her walk and her 'chic of the devil' which lit an expression of admiration in even the cold eyes of American buyers.

Eliane was a quiet girl, pleasant-mannered. She wore a ring with a beautiful emerald on one long, slim finger, and in her small eyes were both intelligence and mystery.

Madame Pecard, the dresser, was seated at the head of the mannequins' table, talking loudly, unlistened to, and gazing benevolently at her flock.

At other tables sat the sewing girls, pale-faced, black-frocked – the workers heroically gay, but with the stamp of labour on them: and the saleswomen. The mannequins, with their sensual, blatant charms and their painted faces were watched covertly, envied and apart.

Babette the blond *enfant* was next to Anna, and having started the conversation with a few good, round oaths at the quality of the sardines, announced proudly that she could speak English and knew London very well. She began to tell Anna the history of her adventures in the city of coldness, dark and fogs. . . . She had gone to a job as a mannequin in Bond Street and the villainous proprietor of the shop having tried to make love to her and she being rigidly virtuous, she had left. And another job, Anna must figure to herself, had been impossible to get, for she, Babette, was too small and slim for the Anglo-Saxon idea of a mannequin.

She stopped to shout in a loud voice to the woman who was serving: '*Hé*, my old one, don't forget your little Babette. . . .'

Opposite, Simone the cat and the sportive Georgette were having a low-voiced conversation about the tristeness of a monsieur of their acquaintance. 'I said to him,' Georgette finished decisively, 'Nothing to be done, my rabbit. You have not looked at me well, little one. In my place would you not have done the same?'

She broke off when she realized that the others were listening, and smiled in a friendly way at Anna.

She too, it appeared, had ambitions to go to London because the salaries were so much better there. Was it difficult? Did they really like French girls? Parisiennes?

The conversation became general.

'The English boys are nice,' said Babette, winking one divinely candid eye. 'I had a chic type who used to take me to dinner at the Empire Palace. Oh, a pretty boy . . .'

'It is the most chic restaurant in London,' she added importantly.

The meal reached the stage of dessert. The other tables were gradually emptying; the mannequins all ordered very strong coffee, several liqueur. Only Mona and Eliane remained silent; Eliane, because she was thinking of something else; Mona, because it was her type, her genre to be haughty.

Her hair swept away from her white, narrow forehead and her small ears: her long earrings nearly touching her shoulders, she sipped her coffee with a disdainful air. Only once, when the blonde *enfant*, having engaged in a passage of arms with the waitress and got the worst of it, was momentarily discomfited and silent, Mona narrowed her eyes and smiled an astonishingly cruel smile.

As soon as her coffee was drunk she got up and went out.

Anna produced a cigarette, and Georgette, perceiving instantly that here was the sportive touch, her genre, asked for one and lit it with a devil-may-care air. Anna eagerly passed her cigarettes round, but the *Mère* Pecard interfered weightily. It was against the rules of the house for the mannequins to smoke, she wheezed.

The girls all lit their cigarettes and smoked. The *Mère* Pecard rumbled on: 'A caprice, my children. All the world knows that mannequins are capricious. Is it not so?' She appealed to the rest of the room.

As they went out Babette put her arm round Anna's waist and whispered: 'Don't answer Madame Pecard. We don't like her. We never talk to her. She spies on us. She is a camel.'

That afternoon Anna stood for an hour to have a dress draped on her. She showed this dress to a stout Dutch lady buying for the Hague, to a beautiful South American with pearls, to a silver-haired American gentleman who wanted an evening cape for his daughter of seventeen, and to a hook-nosed, odd English lady of title who had a loud voice and dressed, under her furs, in a grey jersey and stout boots.

The American gentleman approved of Anna, and said so, and Anna gave him a passionately grateful glance. For, if the *vendeuse* Jeannine had been uniformly kind and encouraging, the other, Madame Tienne, had been as uniformly disapproving and had once even pinched her arm hard.

About five o'clock Anna became exhausted. The four white and gold walls seemed to close in on her. She sat on her high white stool staring at a marvellous nightgown and fighting an intense desire to rush away. Anywhere! Just to dress and rush away anywhere, from the raking eyes of the customers and the pinching fingers of Irene.

'I will one day. I can't stick it,' she said to herself. 'I won't be able to stick it.' She had an absurd wish to gasp for air.

Jeannine came and found her like that.

'It is hard at first, hein? . . . One asks oneself: Why? For what good? It is all idiot. We are all so. But we go on. Do not worry about Irene.' She whispered: 'Madame Vernon likes you very much. I heard her say so.'

At six o'clock Anna was out in the rue de la Paix; her fatigue forgotten, the feeling that now she really belonged to the great,

maddening city possessed her and she was happy in her beautifully cut tailor-made and beret.

Georgette passed her and smiled; Babette was in a fur coat.

All up the street the mannequins were coming out of the shops,
pausing on the pavements a moment, making them as gay and
as beautiful as beds of flowers before they walked swiftly away
and the Paris night swallowed them up.

In the Luxemburg Gardens

H E SAT ON A BENCH, a very depressed young man, meditating on the faithlessness of women, on the difficulty of securing money, on the futility of existence.

A little *bonne*, resting wearily first on one foot, then on the other, screamed: '*Raoul, Raoul, veux-tu te dépêcher.*' Raoul, aged two, dressed in a jade green overcoat and clutching a ball, staggered determinedly in the opposite direction. He sat down suddenly, was captured and received a slap with manly indifference.

'*Sacrés gosses!*' said the young man gazing morosely at all the other Raouls and Pierrots and Jacquelines in their brightly colored overcoats.

He turned his head distastefully away: but instantly interest came into his eyes.

A girl was walking up the steps leading from the fountain, slowly and with a calculated grace. Her hat was as green as Raoul's overcoat, her costume extremely short, her legs . . . 'Not bad!' said the young man to himself. 'In fact . . . one may say pretty!'

The girl walked past slowly, very slowly. She looked back. The young man fidgeted, hesitated, looked at the legs. . . .

He got up and followed. She immediately walked faster and adopted an air of haughty innocence. The young man's hunting instinct awoke and he followed, twirling his little moustache determinedly. Under the trees he caught her up.

'Mademoiselle. . .'

'Monsieur. . .'

Such a waste of time, say the Luxemburg Gardens, to be morose. Are there not always Women and Pretty Legs and Green Hats.

Tea with an Artist

I
T WAS OBVIOUS that this was not an Anglo-Saxon:
he was too gay, too dirty, too unreserved and in his little eyes was
such a mellow comprehension of all the sins and the delights of
life. He was drinking rapidly one glass of beer after another,
smoking a long, curved pipe, and beaming contentedly on the
world. The woman with him wore a black coat and skirt; she had
her back to us.

I said: 'Who's the happy man in the corner? I've never seen
him before.'

My companion who knew everybody answered: 'That's Verhausen. As mad as a hatter.'

'Madder than most people here?' I asked.

'Oh, yes, really dotty. He has got a studio full of pictures that
he will never show to anyone.'

I asked: 'What pictures? His own pictures?'

'Yes, his own pictures. They're damn good, they say.'... Verhausen had started out by being a Prix de Rome and he had had
a big reputation in Holland and Germany, once upon a time. He
was a Fleming. But the old fellow now refused to exhibit, and
went nearly mad with anger if he were pressed to sell anything.

'A pose?'

My friend said: 'Well, I dunno. It's lasted a long time for a
pose.'

He started to laugh.

'You know Van Hoyt. He knew Verhausen intimately in Antwerp, years ago. It seems he already hid his pictures up then....

He had evolved the idea that it was sacrilege to sell them. Then he married some young and flighty woman from Brussels, and she would not stand it. She nagged and nagged: she wanted lots of money and so on and so on. He did not listen even. So she gave up arguing and made arrangements with a Jew dealer from Amsterdam when he was not there. It is said that she broke into his studio and passed the pictures out of the window. Five of the best. Van Hoyt said that Verhausen cried like a baby when he knew. He simply sat and sobbed. Perhaps he also beat the lady. In any case she left him soon afterwards and eventually Verhausen turned up, here, in Montparnasse. The woman now with him he had picked up in some awful brothel in Antwerp. She must have been good to him, for he says now that the Fallen are the only women with souls. They will walk on the necks of all the others in Heaven. . . .' And my friend concluded: 'A rum old bird. But a bit of a back number, now, of course.'

I said: 'It's a perverted form of miserliness, I suppose. I should like to see his pictures, or is that impossible? I like his face.'

My friend said carelessly: 'It's possible, I believe. He sometimes shows them to people. It's only that he will not exhibit and will not tell. I dare say Van Hoyt could fix it up.'

Verhausen's studio was in the real Latin Quarter which lies to the north of the Montparnasse district and is shabbier and not cosmopolitan yet. It was an ancient, narrow street of uneven houses, a dirty, beautiful street, full of mauve shadows. A policeman stood limply near the house, his expression that of contemplative stupefaction: a yellow dog lay stretched philosophically on the cobblestones of the roadway. The concierge said without interest that Monsieur Verhausen's studio was on the *quatrième à droite*. I toiled upwards.

I knocked three times. There was a subdued rustling within. . . . A fourth time: as loudly as I could. The door opened a little and Mr. Verhausen's head appeared in the opening. I read suspicion in his eyes and I smiled as disarmingly as I could. I said something about Mr Van Hoyt – his own kind invitation, my great pleasure.

Verhausen continued to scrutinize me through huge spectacles: then he smiled with a sudden irradiation, stood away from the door and bowing deeply, invited me to enter. The room was big, all its walls encumbered on the floor with unframed canvases, all turned with their backs to the wall. It was very much cleaner than I had expected: quite clean and even dustless. On a table was spread a white cloth and there were blue cups and saucers and a plate of gingerbread cut into slices and thickly buttered. Mr Verhausen rubbed his hands and said with a pleased, childlike expression and in astonishingly good English that he had prepared an English tea that was quite ready because he had expected me sooner.

We sat on straight-backed chairs and sipped solemnly.

Mr Verhausen looked exactly as he had looked in the café, his blue eyes behind the spectacles at once naïve and wise, his waistcoat spotted with reminiscences of many meals.

But a delightful personality – comfortable and comforting. His long, curved pipes hung in a row on the wall; they made the whole room look Dutchly homely. We discussed Montparnasse with gravity.

He said suddenly: 'Now you have drunk your second cup of tea you shall see my pictures. Two cups of tea all English must have before they contemplate works of art.'

He had jumped up with a lightness surprising in a bulky man and with similar alacrity drew an easel near a window and proceeded to put pictures on it without any comment. They were successive outbursts of colour: it took me a little time to get used to them. I imagine that they were mostly, but not all, impressionist. But what fascinated me at first was his way of touching the canvases – his loving, careful hands.

After a time he seemed to forget that I was there and looked at them himself, anxiously and critically, his head on one side, frowning and muttering to himself in Flemish. A landscape pleased

me here and there: they were mostly rough and brilliant. But the
heads were very minutely painted and . . . Dutch! A woman stepping into a tub of water under a shaft of light had her skin turned
to gold.

Then he produced a larger canvas, changed the position of
the easel and turned to me with a little grunt. I said slowly: 'I
think that is a great picture. Great art!'

. . . A girl seated on a sofa in a room with many mirrors held
a glass of green liqueur. Dark-eyed, heavy-faced, with big, sturdy
peasant's limbs, she was entirely destitute of lightness or grace.

But all the poisonous charm of the life beyond the pale was in
her pose, and in her smouldering eyes – all its deadly bitterness
and fatigue in her fixed smile.

He received my compliments with pleasure, but with the quite
superficial pleasure of the artist who is supremely indifferent to
the opinion that other people may have about his work. And, just
as I was telling him that the picture reminded me of a portrait of
Manet's, the original came in from outside, carrying a string bag
full of green groceries. Mr Verhausen started a little when he saw
her and rubbed his hands again – apologetically this time. He
said: 'This, Madame, is my little Marthe. Mademoiselle Marthe
Baesen.'

She greeted me with a reserve and glanced at the picture on
the easel with an inscrutable face. I said to her: 'I have been
admiring Mr Verhausen's work.'

She said: 'Yes, Madame?' with the inflexion of a question and
left the room with her string bag.

The old man said to me: 'Marthe speaks no English and French
very badly. She is a true Fleming. Besides, she is not used to
visitors.'

There was a feeling of antagonism in the studio now. Mr Verhausen fidgeted and sighed restlessly. I said, rather with hesitation: 'Mr Verhausen, is it true that you object to exhibiting and
to selling your pictures?'

He looked at me over his spectacles, and the suspicious look, the look of an old Jew when counting his money, came again into his eyes.

'Object, Madame? I object to nothing. I am an artist. But I do not wish to sell my pictures. And, as I do not wish to sell them, exhibiting is useless. My pictures are precious to me. They are precious, most probably, to no one else.'

He chuckled and added with a glint of malice in his eyes: 'When I am dead Marthe will try to sell them and not succeed, probably. I am forgotten now. Then she will burn them. She dislikes rubbish, the good Marthe.'

Marthe re-entered the room as he said this. Her face was unpowdered but nearly unwrinkled, her eyes were clear with the shrewd, limited expression of the careful housewife – the look of small horizons and quick, hard judgements. Without the flame his genius had seen in her and had fixed for ever, she was heavy, placid and uninteresting – at any rate to me.

She said, in bad French: 'I have bought two artichokes for . . .' I did not catch how many sous. He looked pleased and greedy.

In the street the yellow dog and the policeman had vanished. The café opposite the door had come alive and its gramophone informed the world that:

> *Souvent femme varie*
> *Bien fol est qui s'y fie!*

It was astonishing how the figure of the girl on the sofa stayed in my mind: it blended with the coming night, the scent of Paris and the hard blare of the gramophone. And I said to myself: 'Is it possible that all that charm, such as it was, is gone?'

And then I remembered the way in which she had touched his cheek with her big hands. There was in that movement knowledge, and a certain sureness: as it were the ghost of a time when her business in life had been the consoling of men.

Trio

THEY SAT AT a corner table in the little restaurant, eating with gusto and noise after the manner of simple-hearted people who like their neighbours to see and know their pleasures.

The man was very black – coal black, with a thick silver ring on a finger of one hand. He wore a smart grey lounge suit, cut in at the waist, and his woolly hair was carefully brushed back and brilliantined. The woman was coffee-coloured and fat. She had on the native Martinique turban, making no pretension to fashion. Her bodice and skirt gaped apart and through the opening a coarse white cotton chemise peeped innocently forth. . . . From the Antilles. . . .

Between them was a girl, apparently about fifteen, but probably much younger. She sat very close to the man and every now and then would lay her head on his shoulder for a second. . . . There was evidently much white blood in her veins: the face was charming.

She had exactly the movements of a very graceful kitten, and he, appreciative, would stop eating to kiss her . . . long, lingering kisses, and, after each one she would look round the room as if to gather up a tribute of glances of admiration and envy – a lovely, vicious little thing. . . . From the Antilles, too. You cannot think what home-sickness descended over me. . . .

The fuzzy, negress' hair was exactly the right frame for her vulgar, impudent, startlingly alive little face: the lips were just thick enough to be voluptuous, the eyes with an expression half cunning, half intelligent. She wore a very short red frock and black, patent leather shoes. Her legs were bare. Suddenly she began to sing: *F'en ai marre,* to the huge delight of the coal black man who applauded vigorously.

As she grew more excited she jumped up, swung her slim hips violently, rolled her eyes, stamped her feet, lifted her skirt. Obviously the red dress was her only garment, obviously too she was exquisite beneath it . . . supple, slender, a dancer from the Thousand and One Nights. . . .

F'en ai m-a-r-r-e.

The fat, coffee-coloured woman looked on peacefully, then after a cautious glance at the *patronne* seated behind her counter:

'Keep yourself quiet, Doudou,' she said. 'Keep yourself quiet.' Then with a happy laugh:

Mais . . . ce qu'elle est cocasse, quand même! she said proudly.

It was because these were my compatriots that in that Montparnasse restaurant I remembered the Antilles.

Mixing Cocktails

THE HOUSE in the hills was very new and very ugly, long and narrow, of unpainted wood, perched oddly on high posts, I think as a protection from wood ants. There were six rooms with a veranda that ran the whole length of the house. . . . But when you went up there, there was always the same sensation of relief and coolness – in the ugly house with the beginnings of a rose garden, after an hour's journey by boat and another hour and a half on horse-back, climbing slowly up. . . .

On the veranda, upon a wooden table with four stout legs, stood an enormous brass telescope. With it you spied out the steamers passing: the French mail on its way to Guadeloupe, the Canadian, the Royal Mail, which should have been stately and was actually the shabbiest of the lot. . . . Or an exciting stranger!

At night one gazed through it at the stars and pretended to be interested. . . . 'That's Venus . . . Oh, is that Venus, ... And that's the Southern Cross. . . .' An unloaded shotgun leant up in one corner; there were always plenty of straw rocking-chairs and a canvas hammock with many cushions.

From the veranda one looked down the green valley sloping to the sea, but from the other side of the house one could only see the mountains, lovely but melancholy as mountains always are to a child.

Lying in the hammock, swinging cautiously for the ropes creaked, one dreamt. . . . The morning dream was the best – very early, before the sun was properly up. The sea was then a very tender blue, like the dress of the Virgin Mary, and on it were little white triangles. The fishing boats.

A very short dream, the morning dream – mostly about what one would do with the endless blue day. One would bathe in the pool: perhaps one would find treasure . . . Morgan's Treasure. For who does not know that, just before he was captured and I think hung at Kingston, Jamaica, Morgan buried his treasure in the Dominican mountains. . . . A wild place, Dominica. Savage and lost. Just the place for Morgan to hide his treasure in.

It was very difficult to look at the sea in the middle of the day. The light made it so flash and glitter: it was necessary to screw the eyes up tight before looking. Everything was still and languid, worshipping the sun.

The midday dream was languid too – vague, tinged with melancholy as one stared at the hard, blue, blue sky. It was sure to be interrupted by someone calling to one to come in out of the sun. One was not to sit in the sun. One had been told not to be in the sun. . . . One would one day regret freckles.

So the late afternoon was the best time on the veranda, but it was spoiled for all the rest were there. . . .

So soon does one learn the bitter lesson that humanity is never content just to differ from you and let it go at that. Never. They must interfere, actively and grimly, between your thoughts and yourself – with the passionate wish to level up everything and everybody.

I am speaking to you; do you not hear? You must break yourself of your habit of never listening. You have such an absent-minded expression. Try not to look vague. . . .

So rude!

The English aunt gazes and exclaims at intervals: 'The colours. . . . How exquisite! . . . Extraordinary that so few people should visit the West Indies. . . . That *sea.* . . . Could anything be more lovely?'

It is a purple sea with a sky to match it. The Caribbean. The deepest, the loveliest in the world. . . .

Sleepily but tactfully, for she knows it delights my father, she admires the roses, the hibiscus, the humming birds. Then she starts to nod. She is always falling asleep, at the oddest moments. It is the unaccustomed heat.

I should like to laugh at her, but I am a well-behaved little girl. . . . Too well-behaved. . . . I long to be like Other People! The extraordinary, ungetatable, oddly cruel Other People, with their way of wantonly hurting and then accusing you of being thin-skinned, sulky, vindictive or ridiculous. All because a hurt and puzzled little girl has retired into her shell.

The afternoon dream is a materialistic one. . . . It is of the days when one shall be plump and beautiful instead of pale and thin: perfectly behaved instead of awkward. . . . When one will wear sweeping dresses and feathered hats and put gloves on with ease and delight. . . . And of course, of one's marriage: the dark moustache and perfectly creased trousers. . . . Vague, that.

The veranda gets dark very quickly. The sun sets: at once night and the fireflies.

A warm, velvety, sweet-smelling night, but frightening and disturbing if one is alone in the hammock. Ann Twist, our cook, the old obeah woman has told me: 'You all must'n look too much at de moon. . . .'

If you fall asleep in the moonlight you are bewitched, it seems . . . the moon does bad things to you if it shines on you when you sleep. Repeated often. . . .

So, shivering a little, I go into the room for the comfort of my father working out his chess problem from the *Times Weekly Edition*. Then comes my nightly duty mixing cocktails.

In spite of my absent-mindedness I mix cocktails very well and swizzle them better (our cocktails, in the West Indies, are drunk frothing, and the instrument with which one froths them is called a swizzle-stick) than anyone else in the house.

I measure out angostura and gin, feeling important and happy, with an uncanny intuition as to how strong I must make each separate drink.

Here then is something I can do. . . . Action, they say, is more worthy than dreaming. . . .

Again the Antilles

THE EDITOR OF the *Dominica Herald and Leeward Islands Gazette* lived in a tall, white house with green Venetian blinds which overlooked our garden. I used often to see him looking solemnly out of his windows and would gaze solemnly back, for I thought him a very awe-inspiring person.

He wore gold-rimmed spectacles and dark clothes always – not for him the frivolity of white linen even on the hottest day – a stout little man of a beautiful shade of coffee-colour, he was known throughout the Island as Papa Dom.

A born rebel, this editor: a firebrand. He hated the white people, not being quite white, and he despised the black ones, not being quite black. . . . 'Coloured' we West Indians call the intermediate shades, and I used to think that being coloured embittered him.

He was against the Government, against the English, against the Island's being a Crown Colony and the Town Board's new system of drainage. He was also against the Mob, against the gay and easy morality of the negroes and 'the hordes of priests and nuns that overrun our unhappy Island', against the existence of the Anglican bishop and the Catholic bishop's new palace.

He wrote seething articles against that palace which was then being built, partly by voluntary labour – until, one night his house was besieged by a large mob of the faithful, throwing stones and howling for his blood. He appeared on his veranda, frightened to death. In the next issue of his paper he wrote a long account of the 'riot': according to him it had been led by several well-known

Magdalenes, then, as always, the most ardent supporters of Christianity.

After that, though, he let the Church severely alone, acknowledging that it was too strong for him.

I cannot imagine what started the quarrel between himself and Mr Hugh Musgrave.

Mr Hugh Musgrave I regarded as a dear, but peppery. Twenty years of the tropics and much indulgence in spices and cocktails does have that effect. He owned a big estate, just outside the town of Roseau, cultivated limes and sugar canes and employed a great deal of labour, but he was certainly neither ferocious nor tyrannical.

Suddenly, however, there was the feud in full swing.

There was in the *Dominica Herald and Leeward Islands Gazette* a column given up to letters from readers and, in this column, writing under the pseudonyms of Pro Patria, Indignant, Liberty and Uncle Tom's Cabin, Papa Dom let himself go. He said what he thought about Mr Musgrave and Mr Musgrave replied: briefly and sternly as benefits an Englishman of the governing class. . . . Still he replied.

It was most undignified, but the whole Island was hugely delighted. Never had the *Herald* had such a sale.

Then Mr Musgrave committed, according to Papa Dom, some specially atrocious act of tyranny. Perhaps he put a fence up where he should not have, or overpaid an unpopular overseer or supported the wrong party on the Town Board. . . . At any rate Papa Dom wrote in the next issue of the paper this passionate and unforgettable letter:

'It is a saddening and a dismal sight,' it ended, 'to contemplate the degeneracy of a stock. How far is such a man removed from the ideals of true gentility, from the beautiful description of a contemporary, possibly, though not certainly, the Marquis of Montrose, left us by Shakespeare, the divine poet and genius.

'*He was a very gentle, perfect knight . . .*'

Mr Musgrave took his opportunity:

'Dear Sir,' he wrote

'I never read your abominable paper. But my attention has been called to a scurrilous letter about myself which you published last week. The lines quoted were written, not by Shakespeare but by Chaucer, though you cannot of course be expected to know that, and run

> He never yet no vilonye had sayde
> In al his lyf, unto no manner of wight –
> He was a verray parfit, gentil knyght.

'It is indeed a saddening and a dismal thing that the names of great Englishmen should be thus taken in vain by the ignorant of another race and colour.'

Mr Musgrave had really written 'damn niggers'.

Papa Dom was by no means crushed. Next week he replied with dignity as follows:

'My attention has been called to your characteristic letter. I accept your correction though I understand that in the mind of the best authorities there are grave doubts, very grave doubts indeed, as to the authorship of the lines, and indeed the other works of the immortal Swan of Avon. However, as I do not write with works of reference in front of me, as you most certainly do, I will not dispute the point.

'The conduct of an English gentleman who stoops to acts of tyranny and abuse cannot be described as gentle or perfect. I fail to see that it matters whether it is Shakespeare, Chaucer or the Marquis of Montrose who administers from down the ages the much-needed reminder and rebuke.'

I wonder if I shall ever again read the *Dominica Herald and Leeward Islands Gazette.*

Hunger

L AST NIGHT I took an enormous dose of valerian to make me sleep. I have awakened this morning very calm and rested, but with shaky hands.

It doesn't matter. I am not hungry either: that's a good thing as there is not the slightest prospect of my having anything to eat. I could of course buy a loaf, but we have been living on bread and nothing else for a long time. It gets monotonous. Also, it's damned salt. . . .

Starvation – or rather semi-starvation – coffee in the morning, bread at midday, is exactly like everything else. It has its compensations, but they do not come at once. . . . To begin with it is a frankly awful business.

For the first twelve hours one is just astonished. No money: nothing to eat. . . . *Nothing!* . . . But that's farcical. There must be something one can do. Full of practical common sense you rush about; you search for the elusive 'something'. At night you have long dreams about food.

On the second day you have a bad headache. You feel pugnacious. You argue all day with an invisible and sceptical listener.

I tell you it is *not* my fault. . . . It happened suddenly, and I have been ill. I had no time to make plans. *Can* you not see that one needs money to fight? Even with a hundred francs clear one could make plans.

I said *clear.* . . . A few hundred francs *clear.* There is the hotel

to pay. Sell my clothes? . . . You cannot get any money for wom-
en's clothes in Paris. I tried for a place as a *gouvernante* yesterday. Of course I'm nervous and silly. So'd you be if. . . .

Oh God! leave me alone. I don't care what you think; I don't.

On the third day one feels sick: on the fourth, one starts crying
very easily. . . . A bad habit that; it sticks.

On the fifth day . . .

You awaken with a feeling of detachment; you are calm and
godlike. It is to attain to that state that religious people fast.

Lying in bed, my arms over my eyes, I despise, utterly, my
futile struggles of the last two years. What on earth have I been
making such a fuss about? What does it matter, anyway? Women
are always ridiculous when they struggle.

It is like being suspended over a precipice. You cling for dear
life with people walking on your fingers. Women do not only walk:
they stamp.

Primitive beings, most women.

But I have clung and made huge efforts to pull myself up.
Three times I have . . . acquired resources. Means? Has she
means? She has means. I have been a mannequin. I have been
. . . no: not what you think. . . .

No good, any of it.

Well, you are doomed.

Once down you will never get up. *Did* anyone – did *any*body,
I wonder, ever get up . . . once down?

Every few months there is bound to be a crisis. Every crisis
will find you weaker.

If I were Russian I should long ago have accepted Fate: had
I been French I should long ago have discovered and taken the
back door out. I mean no disrespect to the French. They are logical. Had I been . . . SENSIBLE I should have hung on to being a
mannequin with what it implies. As it is, I have struggled on, not
cleverly. Almost against my own will. Don't I belong to the land
of Lost Causes . . . England. . . .

If I had a glass of wine I would drink to that: the best of toasts:

To a Lost Cause: to All Lost Causes. . . .

Oh! the relief of letting go: tumbling comfortably into the abyss. . .

Not such a terrible place after all. One day, no doubt, one will grow used to it. Lots of jolly people, here. . . .

No more effort.

Retrospection is a waste of the Fifth Day.

The best way is to spend it dreaming over some book like *Dash* or . . . oh, *Dash*, again. . . .

Especially *Dash* number one . . . There are words and sentences one can dream over for hours. . . .

Luckily we have both books: too torn to be worth selling.

I love her most before she has become too vicious.

It is as if your nerves were strung tight. Like violin strings. Anything: lovely words, or the sound of a concertina from the street: even a badly played piano can make one cry. Not with hunger or sadness. No!

But with the extraordinary beauty of life.

I have never gone without food for longer than five days, so I cannot amuse you any longer.

Discourse of a Lady Standing a Dinner to a Down-and-Out Friend

DARLING, I think you are simply wonderful. I always say, if I were in your place I'd go crazy. . . . Have some more soup. . . . Soup is *so* nourishing.

(It is all very well, but she has not forgotten to rouge her lips.)

Of course, I always say one cannot judge by *appearances*. I mean that lots of people who look all right are starving, and all that, I suppose.

What did you say? . . . You cannot buy special clothes to starve in. Naturally not. But it is a question of what people *think*, is it not?

(Now she is not pleased. But is it *my* fault? A woman supposed to be starving ought not to go about in silk stockings and quite expensive shoes.)

I was with Anna at the Galerie yesterday and I saw the sweetest hat. Not *hard*. I bought it to wear with my velvet. But they don't *go* together. It's awful, getting clothes to go together.

(She *does* look a bit thin. I ought to ask her to tea to-morrow. . . . No. To-morrow Albert is coming. I dare say she is all *right*, and she is not his type. But these people with not enough to eat. You can't trust them with *men*. . . . Another day. . . .)

Shall we have some more wine. . . . I wish I could help you. Let me think. I know somebody at Neuilly who wants a mother's help.

(She does not like that. I knew it. It is dreadful to try to help poor people. They will not help themselves.)

It is a friend of Anna's really. We were talking about you the other day. I may tell you that she is not in the least annoyed with you. Indeed she admits that she was a little rude. But . . . darling . . . you can't *afford* to lose your temper like that, can you? You see, Anna and yourself have such very different . . . let us say, temperaments. She is so independent. . . . And Peter really was annoying that day. . . . He flirts so automatically. . . . Such a good-looking fellow: but *what* an irritating husband. . . . Poor Anna! It *was* not your fault. . . . But one must adapt oneself a little, mustn't one? . . . Because you are poor you are not necessarily a . . . What? What did you say? No! I never used that word. . . . You must not look at life in that way. You are too suspicious. I will ring up the woman in Neuilly. I should not do that, should I, if I did not trust you? . . . Cheer up. You will be as happy as possible. . . . (I believe she is going to cry. She irritates me. And there is that man opposite making eyes at her. Quite a good-looking man. Well, if she is that sort . . . Well, why *doesn't* she?)

Of course one has to be *some*thing in this world, hasn't one? I mean . . . There you are. . . . Either one thing or the other. . . . You will have a liqueur? *Deux Kümmel, garçon.*

(I rather hate myself!)

Do you really think this hat suits me? . . . With just a *tack* in the ribbon, here, perhaps. . . . No? . . . Now don't look so sad. I will ring up Anna's friend at Neuilly to-morrow. We will fix you up. I assure you we will fix you up. They pay 150 francs a month. And keep, naturally. . . . Imagine. One hundred and fifty francs. . . . Thirty shillings. . . . Just for pocket money. . . . Good-bye, then, till you hear from Neuilly. . . .

(Poor little devil. Of course it is her own fault. There is one comfort. It is always people's own fault. . . . They lack. . . . Oh, Balance. When people lack Balance there's really nothing to be done.)

A Night

O NE SHUTS ONE'S EYES and sees it written: red letters on a black ground:

Le Saut dans l'Inconnu. . . . Le Saut . . .

Stupidly I think: But why in French? Of course it must be a phrase I have read somewhere. Idiotic.

I screw up my eyes wildly to get rid of it: next moment it is back again.

Red letters on a black ground.

One lies staring at the exact shape of the S.

Dreadfully tired I am too, now this beastly thing won't let me sleep. And because I can't sleep I start to think very slowly and painfully, for I have cried myself into a state of stupor.

No money: rotten. And ill and frightened to death . . . Worse!

But worst of all is the way I hate people: it is as if something in me is shivering right away from humanity. Their eyes are mean and cruel, especially when they laugh.

They are always laughing, too: always grinning. When they say something especially rotten they grin. Then, just for a second, that funny little animal, the Real Person, looks out and slinks away again . . . Furtive.

I don't belong here. I don't belong here. I must get out – must get out.

Le Saut. . . . Le Saut dans l'Inconnu.

One lies very still – staring.

Well, then . . . what?

Make a hole in the water?

In a minute I am sitting up in bed, gasping. I have imagined myself sinking, suffocating, the pain in the lungs horrible. Horrible.

Shoot oneself? . . . I begin again mechanically to plan what would happen. The revolver is in the pawnshop. For twenty francs I could. . . .

I'd sit down. No: lie down. And open my mouth. . . . That's the place: against the roof of one's mouth. How rum it would feel. And pull the trigger.

And then?

L'Inconnu: black, awful. One would fall, down, down, down for ever and ever. Falling.

Frightened. Coward. Do it when you hardly know. Drink perhaps first half a bottle of Cognac.

No: I cannot put up a better fight than that. . . . *Be* ashamed of me.

If I had something to hold on to. Or somebody.

One friend. . . . One!

You know I can't be alone. I can't.

God, send me a friend. . . .

How ridiculous I am. How primitive. . . .

Sneering at myself I start on childishnesses.

I imagine the man I could love. His hands, eyes and voice.

Hullo, he'll say, what's all this fuss about?

– Because I'm hurt and spoilt, and you too late. . . .

– What rot. . . . What rot!

He will buy me roses and carnations and chocolates and a pair of pink silk pyjamas and heaps of books.

He will laugh and say – but nicely:

Finished! What rot!

Just like that.

Saying the Litany to the Blessed Virgin which I learnt at the Convent and have never forgotten.

Mater Dolorosa: Mother most sorrowful. Pray for us, Star of

the Sea. Mother most pitiful, pray for us.
Ripping words.
I wonder if I dare shut my eyes now.
Ridiculous all this. Lord, I am tired. . . .
A devil of a business. . . .

In the Rue de l'Arrivée

HALFWAY UP the Boulevard Montparnasse is a little café called the Zanzi-Bar. It is not one of these popular places swarming with the shingled and long-legged and their partners, who all wear picturesque collars and an incredibly contemptuous expression. No, it is small, half-empty, cheapish. Coffee costs five centimes less than in the Rotonde, for instance. It is a place to know of. It is not gay, except on the rare occasions when some festive soul asks the patron for the Valencia record and puts a ten centimes piece into the gramophone slot.

Here, one evening at eleven o'clock, sat a Lady drinking her fourth *fine à l'eau* and thinking how much she disliked human beings in general and those who pitied her in particular. For it was her deplorable habit, when she felt very blue indeed, to proceed slowly up the right-hand side of the Boulevard, taking a *fine à l'eau* – that is to say a brandy and soda – at every second café she passed. There are so many cafés that the desired effect could be obtained without walking very far, and by thus moving from one to the other she managed to avoid both the curious stares of the waiters and the disadvantage of not accurately knowing just how drunk she was. . . .

From which it will be very easily gathered that the Lady was an Anglo-Saxon. . . . That she was down on her luck. . . . That she lacked strength of character and was doomed to the fate of the feeble who have not found a protector. She rested her elbows on the top of the table to look at the picture of Leda and the Swan hanging opposite her. The walls of the café were covered with the canvases of hopeful artists, numbered and priced, waiting for the possible buyer. An effect of warm reds and greens and yellows and of large numbers of ladies with enormous thighs, well-developed calves and huge feet; the upper part of their bodies very slim and willowy, the faces thin and ascetic with small prim mouths.

But she was a simple soul, so her eyes strayed, puzzled and unsatisfied over these symbols of a point of view and came back to gaze steadily at the red-haired Leda, the curves of her throat and the long, white neck of the Swan lying between her breasts.

Into her vague dream of jade-green water and gently gliding birds with golden beaks, came a disagreeable twinge of loneliness and unhappiness. She sighed heavily, instinctively, as a dog sighs, and ordered another *Fine*. As she waited for it, she took a little mirror out of her bag and observed herself critically. From the small, blurred glass her eyes stared back at her, darkly circled, the whites slightly bloodshot, the clear look of youth going – gone.

Miss Dufreyne, for such was the Lady's name, was a weak, sentimental, very lazy, entirely harmless creature, pathetically incapable of lies or intrigue or even of self-defence – till it was too late. She was also sensual, curious, reckless, and had all her life roused a strong curiosity in men. So much for her.

Inevitably her career had been a series of jerks, very violent and very sudden, and the suddenness of the jerks – even more than their violence – had ended by exhausting her.

Nevertheless, there was still no end to her pathetic and charming illusions. She believed that Gentlemen were Different and to be trusted, that Ladies must not make a Fuss – even when drunk – and that the Lower Classes were the Lower Classes. She believed that Montparnasse, that stronghold of the British and American middle classes, was a devil of a place and what Montmartre used to be. She believed that one day she would rise to fame as a fashion artist, be rescued from her present haphazard existence and restored to a life when afternoon tea, punctually at

five, toast, cakes, maid, rattle of cups in saucers would be a com-
monplace. Such was Miss Dufreyne's strange and secret idea of
bliss.

But there she was stony-broke and with a hand that was rapidly losing its cunning, seeking oblivion in a cheap Montparnasse
café. A bad stage to have reached, useless to disguise it.

Miss Dufreyne drank hastily her fifth *Fine*.

She sat drooping a little on the dark red leather bench, huddled in her black coat with its somewhat ragged fur collar, to all
outer appearance calm, respectable, and mistress of her fate.

But over the unseen, the real Dorothy Dufreyne, a tiny
shrinking thing in a vast, empty space, flowed red waves of despair,
black waves of fatigue, as the brandy crept warmly and treach-
erously to her brain. Waves from a tremendous, booming sea.
And each one would submerge her and then retreat, leaving her
dazed, and as it were, gasping.

Sharp urgings to some violent deed, some inevitable fated end,
and craven fear of life, and utter helpless, childish loneliness.
Never before had drink, which usually warmed and uplifted her,
had this effect on her. Perhaps it was because that afternoon she
had passed a gentleman whom she knew intimately – very intimately indeed – and behold the gentleman had turned his head
aside, and coughing nervously, pretended not to see her. . . . 'If I
want to walk at all straight,' she thought suddenly, 'I'd better go
now.'

She left money on the table, got up and went out in careful
and dignified fashion.

Miss Dufreyne (Dolly to her friends when she had any) stepped
out on to the Boulevard into the soft autumn night, and the night
put out a gentle, cunning hand to squeeze her heart.

As soon as she turned up the side street behind the railway
station which led to her hotel, she began to walk as quickly as
she could. She hated that street.

It was full of cheap and very dirty hotels, of cheaper restaurants where the food smelt of oil and sweat, of coiffeurs' shops haunted by very dark men with five days' blue growth of beard. Never a pretty lady. Not the ghost of a pretty lady in these coiffeurs' shops.

Even the pharmacy at the corner looked sinister and unholy. During the day the waxen head of a gentleman with hollow eyes, thin lips and a tortured and evil expression was exhibited in the window in a little box. A legend on a card under the head read:

'I suffered from diseases of the stomach, liver, kidneys, from neurasthenia, anæmia and loss of vitality before taking the Elixir of Abbé Pierre. . . .'

A street of sordid dramas and horrible men who walked softly behind one for several steps before they spoke.

The Lady sped along, cursing the Paris pavements, almost sobered by her intense wish to get home quickly, and suddenly was aware that she was being followed.

A man was slinking up not quite alongside, a little behind her, cap pulled low over his eyes, crimson scarf knotted round his throat, hands in pockets. His silhouette looked small, almost frail, but as if he would be very quick and active like a cat. Graceful too – like a cat.

He was going to speak to her, and she felt that that night she could not bear it. 'Mademoiselle,' said the man, 'are you walking alone so late?'

'*Allez-vous en!*' she said fiercely, adding without dignity and in a voice that was almost a sob: '*Idiot!*'

Then braced herself up for the inevitable, muttered insult.

But the man, now level with her, only looked with curious, kindly, extremely intelligent eyes and passed on.

She heard him say softly, as if meditatively: '*Pauvre petite, va.*'

And because of the tone of his voice and the glance of his eyes, Miss Dufreyne felt sure that this passer-by in a sordid street knew all about her to the core of her heart and the soul of her soul – the exact meaning of the tears in her eyes and the droop of her head.

It was as if those wary eyes had watched hundreds of women scold and sulk and sob and finally cry themselves into a beaten silence.

Hundreds – all precisely alike – and as if that man himself had become indifferent as Fate – but very wise and infinitely tolerant.

And instead of resenting his knowledge she felt suddenly soothed and calmed. The back of his cap and his supple slouching walk seemed to say: '*Tout s'arrangera, va!*'

And the sympathy which would have maddened her from the happy, the fortunate or the respectable, she strangely and silently accepted coming from someone more degraded than she was, more ignorant, more despised. . . .

She climbed the stairs of the hotel holding tightly to the banisters, and undressed weeping gently but not unhappily.

Her intense desire for revenge on all humanity had given place to an extraordinary clear-sightedness.

For the first time she had dimly realized that only the hopeless are starkly sincere and that only the unhappy can either give or take sympathy – even some of the bitter and dangerous voluptuousness of misery.

That night Dorothy Dufreyne dreamt that she was dead and that a tall, bright angel dressed in a shabby suit and crimson scarf was bearing her to hell.

But what if it were heaven when one got there?

Learning to Be a Mother

THERE WAS a large brass plate on the outside of
the door:

MADAME LABORIAU
Sage-femme des Hôpitaux.
Consultations 12 à 4.

and, when one got past the concierge's loge, a steep flight of
stairs. . . . Interminable, those stairs, as one mounted them, clinging to the banisters, racked with pain. Then there was another
door with a smaller plate: *Sage-femme*.

Inside there was a turmoil – loud voices, mewing of babies, a
warm smell of blankets, a woman moaning. For Madame Laboriau, being a qualified maternity nurse, must, according to the
law, keep one large room for overflowings from the hospitals. . . .
I see the women as I pass the open door – three of them, one
already crazy with pain, the others watching her with white,
curious faces. I turn away my head quickly.

A long passage and I am in my own room. Fortunate me! I
have been able to buy the right to moan in privacy.

It is extraordinary how that electric light hurts one. If only I
could get them to put it out. Painfully I try to remember the French
for light. . . . '*Lumière* . . . *Éteindre la lumière.*' They do not
understand and I begin to cry weakly.

Madame Laboriau sponges my forehead, looks at me with an
expert eye. I look up at her and say again:

'*Anesthésique. . . . On m'a promis. . . .*'

She smiles and pats my hand.

'La la la la,' she says as she hurries away.

I am alone again with the light – yellow and cruel. But now there are two of them, elongated, and round them a quivering halo.

I watch the halo as the giant pain takes me up and squeezes me tighter, tighter, tighter.

'*Regardez*,' says Mme. Laboriau, '*comme il est beau votre fils. . . .*' Look how beautiful is your son!

I look and think weakly: Poor hideous little thing!

Oh do take it away, I say fretfully, and then: Thirsty!

Colette came as soon as I could see visitors, laden of course with flowers and grapes. She had been a friend of my husband and visited me when I first came to Paris, I think out of polite inquisitiveness. . . . But we were curious about each other, so we had gradually become intimate. . . . She had all the qualities. She was beautiful, gay – and she read Tolstoi. Only to put herself to sleep it is true – still she read him. I spent a night at her flat once and actually saw her doing it.

She was more than a Parisienne: she was a Montmartroise, which is a Parisienne raised to the *n*th power.

And generous. . . . She was contemplating marriage, but, I believe, with misgivings.

Well, she came to see the baby and to coo at it. I had to account for my lack of enthusiasm by saying that I had wanted a girl. . . .

'*Ah, mais, non, par exemple!*' she said decidedly, 'A man, a son! that is something. But a woman . . . another *pauvre miserable*. . . . Michel? Is he not proud? And pleased?

I told her: yes. Very pleased. Very proud.

And his name, the poor little cabbage?

'Robert,' I said rather shamefacedly.

'Robayre, *bon*. But I thought it was to be Michel!'

I had meant to call him Michael. Robert had slipped out.

It had been like this:

A couple of days after he was born a little, wizened, dried-up man had come to see me – somebody connected with Mairie. He was smiling and courteous at first.

Was I married – Yes.

My husband's name?

I read carefully from my marriage lines which I had under my pillow: Michel Ivan . . .

Astonishing to see how suddenly the smile left his face.

'Ivan . . . then . . . Your husband is a Russian. A Bolshevik, no doubt!'

I said that my husband was French though born in Russia.

'Ivan . . . Ivan . . . c'est Bolshevik, ça,' he muttered unconvincedly.

Then sharply: 'The name of this child, Madame?'

I stared at him, not being prepared for this.

'The child's name, Madame?' he asked even more sharply.

And, thoroughly frightened, I stammered the first name that came into my head: 'Robert!'

Alone with my son I said to him remorsefully:

'At first I don't like you and now I've been and called you Robert. You poor little devil.'

There it was. I did not like him. I had been too much hurt. I was too tired.

I kept my feelings a profound secret, but with all my efforts I could not bring myself to kiss him. . . . I was thankful that he slept nearly all the time. I spent the days sleeping, reading a book called *Saadha la Marocaine,* talking to Mme. Laboriau whenever she had time to sit with me.

I had grown to admire her. It was impossible not to admire anyone so calm, so efficient, so entirely mistress of herself and of her work. . . . She was fat, with steady, clever, blue eyes, and, underneath her overalls, she wore brightly coloured dresses of velvet. Her hands were small, white, and extraordinarily deft. . . .

With one of them she would lift the baby up, catching him in the middle somewhere, and the little animal, recognizing the touch of the expert, would stop crying at once.

She said with regard to my want of enthusiasm about him: 'That is always so. That will come. That will come. You are still weak. Besides, one must learn.'

She sat comfortably down and began to talk. Suddenly from the next rooms came moans and shrieks.

'*Ça y est!*' she exclaimed, 'the moment I sit down of course.'

'Perhaps,' I said timidly, 'she is suffering very much.'

'Bah. . . . Like you: like me. . . . But the less they pay the more noise they make. That is fated but it is extraordinary.'

'*Jésus! J'aaesus!*' screamed the woman in the next room. '*Mon Dieu . . . Mon Dieu . . . Mon Dieu. . . .*'

She moved towards the door, serene, unhurried, and I pulled the sheet over my head to shut out the shrieks.

What lies people tell about maternity! Sacred Motherhood! *La Femme Sacrée!*

Well, there is *la Femme Sacrée* in the next room. Horrible World. . . .

So I must have slept.

I woke up during the night to hear the little wail of Robert. Because it was a little wail I lifted him out of his crib and held him in my arms. He made a sad, complaining noise that almost stopped as I rocked him backwards and forwards. How warm the room was! How silent! Very far away a dog barking, the horn of a taxi.

Suddenly I realized that I was happy.

There was a nightlight burning. He opened his eyes and looked straight into mine. His were set slantwise, too, and I imagined they looked sad.

He was tied up in the French way like a Red Indian papoose,

only his head out of the bundle. I shall dress him differently when we get home.

Little thing! I must kiss him.

Perhaps that is why he looks sad – because his mother never has kissed him.

The Blue Bird

O<small>N THAT AFTERNOON</small> Carlo and I sat in the Café du Dôme drinking kümmel. The room was comparatively empty, for the weather being hot the Dômites were gathered on the terrace.

There were the usual number of young gentlemen with high voices, carefully shabby trousers, jerseys, caressing gestures, undulating hips, and the usual number of the stony broke sitting haughtily behind *cafés-crème*. The bald waiter with the lecherous eyes trod to and fro, disdainful and flat-footed; the end of a gay scarf floated in the breeze; the high, sharp voice of a respectable English woman discoursed of her uncle the bishop and her hatred of hysteria.

Most of the women were ugly that afternoon. The unpainted faces looked bald and unfinished, the painted – ochre powder, shadowed eyelids, purple lips – were like cruel stains in the sunlight.

In the corner, to redeem humanity, sat one lovely creature, her face framed by a silver turban. Wisps of woolly hair peeped out from beneath it – a nigger – what a pity. Why a pity?

One becomes impressionistic to excess after the third kümmel!

'Another, Carlo?'

'Horrible extravagance!' said Carlo in her deep voice.

Carlo is a mass of contradictions. Her voice is as deep as a man's; her shoulders and hips narrow as those of a fragile schoolgirl, her eyes brown and faithful like a dog's (hence her name).

Her mouth is bitter and tormented. But for her mouth one would not guess that she is a failure, a tragedy, one of the tragedies of Montparnasse.

Montparnasse is full of tragedy – all sorts – blatant, hidden, silent, voluble, quick, slow – even lucrative – A tragedy can be lucrative, I assure you.

On any day of the week you may catch sight of the Sufferers, white-faced and tragic of eye – having a drink in the intervals of expressing themselves – pouring out their souls and exposing them hopefully for sale, that is to say.

Everybody knows Carlo, and nobody blames her, and she is such a *nice* woman really and such a hopeless case.

Poor soul, she loved a Bad Man – and there you are. Such a pity!

I believe her real name is Margaret Tomkins and her birth-place doesn't matter – London probably. But she left England ten years ago when she was about seventeen, and wandered all over Europe, first with the nondescript Greek whom she had married for some extraordinary reason, possibly because she was bored – and then with the Bad Man. She met the Bad Man first in Bucharest. They finally arrived in Paris where Carlo started a desultory career as an artist's model, and came to live in Mont-parnasse. The Bad Man stayed over on the other side of the river, but he would swoop down and carry her off at intervals. People said he took all her money – regardless of how it was earned – but Carlo always swore solemnly that this wasn't true.

On the contrary, she said, he spent all his on her – recklessly.

She had a very varied existence anyway, but has never lost the look of a country clergyman's daughter – which I believe she is. She dresses unimaginatively, with occasional outbreaks into some too vivid colour. She wore that day a red straw hat and in its shadow her face looked very pale, her eyes so clearly brown that they were almost yellow.

She said suddenly: 'Oh, thank God, thank God, it's hot. There are only about two hot days every year. This is one of them. Lovely!'

I agreed without so much enthusiasm. I've never learned the

art of sitting absolutely still, divinely lazy in the golden sun for hours at a time and dreaming vaguely.

Carlo had it, but she had lived so long in hot places and wasn't quite English to start with.

She rested her chin on her hand and gazed at all the familiar faces outside without seeing them.

She said:

'One night last summer when it was hot like this, I was happy. People say you are never utterly happy – but I was.'

She spoke in a low voice.

I was surprised.

Carlo so seldom talked about herself, and never of her loves, which were necessarily many, poor dear. That alone made her unique in Montparnasse, unique amongst women, I think.

She said:

'You see, I hadn't heard from Paul for several weeks, and I was awfully worried.' (Paul was the Bad Man.) 'And then I got a wire from him. He was at Barbizon and he asked me to come. You know Barbizon in Fontainebleau Forest?'

I said: 'Yes. Classical for lovers, my dear.'

'Well,' said Carlo, 'and I went.'

(Of course – you poor devil of a blind and infatuated creature – of course you went.)

'And I got down towards evening and I took a cab from Melun to the hotel. I was simply miserable in the cab. Miserable! You know how one is. I'd such a horrible fear that I was never going to see Paul again – he was one of those people whom one adores and whom one is never sure of because they seem marked out ... fated ... do you know what I mean? No? Well, there are people like that.

'The bedroom at the hotel was full of flowers and all the windows were open – so many windows. It was like being outside.

'And Paul said:

' "Carlo, don't let's talk now – after dinner, after dinner! Let's be happy now. Let's forget everything. Have you brought your little black dress? Put it on."

'So I shut my eyes and I kissed him and I didn't ask a single question – not one, not even if he had money. After all, it didn't matter, for I had some.'

(I repressed a movement of indignation and drank some kümmel. Poor, poor Carlo!)

She went on:

'We had dinner outside on the terrace. The forest begins only a few yards away – the hotel is on the edge of it – and someone has stuck up a sort of shed where people shoot with little guns at something – I don't know what – But we sat with our backs to that, of course.

'I never even noticed the other people. I don't know if the place was full or empty. We ate everything good and drank Sauternes, and I began to feel happy.

'Paul said:

' "Now, we're going into the forest – and will talk, if you like. . . ."

'You know it's extraordinary; the forest near Barbizon is absolutely empty at night. You'd think that all the people from the hotels would drift there after dinner, but they don't. It's empty and still and wonderful. We left the path after a while. The trees got thicker and everything was utterly silent. If I'd been alone I should have been afraid, for I think trees get strange at night, don't you? I love them – but they're strange. I'm sure they are more alive than people imagine. . . .

'And Paul said:

' "We're quite safe here. We're absolutely alone – I'll make a bed for you with my coat."

'He said:

' "Carlo!"

'Do you know how men's eyes look sometimes, as if they were begging desperately and . . . and childishly somehow! . . .

'You can't think how white his face looked under the trees –

And his eyes – they had little lamps in them.

'I thought: Paul looks quite mad.

'I kissed his eyes to make them peaceful.

'And as I was doing that a nightingale began to sing – to sing and sing.

'I was so happy – I've never felt like that before. I never will feel like that again.

'I whispered to Paul: "Wouldn't it be wonderful to die now?" "Carlo, do you mean that? Have you the courage? I'd hold you tight – you wouldn't feel anything."

'I sat up and looked at him and he said: "Have you the courage, Carlo? Tell me – have you?"

'And somehow I was frightened of his eyes and I said: "There's a mosquito – you said there weren't many this year – but there's one."

'It's funny, sometimes a devil talks with one's tongue!

'I wanted to say: "Yes, kill me. It would be worth living to die like this!"

'And instead I said that about the mosquitoes.

'He helped me up and he said: "Let's go back to the hotel."

'All the way home he only spoke once. He said: "Don't worry about money. I've got enough to pay the bill with in my pocketbook."

'He . . .'

Carlo stopped and suddenly began to cry. 'Oh, God, what a fool I was – what a fool! To have been so close to a sweet death and to have pushed it away! Because I was frightened. And went on living – to be a wreck! And to grow old – and to be the butt of a lot of thick fools – I clung on to mean, silly life. Oh! God. . . . That night, you know, when he got up to . . . to go and kill himself, he must have kissed me. . . . In my sleep I felt him kiss me.'

I gave her my handkerchief in sympathetic silence. Hers was so small. . . .

Poor Carlo! The first time I'd ever heard her version. The generally accepted one was that the Bad Man had been a Bad Man to the end – and being wanted by the police for something pretty serious he had shot himself one night at Barbizon, 'having first carefully dragged that unfortunate girl into the business, couldn't even kill himself decently.'

Life is really unsatisfactory and puzzling – very.

All Carlo's friends thought – or pretended to think – that being finally quit of him she'd go up in the world like a skyrocket. And instead of that she went to pieces – absolutely to pieces. She resented fiercely all the well-meant efforts to rouse her to some sense of duty toward life.

There you are! And there she was – the tragedy of Montparnasse – called 'Poor Carlo' by the charitable, and 'that awful woman' by the others. . . .

Now she powdered her face, pulled her hat over her eyes and got up.

She said:

'Well, I've got to go and meet my Arab. D'you know my Arab? He's got a beauty spot on his left cheek like somebody out of the Thousand and One Nights. Awfully good-looking. But a bit of a rotter on the quiet, I should think. . . . Good-bye, dear – sorry I cried – idiotic to cry.'

I watched her red hat in the sun as she crossed the Boulevard.

The Grey Day

ONE OF THOSE cold, heavy days in spring – a hard sky with a glare behind the cloud, all the new green of the trees hanging still and sullen.

A day without joy or romance, or tenderness – when joy and romance and tenderness seem impossible, unthinkable – ridiculous illusions – and sadness itself is only a pale ghost.

The poet walked solemnly along the Boulevard Raspail and longed for the sight of a pretty woman – a useless creature with polished nails, expensive scent and the finest of silk stockings – marked and warranted – For Ornament Fragile –

They cheer one up sometimes. . . . But not one was to be seen.

All the women he met marched heavily with sensible feet and carried parcels. One even held a green broom and looked as if she'd like to sweep the poet out of existence with it.

He groaned, rushed into a café, and ordered a drink. He felt like the Princess who had to spin a beautiful garment out of nothing at all, or have her head cut off.

Imagine being a poet in a world like this!

Imagine being obliged to write one poem (at least) every morning!

Then his despair faded again to greyness in that dark, quiet café, where two men with hooked noses and greasy, curly hair, played draughts.

He shut his eyes and tried hard to think of blue seas in the sunshine, of the white, supple arms of a dancer dressed in red –

of the throb that lives in a violin and the movement of flowers in the wind.

It was quite useless.

Besides, flowers have stupid faces and so have dancers for the matter of that.

He ordered another drink.

It was a grey day – between heat and cold, summer and winter, youth and age.

The poet meditated on all the sensible people in the world, on all the lumps of beef waiting to be eaten, on all the children waiting to have their noses blown – on the Ugliness of Virtue and the Sad Reaction after Vice.

On Mornings. On Getting Up.

He was a young poet and he realized that before him in all probability stretched endlessly thousands of mornings. On every one of which he'd have to get up and bathe. No, he could not bathe, for he was poor and lived in Paris. Get up and wash then – slowly – bit by bit.

It was the last straw.

The poet paid for his drinks. . . .

The Sidi

Iт was four o'clock on a Sunday afternoon.
Soon a bell would warn the prisoners that officially it was night and time to sleep in the prison of the Santé.

No. 54 made his simple preparations for repose. He spread his mattress on the floor, for the bars of the iron bed were broken, and to lie on it was torture. Then he stretched himself out fully dressed, eyes wide open, staring at the damp, dirty white walls of his cell. Further and further the walls seemed to recede into the shadow. . . .

His neighbour on the right began a persistent drumming on the wall: Tap, tap, tap, tap, tap, tap, tap, tap. . . .

A code, doubtless; it happened every night.

No. 54 did not answer. The drumming became faster, redoubled its vigour for a time, then stopped slowly as if regretfully.

A heavy step followed by someone walking quickly and lightly. No. 54 heard the door on the left open with loud creaking of its rusty hinges. He heard the warder's voice explaining the way the bed must be made and unmade, the exhortations to be of good behaviour, obedient, orderly, clean – above all clean: the same exhortations he had heard when he had been entombed in his own cell, the walls of which swarmed with vermin, oozed with a black damp.

'*Tiens*, a new one,' thought No. 54.

He began to picture the new one in the obscurity, preparing

to lie down on his horrible bed, the mattress stained, the sheets grey and damp, the coverlet foul. . . .

No. 54 dozed. But in the middle of the night he was awakened by a monotonous chant, a plaintive, minor chant, tuneless, wordless, without other rhythm than that of a high, sharp note at intervals.

It sounded like a dirge in the obscene darkness, and the silent walls of the prison began to wake. The other prisoners were banging with angry fists for silence. But the chant persisted, a wave of sound without end or beginning – an obsession.

When it stopped at last No. 54 was unable to sleep and he lay making conjectures about his neighbour for the rest of the night. A madman, perhaps – there were madmen in the prison – or a habitué who wanted to show that he did not give a dam.

Not that he had sounded joyful or even defiant – it was more like someone praying. And suddenly No. 54 remembered the days before the war when it was fashionable to represent scenes from Moroccan life on the stages of Paris music-halls, and the Moroccan troops on the French front in 1914.

He thought:

'Of course, a Sidi, a Bicot.'

Why not? One of those Arabs who came over in masses during the war, who stayed in France the war over 'to become good Frenchmen.' They stayed, naïvely hoping to make fortunes out of the lowest and the worst paid work, living in colonies in the popular quarters of Paris, always at odds with the law which they did not understand, and with the 'Roumis' whose wives and daughters they coveted in defiance of Allah – drinking wine in floats notwithstanding the Koran.

One of those Arabs – ragged, verminous, thieves, quarrelsome. That was it. That monotonous complaint in the night – he had already heard it when the Bicots on the front chanted their invocations to Allah, the Compassionate.

During the morning exercise No. 54 caught sight of his neighbour. He was an Arab, but not an Arab of the expected type,

haggard with privations and drink, covered with vermin, devoured
by a secret malady. This was quite a young man and beautiful as
some savage Christ. A head sharply cut, as it were, out of ivory
and ebony, two long, very black eyes under heavy eyelids and
long eyelashes, a red-lipped mouth with teeth marvellously white
and even in the emaciated, copper-coloured face. Among his
squalid companions he looked like a chief, a king.

As the prisoners descended the staircase in Indian file the
Sidi turned:

'You – tobacco?' he demanded.

'Yes,' answered No. 54, deftly handing him a little tobacco
hidden in the hollow of his palm.

At the turn of the staircase a warder bawled:

'Ah! You there! You, le Bicot, forward! Eyes front!'

The Sidi shrugged his shoulders disdainfully and spat on the
ground.

As soon as they were out of the sight of the warder he spoke
again:

'Me – not guilty – me not know why in prison – Me sick, very
sick.'

'They all say that,' thought No. 54. 'They don't understand,
naturally, poor devils.'

'You a long time here?' asked the Sidi again.

But another guardian appeared making any answer impossible.

About ten o'clock, after the distribution of the morning soup,
at the hour when all the prisoners whose turn it was to appear at
the Palais de Justice had left their cells and the day's canteen had
been given out, the Sidi began to chant again: the long, gutteral
complaint filled No. 54's cell, made there as it were a thick curtain of melancholy which smothered the power of thought. It was
lugubrious as the howling of a dog in a still country night, and it
broke off suddenly without an end, without a final note.

A tap on the wall – one, two, three taps. In the prisoners'
code: letter C No. 54 rapped in answer. The Sidi knocked seventeen times – Q – Then eight times – H.

No. 54 did not reply. C-Q-H did not make a word. The Arab could not know the letters of the alphabet, useless after all to try to communicate with him.

About four o'clock in the afternoon the Sidi intoned his prayer, always the same, the only recognizable word:

Allah – Allah – Allah!

It was a persecution, something relentless and terrible.

He chanted regularly at stated hours. At night the sound dragged like an uneasy and agonizing dream; in the day it was fierce, obstinate, high, shrill above all the noises of the cells:

Allah – Allah – Allah! . . .

Every morning No. 54 saw the Arab. Every morning they had the same conversation:

'You – tobacco?'

'Yes.'

'Me – not guilty – me not know why in prison.'

One morning the Sidi was absent when the prisoners went for their morning exercise.

'He must be at the Palais de Justice,' thought No. 54.

(For it is at the Santé that the accused spend the time, sometimes months, which elapses between their arrest and their trial at the Palais de Justice.)

But back in the cell he heard a warder unlock his neighbour's door.

'*Comment, salaud,* in bed! *Espèce de sale Bicot!* Get up and get a move on you!'

'Very sick!' moaned the Arab.

'Sick! Couldn't you have said so this morning? Get up! *Allez! Oust!*'

'Sick,' repeated the Sidi.

The warder's voice swelled with rage and pompous irritation:

'Wait a bit – I'll give you sick, you lazy devil you – *Tu te f— du monde* – Wait a bit, you lousy nigger – *espèce de c—*'

The dull thud of a blow – another – another. . . . Not a sound from the Arab. Then a chair overturned, a heavy fall.

The hinges of the door creaked again:

'You want to stay on the floor; well, stay on the floor, but leave the bed alone or I'll give you bed, *salaud.*'

The door of the cell shut, the heavy clump of hobnailed boots along the corridor – silence.

That day the Sidi did not chant, but his life seemed to be draining itself away in a plaintive, endless litany of moans.

When the hour came for food to be served:

'*Tiens,*' said the warder, 'he is still on the floor, the *salaud* – He'd better be careful – *faut pas qu'il m'em—!*'

And to the auxiliary who was serving a quarter of a tin bowl of uneatable rice soup to each prisoner:

'The Bicot doesn't need to eat. *Il peut crever!*'

All that night the frail, thin, moaning sound continued with the regularity of water dripping from a leak. Towards morning it stopped.

'Gone to sleep, poor devil,' thought No. 54 with relief.

At seven o'clock, when the warder came to inspect the beds, there were again loud curses from the direction of the Sidi's cell.

Then a cry – half astounded, half annoyed:

M—, il a clamsé, le Bicot!' (He's kicked the bucket.)

Then No. 54, horrified, knew that his beautiful neighbour was dead. He began to imagine those big, laughing eyes which had been full of images of the vivid colours and the hot light of Morocco, closing on the cold, sombre walls of a French prison, the untidy, dirty bed, the fat fist – black-nailed, the red, furious face and the loose mouth that spat curses of a 'Roumi' functionary.

At the Villa d'Or

SARA OF MONTPARNASSE had arrived that after-noon at the Villa d'Or, and it was now 9:30 P.M.; dinner was just over, it was the hour of coffee, peace, optimism.

From the depths of a huge arm-chair Sara admired the warmly lovely night which looked in through the open windows, the sea, the moon, the palms – the soft lighting of the room.

The very faint sound of music could be heard from the distant Casino at intervals, and on the sofa opposite Mrs. Robert B. Valentine reclined, dressed in a green velvet gown with hanging sleeves lined with rosy satin. Mr. Robert B. Valentine, the Boot-Lace King, sprawled in another huge arm-chair, and five Pekinese were distributed decoratively in the neighbourhood of Mrs. Valentine. It might have been the Villa of the Golden Calf.

'And very nice too,' thought Sara.

Charles came in to take away the coffee-tray, and to present Mr. Valentine with a large, blue book.

Charles was like the arm-chairs, English. He was also, strange to say, supple, handsome, carefully polite. But then Charles was definitely of the lower classes (as distinct from the middle).

'The chef is there, sir,' said he – and 'Anything more, Mad-ame?'

'Nothing, Charles,' said Mrs. Valentine with a hauteur touched with sweetness.

Charles retreated with grace, carrying the tray. He looked as though he enjoyed the whole thing immensely. His good looks, his supple bow from the waist, his livery. . . .

'It must be fun,' thought Sara, 'to be butler in a place where everything is so exactly like a film.'

Mrs. Valentine's daughter of Los Angeles, Cal., was the most famous of movie stars. She received a thousand love-letters per month. In London she was mobbed when she went out. . . . There was a glamour as distinct from money over the household. . . .

Mr. Valentine put on horn-rimmed spectacles and opened the blue book which told of risotto of lobster, of *bécassine glacée sur lac d'or,* of green peppers stuffed with rice.

After a prolonged study of it he announced like some saint turning his back on the false glitter of this world:

'He's got haricots verts down for to-morrow, darling – wouldn't you like some rice for a change?'

Mr. Valentine was a vegetarian, a teetotaller, a non-smoker, an example of the law of compensation like most American millionaires.

Mrs. Valentine moved a little impatiently on her sofa, and through her dignified charm pierced a slight fretfulness.

'I'm just dead sick of rice, Bobbie,' said she. 'Couldn't we have some ham for a change?'

'He says he can't get a ham,' said Mr. Valentine doubtfully. 'He says he'll have to send to Paris for a ham.'

The lady sat up suddenly and announced with energy that it was all nonsense, that she had seen lovely hams in the corner shop in Cannes – that anyone who couldn't get a ham in Cannes couldn't get one anywhere.

'I'll speak to him, darling,' Mr. Valentine told her soothingly.

He got up and walked alertly out. He wore a purple smoking suit and under the light his perfectly bald head shone as if it were polished. He was extremely like some cheerful insect with long, thin legs.

When he had gone, Mrs. Valentine leant back on to her sofa and half closed her eyes. She was such a slender lady that, sunk into the soft cushions she seemed ethereal, a creature of two dimensions, length and breadth, without any thickness. Her shoes were of gold brocade and round her neck glittered a long necklace of green beads with which she fidgeted incessantly – her hands being white and well manicured, but short, energetic and capable, with broad, squat nails.

A Romantic, but only on the surface; also an active and energetic patroness of the Arts, fond of making discoveries in Montparnasse and elsewhere. So Mr. Pauloff, a little Bulgarian who lived in Vienna, occupied a sumptuous bedroom on the second floor. He painted.

Sara, who sang, was installed on the third floor, though, as she was a female and relatively unimportant, her room was less sumptuous.

'It makes me feel sad, that music in the night,' declared Mrs. Valentine. 'The man who is singing at the Casino this week is Mr. van den Cleef's gardener. Isn't it just too strange? A Russian – a prince or something. Yes. And he only gets – what does a gardener get? I don't know – so he sings at the Casino in the evening. Poor man! And so many of them – all princes or generals or Grand Dukes. . . . Of course most unreliable. . . . Why, my dear Miss Cohen, I could tell you stories about the Russians on the Riviera – Well! Strange people – very strange. Not like us. Always trying to borrow money.'

She went on to talk of the Russian character, of her tastes in music, of Mr. Valentine's eighteenth century bed, of the emptiness of life before she became a spiritualist, of automatic writing.

'Yes, yes,' said Sara patiently at intervals.

After all, this was a tremendous reaction from Paris. In Paris one was fear-hunted, insecure, one caught terrifying glimpses of the Depths and the monsters who live there. . . . At the Villa d'Or life was something shallow . . . that tinkled meaninglessly . . . shallow but safe.

Through Mrs. Valentine's high-pitched drawl she strained her ears to hear some faint sound of the sea and imagined the silken caress of the water when she would bathe next morning. Bathing in that blue jewel of a sea would be a voluptuousness, a giving of oneself up. And coming out of it one would be fresh, purified from how many desecrating touches.

Poor Sara . . . also a Romantic!

As Mrs. Valentine was describing the heroism of a famous American dancer who acted as a secret service agent during the war and averted catastrophe to the Allies by swallowing important documents at the right moment, Mr. Pauloff and Mr. Valentine came in.

'Well, I've told him about that ham, darling,' said the Boot-Lace King brightly.

He added in a lower tone: 'Yes, nood, but not too nood, Mr. Pauloff.'

'There will be a drapery,' the Bulgarian assured him.

Mr. Pauloff had painted Mrs. Valentine two years ago surrounded by her Pekinese, and made her incredibly beautiful. Then he had painted Mr. Valentine with exquisite trousers and the rest, brown boots and alert blue eyes.

He was now decorating the panels of Mr. Valentine's bedroom door with figures of little ladies. And a tactful drapery was to float round the little ladies waists. After all he had been a court painter and he had learned to be miraculously tactful. A polite smile was always carved – as it were – on his ugly little face; in his brown, somewhat pathetic eyes was a look of strained attention.

'In courts and places like that,' as Mr. Valentine said, 'they learn nice manners. Well, I guess they just have to. . . .

'I understand, I quite understand,' the artist said diffidently, but with finality, 'I will drape the figures.'

Then he handled a bundle of press-cuttings which he was holding to Sara and asked if she could read them aloud.

'You have so nice, so charming a voice, Miss Sara.'

Sara, overcome by this compliment, proceeded to read the cuttings which were from the English papers of fifteen years before.

'Mr. Yvan Pauloff, the famous Bulgarian artist . . .'

As Sara read Mrs. Valentine closed her eyes and seemed to

sleep, but Mr. Valentine, crossing his legs, listened with great attention; as to the artist himself, he heard it all with a pleased smile, fatuous but charming.

Then he went – radiant – to fetch some photographs of his most celebrated pictures. Mr. Valentine said quickly: 'You see, deary, there you are; he is a great artist. His name on a picture means something – means dollars.'

'Dollars aren't Art, Bobbie,' answered Mrs. Valentine loftily.

Mr. Valentine muttered something, and walking to the window surveyed the view with a proprietor's eyes.

'Come out on the terrace and look at the stars, Miss Sara,' said he. 'Now that star there, it's green, ain't it?'

'Quite green,' she agreed politely, following him out.

He glanced sideways at her, admiring the curves of her figure – he liked curves – the noble and ardent sweep of her nose – that saving touch of Jewish blood!

He proceeded to pour out his soul to the sympathetic creature:

'My wife's always talking about Art. She thinks I don't understand anything about it. Well, I do. Now, for instance: Bottles – the curve of a bottle, the shape of it – just a plain glass bottle. I could look at it for hours. . . . I started life in a chemist's shop –I was brought up amongst the bottles. Now the pleasure I get in looking at a bottle makes me understand artists. . . . D'you get me?'

'Why, that's absolutely it,' said Sara warmly in response to the note of appeal in his voice. 'You understand perfectly.'

'Would you like to come to Monte with me Sunday?' asked Mr. Valentine in a lower tone, grasping Sara's arm above the elbow. 'I'll teach you to play roulette.'

'Yes, it would be fun,' said Sara without a great deal of enthusiasm.

From inside the Villa came the sweet and mocking music of 'La Berggere Légère.'

'And there's my wife playing the Victrola – Time for my billiards,' chirped Mr. Valentine.

He went briskly up the steps and hauled away an unwilling Mr. Pauloff to the billiard-room.

'Sometimes,' said Mrs. Valentine to Sara, 'I play the Victrola for hours all by myself when Bobbie is in the billiard-room, and I think how strange it is that lovely music – and voices of people who are dead – like Caruso – coming out of a black box. Their voices – Themselves in fact – And I just get frightened to death – terrified. I shut it up and run up the stairs and ring like mad for Marie.'

The marble staircase of the Villa d'Or was dim and shadowy, but one or two electric lights were still lit near the famous (and beautiful) portrait of Mrs. Valentine.

'When I see that portrait,' said the lady suddenly, 'I'm glad to go to bed sometimes.'

In her huge bedroom where the furniture did not quite match, where over the bed hung a picture representing a young lady and gentleman vaguely Greek in costume, sitting on a swing with limbs entwined in a marvellous mixture of chastity and grace – this was a relic of the days before Mrs. Valentine had learned to appreciate Picasso – Sara opened the windows wide and looked out on the enchanted night, then sighed with pleasure at the glimpse of her white, virginal bathroom through the open door – the bath-salts, the scents, the crystal bottles.

She thought again: 'Very nice too, the Villa d'Or.'

La Grosse Fifi

T HE SEA,' said Mark Olsen, 'is exactly the colour
of Reckett's blue this morning.'

Roseau turned her head to consider the smooth Mediterranean.

'I like it like that,' she announced, 'and I wish you wouldn't
walk so fast. I loathe tearing along, and this road wasn't made to
tear along anyhow.'

'Sorry,' said Mark, 'just a bad habit.'

They walked in silence, Mark thinking that this girl was a
funny one, but he'd rather like to see a bit more of her. A pity
Peggy seemed to dislike her – women were rather a bore with
their likes and dislikes.

'Here's my hotel,' said the funny one. 'Doesn't it look awful?'

'You know,' Mark told her seriously, 'you really oughtn't to
stay here. It's a dreadful place. Our *patronne* says that it's got a
vile reputation – someone got stabbed or something, and the
patron went to jail.'

'You don't say!' mocked Roseau.

'I do say. There's a room going at the pension.'

'Hate pensions.'

'Well, move then, come to St Paul or Juan les Pins – Peggy
was saying yesterday. . . .'

'Oh Lord!' said Roseau rather impatiently, 'my hotel's all right.
I'll move when I'm ready, when I've finished some work I'm doing.
I think I'll go back to Paris – I'm getting tired of the Riviera, it's
too tidy. Will you come in and have an aperitif?'

Her tone was so indifferent that Mark, piqued, accepted the invitation though the restaurant of that hotel really depressed him. It was so dark, so gloomy, so full of odd-looking, very odd-looking French people with abnormally loud voices even for French people. A faint odour of garlic floated in the air.

'Have a Deloso,' said Roseau, 'It tastes of anis,' she explained, seeing that he looked blank. 'It's got a kick in it.'

'Thank you,' said Mark. He put his sketches carefully on the table, then looking over Roseau's head his eyes became astonished and fixed. He said: 'Oh my Lord! What's that?'

'That's Fifi,' answered Roseau in a low voice and relaxing into a smile for the first time.

'Fifi! Of course – it would be – Good Lord! – Fifi!' His voice was awed. 'She's – she's terrific, isn't she?'

'She's a dear,' said Roseau unexpectedly.

Fifi was not terrific except metaphorically, but she was stout, well corseted – her stomach carefully arranged to form part of her chest. Her hat was large and worn with a rakish sideways slant, her rouge shrieked, and the lids of her protruding eyes were painted bright blue. She wore very long silver earrings; nevertheless her face looked huge – vast, and her voice was hoarse though there was nothing but Vichy water in her glass.

Her small, plump hands were covered with rings, her small, plump feet encased in very high-heeled patent leather shoes.

Fifi was obvious in fact – no mistaking her mission in life. With her was a young man of about twenty-four. He would have been a handsome young man had he not plastered his face with white powder and worn his hair in a high mass above his forehead.

'She reminds me,' said Mark in a whisper, 'of Max Beerbohm's picture of the naughty lady considering Edward VII's head on a coin – You know, the "Ah! well, he'll always be Tum-Tum to me" one.'

'Yes,' said Roseau, 'she is Edwardian, isn't she?' For some unexplainable reason she disliked these jeers at Fifi, resented them even more than she resented most jeers. After all the lady looked so good-natured, such a good sort, her laugh was so jolly.

She said: 'Haven't you noticed what lots there are down here? Edwardian ladies, I mean – Swarms in Nice, shoals in Monte Carlo! . . . In the Casino the other day I saw. . . .'

'Who's the gentleman?' Mark asked, not to be diverted. 'Her son?'

'Her son?' said Roseau, 'Good Heavens, no! That's her gigolo.'

'Her – what did you say?'

'Her gigolo,' explained Roseau coldly. 'Don't you know what a gigolo is? They exist in London, I assure you. She keeps him – he makes love to her, I know all about it because their room's next to mine.'

'Oh!' muttered Mark. He began to sip his apertif hastily.

'I love your name anyway,' he said, changing the conversation abruptly – 'It suits you.'

'Yes, it suits me – it means a reed,' said Roseau. She had a queer smile – a little sideways smile. Mark wasn't quite sure that he liked it – 'A reed shaken by the wind. That's my motto, that is – are you going? Yes, I'll come to tea soon – sometime: goodbye!'

'He's running off to tell his wife how right she was about me,' thought Roseau, watching him. 'How rum some English people are! They ask to be shocked and long to be shocked and hope to be shocked, but if you really shock them . . . how shocked they are!'

She finished her aperitif gloomily. She was waiting for an American acquaintance who was calling to take her to lunch. Meanwhile the voices of Fifi and the gigolo grew louder.

'I tell you,' said the gigolo, 'that I must go to Nice this afternoon. It is necessary – I am forced.'

His voice was apologetic but sullen, with a hint of the bully. The male straining at his bonds.

'But *mon chéri*,' implored Fifi, 'may I not come with you? We will take tea at the Negresco afterwards.'

The gigolo was sulkily silent. Obviously the Negresco with Fifi did not appeal to him.

She gave way at once.

'Marie!' she called, 'serve Monsieur immediately. Monsieur must catch the one-thirty to Nice . . . You will return to dinner, my Pierrot?' she begged huskily.

'I think so, I will see,' answered the gigolo loftily, following up his victory as all good generals should – and at that moment Roseau's American acquaintance entered the restaurant.

They lunched on the terrace of a villa looking down on the calmly smiling sea.

'That blue, that blue!' sighed Miss Ward, for such was the American lady's name – 'I always say that blue's wonderful. It gets right down into one's soul – don't you think, Mr Wheeler?'

Mr Wheeler turned his horn spectacles severly on the blue.

'Very fine,' he said briefly.

'I'm sure,' thought Roseau, 'that he's wondering how much it would sell for – bottled.'

She found herself thinking of a snappy advertisement: 'Try our Bottled Blue for Soul Ills.'

Then pulling herself together she turned to M. Leroy, the fourth member of the party, who was rapidly becoming sulky.

Monsieur Leroy was what the French call *'un joli garçon'* – he was even, one might say, a very pretty boy indeed – tall, broad, tanned, clean looking as any Anglo-Saxon. Yet for quite three-quarters of an hour two creatures of the female sex had taken not the faintest notice of him. Monsieur Leroy was puzzled, incredulous. Now he began to be annoyed.

However, he responded instantly to Roseau's effort to include him in the conversation.

'Oh, Madame,' he said, 'I must say that very strong emotion is an excuse for anything – one is mad for the moment.'

'There!' said Roseau in triumph, for the argument had been about whether anything excused the Breaking of Certain Rules.

'That's all nonsense,' said Mr Wheeler.

'But you excuse a sharp business deal?' persisted Roseau.

'Business,' said Mr Wheeler, as if speaking to a slightly idiotic child, 'is quite different, Miss . . . er . . .'

'You think that,' argued Roseau, 'because it's your form of emotion.'

Mr Wheeler gave her up.

'Maurice,' said Miss Ward, who loved peace, to the young Frenchman, 'fetch the gramophone, there's a good child!'

The gramophone was fetched and the strains of 'Lady, be Good' floated out towards the blue.

The hotel seemed sordid that night to Roseau, full of gentlemen in caps and loudly laughing females. There were large lumps of garlic in the food, the wine was sour. . . . She felt very tired, bruised, aching, yet dull as if she had been defeated in some fierce struggle.

'Oh God, I'm going to think, don't let me think,' she prayed.

For two weeks she had desperately fought off thoughts. She drank another glass of wine, looked at Fifi sitting alone at the mimosa-decorated table with protruding eyes fixed on the door; then looked away again as though the sight frightened her. Her dinner finished she went straight up into her bedroom, took three cachets of veronal, undressed, lay down with the sheet over her head.

Suddenly she got up, staggered against the table, said 'Damn', turned the light on and began to dress, but quietly, quietly. Out through the back door. And why was she dressing anyway? Never mind – done now. And who the hell was that knocking?

It was Fifi. She was wonderfully garbed in a transparent nightgown of a vivid rose colour trimmed with yellow lace. Over this she had hastily thrown a dirty dressing-gown, knotting the sleeves round her neck.

She stared at Roseau, her eyes full of a comic amazement.

'I hope I do not disturb you, Madame,' she said politely. 'But I heard you – *enfin* – I was afraid that you were ill. My room is next door.'

'Is it?' said Roseau faintly. She felt giddy and clutched at the corner of the table.

'You are surely not thinking of going out now,' Fifi remarked. 'I think it is almost midnight, and you do not look well, Madame.'

She spoke gently, coaxingly, and put her hand on Roseau's arm.

Roseau collapsed on the bed in a passion of tears.

'Ma petite,' said Fifi with decision, 'you will be better in bed, believe me. Where is your *chemise de nuit?* Ah!'

She took it from the chair close by, looked rapidly with a calculating eye at the lace on it, then put a firm hand on Roseau's skirt to help her with the process of undressing.

'La,' she said, giving the pillow a pat, 'and here is your pocket handkerchief.'

She was not dismayed, contemptuous or curious. She was comforting.

'To cry is good,' she remarked after a pause. 'But not too much. Can I get anything for you, my little one? Some hot milk with rum in it?'

'No, no,' said Roseau, clutching the flannel sleeve, 'don't go – don't leave me – lonely –'

She spoke in English, but Fifi responding at once to the appeal answered:'*Pauvre chou – va,*' and bent down to kiss her.

It seemed to Roseau the kindest, the most understanding kiss she had ever had, and comforted she watched Fifi sit on the foot of the bed and wrap her flannel dressing-gown more closely round her. Mistily she imagined that she was a child again and that this was a large, protecting person who would sit there till she slept.

The bed creaked violently under the lady's weight.

'Cursed bed,' muttered Fifi. 'Everything in this house is broken, and then the prices they charge! It is shameful . . .'

'I am very unhappy,' remarked Roseau in French in a small, tired voice. Her swollen eyelids were half shut.

'And do you think I have not seen?' said Fifi earnestly, laying one plump hand on Roseau's knee. 'Do you think I don't know when a woman is unhappy' – I – Besides, with you it is easy to see. You look *avec les yeux d'une biche* – It's naturally a man who makes you unhappy?'

'Yes,' said Roseau. To Fifi she could tell everything – Fifi was as kind as God.

'Ah! *le salaud*: ah! *le monstre.*' This was said mechanically, without real indignation. 'Men are worth nothing. But why should he make you unhappy? He is perhaps jealous?'

'Oh, no!' said Roseau.

'Then perhaps he is *méchant* – there are men like that – or perhaps he is trying to disembarrass himself of you.'

'That's it,' said Roseau. 'He is trying to – disembarrass himself of me.'

'Ah!' said Fifi wisely. She leant closer. *'Mon enfant,'* said she hoarsely, 'do it first. Put him at the door with a *coup de pied quelque part.'*

'But I haven't got a door,' said Roseau in English, beginning to laugh hysterically. 'No vestige of a door I haven't – no door, no house, no friends, no money, no nothing.'

'Comment?' said Fifi suspiciously. She disliked foreign languages being talked in her presence.

'Supposing I do – what then?' Roseau asked her.

'What then?' screamed Fifi. 'You ask what then – you who are pretty. If I were in your place I would not ask "what then", I tell you – I should find a chic type – and quickly!'

'Oh!' said Roseau. She was beginning to feel drowsy.

'Un clou chasse l'autre,' remarked Fifi, rather gloomily. 'Yes, that is life – one nail drives out the other.'

She got up.

'One says that.' Her eyes were melancholy. 'But when one is caught it is not so easy. No, I adore my Pierrot. I adore that child – I would give him my last sou – and how can he love me? I am old, I am ugly. Oh, I know. *Regarde moi ces yeux là!'* She pointed to the caverns under her eyes – *'Et ça!'* She touched her enormous chest. 'Pierrot who only loves slim women. *Que voulez-vous?'*

Fifi's shrug was wonderful!

'I love him – I bear everything. But what a life! What a life! . . . You, my little one, a little courage – we will try to find you a chic type, a –'

She stopped seeing that Roseau was almost asleep. 'Alors – I am going – sleep well.'

Next morning Roseau, with a dry tongue, a heavy head, woke to the sound of loud voices in the next room.

Fifi, arguing, grumbling, finally weeping – the gigolo who had obviously just come in, protesting becoming surly.

'*Menteur, menteur,* you have been with a woman!'

'I tell you no. You make ideas for yourself.'

Sobs, kisses, a reconciliation

'Oh Lord! Oh Lord!' said Roseau. She put the friendly sheet over her head thinking: 'I must get out of this place.'

But when an hour afterwards the stout lady knocked and made her appearance she was powdered, smiling and fresh – almost conventional.

'I hope you slept well last night, Madame; I hope you feel better this morning? Can I do anything for you?'

'Yes, sit and talk to me,' said Roseau. 'I'm not getting up this morning.'

'You are right,' Fifi answered. 'That reposes, a day in bed.' She sat heavily down and beamed. 'And then you must amuse yourself a little,' she advised. 'Distract yourself. If you wish I will show you all the places where one amuses oneself in Nice.'

But Roseau, who saw the 'chic type' lurking in Fifi's eyes, changed the conversation. She said she wished she had something to read.

'I will lend you a book,' said Fifi at once. 'I have many books.'

She went to her room and came back with a thin volume.

'Oh, poetry!' said Roseau. She had hoped for a good detective story. She did not feel in the mood for French poetry.

'I adore poetry,' said Fifi with sentiment. 'Besides, this is very beautiful. You understand French perfectly? Then listen.'

She began to read:

'*Dans le chemin libre de mes années*
Je marchais fière et je me suis arrêtée . . .

'Thou hast bound my ankles with silken cords.

'Que j'oublie les mots qui ne disent pas mon amour,
Les gestes qui ne doivent pas t'enlacer,
Que l'horizon se ferme à ton sourire . . .

'Mais je t'en conjure, ô Sylvius, comme la plus hum-
ble des choses qui ont une place dans ta maison
– garde-moi.'

In other words: you won't be rotten – now. Will you, will you?
I'll do anything you like, but be kind to me, won't you, won't you?
Not that it didn't sound better in French.
'Now,' read Fifi,

'I can walk lightly for I have laid my life in the hands
of my lover.

'Change, chante ma vie, aux mains de mon amant!'

And so on, and so on.

Roseau thought that it was horrible to hear this ruin of a woman
voicing all her own moods, all her own thoughts. Horrible.

'Sylvius, que feras-tu à travers les jours de cet
être que t'abandonne sa faiblesse?
Il peut vivre d'une sourire, mourir d'une parole.
Sylvius, qu'en feras-tu?'

'Have you got any detective stories?' Roseau interrupted suddenly. She felt that she could not bear any more.

Fifi was surprised but obliging. Yes – she had Arsène Lupin,
several of Gaston Leroux; also she had 'Shaerlock 'Olmes'.

Roseau chose *Le Fantôme de l'Opéra*, and when Fifi had left
the room, stared for a long time at the same page:

'Sylvius, qu'en feras-tu?'

Suddenly she started to laugh and she laughed long, and very loudly for Roseau, who had a small voice and the ghost of a laugh.

That afternoon Roseau met Sylvius, *alias* the gigolo, in the garden of the hotel.

She had made up her mind to detest him. What excuse for the gigolo? None – none whatever.

There he was with his mistress in Cannes and his mistress in Nice. And Fifi on the rack. Fifi, with groans, producing a *billet de mille* when the gigolo turned the screw. Horrible gigolo!

She scowled at him, carefully thinking out a gibe about the colour of his face powder. But that afternoon his face was unpowdered and reluctantly she was forced to see that the creature was handsome. There was nothing of the blond beast about the gigolo – he was dark, slim, beautiful as some Latin god. And how soft his eyes were, how sweet his mouth. . . .

Horrible, horrible gigolo!

He did not persist, but looking rather surprised at her snub, went away with a polite murmur: '*Alors,* Madame.'

A week later he disappeared.

Fifi in ten days grew ten years older and she came no more to Roseau's room to counsel rum and hot milk instead of veronal. But head up, she faced a hostile and sneering world.

'Have you any news of Monsieur Rivière?' the *patronne* of the hotel would ask with a little cruel female smile.

'Oh, yes, he is very well,' Fifi would answer airily, knowing perfectly well that the *patronne* had already examined her letters carefully. 'His grandmother, alas! is much worse, poor woman.'

For the gigolo had chosen the illness of his grandmother as a pretext for his abrupt departure.

One day Fifi despatched by post a huge wreath of flowers – it appeared that the gigolo's grandmother had departed this life.

Then silence. No thanks for the flowers.

Fifi's laugh grew louder and hoarser, and she gave up Vichy for champagne.

She was no longer alone at her table – somehow she could collect men – and as she swam into the room like a big vessel with all sails set, three, four, five would follow in her wake, the party making a horrible noise.

'That dreadful creature!' said Peggy Olsen one night. 'How does she get all those men together?'

Mark laughed and said: 'Take care, she's a pal of Roseau's.'

'Oh! is she?' said Mrs Olsen. She disliked Roseau and thought the hotel with its *clientèle* of chauffeurs – and worse – beyond what an English gentlewoman should be called upon to put up with.

She was there that night because her husband had insisted on it.

'The girl's lonely – come on, Peggy – don't be such a wet blanket.'

So Peggy had gone, her tongue well sharpened, ready for the fray.

'The dear lady must be very rich,' she remarked. 'She's certainly most hospitable.'

'Oh, she isn't the hostess,' said Roseau, absurdly anxious that her friend's triumph should be obvious. 'The man with the beard is host, I'm sure. He adores Fifi.'

'Extraordinary!' said Mrs Olsen icily.

Roseau thought: 'You sneering beast, you little sneering beast. Fifi's worth fifty of you!' – but she said nothing, contenting her self with one of those sideway smiles which made people think: 'She's a funny one.'

The electric light went out.

The thin, alert, fatigued-looking bonne brought candles. That long drab room looked ghostly in the flickering light – one had an oddly definite impression of something sinister and dangerous – all these heavy jowls and dark, close-set eyes, coarse hands, loud, quarrelsome voices. Fifi looked sinister too with her vital hair and ruined throat.

'You know,' Roseau said suddenly, 'you're right. My hotel is a rum place.'

'Rum is a good word,' said Mark Olsen. 'You really oughtn't to stay here.'

'No, I'm going to leave. It's just been sheer laziness to make the move and my room is rather charming. There's a big mimosa tree just outside the window. But I will leave.'

As the electric light came on again they were discussing the prices of various hotels.

But next morning Roseau, lying in bed and staring at the mimosa tree, faced the thought of how much she would miss Fifi.

It was ridiculous, absurd, but there it was. Just the sound of that hoarse voice always comforted her; gave her the sensation of being protected, strengthened.

'I must be dotty,' said Roseau to herself. 'Of course I would go and like violently someone like that – I must be dotty. No. I'm such a coward, so dead frightened of life, that I must hang on to some body – even Fifi. . . .'

Dead frightened of life was Roseau, suspended over a dark and terrible abyss – the abyss of absolute loss of self-control.

'Fifi,' said Roseau talking to herself, 'is a pal. She cheers me up. On the other hand she's a dreadful-looking old tart, and I oughtn't to go about with her. It'll be another good old Downward Step if I do.'

Fifi knocked.

She was radiant, bursting with some joyful tidings.

'Pierrot is returning,' she announced.

'Oh!' said Roseau interested.

'Yes, I go to meet him at Nice this afternoon.'

'I am glad!' said Roseau.

It was impossible not to be glad in that large and beaming presence. Fifi wore a new black frock with lace at the neck and wrists and a new hat, a small one.

'My hat?' she asked anxiously. 'Does it make me ridiculous? Is it too small? Does it make me look old?'

'No,' said Roseau, considering her carefully – 'I like it, but put the little veil down.'

Fifi obeyed.

'Ah, well,' she sighed, 'I was always ugly. When I was small my sister called me the devil's doll. Yes – always the compliments like that are what I get. Now – alas! You are sure I am not ridiculous in that hat?'

'No, no,' Roseau told her. 'You look very nice.'

Dinner that night was a triumph for Fifi – champagne flowed – three bottles of it. An enormous bunch of mimosa and carnations almost hid the table from view. The patronne looked sideways, half enviously; the patron chuckled, and the gigolo seemed pleased and affable.

Roseau drank her coffee and smoked a cigarette at the festive table, but refused to accompany them to Nice. They were going to a *boîte de nuit,* 'all that was of the most chic.'

'Ah, bah!' said Fifi good-naturedly scornful, 'she is droll the little one. She always wishes to hide in a corner like a little mouse.'

'No one,' thought Roseau, awakened at four in the morning, 'could accuse Fifi of being a little mouse.' Nothing of the mouse about Fifi.

'I'm taking him to Monte Carlo,' the lady announced next morning. She pronounced it Monte Carl'.

'Monte Carlo – why?'

'He wishes to go. Ah! la la – it will cost me something!' She made a little rueful, clucking noise. 'And Pierrot, who always gives such large tips to the waiters – if he knew as I do what *salauds* are the *garçons de café—,*

'Well, enjoy yourself,' Roseau said laughing. 'Have a good time.'

The next morning she left the hotel early and did not return till dinner-time, late, preoccupied.

As she began her meal she noticed that some men in the restaurant were jabbering loudly in Italian – but they always jabbered.

The patron was not there – the *patronne,* looking haughty, was talking rapidly to her *lingère.*

But the bonne looked odd, Roseau thought, frightened but bursting with importance. As she reached the kitchen she called in a shrill voice to the cook: 'It is in the *Eclaireur.* Have you seen?'

Roseau finished peeling her apple. Then she called out to the *patronne* – she felt impelled to do it.

'What is it, Madame? Has anything happened?'

The *patronne* hesitated.

'Madame Carly – Madame Fifi – has met with an accident,' she answered briefly.

'An accident? An automobile accident? Oh, I do hope it isn't serious.'

'It's serious enough – *assez grave,*' the *patronne* answered evasively.

Roseau asked no more questions. She took up the *Éclaireur de Nice* lying on the table and looked through it.

She was looking for the 'Fatal Automobile Accident'.

She found the headline:

YET ANOTHER DRAMA OF JEALOUSY

'Madame Francine Carly, aged 48, of 7 rue Notre Dame des Pleurs, Marseilles, was fatally stabbed last night at the hotel – Monte Carlo, by her lover Pierre Rivière, aged 24, of rue Madame Tours. Questioned by the police he declared that he acted in self-defence as his mistress, who was of a very jealous temperament, had attacked him with a knife when told of his approaching marriage, and threatened to blind him. When the proprietor of the hotel, alarmed by the woman's shrieks, entered the room accompanied by two policemen, Madame Carly was lying unconscious, blood streaming from the wounds in her throat. She was taken to the hospital, where she died without recovering consciousness.

'The murderer has been arrested and taken to the Depôt.'

Roseau stared for a long time at the paper.

'I must leave this hotel,' was her only thought, and she slept soundly that night without fear of ghosts.

A horrible, sordid business. Poor Fifi! Almost she hated herself for feeling so little regret.

But next morning while she was packing she opened the book of poems, slim, much handled, still lying on the table, and searched for the verse Fifi had read:

> '*Maintenant je puis marcher légère,*
> *J'ai mis toute ma vie aux mains de mon amant.*
> *Chante, change ma vie aux mains de mon amant.*'

Suddenly Roseau began to cry.

'O poor Fifi! O poor Fifi!'

In that disordered room in the midst of her packing she cried bitterly, heartbroken.

Till, in the yellow sunshine that streamed into the room, she imagined that she saw her friend's gay and childlike soul, freed from its gross body, mocking her gently for her sentimental tears.

'Oh well!' said Roseau.

She dried her eyes and went on with her packing.

Vienne

FUNNY HOW it's slipped away, Vienna. Nothing left but a few snapshots.

Not a friend, not a pretty frock – nothing left of Vienna.

Hot sun, my black frock, a hat with roses, music, lots of music –

The little dancer at the Parisien with a Kirchner girl's legs and a little faun's face.

She was so exquisite that girl that it clutched at one, gave one pain that anything so lovely could ever grow old, or die, or do ugly things.

A fragile child's body, a fluff of black skirt ending far above the knee. Silver straps over that beautiful back, the wonderful legs in black silk stockings and little satin shoes, short hair, cheeky little face.

She gave me the *songe bleu*. Four, five feet she could jump and come down on that wooden floor without a sound. Her partner, an unattractive individual in badly fitting trousers, could lift her with one hand, throw her in the air – catch her, swing her as one would a flower.

At the end she made an adorable little '*gamine*'s' grimace.

Ugly humanity, I'd always thought. I saw people differently afterwards – because for once I'd met sheer loveliness with a flame inside, for there was 'it' – the spark, the flame in her dancing.

Pierre (a damn good judge) raved about her. André also, though cautiously, for he was afraid she would be too expensive.

All the French officers coveted her – night after night the place was packed.

Finally she disappeared. Went back to Budapest where afterwards we heard of her.

Married to a barber. Rum.

Pretty women, lots. How pretty women here are. Lovely food. Poverty gone, the dread of it – going.

'I call them war material,' said Colonel Ishima, giggling.

He meant women, the Viennese women. But when I asked him about the Geisha – I thought it might be amusing to hear about the Geisha first hand as it were. Europeans are so very contradictory about the subject – he pursed up his mouth and looked prim.

'We don't talk about these people – shameful people.'

However, he added after looking suspiciously at a dish of kidneys and asking what they were:

'The Geisha were good people during the war, patriotic people. The Geisha served Nippon well.'

He meant the Russo-Japanese War. One had visions of big blond Russian officers and slant-eyed girls like exotic dolls stabbing them under the fifth rib, or stealing their papers when they were asleep . . .

Every fortnight the Japanese officers solemnly entertained their following at Sacher's Hotel, and they were entertained one by one in return, because in a mass they were really rather overwhelming.

Of course, there it was – the Japanese had to have a following. To begin with, not one of them could speak the three necessary languages, English, German and French, properly. It meant perpetual translation and arguments. And they were dreadfully afraid of not being as tactful as an Asiatic power ought to be, or of voting with the minority instead of the majority, which would have been the end of them at Tokio.

Si Ishima had his secretary and confidential adviser (that was Pierre) and Hato had his, and Matsjijiri had his, not to speak of three typists, a Hungarian interpreter and various other hangers-on.

Every fortnight they gave a dinner to the whole lot. It began with caviare and ended with Tokayer and Hato singing love songs, which was the funniest thing I ever heard.

He only had one eye, poor dear; the other disappeared during the Russo-Japanese War. He sang in a high bleat, holding tightly on to one foot and rocking backwards and forwards.

He was very *vieux jeu, arrière,* a Samurai or something, he wore a kimono whenever he could get into it and he loved making solemn proclamations to the delegation. He called them: *Ordres du jour.*

He made one to the typists, *à propos* of the temptation of Vienne, which began like this:

'*Vous êtes jeunes, vous êtes femmes, vous êtes faibles. Pour l'honneur du Nippon,*' etc, etc.

Through some mistake this *ordre du jour* was solemnly brought to an elderly, moustached French general, whilst the Commission was having a meeting to decide some minor detail of the fate of the conquered country. He opened it and read: '*Vous êtes, jeunes, vous êtes femmes, vous êtes faibles.*'

'*Merde, alors!*' said the general, '*qu' est-ce c'est que ca?*'

Hato was a great joy. He despised Europeans heartily. They all did that, exception made in favour of Germany – for the Japanese thought a lot of the German Army and the German way of keeping women in their place. They twigged that at once. Not much they didn't twig.

But they were all bursting with tact and Ishima, immediately after his remark about war material, paid me many flowery compliments. He hoped, he said, to see me one day in Japan. The Lord forbid!

After dinner we went to the Tabarin. He stared haughtily with boot-button eyes at a very pretty little girl, a girl like a wax doll, who was strolling aimlessly about, and who smiled at him very pitifully and entreatingly when she thought I was not looking.

I knew all about her. She had been Ishima's friend, his

acknowledged friend – *en titre*. She really was pretty and young. The odd thing is that the Japanese have such good taste in European women, whereas European tastes in Japanese women is simply atrocious, or so the Japanese say.

Well, and Ishima had got rid of her because she was faithful to him. Odd reason.

It happened like this: he had a visit from a friend from Japan – a prince of the blood, who adored plain boiled fish and ate them in a simple and efficient way, holding them up by the tail with one hand and using his fork vigorously with the other. Ishima offered him with Eastern hospitality everything he possessed – his suite of rooms at the Sacher and the services of his little friend. But the little friend, thinking perhaps to enhance her value, objected – objected with violence, made a scene in fact, and Ishima, more in sorrow than anger, never saw her again.

He just couldn't get over it.

Pierre told me that one day, after meditating for a long time, he asked: 'Was she mad, poor girl, or would others have done the same?'

Pierre answered cautiously that it depended. The ones with temperament would all have made a fuss if only for pride's sake, and the Viennese have nearly as much temperament as the French, the Hungarians even more. On the other hand, the Germans – enfin, it depended.

Ishima meditated a long time. Then he shook his head and said: '*Tiens, tiens, c'est bizarre!*' . . .

I thought of the story that night and hated him. He was so like a monkey, and a fattish monkey which was worse . . .

On the other hand there was Kashua, who looked even more like a monkey and he was a chic type who had rescued another unfortunate bit of war material deserted without a penny by an Italian officer. Not only did Kashua giver her a fabulous sum in yen, but also he paid her expenses at a sanatorium for six months – she was consumptive.

There you are! How can one judge!

Kashua came up grinning and bowing and sat with us. He

showed me photographs of his wife – she looked a darling – and of his three daughters. Their names meant; Early Rising, Order, and Morning Sun. And he had bought them each a typewriter as a present.

Then, with tears in his eyes and a quaver of pride in his voice – his little son.

'I think your wife is very pretty,' I told him.

He said, grinning modestly: 'Not at all, not at all.'

'And I am sure she will be very happy when you will go back to Japan,' I said.

'Very happy, very happy,' he told me. 'Madame Kashua is a most happy woman, a very fortunate woman.'

I said: 'I expect she is.'

Well, Kashua is a chic type, so I expect she is too.

But I believe my dislike of the Viennese nightplaces started at that moment.

We found a flat – the top floor of General von Marken's house in the Razunoffskygasse, and André shared it with us for a time.

He was a little man, his legs were too short, but he took the greatest trouble to have his suits cut to disguise it.

I mean, with the waist of his coat very high, almost under the arms, the chest padded, decided heels to his shoes.

After all these pains what Tilly called his *'silhouette'* was not unattractive.

One could tell a Frenchman, Parisian, a mile off. Quantities of hair which he had waved every week, rather honest blue eyes, a satyr's nose and mouth.

That's what André was, a satyr – aged twenty-four.

He'd stiffen all over when he saw a pretty woman, like those dogs – don't they call them pointers – do when they see a rabbit. His nose would go down over his mouth.

It was the oddest thing to watch him at the Tabarin where there was a particularly good dancer.

He spent hours, all his spare time, I believe, pursuing, searching.

One day walking in the Kärntnerstrasse we saw the whole

proceedings – the chase, the hat raising, the snub. He often got snubbed.

He was so utterly without pretence or shame that he wasn't horrid.

He lived for women; his father had died of women and so would he. *Voilà tout.*

When I arrived in Vienna his friend was a little dancer called Lysyl.

Lysyl and Ossi was her turn – an Apache dance.

She had a wonderfully graceful body, and a brutal peasant's face – and André was torn between a conviction that she wasn't 'chic' enough and a real appreciation of the said grace – he'd lean over the loge when she was dancing, breathing, hard eyes popping out of his head.

One night we went with him to some out-of-the-way music-hall to see her, and after her turn was over she came to visit our loge – on her best behaviour of course.

I took a sudden fancy to her that night – to her grace and her little child's voice saying: *'Ach, meine blumen* – André, André. *Ich hab' meine blumen vergessen'* – so I snubbed André when he started to apologize, I suppose for contaminating me, and told him of course he could bring her back to supper.

We squashed up together in one of those Viennese cabs with two horses that go like hell. She sat in a big coat and little hat, hugging her *blumen* – in the dark one couldn't see her brute's face.

She really was charming that night.

But next morning, when she came to say good-bye before going, the charm wasn't at all in evidence.

She took half my box of cigarettes, asked by signs how much my dress had cost, 'Why is this woman polite to me,' said her little crafty eyes.

Also, most unlucky of all, she met Blanca von Marken on the stairs.

An hour afterwards Madame von Marken had come to see me, to protest.

Blanca was a *jeune fille.* Surely I understood . . . I would forgive her, but in Vienna they were old-fashioned. . . .

Of course I understood, and against all my sense of fairness and logic apologized and said I agreed.

For God knows, if there's one hypocrisy I loathe more than another, it's the fiction of the 'good' woman and the 'bad' one.

André apologized too, but I'm sure he had no sense of being wanting in logic.

So he grovelled with gusto, feeling chivalrous as he did so, and a protector of innocence. Oh, Lord!

'Vous savez, mon vieux, je n'ai pas pensé – une jeune fille!'

However, not being Don Quixote I did not even try to protect Lysyl.

I think she could take care of herself.

But though she got on as a dancer and became *mondäne Tänzerin* – I think that's how they spell it – André was done with her.

The fiat had gone forth.

Elle n'a pas de chic.

Because I liked Blanca and Madame von Marken, I even tried to make up for the shock to their virtue by hanging up Franz Josef and all the ancestors in the sitting-room.

I'd taken them all down in an effort to make the place less gloomy and whiskery and antimacassary – but I saw it hurt that poor pretty lady so up they went again and I started living in my bedroom, which was charming.

Very big, polished floor, lots of windows, little low tables to make coffee – some lovely Bohemian glass.

Also I spent much time in the Prater.

Quantities of lilac, mauve and white –

Always now I'll associate lilac with Vienna.

The Radetsky Hotel was perhaps twenty minutes or half an hour from Vienna by car – and it was real country.

But that is one of the charms of the place – no suburbs.

It wasn't really comfortable; there wasn't a bathroom in the whole establishment, but for some reason it was exciting and gay and they charged enormous prices accordingly.

All the men who made money out of the 'change came there to spend it, bringing the woman of the moment.

All the pretty people with doubtful husbands or no husbands, or husbands in jail (lots of men went to jail – I don't wonder. Every day new laws about the exchange and smuggling gold).

Everybody, in fact.

Very vulgar, of course, but all Vienna was vulgar.

Gone the *'Aristokraten'*.

They sat at home rather hungry, while their women did the washing.

The ugly ones.

The pretty ones tried to get jobs as *mondäne Tänzerinnen*.

Quite right too – perhaps.

Just prejudice to notice podgy hands and thick ankles – keep your eyes glued on the pretty face.

Also prejudice to see stark brutality behind the bows and smiles of the men.

Also prejudice to watch them eat or handle a toothpick.

Stupid too – so much better not to look.

The girls were well dressed, not the slightest bit made up – that seemed odd after Paris.

Gorgeous blue sky and green trees and a good orchestra.

And heat and heat.

I was cracky with joy of life that summer of 1921.

I'd darling muslin frocks covered with frills and floppy hats – or a little peasant dress and no hat.

Well, and Tillie was a queen of the Radetzky. It was through her (she told André) that we got to know of it.

Tillie possessed wonderful eyes, grey-blue – hair which made her look like Gaby Deslys, a graceful figure.

And with that she made one entirely forget the dreadful complexion, four gold teeth, and enormous feet.

This sounds impossible in a place where competition was, to

say the least of it, keen, but is strictly true.

Every time one saw Tillie one would think – 'Gee, how pretty she is.' In the midst of all the others everyone would turn to look at her and her gorgeous hair.

And behind walked André, caught at last, held tight 'by the skin', as the French say.

All his swank was gone – he watched her as a dog watches his master, and when he spoke to her his voice was like a little boy's.

She'd flirt outrageously with somebody else (half the men there had been her lovers so it was an exciting renewal of old acquaintanceships), and André would sit so miserable that the tears were nearly there.

One night in fact they did come when I patted him on the arm and said 'Poor old André – cheer up.'

'*Une grue,*' said Pierre brutally, 'André is a fool – and Frances, leave that girl alone –'

But I didn't leave her alone at once, too interested to watch the comedy.

Next Saturday evening we were dining at Radetzky with a German acquaintance of Pierre's.

Excessively good-looking, but, being a Prussian, brutal, of course.

'*Donner-r-r- wetter-r-r-,*' he'd bawl at the waiters, and the poor men would jump and run.

But perhaps I exaggerated the brutality for he'd done something I'm still English enough to loathe: he'd discussed Tillie with great detail and openness – he'd had a love affair with her.

Just as we were talking about something else, herself and André hove in sight.

André walked straight to our table and asked if they might join us.

Impossible to refuse without being brutal, though Pierre wasn't cordial, and the other man kissed her hand with a sneer that gave the whole show away.

As for Tillie, she behaved perfectly – not a movement, not the flicker of an eyelash betrayed her – though it must have been trying, just as she was posing as a mondaine, to meet this enemy openly hostile.

Nor did she let it interfere in the slightest with her little plan for the evening, well thought out, well carried out.

She owned a beautiful necklace which she always wore, and that night she firmly led the conversation in the direction of pearls.

I couldn't do much 'leading', or indeed much talking in German. I gathered the drift of things, and occasionally Pierre translated.

Tillie's pearls (she told us) were all she had left of a marvellous stock of jewels (*wunderschön!*).

In fact, all she had between herself and destitution, all and all –

Ach – the music chimed in a mournful echo . . .

She was sad that evening, subdued, eyes almost black, voice sweet and quivery.

After dinner she asked me charmingly if I would mind 'a little walking' – it was so hot – they weren't playing well.

I was quite ready – it was hot – and Tillie went up to her room and came down with a scarf very tightly wrapped round her throat.

We set out. Myself, Pierre and Lieutenant – I've completely forgotten his name – walking together, André and Tillie some little way in front.

Pitch dark in the woods round the hotel – so dark that it frightened me after a while, and I suggested going back.

Shouted to the others, no answer, too far ahead.

We'd got back and were sitting comfortably in the hall drinking liqueurs (alone, for everybody assembled in the bar after dinner to dance) when André came in running, out of breath, agitated.

'The pearls, Tillie's pearls, lost – *Bon Dieu de bon Dieu*. She's dropped them –'

He spoke to me, the only sympathetic listener.

Then entered Tillie. Gone the pathos. She looked ugly and dangerous with her underlip thrust out.

A torrent of German to Pierre who listened and said in a non-committal way: 'She says that André kissed her in the woods and was rough, and that the clasp of the pearls wasn't sure. It's André's fault, she says, and he'll have to pay up.'

The other man laughed. Suddenly she turned on him like a fury.

'*Mein lieber Herr.* . . .' I couldn't understand the words; I did the tone.

'Mind your own business if you know what's good for yourself.'

Meanwhile Pierre, whose instinct is usually to act while other people talk, had gone off and come back with two lanterns and a very sensible proposition.

We would go at once, all four of us, holding hands so that not an inch of the ground should be missed, over exactly the same road.

Too dark for anyone else to have picked them up.

Tillie, to my astonishment, didn't seem very keen.

However, we set out in a long row stooping forward. André held one lantern, Pierre the other.

I looked at first perfectly seriously, straining my eyes.

Then André moved his lantern suddenly and I saw Tillie's face. She was smiling, I could swear – she certainly wasn't looking on the ground.

I looked at Pierre – his search was very perfunctory; the other man wasn't even pretending to look.

At that moment I liked André – I felt sorry for him, akin to him.

He and I of the party had both swallowed the story; we were the Fools.

I could have shaken his hand and said: 'Hail, brother Doormat, in a world of Boots.'

But I'd been too sure of the smile to go on looking.

After that I gave all my attention to the little game the German was playing with my hand.

He'd reached my wrist – my arm – I pulled away –

My hand again, but the fingers interlocked.

Very cool and steady he was – and a tiny pulse beating somewhere.

A dispute. We didn't come this way Tillie was saying.

But it had become a farce to everybody but the faithful André.

We went back, but before we'd come within hearing of the
music from the hotel, he had comforted her with many promises.

And he kept them too. He turned a deaf ear to all hints that it
was or might be a trick.

When we went to Budapest Tillie came. Later on to Berlin,
she went too.

She never left him till she could arrange to do so, taking with
her every sou he possessed, and a big diamond he'd bought.

This sequel we heard only later.

Poor André! Let us hope he had some compensation for forgetting for once that 'eat or be eaten' is the inexorable law of life.

The next girl, perhaps, will be sweet and gentle. His turn to
be eater.

Detestable world.

Simone and Germaine, two of the typists at the delegation,
were having a *succès fou*. Simone at least deserved it.

She specialized in English, Americans and French.

Germaine on the other hand had a large following among the
Italians, Greeks, and even a stray Armenian who (she said) had
offered her fifty thousand francs for one night.

Simone was sublimely conceited.

She told me once that Captain La Croix had called her the
quintessence of French charm, Flemish beauty and Egyptian
mystery. (She was born in Cairo, French mother, Belgian father.)

Both girls looked at me a little warily, but they were too anxious to keep in with Pierre to be anything but polite. I'd noticed
people growing more and more deferential to Pierre, and inciden-
tally to me. I'd noticed that he seemed to have money – a good
deal – a great deal.

He made it on the 'change, he told me.

Then one day in the spring of 1921 we left the flat in Razun-offskygasse for rooms in the Imperial.

We sent off the cook and D—, promoted to be my maid, came with us.

Nice to have lots of money – nice, nice. Goody to have a car, a chauffeur, rings, and as many frocks as I liked.

Good to have money, money. All the flowers I wanted. All the compliments I wanted. Everything, everything.

Oh, great god money – you make possible all that's nice in life. Youth and beauty, the envy of women, and the love of men.

Even the luxury of a soul, a character and thoughts of one's own you give, and only you. To look in the glass and you think I've got what I wanted.

I gambled when I married and I've won.

As a matter of fact I wasn't so exalted really, but it was exceedingly pleasant.

Spending and spending. And there was always more.

One day I had a presentiment.

Pierre gave an extra special lunch to the Japanese officers, Shogun, Hato, Ishima and Co.

We lunched in a separate room, which started my annoyance, for I preferred the restaurant, especially with the Japanese, who depressed me.

It was rather cold and dark and the meal seemed interminable.

Shogun in the intervals of eating enormously told us a long history of an officer in Japan who 'hara-kari'd' because his telephone went wrong during manoeuvres.

Rotten reason I call it, but Shogun seemed to think him a hero.

Escaped as soon as I could upstairs.

I was like Napoleon's mother suddenly: 'Provided it lasts.'

And if it does not? Well, thinking that was to feel the authentic 'cold hand clutching my heart'.

And a beastly feeling too – let me tell you.

So damned well I knew that I could never be poor again with courage or dignity.

I did a little sum; translated what we were spending into francs – into pounds – I was appalled. (When we first arrived in Vienna the crown was thirteen to the franc – at that time it was about sixty.)

As soon as I could I attacked Pierre.

First he laughed, then he grew vexed.

Frances, I tell you it's all right. How much am I making? A lot.

How much exactly? Can't say. How? You won't understand.

Don't be frightened, it – brings bad luck. You'll stop my luck.

I shut up. I know so well that presentiments, fears, are unlucky.

'Don't worry,' said Pierre, 'soon I will pull it quite off and we will be rich, rich.'

We dined in a little corner of the restaurant.

At the same table a few days before we came, a Russian girl twenty-four years of age had shot herself.

With her last money she had a decent meal and then bang! Out –

And I made up my mind that if ever it came to it I should do it too.

Not to be poor again. No and No and No.

So darned easy to plan that – and always at the last moment – one is afraid. Or cheats oneself with hope.

I can still do this and this. I can still clutch at that or that.

So-and-So will help me.

How you fight, cleverly and well at first, then more wildly – then hysterically.

I can't go down, I won't go down. Help me, help me!

Steady – I must be clever. So-and-So will help.

But So-and-So smiles a worldly smile.

You get nervous. He doesn't understand, I'll make him –

But So-and-So's eyes grow cold. You plead.

Can't you help me, won't you, please? It's like this and this –

So-and-So becomes uncomfortable; obstinate.

No good.

I mustn't cry, I won't cry.

And that time you don't. You manage to keep your head up, a smile on your face.

So-and-So is vastly relieved. So relieved that he offers at once the little help that is a mockery, and the consoling compliment.

In the taxi still you don't cry.

You've thought of someone else.

But at the fifth or sixth disappointment you cry more easily.

After the tenth you give it up. You are broken – no nerves left.

And every second-rate fool can have their cheap little triumph over you – judge you with their little middle-class judgement.

Can't do anything for them. No good.

C'est rien – c'est une femme qui se noie!

But two years, three years afterwards. Salut to you, little Russian girl, who had pluck enough and knowledge of the world enough, to finish when your good time was over.

The day before we left Vienna for Budapest was thundery and colder.

I'd spent nearly two hours in a massage place the Russian girl had told me of.

The Russian girl was introduced to me to replace Tillie. She had two advantages: a husband, and a slight knowledge of French.

We'd sat up night after night in the Radetzky bar. (Pierre always gathered swarms of people round him.) The most amusing of the party being an old lady over seventy who wore a bright yellow wig. She'd been an actress and still had heaps of temperament left.

There she sat night after night, drinking punch and singing about *Liebe* and *Frauen* with the best.

I came out of the shop and walked down the *strasse* – face like a doll's – not a line, not a shadow, eyes nicer than a doll's. Hadn't I had stuff dropped in to make the pupils big and black?

Highly pleased with everything I was that afternoon – with

the massage place, with the shortness of my frock, with life in general.

Abruptly the reaction came when I sat down to dinner. I was alone that evening – the presentiment, the black mood, in full swing.

A gentleman with a toothpick gazed fondly at me (in the intervals of serious excavating work), I glued my eyes on my plate.

Oh, abomination of desolation, to sit for two hours being massaged, to stand for hours choosing a dress. All to delight the eyes of the gentleman with the toothpick.

(Who finding me unresponsive has already turned his attention elsewhere.)

I hate him worse than ever.

Franzi is in the hall. The Herr has told him to bring the car and take me for a drive.

Nice Franzi.

I climb in – go quick, Franzi. *Schnell – eine andere platz neit Prater neit weg zum Baden – neit Weiner Wald.*

This is my German after two years! I mean go fast. Go to a new place, not the Prater, not the way to Baden –

Yes, that night was the last frenzied effort of my guardian angel, poor creature. I've never seen so clearly all my faults and failures and utter futility. I've never had so strong a wish to pack my trunks and clear.

Clear off – different life, different people.

Work.

Go to England – be quite different.

Even clearly and coldly the knowledge that I was not being sincere.

That I didn't want to work.

Or wear ugly clothes.

That for ten years I'd lived like that – and that except for a miracle, I couldn't change.

'Don't want to change,' defiantly.

I've compensations.

Oh, yes, compensations – moments.

No one has more.

'Liar, Liar,' shrieked the angel, 'pack your trunks and clear.'
Poor angel – it was hopeless. You hadn't a chance in that lovely
night of Vienne.

Especially as in the midst of it came a terrific bump.

In his zeal to find an *andere weg* Franzi had taken me along
a road that hadn't been repaired since the year dot. We'd gone
right over a stone, so big that I jumped, not being solid, a good
three feet into the air. Fell back luckily into the car.

Franzi has stopped and looks behind frightened. I tell him to
go home.

It's not my fault.

Men have spoilt me – always disdaining my mind and con-
centrating on my body. Women have spoilt me with their sense-
less cruelties and stupidities. Can I help it if I've used my only
weapon?

Yes, my only one.

Lies everything else – lies –

Lord, how I hate most women here, their false smiles, their
ferocious jealousies of each other, their cunning – like animals.

They are animals, probably. Look at all the wise men who
think so and have thought so.

Even Jesus Christ was kind but cold and advised having as
little as possible to do with them.

Besides, if I went back to London –

I go back to what, to who?

How lonely I am – how lonely I am.

Tears.

Self-pity, says the little thing in my brain coldly, is the most
ridiculous and futile of emotions. Go to bed, woman.

I creep in and am comforted. How I adore nice sheets; how
good the pillow smells.

I'm awfully happy really – why did I suddenly get the blues?
Tomorrow I'll see Budapest.

Ridiculous idea to go to London. What should I do in London –

Good-bye Vienna, the lilac, the lights looking down from Kahlenberg, the old lady with the yellow wig singing of *Frauen*.

Will I ever be like that old lady? And run to the massage shop because I have to prop up the failing structure? Possibly, probably.

Lovely Vienna. Never see you again.

Nice linen sheets.

Sleep.

Well, we all have our illusions. God knows it would be difficult to look in the glass without them.

I, that my life from seventeen to twenty-two is responsible for my damned weakness, and Simone that she has the prettiest legs in Paris. Good women that they're not really spiteful, bad ones that they're not really growing older or the latest lover growing colder.

I can't imagine winter in Budapest. Can't imagine it anything else but hot summer.

Heat and a perpetual smell, an all-pervading smell – in the hotels, in the streets, on the river, even outside the town I still imagined I smelt it.

The Hungarians told us it used to be the cleanest city in Europe till the Bolsheviks made it dirty – the Bolsheviks and 'the cursed, the horrible Roumanians'.

It was now being cleaned gradually – very gradually, I should say.

Haughton used to bark loudly (he did bark!) about the exact reasons why it had always been, and still was the most interesting city in Europe, with the exception of Petersburg before the war. '*Les femmes ici ont du chien*' – that's how the French officers explained the matter.

Anyway, I liked it – I liked it better than Vienna.

Haughton lived in the same hotel as we did. We took our meals together and every night we made up a party for the Orpheum or one of the dancing places. He generally brought along a bald Italian with kind brown eyes, a sailor, and a Polish woman and her husband.

He was in the Commission because he spoke Russian, German, French, Italian, even a little Hungarian. Marvellous person!

He had lived in Russia for years, tutor or something to one of the Grand Dukes, and I admired his taste in ladies. He liked them slim, frail, graceful, scented, vicious, painted, charming – and he was chic with them from first to last – un-English in fact, though he remained English to look at.

But sometimes he spoilt those perfect nights when we dined outside Buda with his incessant, not very clever cynicisms.

'Ha, ha, ha! Good Lord! Yes. Damn pretty woman. What?'

When the *tziganes* were playing their maddest and saddest – he'd still go on happily barking. . . .

Budapest looks theatrically lovely from a distance. I remember the moon like a white bird in the afternoon sky; the greyish-green trunks of sycamore trees, the appalling bumps in the road.

'Not too fast, Franzi; don't go too fast!' . . .

Then back to the city and its vivid smells, the wail of *tzigane* orchestras, the little dancer of the Orpheum – what was her name? . . . Ilonka – nice name, sounds like a stone thrown into deep water. She would come smiling and silent – she could speak neither French nor German – to sit with us when her turn was over.

'Awfully monotonous this *tzigane* stuff, what?' Haughton would say, fidgeting.

It was, I suppose. It seemed to be endless variations and inversions of a single chord – tuneless, plaintive, melancholy; the wind over the plain, the hungry cry of the human heart and all the rest of it . . . Well, well . . . .

There was a hard, elegant, little sofa in our room, covered with striped yellow silk – sky-blue cushions. I spent long afternoons lying on that sofa plunged in a placid dream of maternity.

I felt a calm sense of power lying in that dark, cool room, as though I could inevitably and certainly draw to myself all I had ever wished for in life – as though I were mysteriously irresistible, a magnet, a *Femme Sacrée*.

One can become absorbed . . . exalted . . . lost as it were, when one is going to have a baby, and one is extremely pleased about it.

One afternoon Pierre said: 'If anyone comes here from the Allgemeine Verkehrsbank you must say that I'm not in and that you don't know when I'll be back.'

Someone called from the bank – a fat, short man, insisting, becoming rude in bad French. He would see Monsieur. He must see Monsieur. Madame could not say when Monsieur would be back. *'Très bien – très bien.'* He would go to Monsieur's office to make inquiries.

He departed. His back looked square, revengeful – catastrophic – that's the word. I believe that looking at the man's back I guessed everything, foresaw everything.

I attacked Pierre as soon as he came home. I mean questioned him – but he was so evasive that I turned it into an attack. Evasion has always irritated me.

'Tell me, for Heaven's sake, have you lost a lot of money, or something? You have. I know you have – you must tell me.'

He said: 'My dear, let me alone, I'll pull it off if you let me alone – but I don't want to talk about it. . . . Haughton has asked us to dine at the Ritz. . . . *Et qu'importent les jours pourvu que les nuits soient belles?'*

He made a large and theatrical gesture.

I let him alone, weakly, I suppose. But one gets used to security and to thinking of one's husband as a money-maker, a juggler, performing incredible and mysterious feats with yen, with lire, with francs and sterling . . . 'change on Zurich. . . .

I let him alone – but I worried. I caught Haughton looking at me as if he were sorry for me. . . . Sorry for me. Haughton!

Ten days after the man of the Bank had called, I went up to my bedroom at half-past six to change my frock and found Pierre sitting on the striped yellow sofa hunched up, staring at the revolver in his hand.

I always hated revolvers, little, vicious, black things. Just to look at a revolver or a gun gives me a pain deep down in my head; not because they're dangerous – I don't hate knives – but because the noise of a shot hurts my ears.

I said: 'Oh, Pierre, put that thing away! How horribly unkind you are to frighten me!'

Stupid to cry at the very moment one should keep calm.

He was silent, rather surly.

Well, I dragged the truth out of him. He told me, moving one foot restlessly and looking rather like a schoolboy, that he had lost money – other people's money – the Commission's money – Ishima had let him down. . . .

Then followed the complicated history of yens – of francs – of krönen. He interrupted himself to say: 'You don't understand a thing about money. What is the good of asking me to explain? I'm done, I tell you, tried everything . . . no good! I may be arrested any time now.'

I was calm, cool, overflowing with common sense. I believe people who are badly wounded must be like that before the wound begins to hurt. . . . Now then, what is the best way to stop this bleeding? . . . Bandages. . . . Impossible that this and no other is the shot that is going to finish one. . . .

I sat on the sofa beside him and said: 'Tell me how much you need to put yourself straight? I can understand that much at any rate.'

He told me, and there was a dead silence.

'Leave me alone,' he said. 'Let me put a bullet in my head. You think I want to go to jail in Budapest? I haven't a chance!'

I explained, still calmly and reasonably, that he must not kill himself and leave me alone – that I was frightened – that I did not want to die – that somehow I would find the money to pay his debts.

All the time I was speaking he kept his eyes on the door as if he were watching for it to open suddenly and brutally. Then repeated as if I had not spoken: 'I'm *fichu*. . . . Go away and let me get out of it the only way I can. . . . I've saved four thousand francs ready for you. . . . And your rings. . . . Haughton will help you. . . . I'm *fichu*. . . .'

I set my mouth: 'You aren't. Why can't you be a man and fight?'

'I won't wait here to be arrested,' he answered me sulkily, 'they shan't get me, they shan't get me, I tell you.'

My plan of going to London to borrow money was already complete in my head. One thinks quickly sometimes.

'Don't let's wait then. Pierre, you can't do such a rotten thing as to leave me alone?'

'*Mon petit,*' he said, 'I'm a damn coward or I would have finished it before. I tell you I'm right – I'm done. Save yourself. . . . You can't save me!'

He laughed with tears in his eyes. 'My poor Francine, wait a bit. . . .'

'Let's go, let's get away,' I said, 'and shut up about killing yourself. If you kill yourself you know what will happen to me?'

We stared at each other.

'You know damn well,' I told him.

He dropped his eyes and muttered: 'All right – all right! . . . Only don't forget I've warned you, I've told you. It's going to be hell. . . . You're going to blame me one day for not getting out quick and leaving you to save yourself.'

He began to walk restlessly up and down the room.

We decided that we could leave early the next morning. Just to go off. Like that. We made plans – suddenly we were speaking in whispers. . . .

We had dinner upstairs that night, I remember – paprika, *canard sauvage,* two bottles of Pommery.

'*Allons,* Francine, cheer up! *Au mauvais jeu il faut faire bonne mine.*'

I've always loved him for these sudden, complete changes of mood. No Englishman could change so suddenly – so completely. I put out my hand, and as I touched him my courage, my calm, my insensibility left me and I felt a sort of vague and bewildered fright. Horrible to feel that henceforth and for ever one would live with the huge machine of law, order, respectability against one. Horrible to be certain that one was not strong enough to fight it.

'*Au mauvais jeu bonne mine*'. . . . A good poker face, don't they call it? . . . The quality of not getting rattled when anything goes wrong. . . .

When we opened our second bottle of Pommery I had become comfortingly convinced that I was predestined – a feather on the sea of fate and all the rest. And what was the use of worrying – anyway? . . .

As I was drinking a fourth glass, hoping to increase this comforting feeling of irresponsibility, Haughton knocked and came in to see us.

There was a moment that night when I nearly confided in Haughton.

Pierre had gone away to telephone, to see the chauffeur, and I've always liked those big men with rather hard blue eyes. I trust them instinctively – and probably wrongly. I opened my mouth to say: Haughton, this and that is the matter. . . . I'm frightened to death, really. . . . What am I to do?'

And as I was hesitating Pierre came back.

At one o'clock we began to pack, making as little noise as possible. We decided to take only one trunk.

I remember the table covered with cigarette ends and liqueur glasses, the two empty bottles of champagne, and the little yellow sofa looking rather astonished and disapproving.

At half-past six in the morning we left the hotel.

That journey to Prague was like a dream. Not a nightmare; running away can be exhilarating but endless as are certain dreams, and unreal.

While I dressed and finished packing my hands had trembled with fright and cold, but before we left Budapest behind us the hunted feeling had vanished.

There is no doubt that running away on a fresh, blue morning can be exhilarating.

I patted the quivering side of the car, gazed at Franzi's stolid back, wondered if he guessed anything, and decided he probably

did, sung *'Mit ihrem roten Chapeau'*. After all, when one is leaving respectability behind one may as well do it with an air.

The country stretched flatly into an infinite and melancholy
distance, but it looked to me sunlit and full of promise, like the
setting of a fairy tale.

About noon we passed through a little plage on the Danube;
it must have been Balaton, and there were groups of men and
girls walking about in short bathing-suits. Nice their brown legs
and arms looked and the hair of the girls in the fierce sun.

Pierre called out: 'Hungry?'

I said: 'Yes.'

But I grew uneasy again when we stopped for lunch at some
little village of which I was never to know the unpronounceable
name.

Through the open door of the restaurant the village looked
bleak in the sunlight and pervaded with melancholy; flocks of
geese, countless proud geese, strolled about; several old women
sat on a long, low stone bench under a lime tree, on another
bench two or three old men. The old women were really alarming. Their brown, austere faces looked as though they were carved
out of some hard wood, the wrinkles cut deep. They wore volu-
minous dark skirts, handkerchiefs tied round their heads, and
they sat quite silent, nearly motionless. How pitiless they would
be, those ancient ones, to a sinner of their own sex – say a thief
– how fiercely they would punish her. Brrrrr! Let us not think of
these things.

Pierre said: 'What a life they must have, these people!'

I agreed: 'Dreadful!' looked away from the stone bench, drank
my horrible coffee, and went outside. There was a girl, a maid of
the inn perhaps, or a goose-girl, going in and out of the back door,
carrying pails and tubs. She wore a white bodice so thin that one
could plainly see the shape of her breasts, a dark skirt, her feet
were bare, her head was small, set on a very long neck, her eyes
slanted like Ishima's – I watched her with an extraordinary pleasure because she was so slim and young and finely drawn. And
because I imagined that when she glanced at me her eyes had

the expression of some proud, wild thing – say a young lioness – instead of the usual stupid antagonism of one female looking at another.

I said to Pierre: 'Oh, I do think that Hungarians can be lovely; they beat the Austrians hollow.'

He answered so indifferently: 'Another type,' that I began to argue.

'The Austrians are always trotting out their rotten old charm that everybody talks about. Hate people who do that. And they're fat and female and *rusé* and all the rest.'

'Oh!' said Pierre, 'and if you think that Hungarians aren't *rusé*, my dear, *zut!* – they are the most *rusé* of the lot, except the Poles.'

I insisted: 'In a different way. . . . Now look at that girl; isn't she lovely, lovely?'

'*Un beau corps,*' judged Pierre. 'Come on, Francine, let's get off if you are ready.'

I heard the apprehension in his voice and climbed into the car a little wearily. A grind . . . and we had left behind us that goose-girl out of a fairy tale against her background of blue distances quivering with heat.

I began to play my triumphant return to Hungary with money to pay Pierre's debts. I saw myself sitting at the head of a long table handing little packets of notes to everyone concerned, with the stern countenance of a born business woman: 'Will you sign this, please?'

Then I must have slept, and when I woke I'd begun to feel as if the flight had lasted for days, as though I could not remember a time when I hadn't been sitting slightly cramped, a little sick, watching the country fly past and feeling the wind in my face.

Pierre turned and asked if I were tired or cold.

'No, I'm all right. . . . Are you going to drive? Well, don't go too fast . . . don't break our necks after all this.'

We left the flat country behind and there was a sheer drop on one side of the road. The darkness crept up, the wind was cold. Now I was perfectly sure that it was all a dream and could wait calmly for the moment of waking.

We flitted silently like ghosts between two rows of dark trees.

I strained my eyes to see into the frightening mystery of the woods at night, then slept again and the car had stopped when I woke.

'What is it?'

'The frontier . . . keep still. . . .'

An unexpected fuss at the frontier. There was a post. A number of men with rifles round a wood fire, an argument which became very loud and gutteral. Our passports were produced: '*Kommission – Kurrier.*'

'What is it, Pierre?'

He got out of the car without answering and followed one of the men into the shelter.

It was horrible waiting there in the night for what seemed hours, my eyes shut, wondering what jail would be like.

Then Pierre reappeared, still arguing, and got in beside me.

He muttered: '*Je m'en fiche, mon vieux,*' and yelled to the chauffeur.

The car jumped forward like a spurred horse. I imagined for one thrilling moment that we would be fired on, and the nape of my neck curled itself up. But when I looked back over my shoulder I saw the knot of men by the light of the fire looking after us as if they were puzzled.

'Frightened?'

'No, only of being sent back. What was it? Had they been told to stop us?'

'No, but nobody is supposed to pass. The frontier is shut, something has happened.'

I said: 'What can it be, I wonder,' without the slightest interest.

'Well,' said Pierre, 'here is Czechoslovakia, and good-bye Hungary!'

'Good-bye, Hungary!' Tears were in my eyes because I felt so tired, so deathly sick.

'You're awfully tired, aren't you, Francine?'

'A bit. I'd like to rest. Let's stop soon. Where will we spend the night?'

'At Presburg. We're nearly there.'

I huddled into a corner of the car and shut my eyes.

It was late when we found a room in the Jewish quarter of the town. All the good hotels were full; and in the hardest, narrowest bed I have ever imagined I lay down and was instantly asleep.

Next morning something of the exhilaration had come back. We went out to breakfast and to buy maps. It had been decided that we would go to Prague and there sell the car, and then. . . .

'I want to go to Warsaw,' announced Pierre.

I said dismayed: 'Warsaw? but, my dear. . . .'

The coffee was good, the rolls fresh; something in the air of the clean, German-looking little town had given me back my self-confidence.

I began to argue: 'We must go to London . . . in London. . . .'

'*Mon petit,*' said Pierre, lighting his pipe, 'I don't believe in your friends helping us. I know how naïve you are. Wait, and you will see what your famous friends are worth. You will be *roulée* from the beginning to the end. Let's go to Warsaw. I believe I can arrange something from there; Francine, do what I say for once.'

I told him obstinately that I did not like Poles. He shrugged his shoulders.

We found the car and Franzi waiting at the hotel.

'Off we go,' said Pierre, cheerfully, 'en route! Here's the brandy flask.'

The road was vastly better, but I had no comforting sensation of speed, of showing a clean pair of heels. Now we seemed to be crawling, slowly and painfully, ant-like, across a flat, grey and menacing country. I pictured that dreary flatness stretching on and on for miles to the north of Russia, and shivered.

I kept repeating to myself: 'I won't go and be buried in Poland . . . I won't go . . . I don't care . . . I will not. . . .'

The wind was cold; it began to drizzle persistently.

'Pierre we're off the road, I'm sure. That woman put us wrong. This is only a cattle-track.'

It was. And time was wasted going backwards. Pierre cursed violently all the while. He had begun to be in a fever of anxiety to reach Prague.

The walls of the bedroom where we slept that night were covered with lurid pictures of Austrian soldiers dragging hapless Czechoslovakians into captivity. In the restaurant downstairs a pretty girl, wearing a black cape lined with vivid purple, sat talking to two loutish youths. She smoked cigarette after cigarette with pretty movements of her hands and arms and watched us with bright blue, curious eyes.

We drank a still wine, sweetish, at dinner. It went to my head and again I could tell myself that my existence was a dream. After all it mattered very little where we went. Warsaw, London. . . . London, Warsaw. . . . Words! Quite without the tremendous significance I had given them.

It was still raining when we reached Prague at last. We made the dreary round of the hotels; they were all full, there were beds in the bathrooms of the Hotel du Passage; it was an hour before we discovered a room in a small hotel in a dark, narrow street.

Pierre began to discuss the sudden return of King Karl to Hungary. We heard the news at the Passage.

That was the trouble at the frontier, of course.

I said indifferently – I was lying down – 'Yes, probably'.

Karl – the Empress Zita – the Allies – Commission – the Whites – the Reds – Pierre himself . . . shadows! Marionnettes gesticulating on a badly lit stage, distracting me from the only reality in life . . . the terrible weight that bowed me down . . . the sickness that turned me cold and mounted up to cloud my brain.

Pierre advised me to have some strong coffee. He rang the bell and a short, fat waiter appeared who looked at me with that peculiar mixture of insolence, disdain, brutality and sentimentality only to be found amongst those of German extraction.

Then he departed to fetch the coffee.

It was an odd place, that hotel, full of stone passages and things. I lay vaguely wondering why Prague reminded me of witches. . . . I read a book when I was a kid – *The Witch of Prague*. No. It reminded me of witches anyhow. Something dark, secret and grim.

'I think Prague is a rum place,' I told Pierre. 'What's that bell that keeps ringing next door?'

'A cabaret, cinema perhaps. . . . Listen, Frances, it's just the best of luck for us, that business of Karl. Nobody will worry about me just now. Ishima will be far too busy voting with the majority. . . . *Sacré* little Japanese!'

'Probably,' I agreed.

He asked me if I felt ill, suggested a doctor.

'A Czech doctor, my God!'

I pulled the sheets over my head. I only wanted to be left alone, I told him.

'Francine,' said he gently, 'don't be a silly little girl. The doctors are good here if you want one.'

He put the rug over me: 'Rest a bit while I go and see about the car. We'll dine at the Passage and find a place for dancing afterwards. Yes?'

I emerged from under the sheets to smile because his voice sounded so wistful, poor Pierre.

About six that evening I felt suddenly better and began to dress.

Because I noticed at lunch that the grand chic at Prague seemed to be to wear black I groped in the trunk for something similar, powdered carefully, rouged my mouth, painted a beauty spot under my left eye.

I was looking at the result when Pierre came in.

'My pretty Francine, wait a bit! I have something here to make you chic . . . but chic. . . .'

He felt into his pocket, took out a long case, handed it to me.

'Pierre!'

'Nice *hé*?'

'Where did you get them?'

He did not answer.

I looked from the pearls to his dark, amused face, and then I blushed – blushed terribly all over my face and neck. I shut the case and gave it back to him and said: 'How much money have we got left?' And he answered without looking at me: 'Not much; the worst is this war-scare. Czechoslovakia is going to mobilize. It won't be so easy to sell the car. We must sell it before we can move. Never mind, Francine.'

I said: 'Never mind!' Then I took the case, opened it, clasped the pearls round my neck. 'If we're going the whole hog, let's go it. Come on.'

One has reactions, of course.

Difficult to go the whole hog, to leave respectability behind with an air, when one lies awake at four o'clock in the morning – thinking.

'Francine, don't cry . . . what is it?'

'Nothing. . . . Oh! do let me alone. . . .'

When he tried to comfort me I turned away. He had suddenly become a dark stranger who was dragging me over the edge of a precipice. . . .

It rained during the whole of the next week, and I spent most of the time in the hotel bedroom staring at the wallpaper. Towards evening I always felt better and would start to think with extraordinary lucidity of our future life in London or Paris – of unfortunate speculation and pearls – of a poker face and the affair of King Karl. . . .

One day at the end of our second week in Prague Pierre arrived with two tickets which he threw on the bed: 'There you are, to Liège, to London. . . . I sold it and did not get much; I tell you.' . . .

I spent an hour dressing for dinner that night. And it was a gay dinner.

'Isn't the *chef d'orchestre* like a penguin?'

'Yes, ask him to play the Saltimbanques Valse.'

'That old valse?'

'Well, I like it . . . ask him. . . . Listen, Pierre, have we still got the car?'

'Till tomorrow.'

'Well, go to the garage and get it. I'd like to drive like hell tonight. . . . Wouldn't you?'

He shrugged: 'Why not?'

Once more and for the last time we were flying between two lines of dark trees, tops dancing madly in the high wind.

'Faster! Faster! Make the damn thing go!'

We were doing a hundred.

I thought: he understands – began to choose the tree we would crash against and to scream with laughter at the old hag Fate because I was going to give her the slip.

'Get on! . . . get on! . . .'

We slowed up.

'You're drunk, Frances,' said Pierre severely.

I got out, stumbled, laughed stupidly – said: 'Good-bye! Poor old car,' gathered up the last remnants of my dignity to walk into the hotel. . . .

It was: '*Nach* London!'

Till September Petronella

THERE WAS a barrel organ playing at the corner of
Torrington Square. It played 'Destiny' and 'La Palome' and 'Le
Rêve Passe', all tunes I liked, and the wind was warm and kind
not spiteful, which doesn't often happen in London. I packed the
striped dress that Estelle had helped me to choose, and the cheap
white one that fitted well, and my best underclothes, feeling very
happy while I was packing. A bit of a change, for that had not
been one of my lucky summers.

I would tell myself it was the colour of the carpet or something about my room which was depressing me, but it wasn't
that. And it wasn't anything to do with money either. I was making nearly five pounds a week – very good for me, and different
from when I first started, when I was walking round trying to get
work. *No* Hawkers, *No* Models, some of them put up, and you
stand there, your hands cold and clammy, afraid to ring the bell.
But I had got past that state; this depression had nothing to do
with money.

I often wished I was like Estelle, this French girl who lived in
the big room on the ground floor. She had everything so cut-and-
dried, she walked the tightrope so beautifully, not even knowing
she was walking it. I'd think about the talks we had, and her
clothes and her scent and the way she did her hair, and that
when I went into her room it didn't seem like a Bloomsbury bed-
sitting room – and when it comes to Bloomsbury bed-sitting rooms
I know what I'm talking about. No, it was like a room out of one
of those long, romantic novels, six hundred and fifty pages of

small print, translated from French or German or Hungarian or something – because few of the English ones have the exact feeling I mean. And you read one page of it or even one phrase of it, and then you gobble up all the rest and go about in a dream for weeks afterwards, for months afterwards – perhaps all your life, who knows? – surrounded by those six hundred and fifty pages, the houses, the streets, the snow, the river, the roses, the girls, the sun, the ladies' dresses and the gentlemen's voices, the old, wicked, hard-hearted women and the old, sad women, the waltz music, everything. What is not there you put in afterwards, for it is alive, this book, and it grows in your head. 'The house I was living in when I read that book,' you think, or 'This colour reminds me of that book.'

It was after Estelle left, telling me she was going to Paris and wasn't sure whether she was coming back, that I struck a bad patch. Several of the people I was sitting to left London in June, but, instead of arranging for more work, I took long walks, zig-zag, always the same way – Euston Road, Hampstead Road, Camden Town – though I hated those streets, which were like a grey nightmare in the sun. You saw so many old women, or women who seemed old, peering at the vegetables in the Camden Town market, looking at you with hatred, or blankly, as though they had forgotten your language, and talked another one. 'My God,' I would think, 'I hope I never live to be old. Anyway, however old I get, I'll never let my hair go grey. I'll dye it black, red, any colour you like, but I'll never let it go grey. I hate grey too much.' Coming back from one of these walks the thought came to me suddenly, like a revelation, that I could kill myself any time I liked and so end it. After that I put a better face on things.

When Marston wrote and I told the landlord I was going away for a fortnight, he said 'So there's a good time coming for the ladies, is there? – a good time coming for the girls? About time too.'

Marston said, 'You seem very perky, my dear. I hardly recognized you.'

I looked along the platform, but Julian had not come to meet me. There was only Marston, his long, white face and his pale-blue eyes, smiling.

'What a gigantic suitcase,' he said. 'I have my motorbike here, but I suppose I'd better leave it. We'll take a cab.'

It was getting dark when we reached the cottage, which stood by itself on rising ground. There were two elm trees in a field near the veranda, but the country looked bare, with low, grassy hills.

As we walked up the path through the garden I could hear Julian laughing and a girl talking, her voice very high and excited, though she put on a calm, haughty expression as we came into the room. Her dress was red, and she wore several coloured glass bangles which tinkled when she moved.

Marston said, 'This is Frankie. You've met the great Julian, of course.'

Well, I knew Frankie Morell by sight, but as she didn't say anything about it I didn't either. We smiled at each other cautiously, falsely.

The table was laid for four people. The room looked comfortable but there were no flowers. I had expected that they would have it full of flowers. However, there were some sprays of honeysuckle in a green jug in my bedroom and Marston, standing in the doorway, said, 'I walked miles to get you that honeysuckle this morning. I thought about you all the time I was picking it.'

'Don't be long,' he said. 'We're all very hungry.'

We ate ham and salad and drank perry. It went to my head a bit. Julian talked about his job which he seemed to dislike. He was the music critic of one of the daily papers. 'It's a scandal. One's forced to down the right people and praise the wrong people.'

'Forced?' said Marston.

'Well, they drop very strong hints.'

'I'll take the plates away,' Frankie told me. 'You can start tomorrow. Not one of the local women will do a thing for us.

We've only been here a fortnight, but they've got up a hate you wouldn't believe. Julian says he almost faints when he thinks of it. I say, why think of it?'

When she came back she turned the lamp out. Down there it was very still. The two trees outside did not move, or the moon.

Julian lay on the sofa and I was looking at his face and his hair when Marston put his arms round me and kissed me. But I watched Julian and listened to him whistling – stopping, laughing, beginning again.

'What was that music?' I said, and Frankie answered in a patronizing voice, 'Tristan, second act duet.'

'I've never been to that opera.'

I had never been to any opera. All the same, I could imagine it. I could imagine myself in a box, wearing a moonlight-blue dress and silver shoes, and when the lights went up everybody asking, 'Who's that lovely girl in that box?' But it must happen quickly or it will be too late.

Marston squeezed my hand. 'Very fine performance, Julian,' he said, 'very fine. Now forgive me, my dears, I must leave you. All this emotion –'

Julian lighted the lamp, took a book from the shelf and began to read.

Frankie blew on the nails of one hand and polished them on the edge of the other. Her nails were nice – of course, you could get a manicure for a bob then – but her hands were large and too white for her face. 'I've seen you at the Apple Tree, surely.' The Apple Tree was a night club in Greek Street.

'Oh yes, often.'

'But you've cut your hair. I wanted to cut mine, but Julian asked me not to. He begged me not to. Didn't you, Julian?'

Julian did not answer.

'He said he'd lose his strength if I cut my hair.'

Julian turned over a page and went on reading.

'This is not a bad spot, is it?' Frankie said. 'Not one of those places where the ceiling's on top of your head and you've got to walk four miles in the dark to the lavatory. There are two other

bedrooms besides the one Marston gave you. Come and have a
look at them. You can change over if you want to. We'll never
tear Julian away from his book. It's about the biological inferiority
of women. That's what you told me, Julian, isn't it?'

'Oh, *go* away,' Julian said.

We ended up in her room, where she produced some head
and figure studies, photographs.

'Do you like these? Do you know this man? He says I'm the
best model he's ever had. He says I'm far and away the best model
in London.'

'Beautiful. Lovely photographs.'

But Frankie, sitting on the big bed, said, 'Aren't people swine?
Julian says I never think. He's wrong, sometimes I think quite a
lot. The other day I spent a long time trying to decide which were
worse – men or women.'

'I wonder.'

'Women are worse.'

She had long, calm black hair, drawn away from her face and
hanging smoothly almost to her waist, and a calm, clear little
voice and a calm, haughty expression.

'They'll kick your face to bits if you let them. And shriek with
laughter at the damage. But I'm not going to let them – oh no.
. . . Marston's always talking about you,' she said. 'He's very fond
of you, poor old Marston. Do you know that picture as you go into
his studio – in the entrance place? What's he say it is?'

'The Apotheosis of Lust.'

'Yes, the Apotheosis of Lust. I have to laugh when I think of
that, for some reason. Poor old Andy Marston. . . . But I don't
know why I should say "Poor old Andy Marston". He'll always
have one penny to tinkle against another. His family's very wealthy,
you know.'

'He makes me go cold.'

I thought, 'Why did I say that?' Because I like Marston.

'So that's how you feel about him, is it?' She seemed pleased,
as if she had heard something she wanted to hear, had been waiting to hear.

'Are you tired?' Marston said.

I was looking out of the bedroom window at some sheep feeding in the field where the elm trees grew.

'A bit,' I said. 'A bit very.'

His mouth drooped, disappointed.

'Oh, Marston, thank you for asking me down here. It's lovely to get away from London; it's like a dream.'

'A dream, my God! However, when it comes to dreams, why shouldn't they be pleasant?'

He sat down on the windowsill.

'The great Julian's not so bad, is he?'

'Why do you call him the great Julian? As if you were gibing at him.'

'Gibing at him? Good Lord, far be it from me to gibe at him. He *is* the great Julian. He's going to be very important, so far as an English musician can be important. He's horribly conceited, though. Not about his music, of course – he's conceited about his personal charm. I can't think why. He's a very ordinary type really. You see that nose and mouth and hear that voice all over the place. You rather dislike him, don't you?'

'Do I?'

'Of course you do. Have you forgotten how annoyed you were when I told you that he'd have to *see* a female before he could consent to live at close quarters with her for two weeks? You were quite spirited about it, I thought. Don't say that was only a flash in the pan, you poor devil of a female, female, female, in a country where females are only tolerated at best! What's going to become of you, Miss Petronella Gray, living in a bed-sitting room in Torrington Square, with no money, no background and no nous? . . . Is Petronella your real name?'

'Yes.'

'You worry me, whatever your name is. I bet it isn't Gray.'

I thought, 'What does it matter? If you knew how bloody my home was you wouldn't be surprised that I wanted to change my name and forget all about it.'

I said, not looking at him, 'I was called after my grandmother – Julia Petronella.'

'Oh, you've got a grandmother, have you? Fancy that! Now, for Heaven's sake don't put on that expression. Take my advice and grow another skin or two and sharpen your claws before it's too late. *Before it's too late,* mark those words. If you don't, you're going to have a hell of a time.'

'So that I long for death?'

He looked startled. 'Why do you say that?'

'It was only the first thing that came into my head from nowhere. I was joking.'

When he did not answer, 'Well, good night,' I said. 'Sleep tight.'

'I shan't sleep,' he said. 'I shall probably have to listen to those two for quite a time yet. When they're amorous they're noisy and when they fight it's worse. She goes for him with a pen-knife. Mind you, she only does that because he likes it, but her good nature is a pretence. She's a bitch really. Shut your door and you won't hear anything. Will you be sad tomorrow?'

'Of course not.'

'Don't look as if you'd lost a shilling and found a sixpence then,' he said, and went out.

That's the way they always talk. 'You look as if you'd lost a shilling and found sixpence,' they say; 'You look very perky, I hardly recognized you,' they say; *'Look gay,'* they say. 'My dear Petronella, I have an entirely new idea of you. I'm going to paint you out in the opulent square. So can you wear something gay tomorrow afternoon? Not one of those drab affairs you usually clothe yourself in. Gay – do you know the meaning of the word? Think about it, it's very important.'

The things you remember. . . .

Once, left alone in a very ornate studio, I went up to a plaster cast – the head of a man, one of those Greek heads – and kissed it, because it was so beautiful. Its mouth felt warm, not cold. It was smiling. When I kissed it the room went dead silent and I was frightened. I told Estelle about this one day. 'Does that sound mad?' She didn't laugh. She said, 'Who hasn't kissed a picture or a photograph and suddenly been frightened?'

The music Julian had been whistling was tormenting me. That, and the blind eyes of the plaster cast, and the way the sun shone on the black iron bedstead in my room in Torrington Square on fine days. The bars of the bedstead grin at me. Sometimes I count the knobs on the chest of drawers three times over. 'One of those drab affairs! . . .'

I began to talk to Julian in my head. Was it to Julian? 'I'm not like that. I'm not at all like that. They're trying to make me like that, but I'm not like that.'

After a while I took a pencil and paper and wrote, 'I love Julian. Julian, I kissed you once, but you didn't know.'

I folded the paper several times and hid it under some clothes in my suitcase. Then I went to bed and slept at once.

Where our path joined the main road there were some cottages. As Marston and I came back from our walk next morning we passed two women in their gardens, which were full of lupins and poppies. They looked at us sullenly, as though they disliked us. When Marston said 'Good morning', they did not answer.

'Surly, priggish brutes,' he muttered, 'but that's how they are.'

The grass round our cottage was long and trampled in places. There were no flowers.

'They're back,' Marston said. 'There's the motorbike.'

They came out on to the veranda, very spruce; Frankie in her red frock with her hair tied up in a red and blue handkerchief, Julian wearing a brown coat over a blue shirt and shabby grey trousers like Marston's. Very gay, I thought. (Gay – do you know the meaning of the word?)

'What's the matter with you, Marston?' Julian said. 'You look frightful.'

'You do seem a bit upset,' Frankie said. 'What happened? Do tell.'

'Don't tell her anything,' said Marston. 'I'm going to dress up too. Why should I be the only one in this resplendent assembly with a torn shirt and stained bags? Wait till you see what I've got – and I don't mean what you mean.'

'Let's get the food ready,' Frankie said to me.

The kitchen table was covered with things they had brought from Cheltenham, and there were several bottles of white wine cooling in a bucket of water in the corner.

'What have you done to Marston?'

'Nothing. What on earth do you mean?'

Nothing had happened. We were sitting under a tree, looking at a field of corn, and Marston put his head in my lap and then a man came along and yelled at us. I said, 'What do you think we're doing to your corn? Can't we even look at your corn?' But Marston only mumbled, 'I'm fearfully sorry. I'm dreadfully sorry,' and so on. And then we went walking along the main road in the sun, not talking much because I was hating him.

'Nothing happened,' I said.

'Oh well, it's a pity, because Julian's in a bad mood today. However, don't take any notice of him. Don't start a row whatever you do, just smooth it over.'

'Look at the lovely bit of steak I got,' she said. 'Marston says he can't touch any meat except cold ham, I ask you, and he does the cooling. Cold ham and risotto, risotto and cold ham. And curried eggs. That's what we've been living on ever since we came down here.'

When we went in with the food they had finished a bottle of wine. Julian said, 'Here's luck to the ruddy citizens I saw this morning. May they be flourishing and producing offspring exactly like themselves, but far, far worse, long after we are all in our dishonoured graves.'

Marston was now wearing black silk pyjamas with a pattern of red and green dragons. His long, thin neck and sad face looked extraordinary above this get-up. Frankie and I glanced at each other and giggled. Julian scowled at me.

Marston went over to the mirror. 'Never mind,' he said softly to his reflection, 'never mind, never mind.'

'It's ham and salad again,' Frankie said. 'But I've got some prunes.'

The table was near the window. A hot, white glare shone in our eyes. We tried pulling the blinds down, but one got stuck and we went on eating in the glare.

Then Frankie talked about the steak again. 'You must have your first bite tonight, Marston.'

'It won't be my first bite,' Marston said. 'I've been persuaded to taste beef before.'

'Oh, you never told me that. No likee?'

'I thought it would taste like sweat,' Marston said, 'and it did.'

Frankie looked annoyed. 'The trouble with you people is that you try to put other people off just because you don't fancy a thing. If you'd just not like it and leave it at that, but you don't *rest* till you've put everybody else off.'

'Oh God, let's get tight,' Julian said. 'There are bottles and bottles of wine in the kitchen. Cooling, I hope.'

'We'll get them,' Frankie said, 'we'll get them.'

Frankie sat on the kitchen table. 'I think Julian's spoiling for a fight. Let him calm down a bit . . . you're staving Marston off, aren't you? And he doesn't like it; he's very disconsolate. You've got to be careful of these people, they can be as hard as nails.'

Far away a dog barked, a cock crew, somebody was sawing wood. I hardly noticed what she had said because again it came, that feeling of happiness, the fish-in-water feeling, so that I couldn't even remember having been unhappy.

Frankie started on a long story about a man called Petersen who had written a play about Northern gods and goddesses and Yggdrasil.

'I thought Yggdrasil was a girl, but it seems it's a tree.'

Marston and Julian and all that lot had taken Petersen up, she said. They used to ask him out and make him drunk. Then he would take his clothes off and dance about and if he did not do it somebody would be sure to say, 'What's the matter? Why don't you perform?' But as soon as he got really sordid they had dropped him like a hot brick. He simply disappeared.

'I met an old boy who knew him and asked what had happened. The old boy said, "A gigantic maw has swallowed Petersen. . . ." Maw, what a word! It reminds me of Julian's mother – she's a maw if you like. Well, I'd better take these bottles along now.'

So we took the four bottles out of the bucket and went back into the sitting-room. It was still hot and glaring, but not quite so bad as it had been.

'Now it's my turn to make a speech,' said Marston. 'But you must drink, pretty creatures, drink.' He filled out glasses and I drank mine quickly. He filled it up again.

'My speech,' he said, 'my speech. . . . Let's drink to afternoon, the best of all times. Cruel morning is past, fearful, unpredictable, lonely night is yet to come. Here's to heartrending afternoon. . . . I will now recite a poem. It's hackneyed and pawed about, like so many other things, but beautiful. "*C'est bien la pire peine de ne savoir pourquoi –*" '

He stopped and began to cry. We all looked at him. Nobody laughed; nobody knew what to say. I felt shut in by the glare.

Marston blew his nose, wiped his eyes and gabbled on: ' "*Pourquoi, sans amour et sans haine, Mon coeur a tant de peine. . . .*" '

' "*Sans amour*" is right,' Julian said, staring at me. I looked back into his eyes.

' "But for loving, why, you would not, Sweet," ' Marston went on, ' "Though we prayed you, Paid you, brayed you. In a mortar – for you could not, Sweet." '

'The motorbike was altogether a bit of luck,' Frankie said. 'Julian had a fight with a man on the bus going in. I thought he'd have a fit.'

'Fight?' Julian said. 'I never fight. I'm frightened.'

He was still staring at me.

'Well then, you were very rude.'

'I'm never rude, either,' Julian said. 'I'm far too frightened ever to be rude! I suffer in silence.'

'I shouldn't do that if I were you,' I said. The wine was making me giddy. So was the glare, and the way he was looking at me.

'What's this young creature up to?' he said. 'I can't quite make her out.'

'Ruddy respectable citizens never can.'

'Ha-hah,' Frankie said. 'One in the eye for you, Julian. You're always going on about respectable people, but you know *you* are respectable, whatever you say and whatever you do, and you'll be respectable till you die, however you die, and that way you miss something, believe it or not.'

'You keep out of this, Phoenician,' Julian said. 'You've got nothing to say. Retire under the table, because that's where I like you best.'

Frankie crawled under the table. She darted her head out now and again, pretending to bit his legs, and every time she did that he would shiver and scream.

'Oh, come on out,' he said at last. 'It's too hot for these antics.'

Frankie crawled out again, very pleased with herself, went to the mirror and arranged the handkerchief round her hair. 'Am I really like a Phoenician?'

'Of course you are. A Phoenician from Cornwall, England. Direct descent, I should say.'

'And what's she?' Frankie said. Her eyes looked quite different, like snake's eyes. We all looked quite different – it's funny what drink does.

'That's very obvious too,' Julian said.

'All right, why don't you come straight out with it?' I said. 'Or are you frightened?'

'Sometimes words fail.'

Marston waved his arms about. 'Julian, you stop this. I won't have it.'

'You fool,' Julian said, 'you fool. Can't you see she's fifth rate. Can't you see?'

'You ghastly cross between a barmaid and a chorus-girl,' he

said. 'You female spider,' he said; 'You've been laughing at him for weeks,' he said, 'jeering at him, sniggering at him. Stopping him from working – the best painter in this damnable island, the only one in my opinion. And then I try to get him away from you, of course you follow him down here.'

'That's not it at all,' Marston said. 'You're not being fair to the girl. You don't understand her a bit.'

'She doesn't care,' Julian said. 'Look at her – she's giggling her stupid head off.'

'Well, what are you to do when you come up against a mutual admiration society?' I said.

'You're letting your jealousy run away with you,' said Marston.

'Jealousy?' Julian said. 'Jealousy!' He was unrecognizable. His beautiful eyes were little, mean pits and you looked down them into nothingness.

'Jealous of what?' he shrieked. 'Why, do you know that she told Frankie last night that she can't bear you and that the only reason she has anything to do with you is because she wants money. What do you think of that? Does that open your eyes?'

'Now, *Julian!*' Frankie's voice was as loud and high as his. 'You'd no right to repeat that. You promised you wouldn't and anyway you've exaggerated it. It's all very well for you to talk about how inferior women are, but you get more like your horrible mother every moment.'

'You do,' Marston said, quite calm now. 'Julian, you really do.'

'Do you know what all this is about?' Frankie said, nodding at Julian. 'It's because he doesn't want me to go back to London with him. He wants me to go and be patronized and educated by his detestable mother in her dreary house in the dreary country, who will then say that the case is hopeless. Wasn't she a good sort and a saint to try? But the girl is *quite impossible*. Do you think I don't know that trick? It's as old as the hills.

'You're mean,' she said to Julian, 'and you hate girls really. Don't imagine I don't see through you. You're trying to get me down. But you won't do it. If you think you're the only man in the world who's fond of me *or* that I'm a goddamned fool, you're making the hell of a big mistake, you and your mother.'

She plucked a hairpin from her hair, bent it into the shape of pince-nez and went on in a mincing voice, 'Do Ay understend you tew say thet *may* sonn –' she placed the pince-nez on her nose and looked over it sourly '– with *one* connection –'

'Damn you,' said Julian, 'damn you, damn you.'

'Now they're off,' Marston said placidly. 'Drinking on a hot afternoon is a mistake. The pen-knife will be out in a minute. . . . Don't go. Stay and watch the fun. My money on Frankie every time.'

But I went into the bedroom and shut the door. I could hear them wrangling and Marston, very calm and superior, putting in a word now and again. Then nothing. They had gone on to the veranda.

I got the letter I had written and tore it very carefully into four pieces. I spat on each piece. I opened the door – there was not a sign of them. I took the pieces of paper to the lavatory, emptied them in and pulled the plug. As soon as I heard the water gushing I felt better.

The door of the kitchen was open and I saw that there was another path leading to the main road.

And there I was, walking along, not thinking of anything, my eyes fixed on the ground. I walked a long way like that, not looking up, though I passed several people. At last I came to a sign-post. I was on the Cirencester road. Something about the word 'miles' written made me feel very tired.

A little farther on the wall on one side of the road was low. It was the same wall on which Marston and I had sat that morning, and he had said, 'Do you think we could rest here or will the very stones rise up against us?' I looked round and there was nobody in sight, so I stepped over it and sat down in the shade. It was pretty country, but bare. The white, glaring look was still in the sky.

Close by there was a dove cooing. 'Coo away, dove,' I thought.

'It's no use, no use, still coo away, coo away.'

After a while the dazed feeling, as if somebody had hit me on the head, began to go. I thought 'Cirencester – and then a train to London. It's as easy as that.'

Then I realized that I had left my handbag and money, as well as everything else, in the bedroom at the cottage, but imagining walking back there made me feel so tired that I could hardly put one foot in front of the other.

I got over the wall. A car that was coming along slowed down and stopped and the man driving it said, 'Want a lift?'

I went up to the car.

'Where do you want to go?'

'I want to go to London.'

'To London? Well, I can't take you as far as that, but I can get you into Cirencester to catch a train if you like.'

I said anxiously, 'Yes – but I must go back first to the place where I've been staying. It's not far.'

'Haven't time for that. I've got an appointment. I'm late already and I mustn't miss it. Tell you what – come along with me. If you'll wait till I've done I can take you to fetch your things.'

I got into the car. As soon as I touched him I felt comforted. Some men are like that.

'Well, you look as if you'd lost a shilling and found sixpence.'

Again I had to laugh.

'That's better. Never does any good to be down in the mouth.'

'We're nearly in Cirencester now,' he said after a while. 'I've got to see a lot of people. This is market day and I'm a farmer. I'll take you to a nice quiet place where you can have a cup of tea while you're waiting.'

He drove to a pub in a narrow street. 'This way in.' I followed him into the bar.

'Good afternoon, Mrs Strickland. Lovely day, isn't it? Will you give my friend a cup of tea while I'm away, and make her comfortable? She's very tired.'

'I will, certainly,' Mrs Strickland said, with a swift glance up and down. 'I expect the young lady would like a nice wash too, wouldn't she?' She was dark and nicely got up, but her voice had a tinny sound.

'Oh, I would.'

I looked down at my crumpled white dress. I touched my face for I knew there must be a red mark where I had lain with it pressed against the ground.

'See you later,' the farmer said.

There were brightly polished taps in the ladies' room and a very clean red and black tiled floor. I washed my hands, tried to smooth my dress, and powdered my face – *Poudre Nildé basané* – but I did it without looking in the glass.

Tea and cakes were laid in a small, dark, stuffy room. There were three pictures of Lady Hamilton, Johnny Walker advertisements, china bulldogs wearing sailor caps and two calendars. One said January 9th, but the other was right – July 28th, 1914.

'Well, here I am!' He sat heavily down beside me. 'Did Mrs Strickland look after you all right?'

'Very well.'

'Oh, she's a good sort, she's a nice woman. She's known me a long time. Of course, you haven't, have you? But everything's got to have a start.'

Then he said he hadn't done so badly that afternoon and stretched out his legs, looking pleased, looking happy as the day is long.

'What were you thinking about when I came in? You nearly jumped out of your skin.'

'I was thinking about the time.'

'About the time? Oh, don't worry about that. There's plenty of time.'

He produced a large silver case, took out a cigar and lighted it, long and slow. 'Plenty of time,' he said. 'Dark in here, isn't it? So you live in London, do you?'

'Yes.'

'I've often thought I'd like to know a nice girl up in London.'

His eyes were fixed on Lady Hamilton and I knew he was imagining a really lovely girl – all curves, curls, heart and hidden claws. He swallowed, then put his hand over mine.

'I'd like to feel that when I go up to Town there's a friend I could see and have a good time with. You know. And I could give her a good time too. By God, I could. I know what women like.'

'You do?'

'Yes, I do. They like a bit of loving, that's what they like, isn't it? A bit of loving. All women like that. They like it dressed up sometimes – and sometimes not, it all depends. You have to know, and I know. I just know.'

'You've nothing more to learn, have you?'

'Not in that way I haven't. And they like pretty dresses and bottles of scent, and bracelets with blue stones in them. I know. Well, what about it?' he said, but as if he were joking.

I looked away from him at the calendar and did not answer, making my face blank.

'What about it?' he repeated.

'It's nice of you to say you want to see me again – very polite.'

He laughed. 'You think I'm being polite, do you? Well, perhaps – perhaps not. No harm in asking, was there? No offence meant – or taken, I hope. It's all right. I'll take you to get your things and catch your train – and we'll have a bottle of something good before we start off. It won't hurt you. It's bad stuff hurts you, not good stuff. You haven't found that out yet, but you will. Mrs Strickland has some good stuff, I can tell you – good enough for me, and I want the best.'

So we had a bottle of Clicquot in the bar.

He said, 'It puts some life into you, doesn't it?'

It did too. I wasn't feeling tired when we left the pub, nor even sad.

'Well,' he said as we got into the car, 'you've got to tell me where to drive to. And you don't happen to know a little song, do you?'

'That was very pretty,' he said when I stopped. 'You've got a very pretty voice indeed. Give us some more.'

But we were getting near the cottage and I didn't finish the next song because I was nervous and worried that I wouldn't be able to tell him the right turning.

At the foot of the path I thought, 'The champagne worked all right.'

He got out of the car and came with me. When we reached the gate leading into the garden he stood by my side without speaking.

They were on the veranda. We could hear their voices clearly.

'Listen, fool,' Julian was saying, 'listen, half-wit. What I said yesterday has nothing to do with what I say today or what I shall say tomorrow. Why should it?'

'That's what you think,' Frankie said obstinately. 'I don't agree with you. It might have something to do with it whether you like it or not.'

'Oh, stop arguing, you two,' Marston said. 'It's all very well for you, Julian, but I'm worried about that girl. I'm responsible. She looked so damned miserable. Supposing she's gone and made away with herself. I shall feel awful. Besides, probably I shall be held up to every kind of scorn and obloquy – as usual. And though it's all your fault you'll escape scot-free – also as usual.'

'Are those your friends?' the farmer asked.

'Well, they're my friends in a way. . . . I have to go in to get my things. It won't take long.'

Julian said, 'I think, I rather think, Marston, that I hear a female pipe down there. You can lay your fears away. She's not the sort to kill herself. I told you that.'

'Who's that?' the farmer said.

'That's Mr Oakes, one of my hosts.'

'Oh, is it? I don't like the sound of him. I don't like the sound of any of them. Shall I come with you?'

'No, don't. I won't be long.'

I went round by the kitchen into my room, walking very softly. I changed into my dark dress and then began to throw my things into the suitcase. I did all this as quickly as I could, but before I had finished Marston came in, still wearing his black pyjamas crawling with dragons.

'Who were you talking to outside?'

'Oh, that's a man I met. He's going to drive me to Cirencester to catch the London train.'

'You're not offended, are you?'

'Not a bit. Why should I be?'

'Of course, the great Julian can be so difficult,' he murmured. 'But don't think I didn't stick up for you, because I did. I said to him. "It's all very well for you to be rude to a girl I bring down, but what about your loathly Frankie, whom you inflict upon me day after day and week after week and I never say a word? I'm never even sharp to her –" What are you smiling at?'

'The idea of your being sharp to Frankie.'

'The horrid little creature!' Marston said excitedly, 'the unspeakable bitch! But the day will come when Julian will find her out and he'll run to me for sympathy. I'll not give it him. Not after this. . . . Cheer up,' he said. 'The world is big. There's hope.'

'Of course.' But suddenly I saw the women's long, scowling faces over their lupins and their poppies, and my room in Torrington Square and the iron bars of my bedstead, and I thought, 'Not for me.'

'It may all be necessary,' he said, as if he were talking to himself. 'One has to get an entirely different set of values to be any good.'

I said, 'Do you think I could go out through the window? I don't want to meet them.'

'I'll come to the car with you. What's this man like?'

'Well, he's a bit like the man this morning, and he says he doesn't care for the sound of you.'

'Then I think I won't come. Go through the window and I'll hand your suitcase to you.'

He leaned out and said, 'See you in September, Petronella. I'll be back in September.'

I looked up at him. 'All right. Same address.'

The farmer said, 'I was coming in after you. You're well rid of that lot – never did like that sort. Too many of them about.'

'They're all right.'

'Well, tune up,' he said, and I sang 'Mr Brown, Mr Brown, Had a violin, Went around, went around, With his violin.' I sang all the way to Cirencester.

At the station he gave me my ticket and a box of chocolates.

'I bought these for you this afternoon, but I forgot them. Better hurry – there's not much time.

'Fare you well,' he said. 'That's what they say in Norfolk, where I come from.'

'Good-bye.'

'No, say fare you well.'

'Fare you well.'

The train started.

'This is very nice,' I thought, 'My first-class carriage,' and had a long look at myself in the glass for the first time since it had happened. 'Never mind,' I said, and remembered Marston saying 'Never mind, never mind.'

'Don't look so down in the mouth, my girl,' I said to myself. *'Look gay.'*

'Cheer up,' I said, and kissed myself in the cool glass. I stood with my forehead against it and watched my face clouding gradually, then turned because I felt as if someone was staring at me, but it was only the girl on the cover of the chocolate-box. She had slanting green eyes, but they were too close together, and she had a white, square, smug face that didn't go with the slanting eyes. 'I bet you could be a rotten, respectable, sneering bitch too, with a face like that, if you had a chance,' I told her.

The train got into Paddington just before ten. As soon as I was on the platform I remembered the chocolates, but I didn't go back for them. 'Somebody will find you, somebody will look after you, you rotten, sneering, stupid, tight-mouthed bitch,' I thought.

London always smells the same. 'Frowsty,' you think, 'but I'm glad to be back.' And just for a while it bears you up. 'Anything's round the corner,' you think. But long before you get round the corner it lets you drop.

I decided that I'd walk for a bit with the suitcase and get tired and then perhaps I'd sleep. But at the corner of Marylebone Road and Edgware Road my arm was stiff and I put down the suitcase and waved at a taxi standing by the kerb.

'Sorry, miss,' the driver said, 'This gentleman was first.'

The young man smiled. 'It's all right. You have it.'

'*You have it,*' *he said. The other one said, 'Want a lift?*'

'I can get the next one. I'm not in any hurry.'

'Nor am I.'

The taxi-driver moved impatiently.

'Well, don't let's hesitate any longer,' the young man said, 'or we'll lose our taximeter-cab. Get in – I can easily drop you wherever you're going.'

'Go along Edgware Road,' he said to the driver. 'I'll tell you where in a minute.'

The taxi started.

'Where to?'

'Torrington Square.'

The house would be waiting for me. 'When I pass Estelle's door,' I thought, 'there'll be no smell of scent now.' Then I was back in my small room on the top floor, listening to the church clock chiming every quarter-hour. 'There's a good time coming for the ladies. There's a good time coming for the girls. . . .'

I said, 'Wait a minute. I don't want to go to Torrington Square.'

'Oh, you don't want to go to Torrington Square?' He seemed amused and wary, but more wary than amused.

'It's such a lovely night, so warm. I don't want to go home just yet. I think I'll go and sit in Hyde Park.'

'Not Torrington Square,' he shouted through the window.

The taxi drew up.

'Damn his eyes, what's he done that for.'

The driver got down and opened the door.

'Here, where am I going to? This is the third time you've changed your mind since you 'ailed me.'

'You'll go where you're damn well told.'

'Well where am I damn well told?'

'Go to Marble Arch.'

''Yde Park,' the driver said, looking us up and down and grinning broadly. Then he got back into his seat.

'I can't bear some of these chaps, can you?' the young man said.

When the taxi stopped at the end of Park Lane we both got out without a word. The driver looked us up and down again scornfully before he started away.

'What do you want to do in Hyde Park? Look at the trees?'

He took my suitcase and walked along by my side.

'Yes, I want to look at the trees and not go back to the place where I live. Never go back.'

'I've never lived in a place I like,' I thought, 'never.'

'That does sound desperate. Well, let's see if we can find a secluded spot.'

'That chair over there will do,' I said. It was away from people under a tree. Not that people mattered much, for now it was night and they are never so frightening then.

I shut my eyes so that I could hear and smell the trees better. I imagined I could smell water too. The Serpentine – I didn't know we had walked so far.

He said, 'I can't leave you so disconsolate on this lovely night – this night of love and night of stars.' He gave a loud hiccup, and then another. 'That always happens when I've eaten quails.'

'It happens to me when I'm tight.'

'Does it?' He pulled another chair forward and sat down by my side. 'I can't leave you now until I know where you're going with that large suitcase and that desperate expression.'

I told him that I had just come back after a stay in the country, and he told me that he did not live in London, that his name was Melville and that he was at a loose end that evening.

'Did somebody let you down?'

'Oh, that's not important – not half so important as the desperate expression. I noticed that as soon as I saw you.'

'That's not despair, it's hunger,' I said, dropping into the backchat. 'Don't you know hunger when you see it?'

'Well, let's go and have something to eat, then. But where?' He looked at me uncertainly. 'Where?'

'We could go to the Apple Tree. Of course, it's a bit early, but we might be able to get kippers or eggs and bacon or sausages and mash.'

'The Apple Tree? I've heard of it. Could we go there?' he said, still eyeing me.

'We could indeed. You could come as my guest. I'm a member. I was one of the first members,' I boasted.

I had touched the right spring – even the feeling of his hand on my arm changed. *Always the same spring to touch before the sneering expression will go out of their eyes and the sneering sound out of their voices. Think about it – it's very important.*

'Lots of pretty girls at the Apple Tree, aren't there?' he said.

'I can't promise anything. It's a bad time of year for the Apple Tree, the singing and the gold.'

'Now what are you talking about?'

'Somebody I know calls it that.'

'But you'll be there.' He pulled his chair closer and looked round cautiously before he kissed me. 'And you're an awfully pretty girl, aren't you? . . . The Apple Tree, the singing and the gold. I like that.'

'Better than "Night of love and night of stars"?'

'Oh, they're not in the same street.'

I thought, 'How do you know what's in what street? How do they know who's fifth-rate, who's fifth-rate and where the devouring spider lives?'

'You don't really mind where we go, do you?' he said.

'I don't mind at all.'

He took his arm away. 'It was odd our meeting like that, wasn't it?'

'I don't think so. I don't think it was odd at all.'

After a silence, 'I haven't been very swift in the uptake, have I?' he said.

'No, you haven't. Now, let's be off to the Apple Tree, the singing and the gold.'

'Oh, damn the Apple Tree. I know a better place than that.'

*'I've been persuaded to taste it before,' Marston said. 'It tasted
exactly as I thought it would.'*

And everything was exactly as I had expected. The knowing
waiters, the touch of the ice-cold wine glass, the red plush chairs,
the food you don't notice, the gold-framed mirror, the bed in the
room beyond that always looks as if its ostentatious whiteness
hides dinginess.

*But Marston should have said, 'It tastes of nothing, my dear,
it tastes of nothing. . . .'*

When we got out into Leicester Square again I had forgotten
Marston and only thought about how, when we had nothing better to do, Estelle and I would go to the Corner House or to some
cheap restaurant in Soho and have dinner. She was so earnest
when it came to food. 'You must have one good meal a day,' she
would say, 'it is *necessary.' Escalope de veau* and fried potatoes
and brussels sprouts, we usually had, and then *crème caramel* or
compôte de fruits. And she seemed to be walking along by my
side, wearing her blue suit and her white blouse, her high heels
tapping. But as we turned the corner by the Hippodrome she
vanished. I thought 'I shall never see her again – I know it.'

In the taxi he said, 'I don't forget addresses, do I?'

'No, you don't.'

To keep myself awake I began to sing 'Mr Brown, Mr Brown,
Had a violin. . . .'

'Are you on the stage?'

'I was. I started my brilliant and successful career like so many
others, in the chorus. But I wasn't a success.'

'What a shame! Why?'

'Because I couldn't say "epigrammatic".'

He laughed – really laughed that time.

'The stage manager had the dotty idea of pulling me out of
my obscurity and giving me a line to say. The line was "Oh, Lot-

tie, Lottie, don't be epigrammatic". I rehearsed it and rehearsed it, but when it came to the night it was just a blank.'

At the top of Charing Cross Road the taxi was held up. We were both laughing so much that people turned round and stared at us.

'It was one of the most dreadful moments of my life, and I shan't ever forget it. There was the stage manager, mouthing at me from the wings – he was the prompter too and he also played a small part, the family lawyer – and there he was all dressed up in grey-striped trousers and a black tail-coat and top hat and silver side-whiskers, and there I was, in a yellow dress and a large straw hat and a green sunshade and a lovely background of an English castle and garden – half ruined and half not, you know – and a chorus of footmen and maids, and my mind a complete blank.'

The taxi started again. 'Well, what happened?'

'Nothing. After one second the other actors went smoothly on. I remember the next line. It was "Going to Ascot? Well, if you don't get into the Royal Enclosure when you *are* there I'm no judge of character".'

'But what about the audience?'

'Oh, the audience weren't surprised because, you see, they had never expected me to speak at all. Well, here we are.'

I gave him my latchkey and he opened the door.

'A formidable key! It's like the key of a prison,' he said.

Everyone had gone to bed and there wasn't even a ghost of Estelle's scent in the hall.

'We must see each other again,' he said. 'Please. Couldn't you write to me at –' He stopped. 'No, I'll write to you. If you're ever – I'll write to you anyway.'

I said, 'Do you know what I want? I want a gold bracelet with blue stones in it. Not too blue – the darker blue I prefer.'

'Oh, well.' He was wary again. 'I'll do my best, but I'm not one of these plutocrats, you know.'

'Don't you dare to come back without it. But I'm going away for a few weeks. I'll be here again in September.'

'All right, I'll see you in September, Petronella,' he said chir-
pily, anxious to be off. 'And you've been so sweet to me.'

'The pleasure was all mine.'

He shook his head. 'Now, Lottie, Lottie, don't be epigrammatic.'

I thought, 'I daresay he would be nice if one got to know him.
I daresay, perhaps . . .' listening to him tapping good-bye on the
other side of the door. I tapped back twice and then started up
the stairs. Past the door of Estelle's room, not feeling a thing as I
passed it, because she had gone and I knew she would not ever
come back.

In my room I stood looking out of the window, remembering
my yellow dress, the blurred mass of the audience and the face
of one man in the front row seen quite clearly, and how I thought,
as quick as lightning. 'Help me, tell me what I have forgotten.'
But though he had looked, as it seemed, straight into my eyes,
and though I was sure he knew exactly what I was thinking, he
had not helped me. He had only smiled. He had left me in that
moment that seemed like years standing there until through the
dreadful blankness of my mind I had heard a high, shrill, cock-
ney voice saying, 'Going to Ascot?' and seen the stage manager
frown and shake his head at me.

'My God, I must have looked a fool,' I thought, laughing and
feeling the tears running down my face.

'What a waste of good tears!' the other girls had told me when
I cried in the dressing-room that night. 'Oh, the waste, the waste,
the waste!'

But that did not last long.

'What's the time?' I thought, and because I wasn't sleepy any
longer I sat down in the chair by the window, waiting for the
clock outside to strike.

The Day They Burned the Books

MY FRIEND Eddie was a small, thin boy. You could see the blue veins in his wrists and temples. People said that he had consumption and wasn't long for this world. I loved, but sometimes despised him.

His father, Mr Sawyer, was a strange man. Nobody could make out what he was doing in our part of the world at all. He was not a planter or a doctor or a lawyer or a banker. He didn't keep a store. He wasn't a schoolmaster or a government official. He wasn't – that was the point – a gentleman. We had several resident romantics who had fallen in love with the moon on the Caribbees – they were all gentlemen and quite unlike Mr Sawyer who hadn't an 'h' in his composition. Besides, he detested the moon and everything else about the Caribbean and he didn't mind telling you so.

He was agent for a small steamship line which in those days linked up Venezuela and Trinidad with the smaller islands, but he couldn't make much out of that. He must have a private income, people decided, but they never decided why he had chosen to settle in a place he didn't like and to marry a coloured woman. Though a decent, respectable, nicely educated coloured woman, mind you.

Mrs Sawyer must have been very pretty once but, what with one thing and another, that was in days gone by.

When Mr Sawyer was drunk – this often happened – he used

to be very rude to her. She never answered him.

'Look at the nigger showing off,' he would say; and she would smile as if she knew she ought to see the joke but couldn't. 'You damned, long-eyed, gloomy half-caste, you don't smell right,' he would say; and she never answered, not even to whisper, 'You don't smell right to me, either.'

The story went that once they had ventured to give a dinner party and that when the servant, Mildred, was bringing in coffee, he had pulled Mrs Sawyer's hair. 'Not a wig, you see,' he bawled. Even then, if you can believe it, Mrs Sawyer had laughed and tried to pretend that it was all part of the joke, this mysterious, obscure, sacred English joke.

But Mildred told the other servants in the town that her eyes had gone wicked, like a soucriant's eyes, and that afterwards she had picked up some of the hair he pulled out and put it in an envelope, and that Mr Sawyer ought to look out (hair is obeah as well as hands).

Of course, Mrs Sawyer had her compensations. They lived in a very pleasant house in Hill Street. The garden was large and they had a fine mango tree, which bore prolifically. The fruit was small, round, very sweet and juicy – a lovely, red-and-yellow colour when it was ripe. Perhaps it was one of the compensations, I used to think.

Mr Sawyer built a room on to the back of this house. It was unpainted inside and the wood smelt very sweet. Bookshelves lined the walls. Every time the Royal Mail steamer came in it brought a package for him, and gradually the empty shelves filled.

Once I went there with Eddie to borrow *The Arabian Nights*. That was on a Saturday afternoon, one of those hot, still afternoons when you felt that everything had gone to sleep, even the water in the gutters. But Mrs Sawyer was not asleep. She put her head in at the door and looked at us, and I knew that she hated the room and hated the books.

It was Eddie with the pale blue eyes and straw-coloured hair – the living image of his father, though often as silent as his mother – who first infected me with doubts about 'home', mean-

ing England. He would be so quiet when others who had never
seen it – none of us had ever seen it – were talking about its
delights, gesticulating freely as we talked – London, the beautiful, rosy-cheeked ladies, the theatres, the shops, the fog, the blazing coal fires in winter, the exotic food (whitebait eaten to the
sound of violins), strawberries and cream – the word 'strawberries' always spoken with a guttural and throaty sound which we
imagined to be the proper English pronunciation.

'I don't like strawberries,' Eddie said on one occasion.

'You *don't like* strawberries?'

'No, and I don't like daffodils either. Dad's always going on
about them. He says they lick the flowers here into a cocked hat
and I bet that's a lie.'

We were all too shocked to say, 'You don't know a thing about
it.' We were so shocked that nobody spoke to him for the rest of
the day. But I for one admired him. I also was tired of learning
and reciting poems in praise of daffodils, and my relations with
the few 'real' English boys and girls I had met were awkward. I
had discovered that if I called myself English they would snub
me haughtily: 'You're not English; you're a horrid colonial.' 'Well,
I don't much want to be English,' I would say. 'It's much more
fun to be French or Spanish or something like that – and, as a
matter of fact, I am a bit.' Then I was too killingly funny, quite
ridiculous. Not only a horrid colonial, but also ridiculous. Heads
I win, tails you lose – that was the English. I had thought about
all this, and thought hard, but I had never dared to tell anybody
what I thought and I realized that Eddie had been very bold.

But he was bold, and stronger than you would think. For one
thing, he never felt the heat; some coldness in his fair skin resisted
it. He didn't burn red or brown, he didn't freckle much.

Hot days seemed to make him feel especially energetic. 'Now
we'll run twice round the lawn and then you can pretend you're
dying of thirst in the desert and that I'm an Arab chieftain bringing you water.'

'You must drink slowly,' he would say, 'for if you're very thirsty
and you drink quickly you die.'

So I learnt the voluptuousness of drinking slowly when you are very thirsty – small mouthful by small mouthful, until the glass of pink, iced Coca-Cola was empty.

Just after my twelfth birthday Mr Sawyer died suddenly, and as Eddie's special friend I went to the funeral, wearing a new white dress. My straight hair was damped with sugar and water the night before and plaited into tight little plaits, so that it should be fluffy for the occasion.

When it was all over everybody said how nice Mrs Sawyer had looked, walking like a queen behind the coffin and crying her eyeballs out at the right moment, and wasn't Eddie a funny boy? He hadn't cried at all.

After this Eddie and I took possession of the room with the books. No one else ever entered it, except Mildred to sweep and dust in the mornings, and gradually the ghost of Mr Sawyer pulling Mrs Sawyer's hair faded, though this took a little time. The blinds were always halfway down and going in out of the sun was like stepping into a pool of brown-green water. It was empty except for the bookshelves, a desk with a green baize top and a wicker rocking-chair.

'My room,' Eddie called it. 'My books,' he would say, 'my books.'

I don't know how long this lasted. I don't know whether it was weeks after Mr. Sawyer's death or months after, that I see myself and Eddie in the room. But there we are and there, unexpectedly, are Mrs Sawyer and Mildred. Mrs Sawyer's mouth tight, her eyes pleased. She is pulling all the books out of the shelves and piling them into two heaps. The big, fat glossy ones – the good-looking ones, Mildred explains in a whisper – lie in one heap. The *Encyclopaedia Britannica, British Flowers, Birds and Beasts*, various histories, books with maps, Froude's *English in the West Indies* and so on – they are going to be sold. The unimportant books, with paper covers or damaged covers or torn pages, lie in another heap. They are going to be burnt – yes, burnt.

Mildred's expression was extraordinary as she said that – half hugely delighted, half shocked, even frightened. And as for Mrs Sawyer – well, I knew bad temper (I had often seen it), I knew rage, but this was hate. I recognized the difference at once and stared at her curiously. I edged closer to her so that I could see the titles of the books she was handling.

It was the poetry shelf. *Poems*, Lord Byron, *Poetical Works*, Milton, and so on. Vlung, vlung, vlung – all thrown into the heap that were to be sold. But a book by Christina Rossetti, though also bound in leather, went into the heap that was to be burnt, and by a flicker in Mrs Sawyer's eyes I knew that worse than men who wrote books were women who wrote books – infinitely worse. Men could be mercifully shot; women must be tortured.

Mrs Sawyer did not seem to notice that we were there, but she was breathing free and easy and her hands had got the rhythm of tearing and pitching. She looked beautiful, too – beautiful as the sky outside which was a very dark blue, or the mango tree, long sprays of brown and gold.

When Eddie said 'no', she did not even glance at him.

'No,' he said again in a high voice. 'Not that one. I was reading that one.'

She laughed and he rushed at her, his eyes starting out of his head, shrieking, 'Now I've got to hate you too. Now I hate you too.'

He snatched the book out of her hand and gave her a violent push. She fell into the rocking-chair.

Well, I wasn't going to be left out of all this, so I grabbed a book from the condemned pile and dived under Mildred's outstretched arm.

Then we were both in the garden. We ran along the path, bordered with crotons. We pelted down the path though they did not follow us and we could hear Mildred laughing – kyah, kyah, kyah, kyah. As I ran I put the book I had taken into the loose front of my brown holland dress. It felt warm and alive.

When we got into the street we walked sedately, for we feared the black children's ridicule. I felt very happy, because I had saved this book and it was my book and I would read it from the beginning to the triumphant words 'The End'. But I was uneasy when I thought of Mrs Sawyer.

'What will she do?' I said.

'Nothing,' Eddie said. 'Not to me.'

He was white as a ghost in his sailor suit, a blue-white even in the setting sun, and his father's sneer was clamped on his face.

'But she'll tell your mother all sorts of lies about you,' he said. 'She's an awful liar. She can't make up a story to save her life, but she makes up lies about people all right.'

'My mother won't take any notice of her,' I said. Though I was not at all sure.

'Why not? Because she's . . . because she isn't white?'

Well, I knew the answer to that one. Whenever the subject was brought up – people's relations and whether they had a drop of coloured blood or whether they hadn't – my father would grow impatient and interrupt. 'Who's white?' he would say. 'Damned few.'

So I said, 'Who's white? Damned few.'

'You can go to the devil,' Eddie said. 'She's prettier than your mother. When she's asleep her mouth smiles and she has your curling eyelashes and quantities and quantities and *quantities* of hair.'

'Yes,' I said truthfully. 'She's prettier than my mother.'

It was a red sunset that evening, a huge, sad, frightening sunset.

'Look, let's go back,' I said. 'If you're sure she won't be vexed with you, let's go back. It'll be dark soon.'

At his gate he asked me not to go. 'Don't go yet, don't go yet.'

We sat under the mango tree and I was holding his hand when he began to cry. Drops fell on my hand like the water from the dripstone in the filter in our yard. Then I began to cry too and when I felt my own tears on my hand I thought, 'Now perhaps we're married.'

'Yes, certainly, now we're married,' I thought. But I didn't say anything. I didn't say a thing until I was sure he had stopped. Then I asked, 'What's your book?'

'It's *Kim*,' he said. 'But it got torn. It starts at page twenty now. What's the one you took?'

'I don't know, it's too dark to see,' I said.

When I got home I rushed into my bedroom and locked the door because I knew that this book was the most important thing that had ever happened to me and I did not want anybody to be there when I looked at it.

But I was very disappointed, because it was in French and seemed dull. *Fort Comme La Mort,* it was called. . . .

Let Them Call It Jazz

ONE BRIGHT Sunday morning in July I have trouble with my Notting Hill landlord because he ask for a month's rent in advance. He tell me this after I live there since winter, settling up every week without fail. I have no job at the time, and if I give the money he want there's not much left. So I refuse. The man drunk already at that early hour, and he abuse me – all talk, he can't frighten me. But his wife is a bad one – now she walk in my room and say she must have cash. When I tell her no, she give my suitcase one kick and it burst open. My best dress fall out, then she laugh and give another kick. She say month in advance is usual, and if I can't pay find somewhere else.

Don't talk to me about London. Plenty people there have heart like stone. Any complaint – the answer is 'prove it'. But if nobody see and bear witness for me, how to prove anything? So I pack up and leave. I think better not have dealings with that woman. She too cunning, and Satan don't lie worse.

I walk about till a place nearby is open where I can have coffee and a sandwich. There I start talking to a man at my table. He talk to me already, I know him, but I don't know his name. After a while he ask, 'What's the matter? Anything wrong?' and when I tell him my trouble he say I can use an empty flat he own till I have time to look around.

This man is not at all like most English people. He see very quick, and he decide very quick. English people take long time to decide – you three-quarter dead before they make up their mind about you. Too besides, he speak very matter of fact, as if it's nothing. He speak as if he realize well what it is to live like I do – that's why I accept and go.

He tell me somebody occupy the flat till last week, so I find everything all right, and he tell me how to get there – three-quarters of an hour from Victoria Station, up a steep hill, turn left, and I can't mistake the house. He give me the keys and an envelope with a telephone number on the back. Underneath is written 'After 6 P.M. ask for Mr Sims'.

In the train that evening I think myself lucky, for to walk about London on a Sunday with nowhere to go – that take the heart out of you.

I find the place and the bedroom of the downstairs flat is nicely furnished – two looking glass, wardrobe, chest of drawers, sheets, everything. It smell of jasmine scent, but it smell strong of damp too.

I open the door opposite and there's a table, a couple chairs, a gas stove and a cupboard, but this room so big it look empty. When I pull the blind up I notice the paper peeling off and mushrooms growing on the walls – you never see such a thing.

The bathroom the same, all the taps rusty. I leave the two other rooms and make up the bed. Then I listen, but I can't hear one sound. Nobody come in, nobody go out of that house. I lie awake for a long time, then I decide not to stay and in the morning I start to get ready quickly before I change my mind. I want to wear my best dress, but it's a funny thing – when I take up that dress and remember how my landlady kick it I cry. I cry and I can't stop. When I stop I feel tired to my bones, tired like old woman. I don't want to move again – I have to force myself. But in the end I get out in the passage and there's a postcard for me. 'Stay as long as you like. I'll be seeing you soon – Friday probably. Not to worry.' It isn't signed, but I don't feel so sad and I think, 'All right, I wait here till he come. Perhaps he know of a job for me.'

Nobody else live in the house but a couple on the top floor – quiet people and they don't trouble me. I have no word to say against them.

First time I meet the lady she's opening the front door and she give me a very inquisitive look. But next time she smile a bit and I smile back – once she talk to me. She tell me the house very old, hundred and fifty year old, and she had her husband live there since long time. 'Valuable property,' she says, 'it could have been saved, but nothing done of course.' Then she tells me that as to the present owner – if he is the owner – well he have to deal with local authorities and she believe they make difficulties. 'These people are determined to pull down all the lovely old houses – it's shameful.'

So I agree that many things shameful. But what to do? What to do? I say it have an elegant shape, it make the other houses in the street look cheap trash, and she seem pleased. That's true too. The house sad and out of place, especially at night. But it have style. The second floor shut up, and as for my flat, I go in the two empty rooms once, but never again.

Underneath was the cellar, full of old boards and broken-up furniture – I see a big rat there one day. It was no place to be alone in I tell you, and I get the habit of buying a bottle of wine most evenings, for I don't like whisky and the rum here no good. It don't even *taste* like rum. You wonder what they do to it.

After I drink a glass or two I can sing and when I sing all the misery goes from my heart. Sometimes I make up songs but next morning I forget them, so other times I sing the old ones like 'Tantalizin' ' or 'Don't Trouble Me Now'.

I think I go but I don't go. Instead I wait for the evening and the wine and that's all. Everywhere else I live – well, it doesn't matter to me, but this house is different – empty and no noise and full of shadows, so that sometimes you ask yourself what make all those shadows in an empty room.

I eat in the kitchen, then I clean up everything and have a bath for coolness. Afterwards I lean my elbows on the windowsill and look at the garden. Red and blue flowers mix up with the weeds and there are five-six apple trees. But the fruit drop and lie in the grass, so sour nobody want it. At the back, near the wall, is a bigger tree – this garden certainly take up a lot of room, perhaps that's why they want to pull the place down.

Not much rain all the summer, but not much sunshine either. More of a glare. The grass get brown and dry, the weeds grow tall, the leaves on the trees hang down. Only the red flowers – the poppies – stand up to that light, everything else look weary.

I don't trouble about money, but what with wine and shillings for the slot-meters, it go quickly; so I don't waste much on food. In the evening I walk outside – not by the apple trees but near the street – it's not so lonely.

There's no wall here and I can see the woman next door looking at me over the hedge. At first I say good evening, but she turn away her head, so afterwards I don't speak. A man is often with her, he wear a straw hat with a black ribbon and goldrim spectacles. His suit hand on him like it's too big. He's the husband it seems and he stare at me worse than his wife – he stare as if I'm wild animal let loose. Once I laugh in his face because why these people have to be like that? I don't bother them. In the end I get that I don't even give them one single glance. I have plenty other things to worry about.

To show you how I felt. I don't remember exactly. But I believe it's the second Saturday after I come that when I'm at the window just before I go for my wine I feel somebody's hand on my shoulder and its Mr Sims. He must walk very quiet because I don't know a thing till he touch me.

He says hullo, then he tells me I've got terrible thin, do I ever eat. I say of course I eat but he goes on that it doesn't suit me at all to be so thin and he'll buy some food in the village. (That's the way he talk. There's no village here. You don't get away from London so quick.)

It don't seem to me he look very well himself, but I just say bring a drink instead, as I am not hungry.

He come back with three bottles – vermouth, gin and red wine. Then he ask if the little devil who was here last smash all the glasses and I tell him she smash some, I find the pieces. But not all. 'You fight with her, eh?'

He laugh, and he don't answer. He pour out the drinks then he says, 'Now, you eat up those sandwiches.'

Some men when they are there you don't worry so much.

These sort of men you do all they tell you blindfold because they can take the trouble from your heart and make you think you're safe. It's nothing they say or do. It's a feeling they can give you. So I don't talk with him seriously – I don't want to spoil that evening. But I ask about the house and why it's so empty and he says:

'Has the old trout upstairs been gossiping?'

I tell him, 'She suppose they make difficulties for you.'

'It was a damn bad buy,' he says and talks about selling the lease or something. I don't listen much.

We were standing by the window then and the sun low. No more glare. He puts his hand over my eyes. 'Too big – much too big for your face,' he says and kisses me like you kiss a baby. When he takes his hand away I see he's looking out at the garden and he says this – 'It gets you. My God it does.'

I know very well it's not me he means, so I ask him, 'Why sell it then? If you like it, keep it.'

'Sell what?' he says. 'I'm not talking about this damned house.'

I ask what he's talking about. 'Money,' he says. 'Money. That's what I'm talking about. Ways of making it.'

'I don't think so much of money. It don't like me and what do I care?' I was joking, but he turns around, his face quite pale and he tells me I'm a fool. He tells me I'll get pushed around all my life and die like a dog, only worse because they'd finish off a dog, but they'll let me live till I'm a caricature of myself. That's what he say, 'Caricature of yourself.' He say I'll curse the day I was born and everything and everybody in this bloody world before I'm done.

I tell him, 'No I'll never feel like that,' and he smiles, if you can call it a smile, and says he's glad I'm content with my lot. 'I'm disappointed in you, Selina. I thought you had more spirit.'

'If I contented that's all right,' I answer him. 'I don't see very many looking contented over here.' We're standing staring at each other when the doorbell rings. 'That's a friend of mine,' he says. 'I'll let him in.'

As to the friend, he's all dressed up in stripe pants and a black jacket and he's carrying a brief-case. Very ordinary looking but with a soft kind of voice.

'Maurice, this is Selina Davis,' says Mr Sims, and Maurice smiles very kind but it don't mean much, then he looks at his watch and says they ought to be getting along.

At the door Mr Sims tells me he'll see me next week and I answer straight out, 'I won't be here next week because I want a job and I won't get one in this place.'

'Just what I'm going to talk about. Give it a week longer, Selina.'

I say, 'Perhaps I stay a few more days. Then I go. Perhaps I go before.'

'Oh no you won't go,' he says.

They walk to the gates quickly and drive off in a yellow car. Then I feel eyes on me and it's the woman and her husband in the next door garden watching. The man make some remark and she look at me so hateful, so hating I shut the front door quick.

I don't want more wine. I want to go to bed early because I must think. I must think about money. It's true I don't care for it. Even when somebody steal my savings – this happen soon after I get to the Notting Hill house – I forget it soon. About thirty pounds they steal. I keep it roll up in a pair of stockings, but I go to the drawer one day, and no money. In the end I have to tell the police. They ask me exact sum and I say I don't count it lately, about thirty pounds. 'You don't know how much?' they say. 'When did you count it last? Do you remember? Was it before you move or after?'

I get confuse, and I keep saying, 'I don't remember,' though I remember well I see it two days before. They don't believe me and when a policeman come to the house I hear the landlady tell him, 'She certainly had no money when she came here. She wasn't able to pay a month's rent in advance for her room though it's a rule in this house.' 'These people terrible liars,' she say and I think 'it's you a terrible liar, because when I come you tell me weekly or monthly as you like.' It's from that time she don't speak to me and perhaps it's she take it. All I know is I never see one penny of my savings again, all I know is they pretend I never have any, but as it's gone, no use to cry about it. Then my mind goes to my father, for my father is a white man and I think a lot about him. If I could see him only once, for I too small to remember when he was there. My mother is fair coloured woman, fairer than I am they say, and she don't stay long with me either. She have a chance to go to Venezuela when I three-four year old and she never come back. She send money instead. It's my grandmother take care of me. She's quite dark and what we call 'country-cookie' but she's the best I know.

She save up all the money my mother send, she don't keep one penny for herself – that's how I get to England. I was a bit late in going to school regular, getting on for twelve years, but I can sew very beautiful, excellent – so I think I get a good job – in London perhaps.

However here they tell me all this fine handsewing take too long. Waste of time – too slow. They want somebody to work quick and to hell with the small stitches. Altogether it don't look so good for me, I must say, and I wish I could see my father. I have his name – Davis. But my grandmother tell me, 'Every word that comes out of that man's mouth a damn lie. He is certainly first class liar, though no class otherwise.' So perhaps I have not even his real name.

Last thing I see before I put the light out is the postcard on the dressing table. 'Not to worry.'

Not to worry! Next day is Sunday, and it's on the Monday the people next door complain about me to the police. That evening the woman is by the hedge, and when I pass her she says in very sweet quiet voice, '*Must* you stay? *Can't* you go?' I don't answer. I walk out in the street to get rid of her. But she run inside her house to the window, she can still see me. Then I start to sing, so she can understand I'm not afraid of her. The husband call out: 'If you don't stop that noise I'll send for the police.' I answer them quite short. I say, 'You go to hell and take your wife with you.' And I sing louder.

The police come pretty quick – two of them. Maybe they just round the corner. All I can say about police, and how they behave is I think it all depends who they dealing with. Of my own free will I don't want to mix up with police. No.

One man says, you can't cause this disturbance here. But the other asks a lot of questions. What is my name? Am I tenant of a flat in No. 17? How long have I lived there? Last address and so on. I get vexed the way he speak and I tell him, 'I come here because somebody steal my savings. Why you don't look for my money instead of bawling at me? I work hard for my money. All-you don't do one single thing to find it.'

'What's she talking about?' the first one says, and the other one tells me, 'You can't make that noise here. Get along home. You've been drinking.'

I see that woman looking at me and smiling, and other people at their windows, and I'm so angry I bawl at them too. I say, 'I have absolute and perfect right to be in the street same as anybody else, and I have absolute and perfect right to ask the police why they don't even look for my money when it disappear. It's because a dam' English thief take it you don't look,' I say. The end of all this is that I have to go before a magistrate, and he fine me five pounds for drunk and disorderly, and he give me two weeks to pay.

When I get back from the court I walk up and down the kitchen, up and down, waiting for six o'clock because I have no five pounds left, and I don't know what to do. I telephone at six and a woman answers me very short and sharp, then Mr Sims comes along and he don't sound too pleased either when I tell him what happen. 'Oh Lord!' he says, and I say I'm sorry. 'Well don't panic,' he says, 'I'll pay the fine. But look, I don't think. . . .' Then he breaks off and talk to some other person in the room. He goes on, 'Perhaps better not stay at No. 17. I think I can arrange something else. I'll call for you Wednesday – Saturday latest. Now behave till then.' And he hang up before I can answer that I don't want to wait till Wednesday, much less Saturday. I want to get out of that house double quick and with no delay. First I think I ring back, then I think better now as he sound so vex.

I get ready, but Wednesday he don't come, and Saturday he

don't come. All the week I stay in the flat. Only once I go out and arrange for bread, milk and eggs to be left at the door, and seems to me I meet up with a lot of policemen. They don't look at me, but they see me all right. I don't want to drink – I'm all the time listening, listening and thinking, how can I leave before I know if my fine is paid? I tell myself the police let me know, that's certain. But I don't trust them. What they care? The answer is Nothing. Nobody care. One afternoon I knock at the old lady's flat upstairs, because I get the idea she give me good advice. I can hear her moving about and talking, but she don't answer and I never try again.

Nearly two weeks pass like that, then I telephone. It's the woman speaking and she say, 'Mr Sims is not in London at present.' I ask, 'When will he be back – it's urgent,' and she hang up. I'm not surprised. Not at all. I knew that would happen. All the same I feel heavy like lead. Near the phone box is a chemist's shop, so I ask him for something to make me sleep, the day is bad enough, but to lie awake all night – Ah no! He gives me a little bottle marked *'One or two tablets only'* and I take three when I go to bed because more and more I think that sleeping is better than no matter what else. However, I lie there, eyes wide open as usual, so I take three more. Next thing I know the room is full of sunlight, so it must be late afternoon, but the lamp is still on. My head turn around and I can't think well at all. At first I ask myself how I get to the place. Then it comes to me, but in pictures – like the landlady kicking my dress, and when I take my ticket at Victoria Station, and Mr Sims telling me to eat the sandwiches, but I can't remember everything clear, and I feel very giddy and sick. I take in the milk and eggs at the door, go in the kitchen, and try to eat but the food hard to swallow.

It's when I'm putting the things away that I see the bottles – pushed back on the lowest shelf in the cupboard.

There's a lot of drink left, and I'm glad I tell you. Because I can't bear the way I feel. Not any more. I mix a gin and vermouth and I drink it quick, then I mix another and drink it slow by the window. The garden looks different, like I never see it before. I know quite well what I must do, but it's late now – tomorrow I have one more drink, of wine this time, and then a song comes in my head, I sing it and I dance it, and more I sing, more I am sure this is the best tune that has ever come to me in all my life.

The sunset light from the window is gold colour. My shoes sound loud on the boards. So I take them off, my stockings too and go on dancing but the room feel shut in, I can't breathe, and I go outside still singing. Maybe I dance a bit too. I forget all about that woman till I hear her saying, 'Henry, look at this.' I turn around and I see her at the window. 'Oh yes, I wanted to speak with you,' I say, 'Why bring the police and get me in bad trouble? Tell me that.'

'And you tell me what you're doing here at all,' she says. 'This is a respectable neighbourhood.'

Then the man come along. 'Now young woman, take yourself off. You ought to be ashamed of this behaviour.'

'It's disgraceful,' he says, talking to his wife, but loud so I can hear, and she speaks loud too – for once. 'At least the other tarts that crook installed here were *white* girls,' she says.

'You a dam' fouti liar,' I say. 'Plenty of those girls in your country already. Numberless as the sands on the shore. You don't need me for that.'

'You're not a howling success at it certainly.' Her voice sweet sugar again. 'And you won't be seeing much more of your friend Mr Sims. He's in trouble too. Try somewhere else. Find somebody else. If you can, of course.' When she say that my arm moves of itself. I pick up a stone and bam! through the window. Not the one they are standing at but the next, which is of coloured glass, green and purple and yellow.

I never see a woman look so surprise. Her mouth fall open she so full of surprise. I start to laugh, louder and louder – I laugh like my grandmother, with my hands on my hips and my head back. (When she laugh like that you can hear her to the end of our street.) At last I say, 'Well, I'm sorry. An accident. I get it fixed tomorrow early.' 'That glass is irreplaceable,' the man says. 'Irreplaceable.' 'Good thing,' I say, 'those colours look like they sea-sick to me. I buy you a better windowglass.'

He shake his fist at me. 'You won't be let off with a fine this time,' he says. Then they draw the curtains, I call out at them. 'You run away. Always you run away. Ever since I come here you hunt me down because I don't answer back. It's you shameless.' I try to sing 'Don't Trouble Me Now'.

> *Don't trouble me now*
> *You without honour.*
> *Don't walk in my footstep*
> *You without shame.*

But my voice don't sound right, so I get back indoors and drink one more glass of wine – still wanting to laugh, and still thinking of my grandmother for that is one of her songs.

It's about a man whose doudou give him the go-by when she find somebody rich and he sail away to Panama. Plenty people die there of fever when they make that Panama canal so long ago. But he don't die. He come back with dollars and the girl meet him on the jetty, all dressed up and smiling. Then he sing to her, 'You without honour, you without shame'. It sound good in Martinique patois too: '*Sans honte*'.

Afterwards I ask myself, 'Why I do that? It's not like me. But if they treat you wrong over and over again the hour strike when you burst out that's what.'

Too besides, Mr Sims can't tell me now I have no spirit I don't care, I sleep quickly and I'm glad I break the woman's ugly window. But as to my own song it go *right* away and it never come back. A pity.

Next morning the doorbell ringing wake me up. The people upstairs don't come down, and the bell keeps on like fury self. So I go to look, and there is a policeman and a policewoman outside. As soon as I open the door the woman put her foot in it. She wear sandals and thick stockings and I never see a foot so big or so bad. It look like it want to mash up the whole world. Then she come in after the foot, and her face not so pretty either. The policeman tell me my fine is not paid and people make serious complaints about me, so they're taking me back to the magistrate. He show me a paper and I look at it, but I don't read it. The woman push me in the bedroom, and tell me to get dress quickly, but I just stare at her, because I think perhaps I wake up soon. Then I ask her what I must wear. She say she suppose I had some clothes on yesterday. Or not? 'What's it matter, wear anything,' she says. But I find clean underclothes and stockings and my shoes with high heels and I comb my hair. I start to file my nails, because I think they too long for magistrate's court but she get angry. 'Are you coming quietly or aren't you?' she says. So I go with them and we get in a car outside.

I wait for a long time in a room full of policemen. They come in, they go out, they telephone, they talk in low voices. Then it's my turn, and first thing I notice in the court room is a man with frowning black eyebrows. He sit below the magistrate, he dressed in black and he so handsome I can't take my eyes off him. When he see that he frowns worse than before.

First comes a policeman to testify I cause disturbance, and then comes the old gentleman from next door. He repeat that bit about nothing but the truth so help me God. Then he says I make dreadful noise at night and use abominable language, and dance in obscene fashion. He says when they try to shut the curtains because his wife so terrify of me, I throw stones and break a valuable stain-glass window. He say his wife get serious injury if she'd been hit, and as it is she in terrible nervous condition and the doctor is with her. I think, 'Believe me, if I aim at your wife I hit your wife – that's certain.' 'There was no provocation,' he says. 'None at all.' Then another lady from across the street says this is true. She heard no provocation whatsoever, and she swear that they shut the curtains but I go on insulting them and using filthy language and she saw all this and heard it.

The magistrate is a little gentleman with a quiet voice, but I'm very suspicious of these quiet voices now. He ask me why I don't pay any fine, and I say because I haven't the money. I get the idea they want to find out all about Mr Sims – they listen so very attentive. But they'll find out nothing from me. He ask how long I have the flat and I say I don't remember. I know they want to trip me up like they trip me up about my savings so I won't answer. At last he ask if I have anything to say as I can't be allowed to go on being a nuisance. I think, 'I'm nuisance to you because I have no money that's all.' I want to speak up and tell him how they steal all my savings, so when my landlord asks for month's rent I haven't got it to give. I want to tell him the woman next door provoke me since long time and call me bad names but she have a soft sugar voice and nobody hear – that's why I broke her window, but I'm ready to buy another after all. I want to say all I do is sing in that old garden, and I want to say this in decent quiet voice. But I hear myself talking loud and I see my hands wave in the air. Too besides it's no use, they won't believe me, so I don't finish. I stop, and I feel the tears on my face. 'Prove it.' That's all they will say. They whisper, they whisper. They nod, they nod.

Next thing I'm in a car again with a different policewoman, dressed very smart. Not in uniform. I ask her where she's taking me and she says 'Holloway' just that 'Holloway'.

I catch hold of her hand because I'm afraid. But she takes it away. Cold and smooth her hand slide away and her face is china face – smooth like a doll and I think, 'This is the last time I ask anything from anybody. So help me God.'

The car come up to a black castle and little mean streets are all round it. A lorry was blocking up the castle gates. When it get by we pass through and I am in jail. First I stand in a line with others who are waiting to give up handbags and all belongings to a woman behind bars like in a post office. The girl in front bring out a nice compact, look like gold to me, lipstick to match and a wallet full of notes. The woman keep the money, but she give back the powder and lipstick and she half-smile. I have two pounds seven shillings and sixpence in pennies. She take my purse, then she throw me my compact (which is cheap) my comb and my handkerchief like everything in my bag is dirty. So I think, 'Here too, here too.' But I tell myself, 'Girl, what you expect, eh? They all like that. All.'

Some of what happen afterwards I forget, or perhaps better not remember. Seems to me they start by trying to frighten you. But they don't succeed with me for I don't care for nothing now, it's as if my heart hard like a rock and I can't feel.

Then I'm standing at the top of a staircase with a lot of women and girls. As we are going down I notice the railing very low on one side, very easy to jump, and a long way below there's the grey stone passage like it's waiting for you.

As I'm thinking this a uniform woman step up alongside quick and grab my arm. She say, 'Oh no you don't.'

I was just noticing the railing very low that's all — but what's the use of saying so.

Another long line waits for the doctor. It move forward slowly and my legs terrible tired. The girl in front is very young and she cry and cry. 'I'm scared,' she keeps saying. She's lucky in a way — as for me I never will cry again. It all dry up and hard in me now. That, and a lot besides. In the end I tell her to stop, because she doing just what these people want her to do.

She stop crying and start a long story, but while she is speaking her voice get very far away, and I find I can't see her face clear at all.

Then I'm in a chair, and one of those uniform women is pushing my head down between my knees, but let her push — everything go away from me just the same.

They put me in the hospital because the doctor say I'm sick. I have cell by myself and it's all right except I don't sleep. The things they say you mind I don't mind.

When they clang the door on me I think, 'You shut me in, but you shut all those other dam' devils *out*. They can't reach me now.'

At first it bothers me when they keep on looking at me all through the night. They open a little window in the doorway to do this. But I get used to it and get used to the night chemise they give me. It very thick, and to my mind it not very clean either — but what's that matter to me? Only the food I can't swallow — especially the porridge. The woman ask me sarcastic, 'Hunger striking?' But afterwards I can leave most of it, and she don't say nothing.

One day a nice girl comes around with books and she give me two, but I don't want to read so much. Beside one is about a murder, and the other is about a ghost and I don't think it's at all like those books tell you.

There is nothing I want now. It's no use. If they leave me in peace and quiet that's all I ask. The window is barred but not small, so I can see a little thin tree through the bars, and I like watching it.

After a week they tell me I'm better and I can go out with the others for exercise. We walk round and round one of the yards in that castle – it is fine weather and the sky is a kind of pale blue, but the yard is a terrible sad place. The sunlight fall down and die there. I get tired walking in high heels and I'm glad when that's over.

We can talk, and one day an old woman come up and ask me for dog-ends. I don't understand, and she start muttering at me like she very vexed. Another women tell me she mean cigarette ends, so I say I don't smoke. But the old woman still look angry, and when we're going in she give me one push and I nearly fall down. I'm glad to get away from these people, and hear the door clang and take my shoes off.

Sometimes I think, 'I'm here because I wanted to sing' and I have to laugh. But there's a small looking glass in my cell and I see myself and I'm like somebody else. Like some strange new person. Mr Sims tells me I too thin, but what he say now to this person in the looking glass? So I don't laugh again.

Usually I don't think at all. Everything and everybody seem small and far away, that is the only trouble.

Twice the doctor come to see me. He don't say much and I don't say anything, because a uniform woman is always there. She looks like she thinking, 'Now the lies start.' So I prefer not to speak. Then I'm sure they can't trip me up. Perhaps I there still, or in a worse place. But one day this happen.

We were walking round and round in the yard and I hear a woman singing – the voice come from high up, from one of the small barred windows. At first I don't believe it. Why should any-body sing here? Nobody want to sing in jail, nobody want to do anything. There's no reason, and you have no hope. I think I must be asleep, dreaming, but I'm awake all right and I see all the others are listening too. A nurse is with us that afternoon, not a policewoman. She stop and look up at the window.

It's a smoky kind of voice, and a bit rough sometimes, as if those old dark walls theyselves are complaining, because they see too much misery – too much. But it don't fall down and die in the courtyard; seems to me it could jump the gates of the jail easy and travel far, and nobody could stop it. I don't hear the words – only the music. She sing one verse and she begin another, then she break off sudden. Everybody starts walking again, and nobody says one word. But as we go in I ask the woman in front who was singing. 'That's the Holloway song,' she says. 'Don't you know it yet? She was singing from the punishment cells, and she tell the girls cheerio and never say die.' Then I have to go one way to the hospital block and she goes another so we don't speak again.

When I'm back in my cell I can't just wait for bed. I walk up and down and I think. 'One day I hear that song on trumpets and these walls will fall and rest.' I want to get out so bad I could hammer on the door, for I know now that anything can happen, and I don't want to stay lock up here and miss it.

Then I'm hungry. I eat everything they bring and in the morning I'm still so hungry I eat the porridge. Next time the doctor come he tells me I seem much better. Then I say a little of what really happen in that house. Not much. Very careful.

He look at me hard and kind of surprised. At the door he shake his finger and says, 'Now don't let me see you here again.'

That evening the woman tells me I'm going, but she's so upset about it I don't ask questions. Very early, before it's light she bangs the door open and shouts at me to hurry up. As we're going along the passages I see the girl who gave me the books. She's in a row with others doing exercises. Up Down, Up Down, Up. We pass quite close and I notice she's looking very pale and tired. It's crazy, it's all crazy. This up down business and everything else too. When they give me my money I remember I leave my compact in the cell, so I ask if I can go back for it. You should see that policewoman's face as she shoo me on.

There's no car, there's a van and you can't see through the

windows. The third time it stop I get out with one other, a young
girl, and it's the same magistrates' court as before.

The two of us wait in a small room, nobody else there, and
after a while the girl say, 'What the hell are they doing? I don't
want to spend all day here.' She go to the bell and she keep her
finger press on it. When I look at her she say, 'Well, what are
they *for?*' That girl's face is hard like a board – she could change
faces with many and you wouldn't know the difference. But she
get results certainly. A policeman comes in, all smiling, and we
go in the court. The same magistrate, the same frowning man
sits below, and when I hear my fine is paid I want to ask who
paid it, but he yells at me, 'Silence.'

I think I will never understand the half of what happen, but
they tell me I can go, and I understand that. The magistrate ask
if I'm leaving the neighbourhood and I say yes, then I'm out in
the streets again, and it's the same fine weather, same feeling
I'm dreaming.

When I get to the house I see two men talking in the garden.
The front door and the door of the flat are both open. I go in, and
the bedroom is empty, nothing but the glare streaming inside
because they take the Venetian blinds away. As I'm wondering
where my suitcase is, and the clothes I leave in the wardrobe,
there's a knock and it's the old lady from upstairs carrying my
case packed, and my coat is over her arm. She says she sees me
come in. 'I kept your things for you.' I start to thank her but she
turn her back and walk away. They like that here, and better not
expect too much. Too besides, I bet they tell her I'm terrible person.

I go in the kitchen, but when I see they are cutting down the
big tree at the back I don't stay to watch.

At the station I'm waiting for the train and a woman asks if I
feel well. 'You look so tired,' she says. 'Have you come a long
way?' I want to answer, 'I come so far I lose myself on that journey.' But I tell her, 'Yes, I am quite well. But I can't stand the
heat.' She says she can't stand it either, and we talk about the
weather till the train come in.

I'm not frightened of them any more – after all what else can they do? I know what to say and everything go like a clock works.

I get a room near Victoria where the landlady accept one pound in advance, and next day I find a job in the kitchen of a private hotel close by. But I don't stay there long. I hear of another job going in a big store – altering ladies' dresses and I get that. I lie and tell them I work in very expensive New York shop. I speak bold and smooth faced, and they never check up on me. I make a friend there – Clarice – very light coloured, very smart, she have a lot to do with the customers and she laugh at some of them behind their backs. But I say it's not their fault if the dress don't fit. Special dress for one person only – that's very expensive in London. So it's take in, or let out all the time. Clarice have two rooms not far from the store. She furnish herself gradual and she gives parties sometimes Saturday nights. It's there I start whistling the Holloway Song. A man comes up to me and says, 'Let's hear that again.' So I whistle it again (I never sing now) and he tells me 'Not bad'. Clarice have an old piano somebody give her to store and he plays the tune, jazzing it up. I say, 'No, not like that,' but everybody else say the way he do it is first class. Well I think no more of this till I get a letter from him telling me he has sold the song and as I was quite a help he encloses five pounds with thanks.

I read the letter and I could cry. For after all, that song was all I had. I don't belong nowhere really, and I haven't money to buy my way to belonging. I don't want to either.

But when that girl sing, she sing to me and she sing for me. I was there because I was *meant* to be there. It was *meant* I should hear it – this I *know*.

Now I've let them play it wrong, and it will go from me like all the other songs – like everything. Nothing left for me at all.

But then I tell myself all this is foolishness. Even if they played it on trumpets, even if they played it just right, like I wanted – no walls would fall so soon. 'So let them call it jazz,' I think, and let them play it wrong. That won't make no difference to the song I heard.

I buy myself a dusty pink dress with the money.

Tigers Are Better-Looking

M EIN LIEB, Mon Cher, My Dear, Amigo,' the letter began:

I'm off. I've been wanting to go for some time, as I'm sure you know, but was waiting for the moment when I had the courage to step out into the cold world again. Didn't feel like a farewell scene.

Apart from much that it is *better* not to go into, you haven't any idea how sick I am of all the phoney talk about Communism – and the phoney talk of the other lot too, if it comes to that. You people are exactly alike, whatever you call yourselves – Untouchable. Indispensable is the motto, and you'd pine to death if you hadn't someone to look down on and insult. I got the feeling that I was surrounded by a pack of timid tigers waiting to spring the moment anybody is in trouble or hasn't any money. *But tigers are better-looking, aren't they?*

I'm taking the coach to Plymouth. I have my plans.

I came to London with high hopes, but all I got out of it was a broken leg and enough sneers to last me for the next thirty years if I live so long, which may God forbid.

Don't think I'll forget how kind you were after my accident – having me stay with you and all that. But *assez* means enough.

I've drunk the milk in the refrigerator. I was thirsty after that party last night, though if you call that a party I call it a wake. Besides, I know how you dislike the stuff (Freud! Bow-wow-wow!!). So you'll have to have your tea straight, my dear.

Good-bye. I'll write you again when times are better.

Hans

There was a postscript:

Mind you write a swell article today, you tame grey mare.

Mr Severn sighed. He had always known Hans would hop it sooner or later, so why this taste in his mouth, as if he had eaten dust?

A swell article.

The band in the Embankment Gardens played. It's the same old song again. It's the same old tender refrain. *As the carriage came into sight some of the crowd cheered and a fat man said he couldn't see and he was going to climb a lamp post. The figures in the carriages bowed from right to left – victims bowed to victimized. The bloodless sacrifice was being exhibited, the reminder that somewhere the sun was shining, even if it doesn't shine on everybody.*

' 'E *looked just like a waxwork, didn't 'e?' a woman said with satisfaction. . . .*

No, that would never do.

He looked out of the window at the Lunch Edition placards outside the newspaper shop opposite. 'JUBILEE PICTURES – PICTURES – PICTURES' *and* 'HEAT WAVE COMING'.

The flat over the shop was occupied by a raffish middle-aged woman. But today her lace-curtained windows, usually not unfriendly, added to his feeling of desolation. So did the words 'PICTURES – PICTURES – PICTURES'.

By six o'clock the floor was covered with newspapers and crumpled, discarded starts of the article which he wrote every week for an Australian paper.

He couldn't get the swing of it. The swing's the thing, as everybody knows – otherwise the cadence of the sentence. Once into it, and he could go ahead like an old horse trotting, saying anything that anybody liked.

'The tame grey mare,' he thought. Then he took up one of the newspapers and, because he had the statistical mania, began to count the advertisements. Two remedies for constipation, three for wind and stomach pains, three face creams, one skin food, one cruise to Morocco. At the end of the personal column, in small print, 'I will slay in the day of My wrath and spare not, saith the Lord God.' Who pays to put these things in anyway, who pays?

'This perpetual covert threat,' he thought. 'Everything's based on it. Disgusting. What Will They Say? And down at the bottom of the page you see what will happen to you if you don't toe the line. You will be slain and not spared. Threats and mockery, mockery and threats. . . .' And desolation, desertion and crumpled newspapers in the room.

The only comfort allowed was the money which would buy the warm glow of drink before eating, the jubilee laughter afterwards. Jubilant – Jubilee – Joy. . . . Words whirled round in his head, but he could not make them take shape.

'If you won't, you bloody well won't,' he said to his typewriter before he rushed down the stairs, counting the steps as he went.

After two double whiskies at his usual pub, Time, which had dragged so drearily all day, began to move faster, began to gallop.

At half-past eleven Mr Severn was walking up and down Wardour Street between two young women. The things one does on the rebound.

He knew one of them fairly well – the fatter one. She was often at the pub and he liked talking to her, and sometimes stood her drinks because she was good-natured and never made him feel nervous. That was her secret. If fair was fair, it would be her epitaph: 'I have never made anybody feel nervous – on purpose.' Doomed, of course, for that very reason. But pleasant to talk to and, usually, to look at. Her name was Maidie – Maidie Richards.

He had never seen the other girl before. She was very young and fresh, with a really glittering smile and an accent he didn't quite recognize. She was called Heather Something-or-other. In the noisy pub he thought she said Hedda. 'What an unusual name!' he remarked. 'I said Heather, not Hedda, Hedda! I wouldn't be seen dead with a name like that.' She was sharp, bright, self-confident – nothing flabby there. It was she who had suggested this final drink.

The girls argued. They each had an arm in one of Mr Severn's, and they argued across him. They got to Shaftesbury Avenue, turned and walked back.

'I tell you the place is in this street,' Heather said. 'The 'Jim-Jam' – haven't you ever heard of it?'

'Are you sure?' Mr Severn asked.

'Of course I'm sure. It's on the left-hand side. We've missed it somehow.'

'Well, I'm sick of walking up and down looking for it,' Maidie said. 'It's a lousy hole anyway. I don't particularly want to go, do you?'

'Not particularly,' said Mr Severn.

'There it is,' Heather said. 'We've passed it twice. It's changed it's name, that's what.'

They went up a narrow stone staircase and on the first landing a man with a yellow face appeared from behind drawn curtains and glared at them. Heather smiled. 'Good evening, Mr Johnson. I've brought two friends along.'

'Three of you? That'll be fifteen shillings.'

'I thought it was half a crown entrance,' Maidie said so aggrievedly that Mr Johnson looked at her with surprise and explained, 'This is a special night.'

'The orchestra's playing rotten, anyway,' Maidie remarked when they got into the room.

An elderly woman wearing steel-rimmed glasses was serving behind the bar. The mulatto who was playing the saxophone leaned forward and whooped.

'They play so rotten,' Maidie said, when the party was seated at a table against the wall, 'that you'd think they were doing it on purpose.'

'Oh stop grumbling,' Heather said. 'Other people don't agree with you. The place is packed every night. Besides, why should they play well. What's the difference?'

'Ah-ha,' Mr Severn said.

'There isn't any difference if you ask me. It's all a lot of talk.'

'Quite right. All an illusion,' Mr Severn agreed. 'A bottle of ginger ale,' he said to the waiter.

Heather said, 'We'll have to have a bottle of whisky. You don't mind, do you, dear?'

'Don't worry, child, don't worry,' Mr Severn said. 'It was only my little joke . . . a bottle of whisky,' he told the waiter.

'Will you pay now, if you please?' the waiter asked when he brought the bottle.

'What a price!' Maidie said, frowning boldly at the waiter. 'Never mind, by the time I've had a few goes at this I ought to have forgotten my troubles.'

Heather pinched up her lips. 'Very little for me.'

'Well, it's going to be drunk,' Mr Severn said. 'Play "Dinah," ' he shouted at the orchestra.

The saxophonist glanced at him and tittered. Nobody else took any notice.

'Sit down and have a drink, won't you?' Heather clutched at Mr Johnson's sleeve as he passed the table, but he answered loftily, 'Sorry, I'm afraid I can't just now,' and passed on.

'People are funny about drinking,' Maidie remarked. 'They get you to buy as much as they can and then afterwards they laugh at you behind your back for buying it. But on the other hand, if you try to get out of buying it, they're damned rude. Damned rude, they can be. I went into a place the other night where they have music – the International Café, they call it. I had a whisky and I drank it a bit quick, because I was thirsty and feeling down and so on. Then I thought I'd like to listen to the music – they don't play so badly there because they say they're Hungarians – and a waiter came along, yelling 'Last drinks'. 'Can I have some water?' I said, 'I'm not here to serve you with water,' he said. 'This isn't a place to drink water in,' he said, just like that. So loud! Everybody was staring at me.'

'Well, what do you expect?' Heather said. 'Asking for water! You haven't got any sense. No more for me, thank you.' She put her hand over her glass.

'Don't you trust me?' Mr Severn asked, leering.

'I don't trust anybody. For why? Because I don't want to be let down, that's why.'

'Sophisticated, she is,' said Maidie.

'I'd rather be sophisticated than a damned pushover like you,' Heather retorted. 'You don't mind if I go and talk to some friends over there, do you, dear?'

'Admirable.' Mr Severn watched her cross the room. 'Admirable. Disdainful, debonair and with a touch of the tarbrush too, or I'm much mistaken. Just my type. One of my types. Why is it that she isn't white – Now, why?' He took a yellow pencil out of his pocket and began to draw on the tablecloth.

Pictures, pictures, pictures. . . . Face, faces, faces. . . . Like hyaenas, like swine, like goats, like apes, like parrots. But not tigers, because tigers are better-looking, aren't they? as Hans says.

Maidie was saying, 'they've got an awfully nice "Ladies" here. I've been having a chat with the woman; she's a friend of mine. The window was open and the street looked so cool and peaceful. That's why I've been so long.'

'London is getting very odd, isn't it?' Mr Severn said in a thick voice. 'Do you see that tall female over there, the one in the backless evening gown? Of course, I've got my own theory about backless evening gowns, but this isn't the moment to tell you of it. Well, that sweetpie's got to be at Brixton tomorrow morning at a quarter past nine to give a music lesson. And her greatest ambition is to get a job as stewardess on a line running to South Africa.'

'Well, what's wrong with that?' Maidie said.

'Nothing – I just thought it was a bit mixed. Never mind. And do you see that couple over there at the bar? The lovely dark brown couple. Well, I went over to have a change of drinks and got into conversation with them. I rather palled up with the man, so I asked them to come and see me one day. When I gave them my address the girl said at once, "Is that in Mayfair?" "Good Lord, no; it's in the darkest, dingiest Bloomsbury." "I didn't come to London to go to the slums," she said with the most perfect British accent, high, sharp, clear and shattering. Then she turned her back on me and hauled the man off to the other end of the bar.'

'Girls always cotton on to things quicker,' Maidie asserted.

'The social climate of a place?' said Mr Severn. 'Yes, I suppose they do. But some men aren't so slow either. Well, well, tigers are better-looking, aren't they?'

'You haven't been doing too badly with the whisky, dear, have you?' Maidie said rather uneasily. 'What's all this about tigers?'

Mr Severn again addressed the orchestra in a loud voice. 'Play "Dinah". I hate that bloody tune you keep playing. It's always the same one too. You can't fool me. Play "Dinah, is there anyone finer?" That's a good old tune.'

'I shouldn't shout so loud,' Maidie said. 'They don't like it here if you shout. Don't you see the way Johnson's looking at you?'

'Let him look.'

'Oh, do shut up. He's sending the waiter to us now.'

'Obscene drawings on the tablecloth not allowed here,' the waiter said as he approached.

'Go to hell,' Mr Severn said. 'What obscene drawings?'

Maidie nudged him and shook her head violently.

The waiter removed the tablecloth and brought a clean one. He pursed his lips up as he spread it and looked severely at Mr Severn. 'No drawings of any description on tablecloths are allowed here,' he said.

'I'll draw as much as I like,' Mr Severn said defiantly. And the next thing he knew two men had him by the collar and were pushing him towards the door.

'You let him alone,' said Maidie. 'He hasn't done anything. You are a lot of sugars.'

'Gently, gently,' said Mr Johnson, perspiring. 'What do you want to be so rough for? I'm always telling you to do it quietly.'

As he was being hauled past the bar, Mr Severn saw Heather, her eyes beady with disapproval, her plump face lengthened into something twice the size of life. He made a hideous grimace at her.

'My Lawd,' she said, and averted her eyes. 'My Lawd!'

Only four men pushed them down the stairs, but when they were out in the street it took more like fourteen, and all howling and booing. 'Now, who are all these people?' Mr Severn thought. Then someone hit him. The man who had hit him was exactly like the waiter who had changed the tablecloth. Mr Severn hit back as hard as he could and the waiter, if he was the waiter, staggered against the wall and toppled slowly to the ground. 'I've knocked him down,' Mr Severn thought. 'Knocked him down!'

'Tally-ho!' he yelled in a high voice. 'What price the tame grey mare?'

The waiter got up, hesitated, thought better of it, turned round and hit Maidie instead.

'Shut up, you bloody basket,' somebody said when she began to swear, and kicked her. Three men seized Mr Severn, ran him off the pavement and sprawled him in the middle of Wardour Street. He lay there, feeling sick, listening to Maidie. The lid was properly off there.

'Yah!' the crowd round her jeered. 'Boo!' Then it opened up, servile and respectful, to let two policemen pass.

'You big blanks,' Maidie yelled defiantly. 'You something somethings. I wasn't doing anything. That man knocked me down. How much does Johnson pay you every week for this?'

Mr Severn got up, still feeling very sick. He heard a voice: 'That's 'im. That's the chap. That's 'im what started everything.' Two policemen took him by the arms and marched him along. Maidie, also between two policemen, walked in front, weeping. As they passed through Piccadilly Circus, empty and desolate, she wailed, 'I've lost my shoe. I must stop and pick it up. I can't walk without it.'

The older policeman seemed to want to force her on, but the younger one stopped, picked the shoe up and gave it to her with a grin.

'What's she want to cry for?' Mr Severn thought. He shouted 'Hoi, Maidie, cheer up. Cheer up, Maidie.'

'None of that,' one of his policemen said.

But when they arrived at the police station she had stopped

crying, he was glad to see. She powdered her face and began to argue with the sergeant behind the desk.

'You want to see a doctor, do you?' the sergeant said.

'I certainly do. It's a disgrace, a perfect disgrace.'

'And do you also want to see a doctor?' the sergeant asked coldly polite, glancing at Mr Severn.

'Why not?' Mr Severn answered.

Maidie powdered her face again and shouted, 'God save Ireland. To hell with all dirty sneaks and Comic Cuts and what-have-yous.'

'That was my father speaking,' she said over her shoulder as she was led off.

As soon as Mr Severn was locked into a cell he lay down on the bunk and went to sleep. When they woke him to see the doctor he was cold sober.

'What time is it?' the doctor asked. With a clock over his head, the old fool!

Mr Severn answered coldly, 'A quarter past four.'

'Walk straight ahead. Shut your eyes and stand on one leg,' the doctor demanded, and the policeman watching this performance sneered vaguely, like schoolboys when the master baits an unpopular one.

When he got back to his cell Mr Severn could not sleep. He lay down, stared at the lavatory seat and thought of the black eye he would have in the morning. Words and meaningless phrases still whirled tormentingly round in his head.

He read the inscription on the grim walls. 'Be sure your sins will find you out. B. Lewis.' 'Anne is a fine girl, one of the best, and I don't care who knows it. (Signed) Charlie S.' Somebody else had written up, 'Lord save me; I perish', and underneath, 'SOS, SOS, SOS (signed) G.R.'

'Appropriate,' Mr Severn thought, took his pencil from his pocket, wrote, 'SOS, SOS, SOS (Signed) N.S.,' and dated it.

Then he lay down with his face to the wall and saw, on a level with his eyes, the words, 'I died waiting.'

Sitting in the prison van before it started, he heard somebody whistling 'The Londonderry Air' and a girl talking and joking with the policemen. She had a deep, soft voice. The appropriate adjective came at once into his mind – a sexy voice.

'Sex, sexy,' he thought. 'Ridiculous word! What a giveaway!'

'What is wanted,' he decided, 'is a brand-new lot of words, words that will mean something. The only word that means anything now is death – and then it has to be my death. Your death doesn't mean much.'

The girl said, 'Ah, if I was a bird and had wings, I could fly away, couldn't I?'

'Might get shot as you went,' one of the policemen answered.

'This must be a dream,' Mr Severn thought. He listened for Maidie's voice, but there was not a sound of her. Then the van started.

It seemed a long way to Bow Street. As soon as they got out of the van he saw Maidie, looking as if she had spent the whole night in tears. She put her hand up to her hair apologetically.

'They took my handbag away. It's awful.'

'I wish it had been Heather,' Mr Severn thought. He tried to smile kindly.

'It'll soon be over now, we've only got to plead guilty.'

And it was over very quickly. The magistrate hardly looked at them, but for reasons of his own he fined them each thirty shillings, which entailed telephoning to a friend, getting the money sent by special messenger and an interminable wait.

It was half-past twelve when they were outside in Bow Street. Maidie stood hesitating, looking worse than ever in the yellowish, livid light. Mr Severn hailed a taxi and offered to take her home. It was the least he could do, he told himself. Also the most.

'Oh, your poor eye!' Maidie said. 'Does it hurt?'

'Not at all now. I feel astonishingly well. It must have been good whisky.'

She stared into the cracked mirror of her handbag.

'And don't I look terrible too? But it's no use; I can't do anything with my face when it's as bad as this.'

'I'm sorry.'

'Oh, well,' she said, 'I was feeling pretty bad on account of the way that chap knocked me down and kicked me, and afterwards on account of the way the doctor asked me my age. "This woman's very drunk," he said. But I wasn't, was I? . . . Well, and when I got back into the cell, the first thing I saw was my own name written up. My Christ, it did give me a turn! Gladys Reilly – that's my real name. Maidie Richards is only what I call myself. There it was staring me in the face. "Gladys Reilly, October 15th, 1934. . . ." Besides, I hate being locked up. Whenever I think of all these people they lock up for years I shiver all over.'

'Yes,' Mr Severn said, 'so do I.' *I died waiting.*

'I'd rather die quick, wouldn't you?'

'Yes.'

'I couldn't sleep and I kept on remembering the way the doctor said, "How old are you?" And all the policemen round were laughing, as if it was a joke. Why should it be such a joke. But they're hard up for jokes, aren't they? So when I got back I couldn't stop crying. And when I woke up I hadn't got my bag. The wardress lent me a comb. She wasn't so bad. But I do feel fed up. . . .'

'You know the room I was waiting in while you were telephoning for money?' she said. 'There was such a pretty girl there.'

'Was there?'

'Yes, a very dark girl. Rather like Dolores del Rio, only younger. But it isn't the pretty ones who get on – oh no, on the contrary. For instance, this girl. She couldn't have been prettier – lovely, she was. And she was dressed awfully nicely in a black coat and skirt and a lovely clean white blouse and a little white hat and lovely stockings and shoes. But she was frightened. She was so frightened that she was shaking all over. You saw somehow that she wasn't going to last it out. No, it isn't being pretty that does it. . . . And there was another one, with great hairy legs and no stockings, only sandals. I do think that when people have hairy legs they ought to wear stockings, don't you? Or do something about it. But no, she was just laughing and joking and you saw whatever happened to her she'd come out all right. A great big, red, square face she had, and those hairy legs. But she didn't care a damn.'

'Perhaps it's being sophisticated,' Mr Severn suggested, 'like your friend Heather.'

'Oh, her – no, she won't get on either. She's too ambitious, she wants too much. She's so sharp she cuts herself as you might say. . . . No, it isn't being pretty and it isn't being sophisticated. It's being – adapted, that's what it is. And it isn't any good *wanting* to be adapted, you've got to be born adapted.'

'Very clear,' Mr Severn said. Adapted to the livid sky, the ugly houses, the grinning policemen, the placards in shop windows.

'You've got to be young, too. You've got to be young to enjoy a thing like this – younger than we are,' Maidie said as the taxi drew up.

Mr Severn stared at her, too shocked to be angry.

'Well, good-bye.'

'*Good*-bye,' said Mr Severn, giving her a black look and ignoring her outstretched hand. 'We' indeed!

Two hundred and ninety-six steps along Coptic Street. One hundred and twenty round the corner. Forty stairs up to his flat. A dozen inside it. He stopped counting.

His sitting-room looked well, he thought, in spite of the crumpled papers. It was one of its good times, when the light was just right, when all the incongruous colours and shapes became a whole – the yellow-white brick wall with several of the Museum pigeons perched on it, the silvered drainpipe, the chimneys of every fantastical shape, round, square, pointed, and the odd one with the mysterious hole in the middle through which the grey, steely sky looked at you, the solitary trees – all framed in the silver oilcloth curtains (Hans's idea), and then with a turn of his head he saw the woodcuts from Amsterdam, the chintz-covered armchairs, the fading bowl of flowers in the long mirror.

An old gentleman wearing a felt hat and carrying a walking-stick passed the window. He stopped, took off his hat and coat, and, balancing the stick on the end of his nose, walked backwards and forwards, looking up expectantly. Nothing happened. Nobody thought him worth a penny. He put his hat and coat on again and, carrying the stick in a respectable manner, vanished round the corner. And, as he did so, the tormenting phrases vanished too – 'Who pays? Will you pay now, please? You don't mind if I leave you, dear? I died waiting. I died waiting. (Or was it I died hating?) That was my father speaking. Pictures, pictures, pictures. You've got to be young. But tigers are better-looking, aren't they? SOS, SOS, SOS. If I was a bird and had wings I could fly away, couldn't I? Might get shot as you went. But tigers are better-looking, aren't they? You've got to be younger than we are. . . .' Other phrases, suave and slick, took their place.

The swing's the thing, the cadence of the sentence. He had got it.

He looked at his eye in the mirror, then sat down at the typewriter and with great assurance tapped out 'JUBILEE. . . .'

Outside the Machine

THE BIG CLINIC near Versailles was run on strictly English lines, so every morning the patients in the women's general ward were woken up at six. They had tea and bread-and-butter. Then they lay and waited while the nurses brought tin basins and soap. When they had washed they lay and waited again.

There were fifteen beds in the tall, narrow room. The walls were painted grey. The windows were long but high up, so that you could see only the topmost branches of the trees in the grounds outside. Through the glass the sky had no colour.

At half-past ten the matron, attended by a sister, came in to inspect the ward, walking as though she were royalty opening a public building. She stopped every now and again, glanced at a patient's temperature chart here, said a few words there. The young woman in the last bed but one on the left-hand side was a newcomer. 'Best, Inez,' the chart said.

'You came last evening, didn't you?'

'Yes.'

'Quite comfortable?'

'Oh yes, quite.'

'Can't you do without all those things while you are here?' the matron asked, meaning the rouge, powder, lipstick and hand-mirror on the bed table.

'It's so that I shouldn't look too awful, because then I always feel much worse.'

But the matron shook her head and walked on without smiling, and Inez drew the sheets up to her chin, feeling bewildered and weak. *I'm cold, I'm tired.*

'Has anyone ever told you that you're very much like Raquel Meller?' the old lady in the next bed said. She was sitting up, wrapped in a black shawl embroidered with pink and yellow flowers.

'Am I? Oh, am I really?'

'Yes, very much like.'

'Do you think so?' Inez said.

The tune of 'La Violetera', Raquel Meller's song, started up in her head. She felt happier – then quite happy and rather gay. 'Why should I be so damned sad?' she thought. 'It's ridiculous. The day after I come out of this place something lucky might happen.'

And it was not so bad lying here and having everything done for you. It was only when you moved that you got frightened because you couldn't imagine ever moving again without hurting yourself.

She looked at the row of beds opposite and sighed. 'It's rum here, isn't it?'

'Oh, you'll feel different tomorrow,' the old lady said. She spoke English hesitatingly – not with an accent, but as if her tongue were used to another language.

The two talked a good deal that day, off and on.

'. . . And how was I to know,' Inez complained, 'that on top of everything else, my inside would go *kaput* like this? And of course it must happen at the wrong time.'

'Now, shut up,' she told herself, 'shut up. Don't say, "Just when I haven't any money." Don't give yourself away. What a fool you are!' But she could not stop the flood of words.

At intervals the old lady clicked her tongue compassionately or said 'Poor child'. She had a broad, placid face. Her hair was black – surely dyed, Inez thought. She wore two rings with coloured stones on the third finger of her left hand and one – a thick gold ring carved into an indistinguishable pattern – on the little finger. There was something wrong with her knee, it appeared, and she had tried several other hospitals.

'French hospitals are more easy-going, but I was very lucky to get into this place, it has quite a reputation. There's nothing like English nursing. And, considering what you get, you pay hardly anything. An English matron, a resident English doctor, several of the nurses are English. I believe the private rooms are *most* luxurious, but of course they are very expensive.'

Her name was Tavernier. She had left England as a young girl and had never been back. She had been married twice. Her first husband was a bad man, her second husband was a good man. Just like that. Her second husband was a good man who had left her a little money.

When she talked about the first husband you could tell that she still hated him, after all those years. When she talked about the good one tears came into her eyes. She said that they were perfectly happy, completely happy, never an unkind word and tears came into her eyes.

'Poor old mutt,' Inez thought, 'she really has persuaded herself to believe that.'

Madame Tavernier said in a low voice, 'Do you know what he said in the last letter he wrote to me? "You are everything to me." Yes, that's what he said in the last letter I had.'

'Poor old mutt,' Inez thought again.

Madame Tavernier wiped her eyes. Her face looked calm and gentle, as if she were repeating to herself, 'Nobody can say this isn't true, because I've got the letter and I can show it.'

The fat, fair woman in the bed opposite was also chatting with her neighbour. They were both blonde, very clean and aggressively respectable. For some reason they fitted in so well with their surroundings that they made everyone else seem dubious, out of place. The fat one discussed the weather, and her neighbour's answers were like an echo. 'Hot . . . oh yes, very hot . . . hotter than yesterday . . . yes, much hotter . . . I wish the weather would break . . . yes, I wish it would, but no chance of that . . . no, I suppose not . . . oh, rather fancy so. . . .'

Under cover of this meaningless conversation the fair woman's stare at Inez was sharp, sly and inquisitive. 'An English person? English, what sort of English? To which of the seven divisions, sixty-nine subdivisions, and thousand-and-three sub-subdivisions do you belong? (*But only one sauce, damn you.*) My world is a stable, decent world. If you withhold information, or if you confuse me by jumping from one category to another, I can be extremely disagreeable, and I am not without subtlety and inventive powers when I want to be disagreeable. Don't underrate me. I have set the machine in motion and crushed many like you. Many like you. . . .'

Madame Tavernier shifted uneasily in her bed, as if she sensed this clash of personalities – stares meeting in mid-air, sparks flying. . . .

'Those two ladies just opposite are English,' she whispered.

'Oh, are they?'

'And so is the one in the bed on the other side of you.'

'The sleepy one they make such a fuss about?'

'She's a dancer – a "girl", you know. One of the Yetta Kauffman girls. She's had an operation for appendicitis.'

'Oh, has she?'

'The one with the screen round her bed,' Madame Tavernier chattered on, 'is very ill. She's not expected to – And the one . . .'

Inez interrupted after a while. 'They seem to have stuck all the English down this end, don't they? I wish they had mixed us up a bit more.'

'They never do,' Madame Tavernier answered. 'I've often noticed it.'

'It's a mistake,' said Inez. 'English people are usually pleasanter to foreigners than they are to each other.'

After a silence Madame Tavernier inquired politely, 'Have you travelled a lot?'

'Oh, a bit.'

'And do you like it here?'

'Yes, I like Paris much the best.'

'I suppose you feel at home,' Madame Tavernier said. Her

voice was ironical. 'Like many people. There's something for every taste.'

'No, I don't feel particularly at home. That's not why I like it.'

She turned away and shut her eyes. She knew the pain was going to start again. And, sure enough, it did. They gave her an injection and she went to sleep.

Next morning she woke feeling dazed. She lay and watched two nurses charging about, very brisk and busy and silent. They did not even say 'Come along', or 'Now, ow', or 'Drink that up.'

They moved about surely and quickly. They did everything in an impersonal way. They were like parts of a machine, she thought, that was working smoothly. The women in the beds bobbed up and down and in and out. They too were parts of a machine. They had a strength, a certainty, because all their lives they had belonged to the machine and worked smoothly, in and out, just as they were told. Even if the machine got out of control, even if it went mad, they would still work in and out, just as they were told, whirling smoothly, faster and faster, to destruction.

She lay very still, so that nobody should know she was afraid. Because she was outside the machine they might come along any time with a pair of huge iron tongs and pick her up and put her on the rubbish heap, and there she would lie and rot. 'Useless, this one,' they would say; and throw her away before she could explain, 'It isn't like you think it is, not at all. It isn't like they say it is. Wait a bit and let me explain. You must listen; it's very important.

But in the evening she felt better.

The girl in the bed on the right, who was sitting up, said she wanted to write to a friend at the theatre.

'In French,' she said. 'Can anybody write the letter for me, because I don't know French?'

'I'll write it for you,' Madame Tavernier offered.

' "Dear Lili . . . L-i-l-i. Dear Lili . . ." well, say, "I'm getting on all right again. Come and see me on Monday or Thursday. Any time from two to four. And when you come will you bring me some notepaper and stamps? I hope it won't be long before I get out of this place. I'll tell you about that on Monday. Don't forget the stamps. Tell the others that they can come to see me, and tell how to get here. Your affectionate friend, and so on, Pat." Give it to me and I'll sign it. . . . Thanks.'

The girl's voice had two sounds in it. One was clear and light, and the other heavy and ruthless.

'You seem to be having a rotten time, you in the next bed,' she said.

'I feel better now.'

'Have you been in Paris long?'

'I live here.'

'Ah, then you'll be having your pals along to cheer you up.'

'I don't think so. I don't expect anybody.'

The girl stared. She was not much over twenty and her clear blue eyes slanted upwards a little. She looked as if, standing up, she would be short with sturdy dancer's legs. Stocky, like a little pony.

Oh God, let her go on talking about herself and not looking at me, or sizing me up, or anything like that.

'This French girl, this friend of mine, she's a perfect scream,' Pat said. 'But she's an awfully obliging girl. If I say, "Turn up with stamps," she will turn up with stamps. That's why I'm writing to her and not to one of our lot. Our lot might turn up or they might not. You know. But she's a perfect scream, really. . . . As a matter of fact, she's not bad-looking, but the way she walks is too funny. She's a *femme nue,* and they've taught her to walk like that. It's all right without shoes, but with shoes it's – well . . . you'll see when she comes here. They only get paid half what we do, too. Anyway, she's an awfully obliging kid; she's a sweet kid, poor devil.'

A nurse brought in supper.

'The girls are nice and the actors are nice,' Pat went on, 'but the stage hands hate us. Isn't it funny? You see, one of them tried to kiss one of our lot and she smacked his face. He looked sort of surprised, she said. And then do you know what he did? He hit her back! Well, and do you know what we did? We said to the stage manager, "If that man doesn't get the sack, we won't go on." They tried one show without us and then they gave in. The principals whose numbers were spoilt made a hell of a row. The French girls can't do our stuff because they can't keep together. They're all right alone – very good sometimes, but they don't understand team work. . . . And now, my God, the stage hands don't half hate us. We have to go in twos to the lavatory. And yet, the girls and the actors are awfully nice; it's only the stage hands who hate us.'

The fat woman opposite – her name was Mrs Wilson – listened to all this, at first suspiciously, then approvingly. Yes, this is permissible; it has its uses. Pretty English chorus girl – north country – with a happy, independent disposition and bright, teasing eyes. Placed! All correct.

Pat finished eating and then went off to sleep again very suddenly, like a child.

'A saucy girl, isn't she?' Madame Tavernier said. Her eyes were half-shut, the corners of her mouth turned downwards.

Through the windows the light turned from dim yellow to mauve, from mauve to grey, from grey to black. Then it was dark except for the unshaded bulbs tinted red all along the ward. Inez put her arm round her head and turned her face to the pillow.

'Good night,' the old lady said. And after a long while she said, 'Don't cry, don't cry.'

Inez whispered, 'They kill you so slowly. . . .'

The ward was a long, grey river; the beds were ships in a mist. . . .

The next day was Sunday. Even through those window panes the sky looked blue, and the sun made patterns on the highly polished floor. The patients had breakfast half an hour later – seven instead of half-past six.

'Only milk for you today,' the nurse said. Inez was going to ask why; then she remembered that her operation was fixed for Monday. *Don't think of it yet. There's still quite a long time to go.*

After the midday meal the matron told them that an English Clergyman was going to visit the ward and hold a short service if nobody minded. Nobody did mind, and after a while the parson came in through an unsuspected door, looking as if he felt very cold, as if he had never been warm in his life. He had grey hair and a shy, shut-in face.

He stood at the end of the ward and the patients turned their heads to look at him. The screen round the bed on the other side had been taken away and the yellow-faced, shrunken woman who lay there turned her head like the others and looked.

The clergyman said a prayer and most of the patients said 'Amen'. ('Amen,' they said. 'We are listening,' they said. . . . I am poor bewildered unhappy comfort me I am dying console me of course I don't let on that I know I'm dying but I know I know Don't talk about life as it is because it has nothing to do with me now Say something go on say something because I'm so darned sick of women's voices Christ how I hate women Say something funny that I can laugh at but anything you say will be funny you old geezer you Never mind say something. . . . 'We are listening,' they said, 'we are listening. . . .') But the parson was determined to stick to life as it is, for his address was a warning against those vices which would antagonize their fellows and make things worse for them. Self-pity, for instance. Where does that lead you? Ah, where? Cynicism. So cheap. . . . Rebellion. So useless. . . . 'Let us remember,' he ended, 'that God is a just God and that man, made in His image, is also just. On the whole. And so, dear sisters, let us try to live useful, righteous and God-fearing lives in that state to which it has pleased Him to call us. Amen.'

He said another prayer and then went round shaking hands. 'How do you do, how do you do, how do you do?' All along the two lines. Then he went out again.

After he had gone there was silence in the ward for a few seconds, then somebody sighed.

Madame Tavernier remarked, 'Poor little man, he was so nervous.'

'Well, it didn't last long, anyway,' Pat said. 'On and off like the Demon King. . . .'

'Oh, he doesn't look much like a lover,
But you can't tell a book by its cover.'

Then she sang, 'The Shiek of Araby'. She tied a towel round her head for a turban and began again: 'Over the desert wild and free. . . . Sing up, girls, chorus. I'm the Sheik of Arabee. . . .'

Everybody looked at Pat and laughed; the dying woman's small yellow face was convulsed with laughter.

'There's lots of time before tomorrow,' Inez thought. 'I needn't bother about it yet.'

'I'm the Sheik of Arabee. . . .' Somebody was singing it in French – *'Je cherche Antinéa.'* It was a curious translation – significant when you came to think of it.

Pat shouted, 'Listen to this. Anybody recognize it? Old but good. "Who's that knocking at my door? said the fair young ladye. . . ." '

The tall English sister came in. She had a narrow face, small deep-set eyes of an unusual reddish-brown colour and a large mouth. Her pale lips lay calmly one on the other, as if she were very good-tempered, or perhaps very self controlled. She smiled blandly and said, 'Now then, Pat, you must stop this,' arranged the screen round the bed on the other side and pulled down the blind of the window at the back.

It was really very hot and after she had gone out again most of the women lay in a coma, but Pat went on talking. The sound of her own voice seemed to excite her. She became emphatic, as if someone was arguing with her.

She talked about love and the difference between glamour and dirt. The real difference was £-s-d, she said. If there was some money about there could be some glamour; otherwise, say what you liked, it was simply dirty – as well as foolish.

'Plenty of survival value there,' Inez thought. She lay with her eyes closed, trying to see trees and smooth water. But the pictures she made slipped through her mind too quickly, so that they became distorted and malignant.

That night everybody in the ward was wakeful. Somebody moaned. The nurse rushed about with a bed pan, grumbling under her breath.

2

At nine o'clock on Monday morning the tall English sister was saying, 'You'll be quite all right. I'm going to give you a morphine injection now.'

After this Inez was still frightened, but in a much duller way.

'I hope you'll be there,' she said drowsily. But there was another nurse in the operating room. She was wearing a mask and she looked horrible, Inez thought – like a torturer.

Floating in the air, which was easy and natural after the morphine – *Of course, I've always been able to do this. Why did I ever forget? How stupid of me!* – she watched herself walking across the floor with tears streaming down her cheeks, supported by the terrifying stranger.

'Now don't be silly,' the nurse said irritably.

Inez sat down on the edge of the couch, not floating now, not divided. One, and heavy as lead.

'You don't know why I'm crying,' she thought.

She tried to look at the sky, but there was a mist before her eyes and she could not see it. She felt hands pressing hard on her shoulders.

'No, no, no, leave her alone,' somebody said in French.

The English doctor was not there – only this man, who was also wearing a mask.

'They're so stupid,' Inez said in a high, complaining voice. 'It's terrible. Oh, what's going to happen, what's going to happen?'

'Don't be afraid,' the doctor said. His brown eyes looked kind. '*N'ayez pas peur, n'ayez pas peur.*'

'All right,' Inez said, and lay down.

The English doctor's voice said, 'Now breath deeply. Count slowly. One – two – three – four – five – six. . . .'

3

'Do you feel better today?' the old lady asked.

'Yes, much better.'

The blind at the back of her bed was down. It tapped a bit. She was sleepy; she felt as if she could sleep for weeks.

'Hullo,' said Pat, 'come to life again?'

'I'm much better now.'

'You've been awfully bad,' Pat said. 'You were awfully ill on Monday, weren't you?'

'Yes, I suppose I was.'

The screen which had been up round her bed for three days had shut her away even from her hand mirror; and now she took it up and looked at herself as if she were looking at a stranger. She had lain seeing nothing but a succession of pictures of the past, always sinister, always too highly coloured, always distorted. She had heard nothing but the incoherent, interminable conversation in her head.

'I look different,' she thought.

'I look awful,' she thought, staring anxiously at her thin, grey face and the hollows under her eyes. This was very important; her principal asset was threatened.

'I must rest,' she thought. 'Rest, not worry.'

She passed her powder puff over her face and put some rouge on.

Pat was watching her. 'D'you know what I've noticed? People who look ghastly oughtn't to put make up on. You only look worse if you aren't all right underneath – much older. My pal Lili came along on Monday. You should have seen how pretty she looked. I will say for these Paris girls they do know how to make up. . . .'

Yap, yap, yap. . . .

'Even if they aren't anything much – and often they aren't, mind you – they know how to make themselves look all right. I mean, you see prettier girls in London, but in my opinion. . . .'

The screen round the bed on the opposite side had been taken away. The bed was empty. Inez looked at it and said nothing. Madame Tavernier, who saw her looking at it, also said nothing, but for a moment her eyes were frightened.

4

The next day the ward sister brought in some English novels.

'You'll fine these very soothing,' she said, and there was a twinkle in her eye. A splendid nurse, that one; she knew her job. What they call a born nurse.

A born nurse, as they say. Or you could be a born cook, or a born clown or a born fool, a born this, a born that. . . .

'What's the joke now?' Pat asked suspiciously.

'Oh, nothing. I was thinking how hard it is to believe in free will.'

'I suppose you know what you're talking about,' Pat answered coldly. She had become hostile for some reason. Not that it mattered.

'Everything will be all right; I needn't worry,' Inez assured herself. 'There's still heaps of time.'

And soon she believed it. Lying there, being looked after and waking obediently at dawn, she began to feel like a child, as if the future would surely be pleasant, though it was hardly conceivable. It was as if she had always lain there and had known everyone else in the ward all her life – Madame Tavernier, her shawl, her rings, her crochet and her travel books, Pat and her repertoire of songs, the two fair, fat women who always looked so sanctimonious when they washed.

The room was wide and the beds widely spaced, but now she knew something of the others too. There was a mysterious girl with long plaits and a sullen face who sometimes helped the nurse to make the beds in the morning – mysterious because there did not seem to be anything the matter with her. She ought to have been pretty, but she always kept her head down and if by chance you met her eyes she would blink and glance away. And there

was the one who wore luxury pyjamas, the one who knitted, the
other constant reader – watching her was sometimes a frightening game – the one who had a great many visitors, the ugly one,
rather like a monkey, who all day sewed something that looked
like a pink *crêpe-de-chine* chemise.

But her dreams were uneasy, and if a book fell or a door banged
her heart would jump – a painful echo. And she found herself
disliking some of the novels the sister brought. One day when
she was reading her face reddened with anger. *Why, it's not a
bit like that. My Lord, what liars these people are! And nobody
to stand up and tell them so. Yah, Judas! Thinks it's the truth!
You're telling me.*

She glanced sideways. Pat, who was staring at her, laughed,
raised her eyebrows and tapped her forehead. Inez laughed back,
also tapped her forehead and a moment afterwards was reading
again, peacefully.

The days were like that, but when night came she burrowed
into the middle of the earth to sleep. 'Never wake up, never wake
up,' her wise heart told her. But the morning always came, the
tin basins, the smell of soap, the long, sunlit, monotonous day.

At last she was well enough to walk into the bathroom by
herself. Going there was all right, but coming back her legs gave
way and she had to put her hand on the wall of the passage for
support. There was a weight round the middle of her body which
was dragging her to earth.

She got back into bed again. Darkness, quiet, safety – all the
same, it was time to face up to things, to arrange them neatly.
'One, I feel much worse than I expected; two, I must ask the
matron tomorrow if I can stay for another week; they won't want
me to pay in advance; three, as soon as I know that I'm all right
for another week, I must start writing round and trying to raise
some money. Fifty francs when I get out! What's fifty francs when
you feel like this?'

That night she lay awake for a long time, making plans. But
the next morning, when the matron came round, she became
nervous of a refusal. 'I'll ask her tomorrow for certain.' However,

the whole of the next day passed and she did not say a word.

She ate and slept and read soothing English novels about the respectable and the respected and she did not say a word nor write a letter. Any excuse was good enough: 'She doesn't look in a good temper today. . . . Oh, the doctor's with her; I don't think he liked me much. (Well, I don't like you much either, old cock; your eyes are too close together.) Today's Friday, not my lucky day. . . . I'll write when my head is clearer. . . .'

A long brown passage smelling of turpentine led from the ward to the washroom. There were rows of basins along either white-washed wall, three water closets and two bathrooms at the far end.

Inez went to one of the washbasins. She was carrying a sponge bag. She took out of it soap, a toothbrush, toothpaste and peroxide.

Somebody opened the door stealthily, hesitated for a moment, then walked past and stood over one of the basins at the far end. It was a sullen girl, the one with the long plaits. She was wearing a blue kimono.

'She does look fed up,' Inez thought.

The girl leant over the basin with both hands on its edge. Was she going to be sick? Then she gave a long, shivering sigh and opened her sponge bag.

Inez turned away without speaking and began to clean her teeth.

The door opened again and a nurse came in and glanced round the washroom. It was curious to see the expression on her plump, pink face change in a few moments from indifference to inquisitiveness, to astonishment, to shocked anger.

Then she ran across the room, shouting 'Stop that. Come along Mrs Murphy. Give it up.'

Inez watched them struggling. Something metallic fell to the floor. Mrs Murphy was twisting like a snake.

'Come on, help me, can't you? Hold her arms,' the nurse said breathlessly.

'Oh, leave me alone, leave me alone,' Mrs Murphy wailed. 'Do for God's sake leave me alone. What do you know about it anyway?'

'Go and call the sister. She's in the ward.'

'She's speaking to me,' Inez thought.

'Oh, leave me alone, leave me alone. Oh, please, please, please, please, please,' Mrs Murphy sobbed.

'What's she done?' Inez said. 'Why don't you leave her alone?'

As she spoke two other nurses rushed in at the door and flung themselves on Mrs Murphy, who began to scream loudly, with her mouth open and her head back.

Inez held on to the basins, one by one, and got to the door. Then she held on to the door post, then to the wall of the passage. She reached her bed and lay down shaking.

'What's up? What's the matter?' Pat asked excitedly.

'I don't know.'

'Was it Murphy? You're all right, aren't you? We were wondering if it was Murphy, or. . . .'

' "Or you," she means,' Inez thought. ' "Or you. . . ." '

All that evening Pat and the fair woman, Mrs Wilson, who had been very friendly, talked excitedly. It seemed that they knew all about Mrs Murphy. They knew that she had tried the same thing on before. Suddenly, by magic, they seemed to know all about her. And what a thing to do, to try to kill yourself! If it had been a man, now, you might have been a bit sorry. You might have said, 'Perhaps the poor devil has had a rotten time.' But a woman!

'A married woman with two sweet little kiddies.'

'The fool,' said Pat. 'My God, what would you do with a fool like that?'

Mrs Wilson, who had been in the clinic for some time, explained that there was a medicine cupboard just outside the ward.

'It must have been open,' she said. 'In *which* case, somebody will get into a row. Perhaps Murphy got hold of the key. That's where she might get the morphine tablets.'

But Pat was of the opinion – she said she knew it for a fact, a nurse had told her – that Mrs Murphy had had the hypodermic syringe and the tablets hidden for weeks, ever since she had been in the clinic.

'She's one of these idiotic neurasthenics, neurotics, or whatever you call them. She says she's frightened of life, I ask you. That's why she's here. Under observation. And it only shows you how cunning they are, that she managed to hide the things. . . .'

'I'm so awfully sorry for her husband,' said Mrs Wilson. 'And her children. So sorry. The poor kiddies, the poor sweet little kiddies. . . . Oughtn't a woman like that to be hung?'

Even after the lights had been put out they still talked.

'What's she got to be neurasthenic and neurotic about, anyway?' Pat demanded. 'If she has a perfectly good husband and kiddies, what's she got to be neurasthenic and neurotic about?'

Stone and iron, their voices were. One was stone and one was iron. . . .

Inez interrupted the duet in a tremulous voice. 'Oh, she's neurasthenic, and they've sent her to a place like this to be cured? That was a swell idea. What a place for a cure for neurasthenia! Who thought that up? The perfectly good, kind husband, I suppose.'

Pat said, 'For God's sake! You get on my nerves. Stop always trying to be different from everybody else.'

'Who's everybody else?'

Nobody answered her.

'What a herd of swine they are!' she thought, but no heat of rage came to warm or comfort her. Sized her up, Pat had. *Why should you care about a girl like that? She's as stupid as a foot. But not when it comes to sizing people up, not when it comes to knowing who is done for. I'm cold, I'm tired, I'm tired, I'm cold.*

The next morning Mrs Murphy appeared in time to help make the beds. As usual she walked with her head down and her eyes down and her shoulders stooped. She went very slowly along the opposite side of the ward, and everybody stared at her with hard, inquisitive eyes.

'What are you muttering about, Inez?' Pat said sharply.

Mrs Murphy and the nurse reached the end of the row opposite. Then they began the other row. Slowly they were coming nearer.

'Shut up, it's nothing to do with you,' Inez told herself, but her cold hands were clenched under the sheet.

The nurse said, 'Pat, you're well enough to give a hand, aren't you? I won't be a moment.'

'Idiot,' Inez thought. 'She oughtn't to have gone away. But they never know what's happening. But yes, they know. The machine works smoothly, that's all.'

In silence Pat and Mrs Murphy started pulling and stretching and patting the sheets and pillows.

'Hullo, Pat,' Mrs Murphy said at last in a low voice.

Pat closed her lips with a righteously disgusted expression. They turned the sheet under at the bottom. They smoothed it down at the top. They began to shake the pillows.

Mrs Murphy's face broke up and she started to cry. 'Oh God,' she said, 'they won't let me get out. They won't.'

Pat said, 'Don't snivel over my pillow. People like you make me sick,' and Mrs Wilson laughed like a horse neighing.

The voice and the laughter were so much alike that they might have belonged to the same person. *Greasy and cold, silly and raw, coarse and thin; everything unutterably horrible.*

'Well, here's bad luck to you,' Inez burst out, 'you pair of bitches. Behaving like that to a sad woman! What do you know about her? . . . You hold your head up and curse them back, Mrs Murphy. It'll do you a lot of good.'

Mrs Murphy rushed out of the room sobbing.

'Who was speaking to you?' Pat said.

Inez heard words coming round and full and satisfying out of her mouth – exactly what she thought about them, exactly what they were, exactly what she hoped would happen to them.

'Disgusting,' said Mrs Wilson. 'I *told* you so,' she added triumphantly. 'I knew it, I knew the sort she was from the first.'

At this moment the door opened and the doctor came in accompanied, not as usual by the matron, but by the tall ward sister.

Once more, for a gesture, Inez shouted, 'This and that to the lot of you!' – 'Not the nurse,' she whispered to the pillow, 'I don't mean her.'

Mrs Wilson announced in a loud, clear voice, 'I think that people who use filthy language oughtn't to be allowed to associate with decent people. I think it's a shame that some women are allowed to associate with ladies at all – a shame. It oughtn't to be allowed.'

The doctor blinked, but the sister's long, narrow face was expressionless. The two were round the beds glancing at the temperature charts here, saying a few words there. Best, Inez. . . .

The doctor asked, 'Does this hurt you?'

'No.'

'When I press here does it hurt you?'

'No.'

They were very tall, thin and far away. They turned their heads a little and she could not hear what they said. And when she began, 'I wanted to . . .' she saw that they could not hear her either, and stopped.

5

'You can dress in the washroom after lunch,' the sister said next morning.

'Oh, yes?'

There was nothing to be surprised about. So much time had been paid for and now the time was up and she would have to go. There was nothing to be surprised about.

Inez said, 'Would it be possible to stay two or three days longer? I wanted to make some arrangements. It would be more convenient. I was idiotic not to speak about it before.'

The sister's raised eyebrows were very thin – like two thin new moons.

She said, 'I'm sorry, I'm afraid it's not possible. Why didn't you ask before? I told the doctor yesterday that I don't think you are very strong yet. But we are expecting four patients this evening and several others tomorrow afternoon. Unfortunately we are going to be very full up and he thinks you are well enough to go. You must rest when you get back home. Move as little as possible.'

'Yes, of course,' Inez said; but she thought, 'No, this time I won't be able to pull it off, this time I'm done.' *'We wondered if it was Murphy – or you. . . .' Well, it's both of us.*

Then her body relaxed and she lay and did not think of anything, for there is peace in despair in exactly the same way as there is despair in peace. Everything in her body relaxed. She did not make any more plans, she just lay there.

They had their midday dinner – roast beef, potatoes and beans, and then a milk pudding. Just like England. Inez ate and enjoyed it, and then lay back with her arm over her eyes. She knew that Pat was watching her but she lay peaceful, and thought of nothing.

'Here are your things,' the nurse said. 'Will you get dressed now?'

'All right.'

'I'm afraid you're not feeling up to much. Well, you'll have some tea before you go, won't you? And you must go straight to bed as soon as you get back.'

'Get back where?' Inez thought. 'Why should you always take it for granted that everybody has somewhere to get back to?'

'Oh yes,' she said. 'I will.'

And all the time she dressed she saw the street, the 'buses and taxis charging at her, the people jostling her. She heard their voices, saw their eyes. . . . When you fall you don't ever get up; they take care of that. . . .

She leant against the wall thinking of Mrs Murphy's voice when she said, 'Please, please, please, please, please. . . .'

After a while she wiped the tears off her face. She did not put

any powder on, and when she got into the ward she could only
see the bed she was going to lie on and wait till they came with
the tongs to throw her out.

'Will you come over here for a moment?'

There was a chair at the head of each bed. She sat down and
looked at the fan-shaped wrinkles under Madame Tavernier's
small, dark, melancholy eyes, the swollen blue veins on her hands
and the pattern of the gold ring – two roses, the petals touching
each other. She read a sentence of the open book lying on the
bed: '*De lá-haut le paysage qu'on découvre est d'une indiscripti-
ble beauté. . . .*'

Madame Tavernier said, 'That's a charming dress, and you
look very nice – very nice indeed.'

'My God!' Inez said. 'That's funny.'

Madame Tavernier whispered, 'S-sh, listen! Turn the chair
round. I want to talk to you.'

Inez turned the chair so that her back was towards the rest
of the room.

Madame Tavernier took a handkerchief from under her pillow – a white, old-fashioned handkerchief, not small, of very fine
linen trimmed with lace. She put it into Inez' hands. 'Here,' she
said. 'S-sh . . . here!'

Inez took the handkerchief. It smelled of vanilla. She felt the
notes inside it.

'Take care. Don't let the others see. Don't let them notice you
crying. . . .' She whispered, 'You mustn't mind these people; they
don't know anything about life. You mustn't mind them. So many
people don't know anything about life . . . so many of them . . .
and sometimes I wonder if it isn't getting worse instead of better.'
She sighed. 'You hadn't any money, had you?'

Inez shook her head.

'I thought you hadn't. There's enough there for a week or
perhaps two. If you are careful.'

'Yes, yes,' Inez said. 'Now I'll be quite all right.'

She stopped crying. She felt tired, rested and rather degraded.
She had never taken money from a woman before. She did not

like women, she had always told herself, or trust them.

Madame Tavernier went on talking. 'That is quite a lot of money if you use it carefully,' she meant. But that was not what she said.

'Thank you,' Inez said, 'oh, thank you.'

'You'd like some tea before you go, wouldn't you?' the nurse said.

Inez drank the tea, went into the washroom and made up her face. She went back to the old lady's bed.

'Will you give me a kiss?' Madame Tavernier said.

Her powdered skin was soft and flabby as used elastic; it smelt, like her handkerchief, of vanilla. When Inez said, 'I'll never forget your kindness, it's made such a difference to me,' she closed her eyes in a way that meant, 'All right, all right, all right.'

'I'll have a taxi to the station,' Inez decided.

But in the taxi she could only wonder what Madame Tavernier would say if she were suddenly asked what it is like to be old – perhaps she would answer, 'Sometimes it's peaceful' – and remember the gold ring carved into two roses, and above all wish she were back in her bed in the ward with the sheets drawn over her head. Because you can't die and come to life again for a few hundred francs. It takes more than that. It takes more, perhaps, than anybody is ever willing to give.

The Lotus

G ARLAND SAYS she's a tart.'

'A tart! My dear Christine, have you seen her? After all, there are limits.'

'What, round about the Portobello Road? I very much doubt it.'

'Nonsense,' Ronnie said. 'She's writing a novel. Yes, dearie –' he opened his eyes very wide and turned the corners of his mouth down – 'all about a girl who gets seduced –'

'Well, well.'

'On a haystack.' Ronnie roared with laughter.

'Perhaps we'll have a bit of luck; she may get tight earlier than usual tonight and not turn up.'

'Not turn up? You bet she will.'

Christine said, 'I can't imagine why you asked her here at all.'

'Well, she borrowed a book the other day, and she said she was coming up to return it. What was I to do?'

While they were still arguing there was a knock on the door and he called, 'Come in. . . . Christine, this is Mrs Heath, Lotus Heath.'

'Good evening,' Lotus said in a hoarse voice. 'How are you? Quite well, I hope. . . . Good evening, Mr Miles. I've brought your book. *Most* enjoyable.'

She was a middle-aged woman, short and stout. Her plump arms were bare, the finger nails varnished bright red. She had rouged her mouth unskilfully to match her nails, but her face was very pale. The front of her black dress was grey with powder.

'The way these windows rattle!' Christine said. 'Hysterical, I call it.' She wedged a piece of newspaper into the sash, then sat down on the divan. Lotus immediately moved over to her side and leaned forward.

'You do like me, dear, don't you? Say you like me.'

'Of course I do.'

'I think it's so nice of you to ask me up here,' Lotus said. Her sad eyes, set very wide apart, rolled vaguely round the room, which was distempered yellow and decorated with steamship posters – 'Morocco, Land of Sunshine,' 'Come to Beautiful Bali'. 'I get fed up, I can tell you, sitting by myself in that basement night after night. And day after day if it comes to that.'

Christine remarked primly, 'This is a horribly depressing part of London, I always think.'

Her nostrils dilated. Then she pressed her arms close against her sides, edged away and lit a cigarette, breathing the smoke in deeply.

'But you've got it very nice up here, haven't you? Is that a photograph of your father on the mantelpiece? You are like him.'

Ronnie glanced at his wife and coughed. 'Well, how's the poetry going?' he asked, smiling slyly as he said the word 'poetry' as if at an improper joke. 'And the novel, how's that getting on?'

'Not too fast,' Lotus said, looking at the whisky decanter. Ronnie got up hospitably.

She took the glass he handed to her, screwed up her eyes, emptied it at a gulp and watched him refill it with an absent-minded expression.

'But it's wonderful the way it comes to me,' she said. 'It's going to be a long book. I'm going to get everything in – the whole damn thing. I'm going to write a book like nobody's ever written before.'

'You're quite right, Mrs Heath, make it a long book,' Ronnie advised.

His politely interested expression annoyed Christine. 'Is he trying to be funny?' she thought, and felt prickles of irritation all over her body. She got up, murmuring, 'I'll see if there's any more whisky. It's sure to be needed.'

'The awful thing,' Lotus said as she was going out, 'is not knowing the words. That's the torture – knowing the thing and not knowing the words.'

In the bedroom next door Christine could still hear her monotonous, sing-song voice, the voice of a woman who often talked to herself. 'Springing this ghastly old creature on me!' she thought. 'Ronnie must be mad.'

'This place is getting me down,' she thought. The front door was painted a bland blue. There were four small brass plates and bell-pushes on the right-hand side – Mr and Mrs Garland, Mr and Mrs Miles, Mrs Spender, Miss Reid, and a dirty visiting-card tacked underneath – Mrs Lotus Heath. A painted finger pointed downwards.

Christine powdered her face and made up her mouth carefully. What could the fool be talking about?

'Is it as hopeless as all that?' she said, when she opened the sitting-room door. Lotus was in tears.

'Very good.' Ronnie looked bashful and shuffled his feet. 'Very good indeed, but a bit sad. Really, a bit on the sad side, don't you think?'

Christine laughed softly.

'That's what my friend told me,' Lotus said, ignoring her hostess. ' "Whatever you do, don't be gloomy," he said, "because that gets on people's nerves. And don't write about anything you know, for then you get excited and say too much, and that gets under their skins too. Make it up; use your imagination." And what about my book? That isn't sad, is it! I'm using my imagination. All the same, I wish I could write down some of the things that have happened to me, just write them down straight, sad or not sad. I've had my bit of fun too; I'll say I have.'

Ronnie looked at Christine, but instead of responding she looked away and pushed the decanter across the table.

'Have another drink before you tell us any more. Do, please.

That's what the whisky's here for. Make the most of it, because I'm sorry to say there isn't any more in the kitchen and the pub is shut now.'

'She thinks I'm drinking too much of your Scotch,' Lotus said to Ronnie.

'No, I'm sure she doesn't think that.'

'Well, don't think that, dear – what's your name? – Christine. I've got a bottle of port downstairs and I'll go and get it in a minute.'

'Do,' Christine said. 'Let's be really matey.'

'That's right, dear. Well, as I was saying to Mr. Miles, the best thing I ever wrote was poetry. I don't give a damn about the novel, just between you and me. Only to make some money, the novel is. Poetry's what I really like. All the same, the memory I've got, you wouldn't believe. Do you know, I can remember things people have said to me ever so long ago? If I try, I can hear the words and I can remember the voice saying them. It's wonderful, the memory I've got. Of course, I can't do it as well now as I used to, but there you are, nobody stays young for ever.'

'No, isn't it distressing?' Christine remarked to no one in particular. 'Most people go on living long after they ought to be dead, don't they? Especially women.'

'Sarcastic, isn't she? A dainty little thing, but sarcastic.' Lotus got up, swayed and held on to the mantelpiece. 'Are you a mother, dear?'

'Do you mean me?'

'No, I can see you're not – and never will be if you can help it. You're too fly, aren't you? Well, anyway, I've just finished a poem. I wrote it with the tears running down my face and it's the best thing I ever wrote. It was as if somebody was saying into my ears all the time, "Write it, write it." Just like that. It's about a woman and she's in court and she hears the judge condemning her son to death. "You must die," he says. "No, no, no," the woman says, "he's too young." But the old judge keeps on. "Till you die," he says. And, you see –' her voice rose – 'he's not real. He's a dummy, like one of those things ventriloquists have, he's not *real*.

And nobody knows it. But she knows it. And so she says – wait,
I'll recite it to you.'

She walked into the middle of the room and stood very straight
with her head thrown back and her feet together. Then she clasped
her hands loosely behind her back and announced in a high, artificial voice, 'The Convict's Mother'.

Christine began to laugh. 'This is too funny. You mustn't think
me rude, I can't help it. Recitations always make me behave badly.'
She went to the gramophone and turned over the records. 'Dance
for us instead. I'm sure you dance beautifully. Here's the very
thing – "Just One More Chance". That'll do, won't it?'

'Don't take any notice of her,' Ronnie said. 'You go on with
the poem.'

'Not much I won't. What's the good, if your wife doesn't like
poetry?'

'Oh, she's only a silly kid.'

'Tell me what you laugh at, and I'll tell you what you are,'
Lotus said. 'Most people laugh when you're unhappy, that's when
they laugh. I've lived long enough to know that – and maybe I'll
live long enough to see them laugh the other side of their faces,
too.'

'Don't you take any notice of her,' Ronnie repeated. 'She's like
that.' He nodded at Christine's back, speaking in a proud and
tender voice. 'She was telling me only this morning that she doesn't
believe in being sentimental about other people. Weren't you,
Christine?'

'I didn't tell you anything of the sort.' Christine turned round,
her face scarlet. 'I said I was tired of slop – that's what I said.
And I said I was sick of being asked to pity people who are only
getting what they deserve. When people have a rotten time you
can bet it's their own fault.'

'Go on,' said Lotus. 'You're talking like a bloody fool, dear.
You've never felt anything in your life, or you wouldn't be able to
say that. Rudimentary heart, that's your trouble. Your father may
be a clergyman, but you've got a rudimentary heart all the same.'
She was still standing in the middle of the room, with her hands

behind her back. 'You tell her, Mr What's-your-name? Tell the truth and shame the devil. Go on, tell your little friend she's talking like a bloody fool.'

'Now, now, now, what's all this about?' Ronnie shifted uncomfortably. He reached out for the decanter and tilted it upside down into his glass. 'It's always when you want a drink really badly that there isn't any more. Have you ever noticed it? What about that port?'

The two women were glaring at each other. Neither answered him.

'What about that port, Mrs Heath? Let's have a look at that port you promised us.'

'Oh yes, the port,' Lotus said, 'the port. All right, I'll get it.'

As soon as she had gone Christine began to walk up and down the room furiously. 'What's the idea? Why are you encouraging that horrible woman? "Your little friend," did your hear that? Does she think I'm your concubine or something? Do you like her to insult me?'

'Oh, don't be silly, she didn't mean to insult you,' Ronnie argued. 'She's tight – that's what's the matter with her. I think she's damned comic. She's the funniest old relic of the past I've struck for a long time.'

Christine went on as if she had not heard him. 'This hellish, filthy slum and my hellish life in it! And now you must produce this creature, who stinks of whisky and all the rest better left unsaid, to *talk* to me. To talk to me! There are limits, as you said yourself, there are limits. . . . Seduced on a haystack, my God! . . . She oughtn't to be touched with a barge-pole.'

'I say, look out,' Ronnie said. 'She's coming back. She'll hear you.'

'Let her hear me,' said Christine.

She went on to the landing and stood there. When she saw the top of Lotus' head she said in a clear, high voice, 'I really can't stay any longer in the same room as that woman. The mixture of whisky and mustiness is too awful.'

She went into the bedroom, sat down on the bed and began

to laugh. Soon she was laughing so heartily that she had to put the back of her hand over her mouth to stop the noise.

'Hullo,' Ronnie said, 'so here you are.'

'I couldn't find the port.'

'That's all right. Don't you worry about that.'

'I did have some.'

'That's quite all right. . . . My wife's not very well. She's had to go to bed.'

'I know when I've had the bird, Mr Miles,' Lotus said. 'Only give us another drink. I bet you've got some put away some-where.'

There was some sherry in the cupboard.

'Thanks muchly.'

'Won't you sit down?'

'No, I'm going. But see me downstairs. It's so dark, and I don't know where the lights are.'

'Certainly, certainly.'

He went ahead, turning on the lights at each landing, and she followed him, holding on to the banisters.

Outside the rain had stopped but the wind was still blowing strong and very cold.

'Help me down these damned steps, will you? I don't feel too good.'

He put his hand under her arm and they went down the area steps. She got her key out of her bag and opened the door of the basement flat.

'Come on in for a minute. I've got a lovely fire going.'

The room was small and crowded with furniture. Four straight-backed chairs with rococo legs, armchairs with the stuffing com-ing out, piles of old magazines, photographs of Lotus herself, always in elaborate evening dress, smiling and lifeless.

Ronnie stood rocking himself from heel to toe. He liked the photographs. 'Must have been a good-looking girl twenty years ago,' he thought, and as if in answer Lotus said in a tearful voice, 'I had everything; my God, I had. Eyes, hair, teeth, figure, the whole damned thing. And what was the good of it?'

The window was shut and a brown curtain was drawn across it. The room was full of the sour smell of the three dustbins that stood in the area outside.

'What d'you pay for this place?' Ronnie said, stroking his chin.

'Thirty bob a week, unfurnished.'

'Do you know that woman owns four houses along this street? And every floor let, basements and all. But there you are – money makes money, and if you haven't any you can whistle for it. Yes, money makes money.'

'Let it,' said Lotus. 'I don't care a damn.'

'Now then, don't talk so wildly.'

'I don't care a damn. Tell the world I said it. Not a damn. That was never what I wanted. I don't care about the things you care about.'

'Cracked, poor old soul,' he thought, and said: 'Well, I'll be getting along if you're all right.'

'You know – that port. I really had some. I wouldn't have told you I had some if I hadn't. I'm not that sort of person at all. You believe me, don't you?'

'Of course I do.' He patted her shoulder. 'Don't you worry about a little thing like that.'

'When I came down it had gone. And I don't need anybody to tell me where it went, either.'

'Ah?'

'Some people are blighters; some people are proper blighters. He takes everything he can lay his hands on. Never comes to see me except it's to grab something.' She put her elbows on her knees and her head in her hands and began to cry. 'I've had enough. I've had enough, I can tell you. The things people say! My Christ, the things they say. . . .'

'Oh, don't let them get you down,' Ronnie said. 'That'll never do. Better luck next time.'

She did not answer or look at him. He fidgeted. 'Well, I must be running along, I'm afraid. Cheerio. Remember – better luck next time.'

As soon as he got upstairs Christine called out from the bedroom, and when he went in she told him that they must get away, that it wasn't any good saying he couldn't afford a better flat, he must afford a better flat.

Ronnie thought that on the whole she was right, but she talked and talked and after a while it got on his nerves. So he went back into the sitting-room and read a list of second-hand gramophone records for sale at a shop near by, underlining the titles that attracted him. 'I'm a Dreamer, Aren't We All?' 'I've Got You under My Skin – that one certainly; he underlined it twice. Then he collected the glasses and took them into the kitchen for the charwoman to wash up the next morning.

He opened the window and looked out at the wet street. 'I've got you under my skin,' he hummed softly.

The street was dark as a country lane, bordered with lopped trees. It glistened – rather wickedly, he thought.

'Deep in the heart of me,' he hummed. Then he shivered – a very cold wind for the time of year – turned away from the window and wrote a note to the charwoman: 'Mrs Bryan. Please call me as soon as you get here.' He underlined 'soon' and propped the envelope up against one of the dirty dishes. As he did so he heard an odd, squeaking noise. He looked out of the window again. A white figure was rushing up the street, looking very small and strange in the darkness.

'But she's got nothing on,' he said aloud, and craned out eagerly.

A police whistle sounded. The squeaking continued, and the Garlands' window above him went up.

Two policemen half-supported, half-dragged Lotus along. One of them had wrapped her in his cape, which hung down to her knees. Her legs were moving unsteadily below it. The trio went down the area steps.

Christine had come into the kitchen and was looking over his shoulder. 'Good Lord,' she said. 'Well, that's one way of attracting attention if all else fails.'

The bell rang.

'It's one of the policemen,' said Ronnie.

'What's he want to ring our bell for? We don't know anything about her. Why doesn't he ring somebody else's bell?'

The bell rang again.

'I'd better go down,' Ronnie said.

'Do you know anything about Mrs Heath, Mrs Lotus Heath, who lives in the basement flat?' the policeman asked.

'I know her by sight,' Ronnie answered cautiously.

'She's a bit of a mess,' said the policeman.

'Oh, dear!'

'She's passed out stone cold,' the policeman went on confidentially. 'And she looks as if there's something more than drink the matter, if you ask me.'

Ronnie said in a shocked voice – he did not know why – 'Is she dying?'

'Dying? No!' said the policeman, and when he said 'No!' death became unthinkable, the invention of hysteria, something that simply didn't happen. Not to ordinary people. 'She'll be all right. There'll be an ambulance here in a minute. Do you know anything about the person?'

'Nothing,' Ronnie said, 'nothing.'

'Ah?' The policeman wrote in his notebook. 'Is there anybody else in the house, do you think, who'd give us some information?' He shone a light on the brass plates on the door post. 'Mr Garland?'

'Not Mr Garland,' Ronnie answered hurriedly. 'I'm sure not. She's not at all friendly with the Garlands, I know that for a fact. She didn't have much to do with anybody.'

'Thank you very much,' the policeman said. Was his voice ironical?

He pressed Miss Reid's bell and when no answer came looked upwards darkly. But he didn't get any change out of Number Six, Albion Crescent. Everybody had put their lights out and shut their windows.

'You see –' Ronnie began.

'Yes, I see,' the policeman said.

When Ronnie got upstairs again Christine was in bed.

'Well, what was it all about?'

'She seems to have conked out. They're getting an ambulance.'

'Really? Poor devil.' ('Poor devil' she said, but it did not mean anything.) 'I thought she looked awful, didn't you? That dead-white face, and her lips such a funny colour after her lipstick got rubbed off. Did you notice?'

A car stopped outside and Ronnie saw the procession coming up the area steps, everybody looking very solemn and important. And it was pretty slick, too – the way they put the stretcher into the ambulance. He knew that the Garlands were watching from the top floor and Mrs Spencer from the floor below. Miss Reid's floor was in darkness because she was away for a few days.

'Fully how this street gives me goose-flesh tonight,' he thought. 'Somebody walking over my grave, as they say.'

He could not help admiring the way Christine ignored the whole sordid affair, lying there with her eyes shut and the eider-down pulled up under her chin, smiling a little. She looked very pretty, warm and happy like a child when you have given it a sweet to suck. And peaceful.

A lovely child. So lovely that he had to tell her how lovely she was, and start kissing her.

A Solid House

WHAT'S HAPPENING NOW?' Miss Spearman said loudly. She was very deaf.

'A bit quieter,' Teresa shouted.

Miss Spearman put her hands to her ears and shook her head. She hadn't heard.

'There, love,' she said. Her arms were thin as drumsticks, her chest bony, her hair soft as a cat's fur. 'It's all over. There, love.'

'Cigarette?' Teresa said.

But when she opened her cigarette case it was empty. That was because the tobacconist on the corner had refused to sell her any the evening before. He always refused women customers when there was a shortage – and very pleased he was to be able to do it. She wondered what the old beast would say if he knew that she rather liked him. His open hatred and contempt were a relief from the secret hatreds that hissed from between the lines of newspapers or the covers of books, or peeped from sly smiling eyes. A woman? Yes, a woman. A woman must, a woman shall or a woman will.

Miss Spearman was fussing about something, too.

'I've left my earphone upstairs. Stupid! D'you think it's worthwhile going to get it?'

'No, don't. Better not,' Teresa said. Certainly better not, she thought, as the silence and emptiness gradually filled with fragments of sentences, columns of figures which she was compelled to add up, subtract and multiply – and with the sound of that first scream and crash. The top of her head, which felt very thin anyway, began to rattle and shake.

Miss Spearman said, whispering this time, 'Right overhead now, aren't they? Perhaps they're ours.'

Ours? Perhaps, maybe. . . .

Pressed flat against the cellar wall, they listened to the inexorable throbbing of the planes. And above them the house waited, its long, gloomy passages full of echoes, shadows, creakings – rats, perhaps. But the square outside was calm and indifferent, the trees cleaner than in a London square, not smelling the same, either.

'Anything?' Miss Spearman asked.

'Gone, I think,' Teresa said, and made signs.

She remembered playing hide-and-seek in a cellar very like this one long ago. Curious, that hide-and-seek. It started well. You picked your side (I pick you, I pick you), then suddenly, in the middle, something happened. Everything changed and became horrible and meaningless. But still it went on. You hid, or you ran with a red face, pretending you knew what it was all about. The boys showed off, became brutal; the girls trotted along, imitating, trying to keep up, but with sidelong looks, sudden fits of giggling, which often ended in tears.

'Well,' Miss Spearman said peevishly, 'what are they waiting for? Why don't they hurry up with the All Clear?'

Teresa smiled and shrugged her shoulders. 'They've gone,' she thought, soothed. 'Gone home to get their medals pinned on, gone home to get something to eat.' She had got used to the cellar, she did not want to leave it now. Why leave this good, this perfectly safe, windowless cellar, so like that other long ago?

'Nothing changes much,' she thought, remembering the bellowed orders, contradicted the next minute – Left turn. No, right turn. No, as you were, silly ass – the obligatory grin, the idiotic jokes, repeated over and over again, which you had to laugh at, at first unwillingly, then so hysterically that your jaws ached, and the endless arguments as to whether the girls might carry knives slung to their waists or not. 'Oh, the girls can't have knives.' 'Why not?' 'Well, because they aren't officers. The girls are only common sailors.' 'Yes, but common sailors do have knives,' and Norman, the soft one, the one who liked girls, you suspected. 'That's the great thing about being a common sailor.' At last it was decided that the leader of the girls could have a knife, the others could carry sticks. The worst part of this horrible game came when the frenzy was over and the damage done. Then the boys would cluster in a group, and one of them would be sure to say, 'It was the girls' fault. They started it; they egged us on. They were worse than we were.'

'Well,' she said, 'there you are. That'll be all for this morning.'

Miss Spearman did not answer. She stared straight ahead, strained, listening.

'The All Clear,' Teresa said, speaking carefully. Now she could think again, she could tell herself, 'Don't shout. Pitch your voice right and she'll hear.'

'Ah!' said Miss Spearman. 'Not much of a raid.' Her expression changed, became spiteful. 'You are nervy, aren't you? Look at your hand shaking.'

'It's so cold down here.'

'Come along then. We'll have something to warm us up.'

They went up the steep stone stairs, past the brass gong in the hall, the brass tray for visiting cards, the dim looking glass, malevolent with age, into the kitchen.

2

The kitchen was a large, comfortable room. The owner of the house had gone off when the raids started, to live at an hotel in the Lake District. ('People said she oughtn't to have done it – that is was a bad example. But when they get to that age what can you expect? "They can't stand the racket these devils make when they're her age," I said.') Miss Spearman, who looked like an ex-lady's maid, or housekeeper, perhaps, or poor relation or half-acknowledged relation – there must be some half-acknowledged relations knocking around, even in this holy and blessed isle – was installed and let rooms to select lodgers.

She lit the fire, talking about air raids, land mines and slaughter.

'Why, there wasn't a pane of glass left in the square. Everything down, from St Agnes's to the County Tea Shop. That *was* a night.'

She went into the scullery and came back with tea and bread-and-butter on a black lacquer tray.

'I'll have mine later; I like it strong. I must go and see if my blind old lady's all right.' She said the words 'old lady' in a patronizing, pitying and scornful tone. 'And then perhaps Olly Pearce at Number Seven may have heard the news.'

There were two red plush armchairs near the fire, a patchwork rug, a calendar with a picture of cats, a round table with a wool mat in the middle, a large black cupboard and, on the walls, some old prints of soldiers in full dress – Ensign of His Majesty's Dragoon Guards, Captain of the 78th Foot – fellows of those in Captain Roper's bedroom upstairs, which Teresa always imagined looked down at him so approvingly as he slept. 'Sleep on, chum,' they said. 'Snore well, mate.'

Captain Roper, her fellow lodger, was away on a course. And a very good thing too, for he had turned against her now, and she knew perfectly well why.

On the first night of her stay they had gone together to the nearest cinema. After dinner on the second night they had settled down by the fire – he in the big armchair, she in the smaller one, and he had produced a half bottle of whisky.

'Have s spot?'

'Battledress doesn't do justice to a man's figure,' he said after the second whisky, and it probably didn't to his. He had a small, handsome, cocky, ageless face and a cocky little moustache.

He told her that he thought things were going to be very difficult after this war – worse than last, which was bad enough. In 1920 he had been in Mexico, but in 1921 he was back in London. On his uppers. 'Pop went everything except my dress suit. In 1914. . . .'

'But you must have been very young in 1914,' Teresa said flatteringly.

Captain Roper blinked. 'Well, as a matter of fact I was. However, I remember. . . .'

Yes, pre-war 1914 must have been a golden time.

Teresa stopped listening. When she next heard what he was
saying he was no longer in 1914; he was in 1924, giving lessons
in Mah Jong to keep his body and soul together.

'And some very interesting pupils I had too. I taught Mah
Jong to the prettiest woman I've ever seen. Lovely young creature – dark, very vivacious. She got rather bored with it, of course.
Scoring too complicated.' His hard, shallow, sentimental eyes
looked past her. Perhaps he saw a sunny street and trim steps up
to a freshly painted door and flower boxes in the windows and
the decorative, unattainable young creature in the room inside.
'I can't remember her name. A double-barrelled name. It's on the
tip of my tongue.'

Double-barrelled names raced through Teresa's brain.

'Ah, I've remembered it,' Captain Roper said. 'Barton-Lumley.'

'Barton-Lumley?'

'Yes, Mrs Barton-Lumley. She got bored,' he muttered, and,
after a pause, 'She died.'

Then Teresa had laughed loudly. One of those terrible laughs
which now shook her at the most unexpected moments. It came
from the depths of her – a real devil of a laugh. Every time this
happened she would think 'Who's that laughing?'

She smoothed her face and tried to turn it into a cough.

'Oh, what a shame! Beautiful people oughtn't to die; they ought
to be guarded and protected and kept alive, whoever else dies.
There are so few of them.'

But this was useless. He looked at her with distrust – and he
had gone on looking at her with distrust.

'No,' she was thinking when Miss Spearman came back, 'I'll
never know the rest of the story – what happened in 1925 or
1938, in 1927 or 1931. . . .'

'Norton Street,' Miss Spearman said, pouring out her tea, 'and
I hear they've got Bailey's.'

'Pretty close. That must have been that first bang.'

'Yes. Olly says she's heard that fifteen people were killed, but old Jimmy says thirty. If it's Norton Street, we can go and have a look this afternoon. But it's no use going now, do you think? Well, you seem better already,' she went on. 'You looked very bad in the cellar, I thought, as white as a – as white as a sheet. You mustn't let your nerves get on top of you, you know. It doesn't do. Think of something else. You want a bit of cheering up.'

She walked across the room and opened a cupboard, which was full of dresses, underclothes, sandals, brassieres, kimonos – ladies' second-hand clothes, Miss Spearman's sideline.

'What about this? Three and sixpence.'

She held up a brown felt halo hat with a long veil attached to it.

'Wouldn't I look comic in that?' Teresa said. 'Well, I mean, a bit comic?'

'Yes, perhaps it's not quite your style,' Miss Spearman agreed. She was now wearing her earphone and it seemed to be working perfectly. 'Well, what about this costume? I only got it yesterday. Very smart woman she is – wears some lovely clothes. She wants two pounds for it. Just been cleaned. I'll let you have it for thirty shillings.'

'But I don't like that shade of green. I don't like green at all. It's not my lucky colour.'

'What?' Miss Spearman said. 'I can't hear you. Take it into your room and try it on. A pound to you – and that's giving it away.'

'All right,' Teresa said feebly. She took the hideous thing and hung it at the back of her chair. She thought, 'Yes, I'll end by buying it, and I'll end by walking about in it too, God help me.'

Then she recognized her own black dress in the cupboard. It was hanging next to a shapeless purple coat. A cast-off self, it stared back so forlornly, so threateningly that she turned her eyes away.

'Have another cup,' Miss Spearman said. 'I see you're looking at your old black. I hope to get it off this week. But you can't expect much.'

'No, I suppose not.'

'Black's too depressing. Twelve and six I might get.'

'Well, it cost me quite a lot, you know.'

'Yes, I know it's well cut, but it's a depressing dress all the same. Would you take ten bob?'

Her face looked very sharp and eager, her brown eyes glittered. You wouldn't have thought she was talking about shillings at all.

'If that's all I can get. . . .'

Miss Spearman relaxed.

'Funny how tired these air raids make you, isn't it?' she said, sighing. 'It's afterwards you feel it, I always think. Yes, it's afterwards you feel it.'

'Sit still. I'll wash the cups up,' Teresa said.

But the scullery was like the cellar – dim and dark, with only one small window high up to light the sink, the rusty gas-stove, the stupid moon-faced plates in the rack, the cheerful cups, the gloomy saucepans on hooks. So she was glad to come back into the kitchen, where Miss Spearman was talking to herself about the charwoman.

'I'm sure Nelly won't turn up. I'm sure she'll make this raid an excuse. She always does. Most annoying. And they never go anywhere near the part she lives in.'

'I don't know what the working class is coming to. Haven't you noticed it?' she said. 'And this house is too much for me without any help, officers or no officers.'

'And,' she continued, 'I do it for love, as you might say. How will they manage when people like me are dead and gone? They'll soon find out what it's like.' Something in her mournful and complaining voice made you see all the houses growing dustier, dingier, more silent. 'What's to happen if everything's left to go to rack and ruin?' she lamented. 'Where do they expect people to live? In underground caves, or in concrete barracks, or what?'

'Some will,' said Teresa, 'and some, as they say, will not.'

Don't worry, everything will survive somewhere – the polished floors, the bowls of roses, the scented hair, the painted nails. Some will sink, but others will swim. Trust Bibi. . . .

She put her hand over her eyes, which felt sore, and listening to the noisy clock, thought about that other clock ticking so slowly, the watch on the table ticking so fast. But the same seconds, or they said the same seconds. Not that she believed a word they said.

'I know she isn't coming. An hour and a half late now. The whole trouble is that they promise things that they don't mean to. It's very un-English, very. And she was going to cut the cards for me today, too. She's wonderful at that, I will say.'

She clasped and unclasped her hands in her lap. They were very red and raw, the joints swollen – the only ungraceful things about her.

'Miss Spearman, I admire you so much.'

'Do you?'

'Yes, and I envy you.'

'Envy me?' Miss Spearman said happily. She looked into the little glass over the mantelpiece. 'I never touch my hair or my face with anything but rain water. From that cask outside. Soft water – that's the secret.'

Teresa said, 'Yes – your appearance, of course. But what I meant was that I admire you because you're always so calm, so sure of yourself, and because . . .'

It was a glittering, glaring day outside, the sky blown blue. A heartless, early spring day – acid, like an unripe gooseberry. There was a cold yellow light on the paved garden and the tidy, empty flower beds and on the high wall, where a ginger cat sat staring at birds. You could see his neat paw-marks in the damp mould.

'I feel so well,' Teresa said, 'though a bit sleepy. That shows I'm getting better – feeling well so early in the morning before the break of day. Almost.'

'Have you been ill?' Miss Spearman asked inquisitively. 'A lot of people are feeling it now, a lot of people. Of course, not these young, heartless people.'

Teresa said, 'Do you think young people are heartless? Aren't old people heartless? And people who are getting old – aren't they heartless too?'

'I can see you've been ill. I can see it in your eyes.'

'Oh, nothing much,' said Teresa.

But instead of turning her head away she looked straight at Miss Spearman – straight into a hard bright glitter, hard and bright as the day outside. But behind the glitter there was surely something nebulous, dreamy, soft? Usually the sweetness and softness, if any, was displayed for all to see; but, hidden away, what continents of distrust, what icy seas of silence. Voyage to the Arctic regions. . . .

She thought, 'Shall I tell her about it on this fresh new morning?'

3

But then it was afternoon – a hot afternoon. You know, there does come an afternoon when you think 'I want a rest; I want a good long sleep'. So I took two tablets, and then another two. Then I drank some whisky and it seemed quite clear. Now, my lass, now Hope, the vulture, will have to go and feed on somebody else. I thought, 'I must wear my pretty dress for this.' So I went upstairs and put on my blue dress and powdered my face. I didn't hurry, but when I came down again the hands of the clock hadn't moved at all. Which shows that it's true, what they say: 'Time is made for slaves.' Then I knew I must do it and so I swallowed all the tablets in the bottle with the whisky. Seven grains each they were – strong. And I saw some spilt on the floor. 'I must take these too,' I thought. But before I could take them I don't remember anything more.

When I woke up the first thing I saw was the blue dress on the chair. And the doctor was there. 'What are you doing here?' I said, and he answered, 'It's the afternoon I always come to see you.' So I knew it was Tuesday. A whole night and a day gone, and I shall never know what happened. And afterwards too I don't remember. I had dreams, of course. But were they dreams? . . .

She said, 'I liked this house as soon as I saw it. And you seemed exactly right when you opened the door. Not the sort of person who goes all of a doodah, like me.'

'It's a lovely old house,' Miss Spearman said. 'Solid.'

'Yes, lovely and solid,' Teresa said.

But how can you tell? The other one was solid, too. As you approached it the river, which had been narrow, broadened out, like an avenue, straight, with willows on each bank. The water was covered with dead leaves. The paddle did not make any sound, the dead leaves slowed the punt down. Round a corner was the house – turrets and gables and balconies and green shutters all mixed up. It looked empty and dilapidated. The boards of the landing-stage were broken and rotten. Two statues faced one another – the gentleman wore a cocked hat, knee-breeches and tail-coat, but the lady showed a large breast. She held up her draperies with one hand, the other was raised as if she were listening. The lawn was dark green and smooth and in the middle was a cedar tree. The rocking-horse under it was painted white with red spots. There wasn't a sound. And I knew that if I could pass the statues and touch the tree and walk into the house, I should be well again. But they wouldn't let me do that, the simple thing that always makes you well.

How much shall I tell her? Shall I tell her that in spite of everything they did I died then? Shall I tell her what it feels like to be dead? It's not being sad, it's quite different. It's being nothing, feeling nothing. You don't feel insults, you wouldn't feel caresses if there was anyone to caress you. It's like this – it's like walking along a road in a fog, knowing that you have left everything behind you. But you don't want to go back; you've got to go on. There are moments when you know where you are going, but then you forget and you walk on, torturing yourself, trying to remember, for it's very important. When you start, you often look back to catch them laughing or making faces in the bright lights away from the fog. Later on you don't do that; you don't care any longer. If they were to laugh until their mouths met at the back and the tops of their heads fell off like some loathsome over-ripe fruit – as they doubtless will one day – you wouldn't turn your head to see the horrible but comic sight. . . .

'Yes, I've been ill,' she said. 'I've been having a holiday. I was staying not so far from here and I saw your advertisement in the local paper.'

Miss Spearman said, 'I usually let my rooms to officers. But this happened to be a slack time.'

Teresa smiled. 'Lucky for me.'

How much have I told her? What have I said . . .

Not too much, for Miss Spearman did not seem to be at all surprised.

'Calm?' she said. 'Of course, it's better to be calm. I don't believe in hysteria. Not for women, anyhow. Sometimes a man can get away with hysteria, but not a woman. And then of course don't be too much alone. People don't like it. The things they say if you're alone! You had to have a good deal of money to get away with that. And keep up with your friends. Write letters. And a good laugh always helps, of course.'

'Which helps most – with or at?'

'I don't quite follow you,' Miss Spearman said. 'And then a little bit of gossip.'

. . . See people. Write letters. Join the noble and gallant army of witch-hunters – both sexes, all ages eligible – so eagerly tracking down some poor devil, snouts to the ground. Watch the witch-hunting, witch-pricking ancestor peeping out of those close-set Nordic baby-blues.

But are you telling me the real secret, how to be exactly like everybody else? Tell me, for I am sure you know. If it means being deaf, then I'll be deaf. And if it means being blind, then I'll be blind. I'm afraid of that road, Miss Spearman – the one that leads to madness and to death, they say. That's not true. It's longer than that. But it's a terrible road to put your feet on, and I'm not strong enough; let somebody else try it. I want to go back. Tell me how to get back; tell me what to do and I'll do it.

'And then,' Miss Spearman said, 'there's another thing. . . .'

Teresa leaned forward eagerly.

'Olly Pearce,' Miss Spearman said in a low mysterious voice, 'is a medium.'

'A what? . . . Oh, I see.'

'We have sittings, sometimes at her place; sometimes here, sometimes at Mrs Davis's. I've had messages, and I hear them at night, just before I sleep. Especially since I've grown so deaf. It always starts with a humming, twanging noise in my head.'

'Yes, that's how it starts, isn't it?' Teresa said, staring at her.

'Was that the bell?' Miss Spearman sat very erect. 'It's that slut Nelly. Excuse the word. Over two hours late.'

She went out into the hall, and Nelly could be heard, loudly explaining, arguing, and then becoming aggressive. And Miss Spearman's shrill answers, which ended on a high, thin note.

She came back into the kitchen, looking triumphant.

'Well, what are you going to do while your room's being turned out? Why not go for a walk to Norton Street, and see what's to be seen?'

'No, I don't think I will,' Teresa said. In Norton Street a doll, or a dressmaker's dummy, would stare blankly, a cigarette poster, untouched, flapping in the wind, would smile, beckon, wave a coy finger. The notice would say, 'Danger: No Thoroughfare.'

She heard Nelly outside, shovelling coal violently into a scuttle.

'Why, the old badger!' said Nelly, 'the bloody old . . .'

The radio next door began to sing defiantly 'Now's the time for Paradise, Paradise for two. . . .'

4

'I generally keep it locked,' Miss Spearman said. 'But I opened it up and air it and light a fire every Tuesday.'

'And it's Tuesday today, of course,' Teresa thought. 'Always Tuesday. . . .'

'Captain Roper sits in here sometimes,' Miss Spearman said, 'so why shouldn't you?'

She led the way through the white-painted door into another room – a long, narrow, pathetic room. Gold brocade curtains shut out the square, but the windows which led into the garden were open. There was a freshly lighted fire; no dust sheets – everything was spick and span.

'Aren't they beautiful?' Miss Spearman said, pointing to a case of stuffed birds, neatly labelled in careful, slanting handwriting. There was a card in the corner, in the same writing: 'I believe in the Resurrection of the Dead.' A fanatic birdlover? A joke? Or had Miss Spearman picked it up and put it there to preserve the admirable sentiment?

Teresa came close and looked at the birds which would rise again – White Heron, Lapwing, Great Crested Grebe, Indian Cock Pheasant, Wild Duck and, in a corner, four humming birds. Four humming birds with fierce glass eyes.

"Well, you've grown up now, haven't you?' she said to them. 'You are having you own back.'

Miss Spearman was talking about the pictures in white or faded gold frames which covered the walls. Pictures of blue seas – but not too blue, not a vulgar, tropical blue – of white walls – but not stark – of shadows – but not too black. Pictures of gentlemen with powdered hair and ladies with ringlets falling on long, graceful necks, their mouths mournful, patient or smiling as the case might be. One was holding a violin, another a book.

There was a mirror in a silver-green frame, and glass paperweights through which could be seen roses, carnations and violets. There were white jade vases, and the Woolworth's glass mats they were standing on were as touching as Miss Spearman's red hands or make-up used by an ageing woman. ('Must make the best of the poor old face.')

'Perhaps there's a musical box,' Teresa thought. 'Perhaps it will play "Pink and blue, pink and blue, Do you know what love can do? Love can kill. . . ." '

There was no musical box, but there were Japanese windglasses, again from Woolworth's, hanging over the door into the garden.

'You say you're tired,' Miss Spearman said. 'Why not lie down and have a little rest? Have a little doze. The sofa's quite comfortable.' And left her.

She recognized one of the gentlemen now – the one with china-blue eyes – also the lady with the violin. There were portraits of them in her room, but here they hung straight, with no string visible, with no incongruous text between them – 'The Lord is my Shepherd, and I shall lack nothing.'

She sat down on a gilt chair and saw that there was a small

bookshelf behind a red and gold screen, the only gaudy thing in the room. And the right books were in it – *The Heart of Rome, Wanda, All for the Czar, As a Dream When One Awaketh, From One Generation to Another.* 'Yes, this is paradise,' she thought, and leant forward to touch the books. But next to innocent *Wanda* was a warning – *No Orchids for Miss Blandish.* 'I bet old Cap Roper brought that in here. Not that I've got anything against the book. On the contrary, didn't I win a quid ages ago when I bet it was written by an Englishman, judging entirely by internal evidence and confounding the experts?'

She began to walk restlessly up and down the room, thinking, 'No, if I slept here I'd dream. I'd dream of monstrous humming birds, cellars, flowers under glass, gentlemen with china-blue eyes, ladies with smooth shoulders who will never lack the still pastures and the green waters, the peaceful death, the honoured grave – all this, and Heaven too – who will never, never lack the sense of superiority nor the disciplined reaction nor the proper way to snub nor the heart like a rock nor the wrist surprisingly thick. Nor the flower of the flock to be sacrificed.'

'I must find somewhere else to sleep,' she thought.

And then Miss Spearman opened the door and called 'Ready'.

5

In the dining-room the glass cases round the walls were full of shepherds and shepherdesses, mandarins and small china portrait figures. 'My sister brought me some new laid eggs yesterday. I do my best for you.'

'You do indeed.'

There were two newspapers by the plate, one unfamiliar, and when Miss Spearman came in to clear away the meal she hovered.

'Did you notice that paper? Very good, I think.'

'Yes, awfully good.'

But Miss Spearman did not seem satisfied with this response, or she had not heard it.

'You see,' she said, taking up the paper and pointing to an

article marked with two red lines, 'it's all quite simple and homely
– anyhow at the start. Many people simply won't believe they are
dead, he says. He says it's quite amusing, if one may use the
word.'

'If one may use the word.'

'Of course, it gets more complicated later on.'

'It always does get more complicated later on, don't you think?'
Teresa said.

'We're going to try to sit tonight,' Miss Spearman said. 'We
always get very good results after a raid. One learns not to question these things. Would you care to join us? Olly Pearce, Mrs
Davis, myself and the lady who keeps the wool shop in Modder
Street.'

'No,' Teresa said, 'no. I'm sorry I can't.'

'I'll think about it,' she said, laughing feebly. 'Like the green
suit, I'll think about it.'

Although she was wearing her earphone Miss Spearman looked
so bewildered that Teresa repeated, 'No. Not yet.'

'Of course,' Miss Spearman said stiffly, 'people mustn't be
forced; they must come of their own free will. Just as you like.'

Her friendliness seemed to float away in the act of puting the
dishes on the tray and she slammed the door so violently that the
pictures on the walls and the little figures in the cases trembled.

But silence came and patched up the rent. Olly Pearce's young
niece, wearing a blue overall, was in the front garden of Number
Seven. She pushed her hair off her forehead, stretched, yawned.
She was sleepy too. The ginger cat danced in the cold wind outside – three little steps one way, three little steps the other, backwards and spring.

Teresa lay down on the sofa and shut her eyes. The sound of
the crash in her head became fainter. It was off on its journey,
off on its travels, for ever and ever, world without end.

'My little doze,' she thought. 'At last. My little sleep.'

The Sound of the River

THE ELECTRIC BULB hung on a short flex from the middle of the ceiling, and there was not enough light to read so they lay in bed and talked. The night air pushed out the curtains and came through the open window soft and moist.

'But what are you afraid of? How do you mean afraid?'

She said, 'I mean afraid like when you want to swallow and you can't.'

'All the time?'

'Nearly all the time.'

'My dear, really. You are an idiot.'

'Yes, I know.'

Not about this, she thought, not about this.

'It's only a mood,' she said. 'It'll go.'

'You're so inconsistent. You chose this place and wanted to come here, I thought you approved of it.'

'I do. I approve of the moor and the loneliness and the whole set-up, especially the loneliness. I just wish it would stop raining occasionally.'

'Loneliness is all very well,' he said, 'but it needs fine weather.'

'Perhaps it will be fine tomorrow.'

If I could put it into words it might go, she was thinking. Sometimes you can put it into words – almost – and so get rid of it – almost. Sometimes you can tell yourself I'll admit I was afraid today. I was afraid of the sleek smooth faces, the rat faces, the way they laughed in the cinema. I'm afraid of escalators and dolls' eyes. But there aren't any words for this fear. The words haven't been invented.

She said, 'I'll like it again when the rain stops.'

'You weren't liking it just now, were you? Down by the river?'

'Well,' she said, 'no. Not much.'

'It was a bit ghostly down there tonight. What can you expect? Never pick a place in fine weather.' (Or anything else either he thought.) 'There are too many pines about,' he said. 'They shut you in.'

'Yes.'

But it wasn't the black pines, she thought, or the sky without stars, or the thin hinted moon, or the lowering, flat-topped hills, or the tor and the big stones. It was the river.

'The river is very silent,' she'd said. 'Is that because it's so full?'

'One gets used to the noise, I suppose. Let's go in and light the bedroom fire. I wish we had a drink. I'd give a lot for a drink, wouldn't you?'

'We can have some coffee.'

As they walked back he'd kept his head turned towards the water.

'Curiously metallic it looks by this light. Not like water at all.'

'It looks smooth as if it were frozen. And much wider.'

'Frozen – no. Very much alive in an uncanny way. Streaming hair,' he's said as if he were talking to himself. So he'd felt it too. She lay remembering how the brown broken-surfaced, fast-running river had changed by moonlight. Things are more powerful than people. I've always believed that. (You're not my daughter if you're afraid of a horse. You're not my daughter if you're afraid of being seasick. You're not my daughter if you're afraid of the shape of a hill, or the moon when it is growing old. In fact you're not my daughter.)

'It isn't silent now is it?' she said. 'The river I mean.'

'No, it makes a row from up here.' He yawned. 'I'll put another log on the fire. It was very kind of Ransom to let us have that coal and wood. He didn't promise any luxuries of that sort when we took the cottage. He's not a bad chap, is he?'

'He's got a heart. And he must be wise to the climate after all.'

'Well I like it,' he said as he got back into bed, 'in spite of the rain. Let's be happy here.'

'Yes, let's.'

That's the second time. He said that before. He'd said it the first day they came. Then too she hadn't answered 'yes let's' at once because fear which had been waiting for her had come up to her and touched her, and it had been several seconds before she could speak.

'That must have been an otter we saw this evening,' he said, 'much too big for a water rat. I'll tell Ransom. He'll be very excited.'

'Why?'

'Oh, they're rather rare in these parts.'

'Poor devils, I bet they have an awful time if they're rare. What'll he do? Organize a hunt? Perhaps he won't, we've agreed that he's soft-hearted. This is a bird sanctuary, did you know? It's all sorts of things. I'll tell him about that yellow-breasted one. Maybe he'll know what it was.'

That morning she had watched it fluttering up and down the window pane – a flash of yellow in the rain. 'Oh what a pretty bird.' Fear is yellow. You're yellow. She's got a broad streak of yellow. They're quite right, fear is yellow. 'Isn't it pretty?' And isn't it persistent? It's determined to get in. . . .'

'I'm going to put this light out,' he said. 'It's no use. The fire's better.'

He struck a match to light another cigarette and when it flared she saw the deep hollows under his eyes, the skin stretched taut over his cheekbones, and the thin bridge of his nose. He was smiling as if he knew what she'd been thinking.

'Is there anything you're not afraid of in these moods of yours?'

'You,' she said. The match went out. Whatever happened, she

thought. Whatever you did. Whatever I did. Never you. D'you hear me?

'Good.' He laughed. 'That's a relief.'

'Tomorrow will be fine, you'll see. We'll be lucky.'

'Don't depend on our luck. You ought to know better by this time,' he muttered. 'But you're the sort who never knows better. Unfortunately we're both the sort who never knows better.'

'Are you tired? You sound tired.'

'Yes.' He sighed and turned away, 'I am rather.' When she said, 'I must put the light on, I want some aspirin,' he didn't answer, and she stretched her arm over him and touched the switch of the dim electric bulb. He was sleeping. The lighted cigarette had fallen on to the sheet.

'Good thing I saw that,' she said aloud. She put the cigarette out and threw it through the window, found the aspirin, emptied the ashtray, postponing the moment when she must lie down stretched out straight, listening, when she'd shut her eyes only to feel them click open again.

'Don't go to sleep,' she thought lying there. 'Stay awake and comfort me. I'm frightened. There's something here to be frightened of, I tell you. Why can't you feel it? When you said, let's be happy, that first day, there was a tap dripping somewhere into a full basin, playing a gay and horrible tune. Didn't you hear it? I heard it. Don't turn away and sigh and sleep. Stay awake and comfort me.'

Nobody's going to comfort you, she told herself, you ought to know better. Pull yourself together. There was a time when you weren't afraid. Was there? When? When was that time? Of course there was. Go on. Pull yourself together, pull yourself to pieces. There was a time. There was a time. Besides I'll sleep soon. There's always sleeping, and it'll be fine tomorrow.

'I knew it would be fine today,' she thought when she saw the sunlight through the flimsy curtains. 'The first fine day we've had.'

'Are you awake,' she said. 'It's a fine day. I had such a funny dream,' she said, still staring at the sunlight. 'I dreamt I was walking in a wood and the trees were groaning and then I dreamt of the wind in telegraph wires, well a bit like that, only very loud. I can still hear it – really I swear I'm not making this up. It's still in my head and it isn't anything else except a bit like the wind in telegraph wires.'

'It's a lovely day,' she said and touched his hand.

'My dear, you are cold. I'll get a hot water bottle and some tea. I'll get it because I'm feeling very energetic this morning, you stay still for once!'

'Why don't you answer,' she said sitting up and peering at him. 'You're frightening me,' she said, her voice rising. 'You're frightening me. Wake up,' she said and shook him. As soon as she touched him her heart swelled till it reached her throat. It swelled and grew jagged claws and the claws clutched her driving in deep. 'Oh God,' she said and got up and drew the curtains and saw his face in the sun. 'Oh God,' she said staring at his face in the sun and knelt by the bed with his hand in her two hands not speaking not thinking any longer.

The doctor said, 'You didn't hear anything during the night?'

'I thought it was a dream.'

'Oh! You thought it was a dream. I see. What time did you wake up?'

'I don't know. We kept the clock in the other room because it had a loud tick. About half past eight or nine, I suppose.'

'You knew what had happened of course.'

'I wasn't sure. At first I wasn't sure.'

'But what did you do? It was past ten when you telephoned. What did you do?'

Not a word of comfort. Suspicion. He has small eyes and bushy eyebrows and he looks suspicious.

She said, 'I put on a coat and went to Mr Ransom's, where there's a telephone. I ran all the way but it seemed a long way.'

'But that oughtn't to have taken you more than ten minutes at the most.'

'No, but it seemed very long. I ran but I didn't seem to be moving. When I got there everybody was out and the room where the telephone is was locked. The front door is always open but he locks that room when he goes out. I went back into the road but there was no one there. Nobody in the house and nobody in the road and nobody on the slope of the hill. There were a lot of sheets and men's shirts hanging on a line waving. And the sun of course. It was our first day. The first fine day we've had.'

She looked at the doctor's face, stopped, and went on in a different voice.

'I walked up and down for a bit. I didn't know what to do. Then I thought I might be able to break the door in. So I tried and I did. A board broke and I got in. But it seemed a long time before anybody answered.'

She thought, Yes, of course I knew. I was late because I had to stay there listening. I heard it then. It got louder and closer and it was in the room with me. I heard the sound of the river.

I heard the sound of the river.

I Spy a Stranger

T HE DOWNRIGHT RUDENESS I had to put up with,'
Mrs Hudson said, 'Long before there was any cause for it. And
the inquisitiveness! She hadn't been here a week before they
started making remarks about her, poor Laura. And I had to consider Ricky, hadn't I? They said wasn't his job at the R.A.F Station supposed to be so very hush-hush, and that he oughtn't to
be allowed –'

While her sister talked Mrs Trant looked out of the window
at the two rose beds in the front garden. They reassured her.
They reminded her of last summer, of any day in the summer.
They made her feel that all the frightening changes were not
happening or, if they were happening, that they didn't really matter. The roses were small, flame-coloured, growing four or five
on the same stalk, each with a bud ready to replace it. Every time
an army lorry passed they shivered. They started shivering before
you could see the lorry or even hear it, she noticed. But they were
strong; hardened by the east coast wind, they looked as if they
would last for ever. Against the blue sky they were a fierce, defiant
colour, a dazzling colour. When she shut her eyes she could still
see them as plainly as if they were photographed on her eyelids.

'They didn't stop at nasty remarks either,' said Mrs Hudson.
'Listen to this:

'People in this town are not such fools as you think and unless you
get rid of that crazy old foreigner, that witch of Prague, who *you say* is
a relative, steps will be taken which you will not like. This is a friendly

warning but a good many of us are keeping an eye on her and if you allow her to stay. . . .

This time next year. . . .

You'll be all very much the worse for wear.'

'That was the first,' she said. 'But afterwards – my dear, really! You think who, in a small place like this, who?'

'I might give a guess.'

'Ah, but that's the worst of it. Once start that and there's no end. It's surprising how few can be trusted. Here's a beauty. Written on quite expensive paper, too.'

' "A Gun for the Old Girls. . . ." A gun for the old girls?' Mrs Trant repeated. 'What's that mean?'

'There's a drawing on the other side.'

'Well!'

'Yes. When that came Ricky said "I can't have her any longer. You must tell her so." '

'But why on earth didn't you let me know what was going on? Malvern isn't the other end of the world. Why were you so vague?'

'Because it *was* vague. It was vague at first. And Ricky said "Take no notice of it. Keep quiet and it'll all blow over. And don't go and write a lot of gossip to anybody, because you never know what happens to letters these days. I could tell you a thing or two that would surprise you." So I said "What next? This is a free country, isn't it?" And he said there wasn't much free nowadays except a third-class ticket to Kingdom Come. And what could you have done about it? You couldn't have had her to stay. Why, Tom detests her. No. I thought the best thing was to advise her to go back to London.'

And hadn't she tried to be as nice as possible and to speak as kindly as she could?

'Laura,' she had said, 'I hate to tell you, but Ricky and I think it best that you should leave here, because there's such a lot of chatter going on and it really isn't fair on him. The blitz is over now, and there are all these divan rooms that are advertised round Holland Park or the Finchley Road way. You could be quite com-

fortable. And you can often find such good little restaurants close
by. Don't you remember the one we went to? The food was wonderful. The one where the menu was in English on one side and
Continental on the other?'

'What do you mean by Continental?'

'Well, I mean Continental – German, if you like.'

'Of course you mean German. This Anglo-German love-hate
affair!' she had said. 'You might call it the most sinister love affair
of all time, and you wouldn't be far wrong . . . !'

'She could be very irritating,' Mrs Hudson continued. 'She
went on about London. "I daresay, Laura," I said, "I daresay. But
London's a big place and, whatever its disadvantages, it has one
advantage – there are lots of people. Anybody odd isn't so con-
spicuous, especially nowadays. And if you don't like the idea of
London, why not try Norwich or Colchester or Ipswich? But I
shouldn't stay on here." She asked me why. "Why?" I said – I
was a bit vexed with her pretending as much as all that, she must
have known – "Because somebody has started a lot of nasty talk.
They've found out that you lived abroad a long time and that
when you had to leave – Central Europe, you went to France.
They say you only came home when you were forced to, and
they're suspicious. Considering everything, you can't blame them,
can you?" "No," she said, "it's one of the horrible games they're
allowed to play to take their minds off the real horror." That's the
sort of thing she used to come out with. I told her straight, "I'm
sorry, but it's no use thinking you can ignore public opinion,
because you can't." "Do you wish me to leave at once?" she said,
"or can I have a few days to pack?" Her face had gone so thin.
My dear, it's dreadful to see somebody's face go thin while you're
watching. Of course, I assured her she could have all the time
she wanted to pack. If it hadn't been for Ricky I'd never have
asked her to go, in spite of that hound Fluting.'

'Oh Lord,' said Mrs Trant, 'was Fluting mixed up in it?'

'Was he? But it was her own fault. She got people against her.
She behaved so unwisely. That quarrel with Fluting need never
have happened. You see, my dear, he was dining here and he

said some of the Waafs up at the Station smelt. And he was sarcastic about their laundry allowance. "Pah!" he said. Just like
that – "Pah!" *Most* uncalled for, I thought, especially from a man
in his position. However, what can you do? Smile and change the
subject – that's all you can do. But she flew at him. She said,
"Sir, they smell; you stink." He couldn't believe his ears. "I *beg*
your pardon?" – you know that voice of his. She said "Inverted
commas". He gave her *such* a look. I thought "You've made an
enemy, my girl".'

'I call that very tactless – and badly behaved too.'

'Yes, but tactless and badly behaved on both sides, you must
admit. I told her "It's better not to answer them. Believe me, it's
a mistake." But she thought she knew better. It was one silly
thing like that after another, making enemies all over the place.
. . . And she brooded, she worried,' said Mrs Hudson. 'She worried so dreadfully about the war.'

'Who doesn't?'

'Yes, but this was different. You'd have thought she was per-
sonally responsible for the whole thing. She had all sorts of crack
ideas about why it started and what it meant.'

'Trying to empty the sea with a tin cup,' Mrs Trant said sadly.

'Yes, just like that. "It's too complicated," I said to her one day
when she was holding forth, "for you to talk about the why and
the wherefore." But she had these cracky ideas, or they'd been
put into her head, and she wanted to try to prove them. That's
why she started this book. There was no harm in it: I'm sure
there was no real harm in it.'

'This is the first I've heard about a book,' said Mrs. Trant.
'What book?'

Mrs Hudson sighed. 'It's so difficult to explain. . . . You
remember all those letters she used to write, trying to find out
what happened to her friends? Through the Red Cross and Cook's
and via Lisbon, and goodness knows what?'

'After all, it was very natural.'

'Oh yes. But suddenly she stopped. She never had any news.
I used to wonder how she could go on, week after week and month

after month, poor Laura. But it was curious how *suddenly* she
gave up hope. It was then that she changed. She got this odd
expression and she got very silent. And when Ricky tried to laugh
her out of it she wouldn't answer him. One day when he made a
joke about the Gestapo getting her sweetheart she went so white
I thought she'd faint. Then she took to staying in her room for
hours on end and he didn't like it. "The old girl's got no sense of
humour at all, has she?" he said. "And she's not very sociable.
What on earth does she do with herself?" "She's probably reading," I said. Because she used to take in lots of papers – dailies
and weeklies and so on – and she *hung* about the bookshops and
the library, and twice she sent up to London for books. "She was
always the brainy one of her family." "Brainy?" he said. "That's
one word for it." I used to get so annoyed with him. After all, she
paid for the room and board and the gas meter's a shilling in the
slot. I didn't see that it was anybody's business if she wanted to
stay up there. "If you dislike her so much, it's all to the good, isn't
it?" I said. But that was the funny thing – he disliked her, but he
couldn't let her alone. "Why doesn't she do this, and why doesn't
she do that?" And I'd tell him "Give her time, Ricky. She's more
unhappy than she lets on. After all, she'd made a life for herself
and it wasn't her fault it went to pieces. Give her a chance." But
he'd got his knife into her. "Why should she plant herself on us?
Are you the only cousin she's got? And if she's seen fit to plant
herself on us, why can't she behave like other people?" I told him
she hadn't planted herself on us – I invited her. But I thought I'd
better drop a hint that was the way he felt. And there she was,
my dear, surrounded by a lot of papers, cutting paragraphs out
and pasting them into an exercise-book. I asked what she was
doing and if I could have a look. "Oh, I don't think it will interest
you," she said. Of course, that was the thing that, when the row
came, they had most against her. Here it is – the police brought
it back. Ricky and I must destroy it, but I wanted to show it to
you first.'

Mrs Trant thought 'First those horrible anonymous letters,
now a ridiculous exercise-book!' She said, 'I don't understand all
this.'

'It's what I told you – headlines and articles and advertise-ments and reports of cases in court and jokes. There are a lot of jokes. Look.'

The exercise-book began with what seemed to be a collection of newspaper cuttings, but the last pages were in Laura's hand-writing, clear enough at first, gradually becoming more erratic, the lines slanting upwards, downwards, the letters too large or too small.

'It was only to pass the time away,' Mrs Hudson said. 'There was no harm in it.'

'No, I suppose not.'

Mrs Trant turned to the handwriting at the end.

She said, 'The top part of this page has been torn out. Who did that?'

'I don't know. The police, perhaps. It seems they had a good laugh when they read it. That must have been one of the funniest bits.'

Mrs Trant said 'A forlorn hope? What forlorn hope?'

'. . . a forlorn hope. First impressions – and second?

An unforgiving sky. A mechanical quality about everything and everybody which I found frightening. When I bought a ticket for the Tube, got on to a bus, went into a shop, I felt like a cog in a machine in contact with others, not like one human being associating with other human beings. The feeling that I had been drawn into a mechanism which intended to destroy me became an obsession.

I was convinced that coming back to England was the worst thing I could have done, that almost anything else would have been preferable. I was sure that some evil fate was in store for me and longed violently to escape. But I was as powerless as a useless, worn-out or badly-fitting cog. I told myself that if I left London I should get rid of this obsession – it was much more horrible than it sounds – so I wrote to the only person whose address I still had, my cousin Marion Hudson, hoping that she would be able to tell me of some place in the country where I could stay for a while. She answered offering me a room in her house. This was at the end of what they called the "phoney war" . . .'

'But she seems to be writing to somebody,' said Mrs Trant. 'Who?'

'I've no idea. She didn't tell me much about herself.' Mrs

Hudson added, 'I was pleased to have her. She paid well and she was good about helping me in the house, too. Yes, I was quite pleased to have her – at first.'

'. . . the "phoney war", which was not to last much longer. After I realized I was not going to get answers to my letters the nightmare finally settled on me. I was too miserable to bear the comments on what had happened in Europe – they were like slaps in the face.

I could not stop myself from answering back, saying that there was another side to the eternal question of who let down who, and when. This always ended in a quarrel, if you can call trying to knock a wall down by throwing yourself against it, a quarrel. I knew I was being unwise, so I tried to protect myself by silence, by avoiding everybody as much as possible. I read a great deal, took long walks, did all the things you do when you are shamming dead.

You know how you can be haunted by words, phrases, whole conversations sometimes? Well, I began to be haunted by those endless, futile arguments we used to have when we all knew the worse was coming to the worst. The world dominated by Nordics, German version – what a catastrophe. But if it were dominated by Anglo-Saxons, wouldn't that be a catastrophe too? Then, of course, England and the English. Here everybody, especially Blanca, would become acrimonious. "Their extraordinary attitude to women." "They're all mad." "That's why." And so on. Blanca's voice, her face, the things she used to say haunted me. When I had finished a book I would imagine her sharp criticisms. "What do you think of that? Isn't it unbelievable? What did I tell you? Who was right?" All these things I could hear her saying.

And I began to feel that she wasn't so far wrong. There is something strange about the attitude to women as women. Not the dislike (or fear). That isn't strange of course. But it's all so completely taken for granted, and surely that is strange. It has settled down and become an atmosphere, or, if you like, a climate, and no one questions it, least of all the women themselves. There is *no* opposition. The effects are criticized, for some of the effects are hardly advertisements for the system, the cause is seldom mentioned, and then very gingerly. The few mild ambiguous protests usually come from men. Most of the women seem to be carefully trained to revenge any unhappiness they feel on each other, or on children – or on any individual man who happens to be at a disadvantage. In dealing with men as a whole, a streak of subservience, of servility, usually appears, something cold, calculating, lacking in imagination.

But no one can go against the spirit of a country with impunity, and propaganda from the cradle to the grave can do a lot.

I amused myself by making a collection of this propaganda, sometimes it is obvious, sometimes sly and oblique, but it's constant, it goes
on all the time. "For Blanca." This is one way they do it, not the most
subtle or powerful way of course.

Titles of books to be written ten years hence, or twenty, or forty, or a
hundred: *Woman an Obstacle to the Insect Civilization? The Standard-
ization of Woman, The Mechanization of Woman, Misogyny* – well, call
misogyny – *Misogyny and British Humour* will write itself. (But why
pick on England, Blanca? It's no worse than some of the others.) *Misogyny and War, The Misery of Woman and the Evil in Men or the Great
Revenge that Makes all other Revenges Look Silly*. My titles go all the
way from the sublime to the ridiculous.

I could have made my collection as long as I liked; there is any amount
of material. But why take the trouble? It's only throwing myself against
the wall again. You will never read this, I shall not escape.'

Mrs Trant, who had been frowning at the words *Misogyny
and War*, exclaimed indignantly 'Couldn't she find something
else to occupy her mind – now, of all times?"

'Do you know,' said Mrs Hudson, 'there are moments – don't
laugh – when I see what she meant? All very exaggerated, of
course.'

'Nonsense,' Mrs Trant repeated, examining sketches of narrow, sharp-nosed faces in the margins of the last few pages.

'I am very unpopular in this damned town – they leave me in no
doubt about that. A fantastic story about me has gone the rounds and
they have swallowed every word of it. They will believe anything, except
the truth.

Sometimes people loiter in the street and gape up at this house. The
plane tree outside my window has been lopped and they can look straight
into my room, or I think they can. So I keep the curtains drawn and
usually read and write in a very bad light. I suppose this accounts for
my fits of giddiness.

Why do people so expert in mental torture pretend blandly that it
doesn't exist? Some of their glib explanations and excuses are very familiar.
I often think there are many parallels to be drawn between –'

Here the sentence broke off. Mrs Trant shook her head and
shut the exercise-book. 'What a stifling afternoon!' she said. 'Too
much light, don't you think?'

She glanced at the roses again and decided that their colour was trying. The brilliant, cloudless sky did that. It made them unfamiliar, therefore menacing, therefore, of course, unreal.

'It's all very well to say that nobody liked Laura,' she thought. 'Judy liked her.'

Judy was her youngest daughter and the prettiest. But too moody, too fanciful and self-willed. She had stood up to her father about Laura. It had been amusing at the time, but now she wasn't so sure – a girl ought to play safe, ought to go with the tide, it was a bad sign when a girl liked unpopular people. She imagined Judy growing up to be unhappy and felt weak at the knees, then suddenly angry.

She must have said 'Judy' aloud, because Mrs Hudson remarked 'You worry too much about Judy. She's all right – she's tough.'

'She's *not* tough,' thought Mrs Trant. 'She's the very reverse of tough, you sterile old fool.'

She moved her chair so that she could not see the rose beds and said 'Well, if you told Ricky about these hallucinations, I don't wonder there was a row.'

'I never told him.'

'Well, why was there all this trouble? Did she seem crazy? Did she look crazy?'

'No, not exactly. Only a very strained expression. I don't know why they made such a dead-set at her. Her *gift* for making enemies, I suppose.'

'Fluting?'

'Not only Fluting. She was so careless.'

– Careless! Leaving the wretched book lying about, and that daily woman I had spread a rumour that she was trying to pass information on to the enemy. She got on the wrong side of everybody – everybody –

'You know old Mr Roberts next door – well, she quarrelled with him. You can't imagine why. Because his dog is called Brontë, and he kicks it – well, pretends to kick it. "Here's Emily Brontë or my pet aversion," he says, and then he pretends to kick it. It's only a joke. But Ricky's right; she has no sense of humour. One day they had a shouting match over the fence. "Really, Laura," I told her, "You're making a fool of yourself. What have you got against *him*? He's a dear old man." She gave me such a strange look. "I don't know how you can breathe after a lifetime of this," she said. . . .

'Well, things did go very wrong, and after the anonymous letters came, Ricky said I must get rid of her. "When is she going?" he would say, and I would tell him "One day next week." But the next week came and she didn't go, and the week after that, and she didn't go. . . .'

– I should have insisted on her leaving, I see that now. But somehow I couldn't. And it wasn't the three guineas a week she paid. I said two, but she said it wasn't enough. Three she gave me, and goodness knows it's nice to have a little money in your pocket without asking for it. Mind you, I wouldn't say that Ricky is a mean man, but he likes you to ask; and at my age I oughtn't to have to ask for every shilling I spend, I do think. But it wasn't that. It went right against the grain to turn her out when she was looking so ill. Seven stone ten she weighed when she left. Even the assistant in the chemist's shop looked surprised.

Then the day when I was going to give her another hint, she said 'I've started packing'. And all her things were piled on the floor. Such a lot of junk to travel about the world with – books and photographs and old dresses, scarves and all that, and reels of coloured cotton.

A cork with a face drawn on it, a postcard of the Miraculous Virgin in the church of St Julien-le-Pauvre, a china inkstand patterned with violets, a quill pen never used, a ginger jar, a box full of old letters, a fox fur with the lining gone, silk scarves each with a history – the red, the blue, the brown, the purple – the green box I call my jewel case, a small gold key that fits the case (I'm going to lock my heart and throw away the key), the bracelet bought in Florence because it looked like a stained glass window, the ring he gave me, the old flowered workbox with coloured reels of cotton and silk and my really sharp scissors, the leather ciga-

rette case with a photograph inside it. . . . Last of all, the blue
envelope on which he wrote 'Listen, listen', in red chalk. . . .

'When I told Ricky "She's going, she's packing her things,"
he said "Thank God. That's the best news I've heard for a long
while." But it was the next night that it happened. We were down
in the kitchen. The worst raid we've had – and no Laura. I said
"Do you think she's asleep?" "How could anybody sleep through
this? She'll come when she's ready. I expect the zip in her ruddy
siren suit's got stuck," Ricky said, and I had to laugh. . . . You
know, he really was horrid to her. "What's the old girl want to
clutter up the bathroom for?" he'd say, and I'd say "Well be fair,
Ricky, she must wash, whatever her age is. If she didn't it would
only be another grievance against her. . . . She had some good
clothes when she first came and she used to make the best of
herself. "These refugees!" he'd say, "all dressed up and nowhere
to go." Then she got that she didn't seem to care a damn what
she looked like and he grumbled about that. She aged a lot too.
"Ricky," I said, "if you do your best to get people down you can't
blame them when they look down, can you?" Sometimes I wonder if she wasn't a bit right – if there isn't a very nasty spirit
about.'

'But there always has been,' Mrs Trant said.

'Yes, but it's worse now, much worse. . . . Well, when the lull
came I rushed upstairs. She was smoking and playing the gramophone she'd bought, and as I came in the record stopped and
she started it again. "Laura," I said "*is* this the moment to fool
about with *music*? And your black-out's awful." While I was fix-
ing it I heard the warden banging at the door and shouting that
we were showing lights. "I thought so," she said. "The Universal
Robots have arrived," and something about *R.U.R.* Then she went
to the head of the stairs and called out to the warden "The law?
The law! What about the prophets? Why do you always forget
them?" In the midst of this the All Clear went. Ricky said to me
"That's enough now. She's as mad as a hatter and I won't stand
for it a day longer. She *must* get out." I decided not to go to bed
at all, but to do my shopping early for once, and as soon as I was

in the butcher's I knew it had got round already – I knew it by the way people looked at me. One woman – I couldn't see who – said "That horrible creature ought to be shot." And somebody else said "Yes, and the ones who back her up ought to be shot too; it's a shame. Shooting's too good for them." I didn't give them any satisfaction, I can tell you. I stood there with my head up, as if I hadn't heard a word. But when I got back here the police were in the house. They'd been waiting for a pretext – not a doubt of that. They said it was about the lights, but they had a warrant and they searched her room. They took the book and all her letters. And at lunch-time Fluting telephoned Ricky and said there was so much strong feeling in the town that something must be done to get her away at once. . . . I don't know how I kept so calm. But I look older too, don't you think? Do you wonder? . . . After the police left she went upstairs and locked herself into her room and there she stayed. I knocked and called, but not a sound from her. When Fluting telephoned Ricky wanted to break the door down. I've never seen him in such a state – my dear, green with rage. I said No, we'd get Dr Pratt, he'd know what to do.'

'And did Dr Pratt say she was insane? What a terrible thing!'

'No, he didn't, not exactly. She opened the door to him at once and when he came downstairs Ricky talked about getting her certified. "I'll do nothing of the sort," Pratt said. "There's too much of that going on and I don't like it." '

'Pratt's an old-fashioned man, isn't he?'

'Yes, and obstinate as the devil. Try to rush him and he'll go bang the other way. And I got a strong impression that somebody else has been on at him – Fluting, probably. "She's been treated badly," he said, "from all I can hear." "Well," Ricky said, "why can't she go somewhere where she'll be treated better? I don't want her here." Pratt said he knew that the police weren't going to press any charge. "They hadn't any charge to press," I said, "except the light – and goodness knows it was the *merest glimmer*." And he smiled at me. But he told us it was advisable for Laura to leave the town. Wasn't there any friend she could go and stay with, because it would be better for her not to be alone?

We said we didn't think there was – I remembered what you told me about Tom – and we all went up to her room. Pratt asked her if she was willing to go to a sanatorium for a rest and she said "Why not?" Ricky shouted at her "You get off to your sanatorium pronto. You ought to have been there long ago." "You're being inhuman," Pratt said. Ricky said "Well, will the bloody old fool keep quiet?" Pratt told him he'd guarantee that.'

'Inhuman,' said Mrs Trant. 'That's the word that keeps coming into my head all the time now – inhuman, inhuman.'

Her sister went on 'And she was perfectly all right until the last moment. The taxi was waiting and she didn't come down, so I thought we'd better go and fetch her. "Come along, old girl," Ricky said. "It's moving day." He put his hand on her arm and gave her a tug. That was a mistake – he shouldn't have done that. It was when he touched her that she started to scream at the top of her voice. And swear – oh my dear, it was awful. He got nasty, too. He dragged her along and she clung to the banisters and shrieked and cursed. He hit her, and kicked her, and she kept on cursing – oh, I've *never* heard such curses. And I wanted to say "Don't you dare behave like that, either of you," but instead I found I was laughing. And when I looked at his face and her face and heard myself laughing I thought "Something has gone terribly wrong. I believe we're all possessed by the Devil. . . ." As soon as we got into the garden Ricky let go of her, a bit ashamed of himself, I will say. She stood quietly, looking around, and then – d'you know what? – she started talking about the roses and in quite a natural voice "How exquisite they are!" "Aren't they?" I said, though I was shaking all over. "They weren't here," she said, "last time I went for a walk." I said "They come out so quickly, so unexpectedly. Have one for your buttonhole." "No, let them live," she said. "One forgets the roses – always a mistake." She stood there staring at them as if she had never seen roses before and talking away – something about how they couldn't do it, that it wouldn't happen. "Not while there are roses," she said two or three times. Quite crazy, you see, poor Laura, whatever

Pratt's opinion was. "The taxi's waiting, dear," I said, and she got in without any fuss at all.'

'Is this the place?' Mrs Trant said.

There was a photograph on the cover of a prospectus showing a large, ugly house with small windows, those on the top two floors barred. The grounds were as forbidding as the house and surrounded by a high wall.

'I don't like this place.'

'What was I to do, my dear? The sanatorium Pratt suggested was far too expensive. She's got hardly any money left, you know. I had no idea how little she had. What will happen when it's all gone I daren't think. Then Ricky got on to this place near Newcastle. I showed her the prospectus. I asked her if she minded going and she said "No". "You do realize you need a rest, don't you?" I said. "Yes," she said, "I realize that." She can come away if she wants to.'

'Can she, do you think?'

'Well, I suppose she can. I must say the doctor there doesn't seem – I know I ought to go and see her, but I dread it so. I keep on putting it off. Of course, there's a golf links there. Not much of a garden, but a golf links. They can play golf as soon as they're getting better.'

'But does she play golf?' said Mrs Trant.

'Let's hope,' said Mrs Hudson, 'let's hope. . . .'

Temps Perdi

ROLVENDEN' is a square, red-brick house, and it stands with two others on the farthest outskirts of a good-sized village on the east coast. It belongs to one of the masters of a small public school which has moved to Gloucestershire for safety's sake. There is nothing in the house that you can say is ugly; on the other hand there is nothing that you can say is beautiful, impulsive, impetuous or generous. All is sparse, subdued, quiet and negative, or so you would think – a lawn, a large vegetable garden, an empty garage and, when I first came, a few last sad flowers. Outside the front door a gravel path, once bordered with lavender, leads to a green gate.

The two other houses have been taken over by the Army. The one opposite has large grounds and I never hear a sound from it. But from the one on the side there is often the clatter of men washing up ill-temperedly. How they chuck the things about! This is the time of smash and grab. Some poor devil – or rich devil or stupid devil – had tried hard with that house. There are four bathrooms – pink, black, green and blue. But there is venom in the way those men wash up, and there won't be much left of the pink, black, green and blue bathrooms when the military have got out.

But why be glad? Above all, why be sad? Death brings its own anaesthetic, or so they say. . . .

Behind the garden wall there is land and a row of cottages. Never a sound from them either. At first I thought there wasn't a living soul there, but I learnt better later.

In justice to 'Rolvenden' I must say that it has changed a great deal since I have lived in it, and in fairness to myself I must add that I knew at once that we shouldn't get on and argued that I did not want to live there alone – especially in October, November, December and January. But there are times when one is helpless. However, only the helpless know this – and why preach to the converted?

A few days ago, or a week ago – I have forgotten – it began to snow. Since then I have been quite happy. Yes, since the snow started falling I have been much happier, though I don't trouble to look at it. Why look at it when I remember so well the first time I saw it? It was better then – it was a marvel, the only thing in England that hadn't disappointed me. (Remembering when I used to have to touch and taste it every time it fell. . . .)

Now, on my way to the garage in the morning to bring in coal, I see the black trunks of the trees in the garden and the thin, pointing branches, then hurry in to light the fire and make my bacon sandwich and cup of coffee essence. After that I can lie for a long time watching the neutral sitting-room and the rows of extraordinary books without being angry or afraid or hoping. Now I am almost as wary of books as I am of people. They also are capable of hurting you, pushing you into the limbo of the forgotten. They can tell lies – and vulgar, trivial lies – and when there are so many all saying the same thing they can shout you down and make you doubt, not only your memory, but your senses. However, I have discovered one or two of the opposition. Listen: '. . . to conduct the transposition of the souls of the dead to the White Island, in the manner just described. The White Island is occasionally also called Brea, or Britannia. Does this perhaps refer to White Albion, to the chalky cliffs of the English coast? It would be a very humorous idea if England was designated as the land of the dead . . . as hell. In such a form, in truth, England has appeared to many a stranger.' (To many a stranger . . .)

Also I have discovered how to keep warm. You drape a blanket over the door, which stops the draught from the keyhole and the cracks, and a bolster finishes it off. And now I know how to pile the cushions so that I can sit on the floor in front of the fire without slipping backwards. The solid, uncomfortable chairs help. I am learning how to make use of you, my enemy.

The piano is out of tune. It gives a cracked, shattered and ghostly sound, it complains like a hurt animal when I play 'Mama, I want to make rhythm, I want to make music' and 'Time on my hands', then backwards to '*Si j'avais su – évidemment*', backwards again to the waltz of Nina Rodriguez, never forgotten, heard so long ago.

Said to be twelve, Nina was probably sixteen or seventeen. She was a performer in a Havana circus which was touring the smaller Caribbean islands. It was the first theatrical performance I had ever seen. The circus tent was as huge as a cathedral to me, and the trapeze impossibly high and frail. It was lighted by glaring acetylene lamps.

The Rodriguez family were the stars. Mr Rodriguez, burly and sinister, always wore light-blue tights; Madame Rodriguez, pale, sad and mournful under her make-up, wore pink or red, and lovely Nina – the Only Girl Who Works Without a Net – wore black. Black tights to match her black eyes. And her golden curls were hanging down her back, too. We craned our necks to watch her, a black and gold butterfly caught in a web, weaving in and out of the web, miraculously escaping, miraculously coming to earth again, giving the two little stylized hops, smiling, kissing her hands to us.

Pale Madame Rodriguez worked on a higher trapeze. The net was brought in with much ceremony and there was a big roll of drums for the dangerous bit, but it wasn't the same thing and I don't remember a note of her waltz.

I was in the kitchen making a bacon sandwich when the coal arrived. It had been worrying me – there was so little left in the garage and all the coal in the bin outside the kitchen had disappeared. The people from the cottages in the lane took most of it – at first surreptitiously when I was out; after they had sized me up, openly.

The clatter of coal on zinc. Then a man's voice said, 'That's the bathroom.'

'Well what about it? Why are you looking at it? Is there a woman in the ditch?' said a second voice.

'Why d'you think I'd look at her if there was?' the first voice said, very offended. 'Why should you think I'd look at a blank, blank cow in a blank, blank, blank ditch?'

I walked out of the kitchen and scowled at them. These people are altogether too much. . . . They jeered back at me.

'You shouldn't have put the coal in that bin,' I said in an old shrew's voice. 'You should have asked me. You should have put it in the garage. Every lump of it will get stolen there. It was full when I came and it's all gone now because there are a lot of thieves round here, and mean thieves too. There are meaner thieves here than anywhere I've ever been in my life.'

'A-ah?' said one of them.

'It ought to have a padlock on it,' the second one said, helpfully. 'What can you expect if it hasn't got a padlock on it?'

They both wear the local mask – beige in colour as usual.

'Go to hell,' I said.

The first man answered gently. 'Yes, it's very cold today, isn't it, Miss?'

The second one said, 'Very cold weather. Madam,' he said, winking at the first one.

They went off and I started after them. They must be frozen. Shall I call to them and ask them in to have some coffee essence? They might warm the place.

But before they got to the garden gate – 'Rolvenden' is painted on it – I saw that they were shaking with laughter. Silent, smothered laughter – never, even with them, a good hearty shout or curse, just this silent, sly, shy laughter. I can imagine what they would have said about me if I had asked them indoors.

That's an exaggeration. They don't think or say anything that I would imagine they would think or say. Speak for yourself and no falsities. There are enough falsities; enough harm has been done.

For all that was left of the afternoon I carried scuttles of coal from the bin outside the kitchen to the garage, which can be locked, and the house watched me haughtily, seeing me as I really am. And once or twice I looked back at it and thought that maybe I too saw it as it really was. But it will certainly defeat me, for it has one great quality – it is very cunning. It knows how to hide its hate under a hypocrite's mask – again a beige mask, of course – for all here is beige that can be beige, paint, carpets, curtains, upholstery, bedspreads. Everything wears this neutral mask – the village, the people, the sky, even the trees have not escaped.

But before I had half-emptied the bin I felt as tired as if I had walked fifty miles – tired and in utter despair. This bath will always be a ditch to me now and a dirty ditch at that. I was too tired to eat but went up to bed with a beer-bottle filled with hot water to keep me warm.

All the beds are cold, narrow and hard. There are three bedrooms. Photographs of Greek temples – I suppose they are temples, pillars anyway – decorate the wall of this one. There is a cheap dressing-table with a glass that won't stay put, a wardrobe to match the dressing-table and a straightbacked chair. Here too I have put bolsters along the window-sills, because I remember how well they kept out the cold in Vienna. Slowly I grow calmer, and then quite calm. I know that the second stage of loneliness is over and the bad moment is past.

Looking at the bolsters and remembering the piles of yellow-white snow and that statue of the Holy Ghost. 'Clouds in stone,' said André. 'Very German! Like the insides of a turkey.' Another time he said 'The legs are the most noble, beautiful, harmonious and interesting part of the human body.' I said No, I didn't agree. We argued sitting at a table in the *Parisien* with bottles of German champagne before us. But it was not chic to drink it. Now and again you foamed up your glass with one of those wooden instruments they had and then pretended to sip. I can see us sitting there and I can see my astrakhan coat and the dress I was wearing, but it is not myself inside it. Everything is sharp, bright, clear-cut – a little smaller than life, perhaps, and the voices com-

ing from some way off, but very clear. It is 'Rolvenden' that is
behind me in the mist.

In the bedroom of the flat in the Razumoffskygasse there were
low coffee tables, Bohemian glass, a big picture of Franz Josef
and smaller pictures on either side of General and Madame von
Marken. Pierre came in and said 'Bravo' when he saw me in my
new black dress. There was a smell of lilac when you got out into
the street, of lilac, of drains and of the past. Yes, that's what Vienna
smelt of then. . . .

2. *The Sword Dance and the Love Dance*

Every fortnight the officers of the Japanese Commission
entertained their following at Sacher's Hotel. The Japanese were
very dependent on their following, for not one of them could speak
all three of the necessary languages – French, English, German.
There were perpetual arguments over the exact translation of
documents. They were afraid of not being as tactful as the rep-
resentatives of an Asiatic power ought to be, or of voting with the
minority instead of the majority – that would have been the end
of them in Tokyo. So Colonel Hato had his secretary and confidential adviser – that was André – and Lieutenant-Colonel Matsu
had his – that was Pierre. Then there were four other officers (at
first – the number increased by leaps and bounds later on), a
naval attaché, the typists, who had been carefully chosen by Matsu
in Paris and were all very easy on the eye though by no means all
of them were efficient according to Pierre, a Hungarian interpreter, and various other hangers-on.

At the end of the long, elaborate meal some of the guests would
leave and the rest of us would go into Matsu's sitting-room next
door – high, silk-curtained windows, gilt furniture, shining mirrors. Then bottles of Tokay and kümmel appeared and the Japanese mask dropped. Then photographs would be produced and
handed round.

'This is Madame Yoshi.'

'How pretty she is!'

'She's wearing European clothes.'

'Oh, doesn't she look smiling and happy?'

'Of course she is smiling,' Captain Yoshi said – rather grimly, I thought – 'Madame Yoshi is a most fortunate woman. Madame Yoshi *knows* that she is a most fortunate woman.'

Matsu's photographs were of his little son and of his three daughters, whose names meant Early Rising, Order and Morning Sun. He had bought them each a typewriter as a present. He never told us the son's name, or what present was destined for him. Too sacred?

Captain Oyazu had no photographs, but in next to no time he could transform the evening paper into a frog which looked as if it might start hopping at any moment, and he smiled in a pleased, childlike way when you admired it.

On this particular evening Colonel Hato and Oyazu left after the first glass of Tokay, and as soon as they had gone Yoshi began to dance.

Yoshi was the tallest, handsomest and best-dressed of the Japanese officers and he spoke French and German better than any of the others. First he danced the sword dance, using umbrellas instead of swords, and then what I suppose was a love dance, for, turning his feet out at right angles and holding an umbrella upright, he shuffled past us, looking at the women of the party very slanting-eyed and mocking.

But Simone, who was the prettiest of the typists and only eighteen years of age, answered that challenge at once. She danced opposite him with her hands on her hips, laughing, imitating exactly every step he made, and after a bit of this the strain and defiance went out of his face. He pulled her to him and began a clumsy foxtrot. André played 'Dardanella' for them on the piano.

When 'Dardanella' was finished Matsu announced, 'I will now play you a Japanese song.'

He played it with one finger, striking the notes carefully and gently, with a sad, absorbed, intent expression.

He said – he was the one who spoke English – 'That is a sleep song.'

Matsu had spent a fortnight in London and for a whole day of it he had been lost in the Inner Circle. 'When I came out it was very dark and cold. I grew frightened and sad.' (He was in London in November.)

After the lullaby he went off into a long, monotonous succession of notes, as if he were trying to make a pattern of the keys, black and white. There was music in him somewhere – he touched the piano so gently.

Yoshi and Simone were sitting at a table at the far end of the room. The others were gossiping about Hato. There was always a new story going about him. He was the one who loathed white people and said so, maintaining that contact with them would bring nothing but misfortune to Japan. He was the one who, safe in his bedroom, André said, would at once take off his European clothes, saying that they made him feel unclean, and put on a kimono and slippers with hisses of relief.

He was a small, thin man, much older than any of the others. Really very old, we thought, quite gaga. He had only one eye – he had lost the other in the Russo-Japanese War, and it had not been dolled up, either. On social occasions he would sit bolt upright, silent, staring into the distance.

'What can he be thinking of, André?'

André said, 'The poor devil is supposed to speak French. And he can't. I should say that gives him enough to think about.'

But he, too, liked music. His favourite song was 'Marjolaine'. 'Encore "Marjolaine",' he would shout. (*Si gracile, si fragile. . . .*) 'Encore, encore "Marjolaine".'

When they had finished with Hato, Odette, another of the typists, began to tell us what she thought about Viennese clothes. She said that they were pretty but they had no real chic. "When I went back to Paris on leave last month Maman told me, "You look like a little provincial". Maman is thirty-nine but one would say twenty-five. She cried like a Magdalene when I left –'

André interrupted, 'My God, what's happening over there?'

Yoshi was sprawled on the floor, the table and the bottle of wine were upset. He got up and brushed his clothes down, though

without smiling or looking at us. André rushed forward and picked
up the table and the bottle. Simone said, 'Oh, do excuse me. I'm
such a clumsy girl. I've always been like that. You've no idea –
the trouble I get into because –'

Soon afterwards we said good night and were out in the lilac-
scented street. After we got round the first corner Simone began
to laugh. She had held it in like a good one, but now it had to
come out.

'How did it happen, Simone?' André said at last.

Simone said, 'I don't know how it happened. He was practising kissing the hand and I'd had enough of it and tried to pull
away. He held on and crashed into the table, and down he went.
I expect he'd had too much to drink. Oh, his face when he fell!
Aren't they funny? And those dances with the umbrellas!'

Off she went again.

Pierre said, 'I hope he won't bear you any malice Simone. I'd
hate to be somebody the Japanese bore malice against.'

'Not he,' Simone said. 'He won't bear any malice against me,
poor boy.'

None of us thought of taking cabs home that night. Perhaps
there was a moon. Perhaps the streets were lovelier or more
deserted than usual. Then there was that smell of lilac and of the
past. Vienna still smelt very strongly of the past. We walked along,
keeping rather close together.

'Well,' I said, 'He looked as if he were telling you all his secrets.'

'He was,' Simone said, 'he was. Do you know what he was
saying? He was saying how much he admires the Germans. He
said they'll soon have the best army in Europe, and that they'll
dominate it in a few years.'

'No bouquet for the French?' André asked, laughing. 'And
think how I sweat, translating their idiotic ideas into diplomatic
language!'

Simone answered seriously, 'But he did say something about
the French. He said the French love women too much. He said
only the Germans know how to treat women. The Germans and
the English think the same way about women, he said, but the

French think differently. He said the English and the French together won't last another year, and that they are splitting up already.'

Pierre said, 'Oh, he's found that out, has he? Not much they don't find out.'

We walked on.

Odette said in a sullen voice, 'I'm not Anglophile, me. And why do all their songs sound like hymns?'

'I like them,' Simone said happily. 'Oh, I like some of those boys. Their clothes are so chic and they can be very nice. I like them. I like everything – everybody.' She spread her arms wide open.

'And then you wake up,' I thought.

'What beautiful enthusiasm, Simone!' said André.

Odette said, 'It's true that the English have droll ideas. The other day I was talking to Captain – You know the one, the one with the long nose and the monocle. And he said, 'I've just seen an amazingly pretty woman –" Then he stopped and went as red as fire. So out of spite I pretended I hadn't heard; I made him repeat it. "I've just seen rather an attractive *person*," he said, "in the Kärntnerstrasse." Why should he have to blush like that, when he says the word woman? Is it a dirty word in English?'

'Because he's an idiot,' Pierre said, 'and so are you a little idiot, Odette.'

'All the same,' André said, 'there's something in it. *"Ma femme,"* you say; *"Meine Frau,"* you say. But what would happen if you said "May I introduce my woman, Mrs Colonel?" '

'It depends on Mrs Colonel, but I shouldn't risk it,' I said.

'I used to mix up the words myself when I first learnt English,' André remarked. 'That's how I know the difference is very important. Also there's lady and girl. Very complicated.'

Of course we all knew that there were a lot of sly jokes, misunderstandings, cartoons and so on, about the British in Vienna. It was not altogether their fault – they were severely handicapped. Love affairs with Viennese girls were very much discouraged, so when they occurred they were carried on cautiously

and often ended brutally. On the other hand, 'great friendships'
with boys were winked at – even with the boys who at one café
were to be found heavily made up and dressed in women's evening clothes. But everybody said that you ought to see them in
Berlin; Vienna wasn't their home town.

André said, 'I bet if they knew in Tokyo what Yoshi told Simone
there'd be trouble. They're not orthodox, these confidences.'

'No need for Tokyo,' Pierre said. 'You've only got to tell Hato.
Then Yoshi would have to commit hara-kiri. Hato detests him.'

'Wouldn't that be a feather in Hato's cap?' I said.

And we all knew that not one of us would stick that feather
in Hato's cap. He hated us, so we hated him – it's easy.

We had nearly reached the hotel where the girls were staying.

'Did he really say that, Simone,' asked André. 'About the
English and the French splitting up, and the next war?'

'He did, I assure you,' said Simone, 'he did. He said he gave
it ten to fifteen years, and after that Germany would probably
dominate Europe. He said it would happen because the English
and the French don't trust each other and can't stick together
and that's the only thing that might stop it.'

'Ten to fifteen years is a long time,' Odette said.

'And Japan?' said Pierre. 'And beautiful Nippon? Banzai Nippon!'

'He didn't say anything about Japan,' said Simone, 'now I come
to think of it. Not a word about Nippon.'

We said good night to the girls. We didn't talk for a bit. Then
André said. 'The Japanese! They are not to be taken seriously.
What can they possibly know about it?'

Yes, I can remember all my dresses, except the one on the
chair beside me, the one I wore when I was walking on the cliffs
yesterday. Yesterday – when was yesterday? . . .

I had a striped taffeta dress, with velvet flowers tucked into
the tight waistband. (And the waistband was round the waist,
whatever the English fashion was then.) I had a white satin dress,
very slick and smooth, the prettiest of the lot but the cheapest.

Round the throat there were coloured stones imitating a neck-lace. I had a black satin dress with three flounces bordered with green, hand-sewn. With this dress I had two sashes to wear, each as elaborate as a Japanese *obi*. One was black, boned so that it made my waist look very small; the other was green, to match the borders of the flounces. I had a white muslin dress that washed like a rag, and a blue one too, made just the same. Those were my favourites. Washed and ironed like rags, they did, and always came up as fresh as daisies. I had a dirndl, and a check dress. I had a blue serge dress, the bodice fitting closely but the skirt wide and full. Its sleeves were loose, embroidered in gay colours and finished with a tassel. I had a classic English *tailleur*, but I always hated that. I had a yellow and blue dress to wear when I wanted to lie down, when I was tired. It was long and loose, the neck and sleeves bordered with blue. It was like cornfields and the sky, and looking at it made you feel happy, made you feel free. And thinking of it I am free again, knowing that nobody can stop me thinking, thinking of my dresses, or mirrors and pic-tures, of stones and clouds and mountains and the days that wait for you round the corner to be lived again. Riding round and round the Inner Circle, but unlike Matsu I ride knowing that it will be dark and cold when I come out, that it will be November, and that I shall be a savage person – a real Carib.

But Caribs live under different skies, by a different sea. 'They run and hide when they see anybody,' Nicholas said. Perhaps I shall do that too.

3. *Carib Quarter*

Nicholas was the overseer of Temps Perdi, an estate near the Carib Quarter. Temps Perdi is Creole patois and does not mean, poetically, lost or forgotten time, but, matter-of-factly, wasted time, lost labour. There are places which are supposed to be hostile to human beings and to know how to defend themselves. When I was a child it used to be said that this island was one of them. You are getting alone fine and then a hurricane comes, or a dis-ease of the crops that nobody can cure, and there you are – more

West Indian ruins and labour lost. It has been going on for more than three hundred years – yes, it's more than three hundred years ago that somebody carved 'Temps Perdi' on a tree near by, they say.

The estate house had been empty for so long that a centipede fell out of a book when I opened it. Everything had run wild, but there was still hibiscus growing by the stone garden walls and butterflies made love over the thorny bougainvilea. Every morning Myra, Nicholas's daughter, put little earthenware bowls of fresh flowers along the low partition which separated the veranda from the sitting-room. From the veranda we could see Guadeloupe, the Saints and Marie Galante; sun on dark trees. . . .

But the white-cedars at the end of the garden – the lowest about eighty feet high – had dropped their leaves and were covered with flowers, white flowers very faintly tinged with pink, so light and fragile that they fell with the first high wind and were blown away as soon as they fell. There used to be a famous Creole song about the white-cedar flowers but I can't remember it. 'Here today and gone tomorrow' – something like that, it must be.

'There is nothing to see in the Carib Quarter,' Nicholas insisted. He had a handsome Negro face, a big chest, a deep, booming voice.

'These people,' he said, 'don't even live near together. Their houses are each far away from the other, and all hidden in the bush. There is nothing to see in Salybia. Besides, the new road only goes as far as the river. After that you'll have to ride. It will take a couple of hours or so.'

'But can't it be arranged? Can't we get the horses?'

'Oh yes, it can be arranged,' Nicholas said disapprovingly.

But I wasn't so easily put off. All my life I had been curious about these people because of a book I once read, pictures I once saw.

Whenever the Caribs are talked about, which is not often, the adjective is 'decadent', though nobody knows much about them, one way or the other or ever will now. There are a few hundreds left in the West Indies, or in the world, and they live in the part of this island called Salybia. They had not intermarried much with the Negroes and still have smooth, black hair, small, slanting eyes, high cheekbones, copper-coloured skins. They make baskets, beautifully plaited, light and waterproof, dyed red and brown or black and white. The largest is the island's substitute for a trunk, the smallest would just hold a baby's shoe. Sometimes the baskets are made to fit one inside the other, like Chinese boxes.

Nobody else seemed to want to visit the Carib Quarter, nobody seemed at all anxious to take a long ride in the sun with nothing much to see at the end of it.

'They are supposed to have two languages. The women have a language that the men don't know. So they say.'

'They say so, do they?'

'Well, we'll ask Nicholas. . . . Nicholas, isn't it true that the Carib women have a secret language?'

Nicholas said, grinning, that he thought he had heard something of the sort. Yes, he fancied he had.

Tormented with the fear that I had imagined the closely-printed book, the gaudy illustrations pored over as a child, I produced the special number of *L'Illustration*, 23 November 1935, for the *Tricentenaire des Antilles Françaises* and exhibited '*Homme Caraibe Dessiné d'après natur par le Père Plumier*'. Early eighteenth century, probably. Bow and arrows in his right hand, a club in his left, a huge, muscular body and a strange, small, womanish face. His long, black hair was carefully parted in the middle and hung smoothly to his shoulders. But his slanting eyes, starting from their sockets, looked wild and terrified. He was more the frightened than the frightening savage.

'We had a print very like this – perhaps it was the same one – in the dining-room at home.'

'He isn't very attractive.'

'Everybody used to say that.'

And he always used to look so sad, I thought, when they laughed at him. With his wild, strained eyes and his useless bows and arrows.

'The original West Indian, is he?'

'Oh no, that's a Carib. The original West Indians were killed by the Spaniards or deported to Hispaniola – Haiti. Well, most of the men were. The Spaniards told them they were going to Heaven. So they went. Weren't they suckers? Then the Caribs, the cannibals, came from the mainland of South America and killed off the few men who were left.'

But that book, written by an Englishman in the 1880s, said that some of the women, who had survived both Spaniards and Caribs – people were not so thorough then as they are now – had carried on the old language and traditions, handing them down from mother to daughter. This language was kept a secret from their conquerors, but the writer of the book claimed to have learned it. He said that is was Mongolian in origin, not South American. He said that it definitely established the fact that there was communication between China and what is now known as the New World. But he had a lot of imagination, that man. Wasn't there a chapter about the buried Carib treasure in La Soufrière, St Lucia – one of the mouths of Hell, they say – and another about the snake god, and another about Atlantis? Oh yes, he had a lot of imagination.

The day we went to the Carib Quarter the wind was blowing heavy luminous clouds across the sky, tormenting the thin crooked coconut-palms on the slope of the hill opposite the veranda, so different from the straight, healthy, glossy-green coconuts just round the corner of the road – tame trees, planted in rows to make copra. We arrived punctually at the place where the horses were to wait for us, but it was a long wait before they turned up, so young Charlie, aged sixteen, who was our guide, went on ahead. He was beautifully got up in white shirt, shorts and socks, but hideous, heavy black boots that squeaked with every step he took. There were stepping-stones across the shallowest part of the broad river. On one of these Charlie's horrible boots betrayed him and I thought he had fallen into the water, but he managed to save himself. When he got to the other side it was a relief to see him sit down, take off his boots and socks and hang them round his neck before he walked on.

The horses came at last. They were so thin that every bone showed in their bodies and they had the morose, obstinate expression which is the price of survival in hostile surroundings. Negroes like to be in the movement and hate anything old-fashioned, and horses are now definitely old-fashioned.

However, when we mounted they jerked their necks strongly and clip-clopped without hesitation into the clear, shallow river. I had forgotten the lovely sound of horses' hooves in water, that I hadn't heard for so many damnable years.

Then they heaved and strained us on to a wide, grassy road. There was a flamboyant tree with a few flowers out. Next month, I thought, it will be covered; next month all the flamboyant trees – the flame trees – will be covered, and the immortelles will flower, but I shan't be here to see them. I'll be on my way back to England then, I thought, and felt giddy and sick. There were a lot of iguanas along that road. I shut my eyes and saw one of the illustrations in the book about the Caribs, vivid, complete in ever detail. A brown girl, crowned with flowers, a parrot on her shoulder, welcoming the Spaniards, the long-prophesied gods. Behind her the rest of the population crowded, carrying presents of fruit and flowers, but some of them very scowling and suspicious – and how right they were!

In the midst of this dream, riding through a desolate, arid, lizard-ridden country, different and set apart from the island I knew, I was still sensitive to the opinion of strangers and dreaded hostile criticism. But no, it was approved of, more or less. 'Beautiful, open, park-like country. But what an *extreme* green!'

The road had been gradually rising and, as we came round the shoulder of a hill, smiling Charlie met us, accompanied by a Negro policeman. An official welcome to Salybia? . . . Below us we saw small clearings among the low trees – low for that part of the world – and the bush riddled with narrow paths. But not a human being. ('These people live all separated from each other, and all hidden in the bush. These people hide when they see anybody.')

'That's the king's house,' the policeman announced, and I thought 'So, there's still a king, is there?'

Round another bend in the road we saw below us the big clearing where the police-station stood with five or six other houses, one of them a Catholic church.

In the station the rifles were stacked in a row, bayonets and all. The room was large, almost cool. Everything looked new and clean, and there was a circular set round the palm tree outside.

'We had trouble here,' our policeman told us. 'They burnt the last station and they burnt twenty feet off this one while it was being built.'

'Why?'

'Well, it seems they thought they were going to have a hospital. They had asked the Government for a hospital. A petition, you know. And when they found out that the Government was giving them a police-station and not a hospital, there was trouble.'

'Serious trouble?'

'Pretty serious. They burnt the first one down, and they burnt twenty feet off this one.'

'Yes, but I mean was anybody hurt?'

'Oh no, only two or three Caribs,' he said. 'Two-three Caribs were killed.' It might have been an Englishman talking.

'There is a beautiful Carib girl,' the policeman said, 'in the house over there – the one with the red roof. Everybody goes to see her and photographs her. She and her mother will be vexed if you don't go. Give her a little present, of course. She is very beautiful but she can't walk. It's a pity, that.'

When you went in it was like all their houses. A small room, clean, the walls covered with pictures cut from newspapers and coloured cards of Virgins, saints and angels, Star of the Sea, Refuge of the Distressed, Hope of the Afflicted, Star of the Sea again, Jesus, Mary and Joseph. . . .

The girl appeared in the doorway of the dark little bedroom, posed for a moment dramatically, then dragged herself across the floor into the sun outside to be photographed, managing her useless legs with a desperate, courageous grace; she had white, lovely teeth. There she sat in the sun, brown eyes fixed on us the long brown eyes of the Creole, not the small, black, slanting eyes of the pure Carib. And her hair, which hung to her waist and went through every shade from dark brown to copper and back again, was not a Carib's hair, either. She sat there smiling, and an assortment of brightly-coloured Virgins and saints looked down at her from the walls, smiling too. She had aquiline features, proud features. Her skin in the sun was a lovely colour.

We took a few photographs, then Charlie asked if he might take the rest. We heard his condescending voice: 'Will you turn your side face? Will you please turn your full face? *Don't* smile for this one.' ('These people are quite savage people – quite uncivilized.')

Her mother, who looked like an old Chinese woman, told us that in her youth she had lived in Martinique in service with a French family and then had been taken to Paris.

'I come back here,' she said, 'because I want to see my mother before she die. I loved my mother. Now I must stay because I am old, I am old and who will take me away?'

'She like that since she four,' she said, pointing to her daughter.

'*Hélas!*' she said, gesticulating. She had thin, lovely hands. '*Hélas, hélas!*'

But the girl, sitting in the sun to be photographed, smiled contentedly at us, pushed a strand of hair from her shoulder to her back, smiled again. And all the Virgins and saints on the walls smiled at us too.

The night in Temps Perdi is full of things chirping and fluttering. The fireflies are out – they call them labelles. It is at night, lying caged under a mosquito-net, that you think, 'Now I am home, where the earth is sometimes red and sometimes black. Round about here is ochre – a Carib skin. In some lights like blood, in others just pretty, like a picture postcard coloured by somebody with a child's paintbox and no imagination.'

It is at night that you know old fears, old hopes, that you know unhappiness, turning from side to side under the mosquito-net, like a prisoner in a cell full of small peepholes. Then you think of that plant with thick, fleshy leaves edged with thorns, on which some up-to-the-minute Negro has written over and over again 'Girls muck, girls muck', and other monosyllabic and elementary truths. When I was a child we used to draw hearts pierced with arrows on leaves like that and 'Z loves A'. It all comes to the same thing, probably.

But when you have drunk a good tot of rum nothing dismays you; you know the password and the Open Sesame. You drink a second; then you understand everything – the sun, the flamboyance, the girl crawling (because she could not walk) across the floor to be photographed. And the song about the white-cedar trees. *'Ma belle ka di maman-li –'* (A lot of their songs begin like that – 'My lovely girls said to her mother.') 'Why do the flowers last only a day?' the girl says. 'It's very sad. Why?' The mother says 'One day and a thousand years are the same for the *Bon Dieu.*' I wish I could remember it all but it is useless trying to find out because nobody sings these old songs any more.

It had a sweet sound sometimes, patois. And I can't get the words out of my mind, Temps Perdi.

Before I leave 'Rolvenden' I'll write them up – on a looking glass, perhaps. Somebody might see them who knows about the days that wait round the corner to be lived again and knows that you don't choose them, either. They choose themselves.

Pioneers, Oh, Pioneers

As THE TWO GIRLS were walking up yellow-hot Market Street, Irene nudged her sister and said: 'Look at her!' They were not far from the market, they could still smell the fish.

When Rosalie turned her head the few white women she saw carried parasols. The black women were barefooted, wore gaily striped turbans and highwaisted dresses. It was still the nineteenth century, November 1899.

'There she goes,' said Irene.

And there was Mrs Menzies, riding up to her house on the Morne for a cool weekend.

'Good morning,' Rosalie said, but Mrs Menzies did not answer. She rode past, clip-clop, clip-clop, in her thick, dark riding habit brought from England ten years before, balancing a large dripping parcel wrapped in flannel on her knee.

'It's ice. She wants her drinks cold,' said Rosalie.

'Why can't she have it sent up like everybody else? The black people laugh at her. She ought to be ashamed of herself.'

'I don't see why,' Rosalie said obstinately.

'Oh, you,' Irene jeered. 'You like crazy people. You like Jimmy Longa and you like old maman Menzies. You liked Ramage, nasty beastly horrible Ramage.'

Rosalie said: 'You cried about him yesterday.'

'Yesterday doesn't count. Mother says we were all hysterical yesterday.'

By this time they were nearly home so Rosalie said nothing.

But she put her tongue out as they went up the steps into the long, cool gallery.

Their father, Dr Cox, was sitting in an armchair with a three-legged table by his side.

On the table were his pipe, his tin of tobacco and his glasses. Also *The Times* weekly edition, the *Cornhill Magazine*, the *Lancet* and a West Indian newspaper, the *Dominica Herald and Leeward Islands Gazette*.

He was not to be spoken to, as they saw at once though one was only eleven and the other nine.

'Dead as a door nail,' he muttered as they went past him into the next room so comfortably full of rocking-chairs, a mahogany table, palm leaf fans, a tigerskin rug, family photographs, views of Bettws-y-Coed and a large picture of wounded soldiers in the snow, Napoleon's Retreat from Moscow.

The doctor had not noticed his daughters, for he too was thinking about Mr Ramage. He had liked the man, stuck up for him, laughed off his obvious eccentricities, denied point blank that he was certifiable. All wrong. Ramage, probably a lunatic, was now dead as a door nail. Nothing to be done.

Ramage had first arrived in the island two years before, a handsome man in tropical kit, white suit, red cummerbund, solar topee. After he grew tired of being followed about by an admiring crowd of little Negro boys he stopped wearing the red sash and the solar topee but he clung to his white suits though most of the men wore dark trousers even when the temperature was ninety in the shade.

Miss Lambton, who had been a fellow passenger from Barbados, reported that he was certainly a gentleman and also a king among men when it came to looks. But he was very unsociable. He ignored all invitations to dances, tennis parties and moonlight picnics. He never went to church and was not to be seen at the club. He seemed to like Dr Cox, however, and dined with him one evening. And Rosalie, then aged seven, fell in love.

After dinner, though the children were not supposed to talk

much when guests were there, and were usually not allowed downstairs at all, she edged up to him and said: 'Sing something.' (People who came to dinner often sang afterwards, as she well knew.)

'I can't sing,' said Ramage.

'Yes you can.' Her mother's disapproving expression made her insist the more. 'You can. You can.'

He laughed and hoisted her on to his knee. With her head against his chest she listened while he rumbled gently: 'Baa baa black sheep, have you any wool? Yes sir, yes sir, three bags full.'

Then the gun at the fort fired for nine o'clock and the girls, smug in their stiff white dresses, had to say good night nicely and go upstairs to bed.

After a perfunctory rubber of whist with a dummy, Mrs Cox also departed. Over his whisky and soda Ramage explained that he'd come to the island with the intention of buying an estate. 'Small, and as remote as possible.'

'That won't be difficult here.'

'So I heard,' said Ramage.

'Tried any of the other islands?'

'I went to Barbados first.'

'Little England,' the doctor said. 'Well?'

'I was told that there were several places going along this new Imperial Road you've got here.'

'Won't last,' Dr Cox said. 'Nothing lasts in this island. Nothing will come of it. You'll see.'

Ramage looked puzzled.

'It's all a matter of what you want the place for,' the doctor said without explaining himself. 'Are you after a good interest on your capital or what?'

'Peace,' Ramage said. 'Peace, that's what I'm after.'

'You'll have to pay for that,' the doctor said.

'What's the price?' said Ramage, smiling. He put one leg over the other. His bare ankle was hairy and thin, his hands long and slender for such a big man.

'You'll be very much alone.'

'That will suit me,' Ramage said.

'And if you're far along the road, you'll have to cut the trees down, burn the stumps and start from scratch.'

'Isn't there a half-way house?' Ramage said.

The doctor answered rather vaguely: 'You might be able to get hold of one of the older places.'

He was thinking of young Errington, of young Kellaway, who had both bought estates along the Imperial Road and worked hard. But they had given up after a year or two, sold their land cheap and gone back to England. They could not stand the loneliness and melancholy of the forest.

A fortnight afterwards Miss Lambton told Mrs Cox that Mr Ramage had bought Spanish Castle, the last but one of the older properties. It was beautiful but not prosperous — some said bad luck, others bad management. His nearest neighbour was Mr Eliot, who owned *Malgré Tout*. Now called Twickenham.

For several months after this Ramage disappeared and one afternoon at croquet Mrs Cox asked Miss Lambton if she had any news of him.

'A strange man,' she said, 'very reserved.'

'Not so reserved as all that,' said Miss Lambton. 'He got married several weeks ago. He told me that he didn't want it talked about.'

'No!' said Mrs Cox. 'Who to?'

Then it all came out. Ramage had married a coloured girl who called herself Isla Harrison, though she had no right to the name of Harrison. Her mother was dead and she'd been brought up by her godmother, old Miss Myra, according to local custom. Miss Myra kept a sweet shop in Bay Street and Isla was very well known in the town — too well known.

'He took her to Trinidad,' said Miss Lambton mournfully, 'and when they came back they were married. They went down to Spanish Castle and I've heard nothing about them since.'

'It's not as though she was a nice coloured girl,' everybody said.

So the Ramages were lost to white society. Lost to everyone but Dr Cox. Spanish Castle estate was in a district which he visited every month, and one afternoon as he was driving past he saw Ramage standing near his letter box which was nailed to a tree visible from the road. He waved. Ramage waved back and beckoned.

While they were drinking punch on the veranda, Mrs Ramage came in. She was dressed up to the nines, smelt very strongly of cheap scent and talked loudly in an aggressive voice. No, she certainly wasn't a nice coloured girl.

The doctor tried – too hard perhaps – for the next time he called at Spanish Castle a door banged loudly inside the house and a grinning boy told him that Mr Ramage was out.

'And Mrs Ramage?'

'The mistress is not at home.'

At the end of the path the doctor looked back and saw her at a window peering at him.

He shook his head, but he never went there again, and the Ramage couple sank out of sight, out of mind.

It was Mr Eliot, the owner of Twickenham, who started the trouble. He was out with his wife, he related, looking at some young nutmeg trees near the boundary. They had a boy with them who had lighted a fire and put on water for tea. They looked up and saw Ramage coming out from under the trees. He was burnt a deep brown, his hair fell to his shoulders, his beard to his chest. He was wearing sandals and a leather belt, on one side of which hung a cutlass, on the other a large pouch. Nothing else.

'If,' said Mr Eliot, 'the man had apologized to my wife, if he'd shown the slightest consciousness of the fact that he was stark naked, I would have overlooked the whole thing. God knows one learned to be tolerant in this wretched place. But not a bit of it. He stared hard at her and came out with: "What an uncomfortable dress – and how ugly!" My wife got very red. Then she said: "Mr Ramage, the kettle is just boiling. Will you have some tea?" '

'Good for her,' said the doctor. 'What did he say to that?'

'Well, he seemed rather confused. He bowed from the waist, exactly as if he had clothes on, and explained that he never drank tea. "I have a stupid habit of talking to myself. I beg your pardon," he said, and off he went. We got home and my wife locked herself in the bedroom. When she came out she wouldn't speak to me at first, then she said that he was quite right, I didn't care what she looked like, so now she didn't either. She called me a mean man. A mean man. I won't have it,' said Mr Eliot indignantly. 'He's mad, walking about with a cutlass. He's dangerous.'

'Oh, I don't think so,' said Dr Cox. 'He'd probably left his clothes round the corner and didn't know how to explain. Perhaps we do cover ourselves up too much. The sun can be good for you. The best thing in the world. If you'd seen as I have . . .'

Mr Eliot interrupted at once. He knew that when the doctor started talking about his unorthodox methods he went on for a long time.

'I don't know about all that. But I may as well tell you that I dislike the idea of a naked man with a cutlass wandering about near my place. I dislike it very much indeed. I've got to consider my wife and my daughter. Something ought to be done.'

Eliot told his story to everyone who'd listen and the Ramages became the chief topic of conversation.

'It seems,' Mrs Cox told her husband, 'that he does wear a pair of trousers as a rule and even an old coat when it rains, but several people have watched him lying in a hammock on the veranda naked. You ought to call there and speak to him. They say,' she added, 'that the two of them fight like Kilkenny cats. He's making himself very unpopular.'

So the next time he visited the district Dr Cox stopped near Spanish Castle. As he went up the garden path he noticed how unkempt and deserted the place looked. The grass on the lawn had grown very high and the veranda hadn't been swept for days.

The doctor paused uncertainly, then tapped on the sitting-room door, which was open. 'Hallo,' called Ramage from inside the house, and he appeared, smiling. He was wearing one of his linen suits, clean and pressed, and his hair and beard were trimmed.

'You're looking very well,' the doctor said.

'Oh, yes, I feel splendid. Sit down and I'll get you a drink.'

There seemed to be no one else in the house.

'The servants have all walked out,' Ramage explained when he appeared with the punch.

'Good Lord, have they?'

'Yes, but I think I've found an old woman in the village who'll come up and cook.'

'And how is Mrs Ramage?'

At this moment there was a heavy thud on the side of the house, then another, then another.

'What was that?' asked Dr Cox.

'Somebody throwing stones. They do sometimes.'

'Why, in heaven's name?'

'I don't know. Ask them.'

Then the doctor repeated Eliot's story, but in spite of himself it came out as trivial, even jocular.

'Yes, I was very sorry about that,' Ramage answered casually. 'They startled me as much as I startled them. I wasn't expecting to see anyone. It was a bit of bad luck but it won't happen again.'

'It was bad luck meeting Eliot,' the doctor said.

And that was the end of it. When he got up to go, no advice, no warning had been given.

'You're sure you're all right here?'

'Yes, of course,' said Ramage.

'It's all rubbish,' the doctor told his wife that evening. 'The man's as fit as a fiddle, nothing wrong with him at all.'

'Was Mrs Ramage there?'

'No, thank God. She was out.'

'I heard this morning,' said Mrs Cox, 'that she disappeared. Hasn't been seen for weeks.'

The doctor laughed heartily. 'Why can't they leave those two alone? What rubbish!'

'Well,' said Mrs Cox without smiling, 'it's odd, isn't it?'

'Rubbish,' the doctor said again some days later, for, spurred on by Mr Eliot, people were talking venomously and he could not stop them. Mrs Ramage was not at Spanish Castle, she was not in the town. Where was she?

Old Myra was questioned. She said that she had not seen her god-daughter and had not heard from her 'since long time'. The Inspector of Police had two anonymous letters – the first writer claimed to know 'all what happen at Spanish Castle one night': the other said that witnesses were frightened to come forward and speak against a white man.

The *Gazette* published a fiery article:

'The so-called "Imperial Road" was meant to attract young English-men with capital who would buy and develop properties in the interior. This costly experiment has not been a success, and one of the last of these gentlemen planters has seen himself as the king of the cannibal islands ever since he landed. We have it, on the best authority, that his very eccentric behavior has been the greatest possible annoyance to his neighbour. Now the whole thing has become much more serious. . . .'

It ended: 'Black people bear much; must they also bear beastly murder and nothing be done about it?'

'You don't suppose that I believe all these lies, do you?' Dr Cox told Mr Eliot, and Mr Eliot answered: 'Then I'll make it my business to find out the truth. That man is a menace, as I said from the first, and he should be dealt with.'

'Dear Ramage,' Dr Cox wrote. 'I'm sorry to tell you that stupid and harmful rumours are being spread about your wife and your-self. I need hardly say that no one with a grain of sense takes them seriously, but people here are excitable and very ready to believe mischiefmakers, so I strongly advise you to put a stop to the talk at once and to take legal action if necessary.'

But the doctor got no answer to this letter, for in the morning news reached the town of a riot at Spanish Castle the night before.

A crowd of young men and boys, and a few women, had gone up to Ramage's house to throw stones. It was a bright moonlight night. He had come on to the veranda and stood there facing them. He was dressed in white and looked very tall, they said, like a zombi. He said something that nobody heard, a man had shouted 'white zombi' and thrown a stone which hit him. He went into the house and came out with a shotgun. Then stories differed wildly. He had fired and hit a woman in the front of the crowd. . . . No, he'd hit a little boy at the back. . . . He hadn't fired at all, but had threatened them. It was agreed that in the rush to get away people had been knocked down and hurt, one woman seriously.

It was also rumoured that men and boys from the village planned to burn down Spanish Castle house, if possible with Ramage inside. After this there was no more hesitation. The next day a procession walked up the garden path to the house – the Inspector of Police, three policemen and Dr Cox.

'He must give some explanation of all this,' said the Inspector.

The doors and windows were all open, and they found Ramage and the shotgun, but they got no explanation. He had been dead for some hours.

His funeral was an impressive sight. A good many came out of curiosity, a good many because, though his death was said to be 'an accident', they felt guilty. For behind the coffin walked Mrs Ramage, sent for post-haste by old Myra. She'd been staying with relatives in Guadeloupe. When asked why she had left so secretly – she had taken a fishing boat from the other side of the island – she answered sullenly that she didn't want anyone to know her business, and she knew how people talked. No, she'd heard no rumours about her husband, and the *Gazette* – a paper written in English – was not read in Guadeloupe.

'Eh-eh,' echoed Myra. 'Since when the girl obliged to tell everybody where she go and what she do chapter and verse. . . .'

It was lovely weather, and on their way to the Anglican cemetery many had tears in their eyes.

But already public opinion was turning against Ramage.

'His death was really a blessing in disguise,' said one lady. 'He was evidently mad, poor man – sitting in the sun with no clothes on – much worse might have happened.'

'This is All Souls Day,' Rosalie thought, standing at her bedroom window before going to sleep. She was wishing that Mr Ramage could have been buried in the Catholic cemetery, where all day the candles burnt almost invisible in the sunlight. When night came they twinkled like fireflies. The graves were covered with flowers – some real, some red or yellow paper or little gold cut-outs. Sometimes there was a letter weighted by a stone and the black people said that next morning the letters had gone. And where? Who would steal letters on the night of the dead? But the letters had gone.

The Anglican cemetery, which was not very far away, down the hill, was deserted and silent. Protestants believed that when you were dead, you were dead.

If he had a letter . . . she thought.

'My dear darling Mr Ramage,' she wrote, then felt to sad that she began to cry.

Two hours later Mrs Cox came into the room and found her daughter in bed and asleep; on the table by her side was the unfinished letter. Mrs. Cox read it, frowned, pressed her lips together, then crumpled it up and threw it out of the window.

There was a stiff breeze and she watched it bouncing purposefully down the street. As if it knew exactly where it was going.

Good-bye Marcus,
Good-bye Rose

WHEN FIRST I WORE my old shako,' sang Captain Cardew, 'Ten, twenty, thirty, forty, fifty years ago . . . ' and Phoebe thought what a wonderful bass voice he had. This was the second time he had called to take her for a walk, and again he had brought her a large box of chocolates.

Captain Cardew and his wife were spending the winter in Jamaica when they visited the small island where she lived and found it so attractive and unspoilt that they decided to stay. They even talked of buying a house and settling there for good.

He was not only a very handsome old man but a hero who had fought bravely in some long ago war which she thought you only read about in history books. He'd been wounded and had a serious operation without an anaesthetic. Anaesthetics weren't invented in those days. (Better not think too much about that.)

It had been impressed on her how kind it was of him to bother with a little girl like herself. Anyway she liked him, he was always so carefully polite to her, treating her as though she were a grown-up girl. A calm unruffled man, he only grew annoyed if people called him 'Captain' too often. Sometimes he lost his temper and would say loudly things like: 'What d'you think I'm Captain of now – a Penny a Liner?' What was a Penny a Liner? She never found out.

It was a lovely afternoon and they set out. She was wearing a white blouse with a sailor collar, a long full white skirt, black stockings, black buttoned boots and a large wide-brimmed white hat anchored firmly with elastic under her chin.

When they reached the Botanical Gardens she offered to take him to a shady bench and they walked slowly to the secluded part of the Gardens that she'd spoken of and sat under a large tree. Beyond its shadow they could see the yellow dancing patches of sunlight.

'Do you mind if I take off my hat? The elastic is hurting me,' Phoebe said.

'Then take it off, take it off,' said the Captain.

Phoebe took off her hat and began to talk in what she hoped was a grown-up way about the curator, Mr Harcourt-Smith, who'd really made the Gardens as beautiful as they were. He'd come from a place in England called the Kew. Had he ever heard of it?

Yes he had heard of it. He added: 'How old are you Phoebe?'

'I'm twelve,' said Phoebe, '– and a bit.'

'Hah!' said the Captain. 'Then soon you'll be old enough to have a lover!' His hand, which had been lying quietly by his side, darted towards her, dived inside her blouse and clamped itself around one very small breast. 'Quite old enough,' he remarked.

Phoebe remained perfectly still. 'He's making a great mistake, a great mistake,' she thought. 'If I don't move he'll take his hand away without really noticing what he'd done.'

However the Captain showed no sign of that at all. He was breathing rather heavily when a couple came strolling round the corner. Calmly, without hurry, he withdrew his hand and after a while said: 'Perhaps we ought to be going home now.'

Phoebe, who was in a ferment, said nothing. They walked out of the shade into the sun and as they walked she looked up at him as though at some aged but ageless god. He talked of usual things in a usual voice and she made up her mind that she would tell nobody of what had happened. Nobody. It was not a thing you could possibly talk about. Also no one would believe exactly how it happened, and whether they believed her or not she would be blamed.

If he was as absentminded as all that – for surely it could be nothing but absentmindedness – perhaps there oughtn't to be any more walks. She could excuse herself by saying that she had a headache. But that would only do for once. The walks continued. They'd go into the Gardens or up the Morne, a hill overlooking the town. There were benches and seats there but few houses and hardly anybody about.

He never touched her again but all through the long bright afternoons Captain Cardew talked of love and Phoebe listened, shocked and fascinated. Sometimes she doubted what he said: surely it was impossible, horrifyingly impossible. Sometimes she was on the point of saying, not 'You oughn't to talk to me like this' but babyishly 'I want to go home'. He always knew when she felt this and would at once change the subject and tell her amusing stories of his life when he was a young man and a subaltern in India.

'Hot?' he'd say. 'This isn't hot. India's hot. Sometimes the only thing to do is take off your clothes and see that the punkah's going.'

Or he'd talk about London long ago. Someone – was it Byron? – had said that women were never so unattractive as when they were eating and it was still most unfashionable for them to eat heartily. He'd watch in wonder as the ethereal creatures pecked daintily, then sent away almost untouched plates. One day he had seen a maid taking a tray laden with food up to the bedrooms and the mystery was explained.

But these stories were only intervals in the ceaseless talk of love, various ways of making love, various sorts of love. He'd explain that love was not kind and gentle, as she had imagined, but violent. Violence, even cruelty, was an essential part of it. He would expand on this, it seemed to be his favourite subject.

The walks had gone on for some time when the Captain's wife, Edith, who was a good deal younger than her husband, became suspicious and began making very sarcastic remarks. Early one evening when the entire party had gone up the Morne to watch the sunset, she'd said to her husband, after a long look at Phoebe: 'Do you really find the game worth the candle?' Captain

Cardew said nothing. He watched the sun going down without expression, then remarked that it was quite true that the only way to get rid of a temptation was to yield to it.

Phoebe had never liked Edith very much. Now she began to dislike her. One afternoon they were in a room together and she said: 'Do you see how white my hair's becoming? It's all because of you.' And when Phoebe answered truthfully that she didn't notice any white hairs: 'What a really dreadful little liar you are!'

After this she must have spoken to Phoebe's mother, a silent, reserved woman, who said nothing to her daughter but began to watch her in a puzzled, incredulous, even faintly suspicious way. Phoebe knew that very soon she would be questioned, she'd have to explain.

So she was more than half relieved when Edith Cardew announced that they'd quite given up their first idea of spending the rest of the winter on the island and were going back to England by the next boat. When Captain Cardew said 'Good-bye' formally, the evening before they left, she had smiled and shaken hands, not quite realizing that she was very unlikely ever to see him again.

There was a flat roof outside her bedroom window. On hot fine nights she'd often lie there in her nightgown looking up at the huge brilliant stars. She'd once tried to write a poem about them but had not got beyond the first line: 'My stars. Familiar jewels'. But that night she knew that she would never finish it. They were not jewels. They were not familiar. They were cold, infinitely far away, quite indifferent.

The roof looked onto the yard and she could hear Victoria and Joseph talking and laughing outside the pantry, then they must have gone away and it was quite silent. She was alone in the house for she'd not gone with the others to see the Cardews off. She was sure that now they had gone her mother would be very unlikely to question her, and then began to wonder how he had been so sure, not only that she'd never tell anybody but that she'd make no effort at all to stop him talking. That could only mean that he'd seen at once that she was not a good girl – who would object – but a wicked one – who would listen. He must know. He knew. It was so.

It was so and she felt not so much unhappy about this as uncomfortable, even dismayed. It was like wearing a dress that was much too big for her, a dress that swallowed her up.

Wasn't it quite difficult being a wicked girl? Even more difficult than being a good one? Besides, didn't the nuns say that Chastity, in Thought, Word and Deed was your most precious possession? She remembered Mother Sacred Heart, her second favourite, reciting in her lovely English voice:

'So dear to Heaven is saintly chastity . . . '

How did it go on? Something about 'a thousand liveried angels lackey her . . . '

'A thousand liveried angels' now no more. The thought of some vague irreparable loss saddened her. Then she told herself that anyway she needn't bother any longer about whether she'd get married or not. The older girls that she knew talked a great deal about marriage, some of them talked about very little else. And they seemed so sure. No sooner had they put their hair up and begun going to dances, than they'd marry someone handsome (and rich). Then the fun of being grown-up and important, of doing what you wanted instead of what you were told to do, would start. And go on for a long long time.

But she'd always doubted if this would happen to her. Even if numbers of rich and handsome young men suddenly appeared, would she be one of the chosen?

If no one ever marries me
And I don't see why they should
For nurse says I'm not pretty
And I'm seldom very good . . .

That was it exactly.

Well there was one thing. Now she felt very wise, very grown-up, she could forget these childish worries. She could hardly believe that only a few weeks ago she, like all the others, had secretly made lists of her trousseau, decided on the names of her three children. Jack. Marcus. And Rose.

Now good-bye Marcus. Good-bye Rose. The prospect before her might be difficult and uncertain but it was far more exciting.

The Bishop's Feast

WHEN I'D LEFT Dominica twenty-five years ago there were no hotels, only a small boarding-house run by three sisters. The few people who wished to stay usually rented a house. So I was relieved when I saw the large cool room in the La Paz. There was a bathroom, and flush lavatories. All was well.

The next morning one of my mother's old friends sent me some flowers, and there was a letter from Mother Mount Calvary, the Mother Superior of the convent where I was at school, whom I had loved so much. She wrote 'Welcome back to Dominica. Come to see us at 4 o'clock this afternoon. How could I forget you?'

I asked the driver of the car we had hired to take me to the convent. He told me the old convent I knew had been sold, and the nuns were now living in a much smaller building. They would soon be going back to England and would be replaced by nuns of a Belgian order. 'I hear the old nun says she won't go, but she'll soon find out that she has to.'

'Isn't it rather a shame,' I said, 'to make them leave when they've worked so hard here, all their lives?'

He said 'They're too old for the job, anyway.'

Mother Mount Calvary – Good Mother, we used to call her – was smiling when she welcomed me and looked almost as cheerful as I remembered her. When she stopped smiling I saw that her face was very sombre and old. We sat in the garden with two other nuns who I thought I didn't know. One of them remarked how much I had changed.

'She hasn't changed at all,' Mother Mount Calvary said sharply.

When I looked again at the nun I recognized something in her expression. She was the little Irish nun I had once seen smiling at her reflection in a barrel of water. There were no dimples now. She was a frightened old lady.

So this was the end of the feud between the convent and the bishopric, which had started at the new bishop's feast.

We'd all subscribed towards a present for the new bishop. It was an armchair to be given to him when he came to watch the performance celebrating his feast. We were excited about this performance.

The evening came. We clustered in the wings listening to a girl reciting 'Partant pour la Syrie', which was the first item on the programme. She didn't seem at all nervous. Her voice sounded clear and assured:

> 'Partant pour la Syrie le jeune et beau Dunois
> Venait prier Marie de bénir ses exploits.
> "Faites, Reine Immortelle," lui dit-il en partant,
> "Que j'aime la plus belle et sois le plus vaillant." '

Louise was dressed for her song 'L'Anglaise à Paris', a mild satire on Englishwomen in Paris and the next item, when Mother St Edmund came bustling in and without giving us any reason told us that the programme had been changed. 'L'Anglaise à Paris' was cancelled, instead a selected chorus was to sing 'Killarney'.

Consternation, giggles.

'Don't be silly, children,' said Mother St Edmund. 'Sing up and do your best. You all know the words.'

'He won't like that one either,' said Mother Sacred Heart. But Mother St Edmund urged us on:

> 'By Killarney's lakes and fells,
> Emerald isles and winding bays . . . '

From the stage we could see the bishop enthroned in his new armchair, Mother Mount Calvary by his side. A large audience of parents and friends stretched away to the end of the room.

> ' . . . *Beauty's home, Killarney,*
> *Heaven's reflex, Killarney.*'

The curtain came down.

Somebody played a Chopin mazurka and everything went more or less smoothly on to a series of tableaux vivants, the most important part of the programme.

The first one was of the Last Supper with Mary Magdalene at the feet of Christ. None of the apostles appeared. Delia Paulson's hair was exactly right – she played Mary Magdalene – though her face, which was hidden, wouldn't have done at all. Mildred Watts was Jesus Christ. She was lovely, just like Jesus. The nuns had fixed her up with a little beard and she looked into the distance over Mary's head. (I thought Christ might have looked at Mary but I suppose the nuns told Mildred not to.) However, His hand was raised in a rather absentminded blessing.

The next tableau was the Death of St Cecilia, patron saint of music. There was a statue of her above the piano on which I practised and I always thought she looked at me most severely when I played the waltzes of Rodolphe Berger instead of my scales. St Cecilia lay smiling on the couch with one finger over three to symbolize that she believed in the Three in One.

So the tableaux went on and we peeped at the bishop, but he didn't applaud. The old bishop always clapped loudly and smiled, but this bishop seemed very bored.

When the programme ended we trooped onto the stage to hear the bishop give his little speech of thanks and appreciation. There was a pause, because for some reason he didn't seem able to get up. He put his hands on the arms of the chair, turned round, glared and tried again. No use.

Soon it was plain what had happened; he had stuck to the chair, which had been taken to be varnished and the varnish hadn't quite dried. Some of the nuns looked apprehensive and hurried to help him, but Mother Superior, who dearly loved a joke, couldn't stop herself from smiling broadly. Just as she smiled the bishop looked straight at her, their eyes met, she suppressed the smile but it was too late.

Soon afterwards he came to the school to give us dictation. I liked the colour of his purple skull cap but I hated his face. The old bishop had a light voice, he had a heavy throaty voice. He dictated: 'I have a dog. His name is Toby. He can bark and he can bite. . . . '

That's how it began. He started trying to get rid of them even before I left the island.

Of course Mother Mount Calvary had her friends and must have fought back, but even she couldn't fight old age. It was a sad meeting. When I left them I promised to visit them again before they sailed.

But I never saw them again. I went away to spend a week on the Atlantic side of the island, and when I returned to town the day before they were to leave, I was told that Mother Mount Calvary had died that morning. I felt very sad, but also something like triumph, because in the end she had won. She had always done what she said she'd do. She had said she would never leave the island, and she hadn't.

Heat

ASH HAD FALLEN. Perhaps it had fallen the night before or perhaps it was still falling. I can only remember in patches. I was looking at it two feet deep on the flat roof outside my bedroom. The ash and the silence. Nobody talked in the street, nobody talked while we ate, or hardly at all. I know how that they were all frightened. They thought our volcano was going up.

Our volcano was called the boiling lake. That's what it was, a sheet of water that always boiled. From what fires? I thought of it as a mysterious place that few people had ever seen. In the churchyard where we often went – for death was not then a taboo subject – quite near the grave of my little sister, was a large marble headstone. 'Sacred to the memory of Clive —, who lost his life at the boiling lake in Dominica in a heroic attempt to save his guide'. Aged twenty-seven. I remember that too.

He was a young Englishman, a visitor, who had gone exploring with two guides to the boiling lake. As they were standing looking at it one of the guides, who was a long way ahead, staggered and fell. The other seized hold of the Englishman's hand and said 'Run!' There must have been some local tradition that poisonous gases sometimes came out of the lake. After a few steps the Englishman pulled his hand away and went back and lifted up the man who had fallen. Then he too staggered and they both fell. The surviving guide ran and told what had happened.

In the afternoon two little friends were coming to see us and to my surprise they both arrived carrying large glass bottles. Both the bottles had carefully written labels pasted on: 'Ash collected

from the streets of Roseau on May 8th, 1902.' The little boy asked
me if I'd like to have his jar, but I refused. I didn't want to touch
the ash. I don't remember the rest of the day. I must have gone
to bed, for that night my mother woke me and without saying
anything, led me to the window. There was a huge black cloud
over Martinique. I couldn't ever describe that cloud, so huge and
black it was, but I have never forgotten it. There was no moon,
no stars, but the edges of the cloud were flame-coloured and in
the middle what looked to me like lightning flickered, never stopping. My mother said: 'You will never see anything like this in
your life again.' That was all. I must have gone to sleep at the
window and been carried to bed.

Next morning we heard what had happened. Was it a blue or
a grey day? I only know ash wasn't falling any longer. The Roseau
fishermen went out very early, as they did in those days. They
met the fishermen from Port de France, who knew. That was
how we heard before the cablegrams, the papers and all the rest
came flooding in. That was how we heard of Mont Pelée's eruption and the deaths of 40,000 people, and that there was nothing
left of St Pierre.

As soon as ships were sailing again between Dominica and
Martinique my father went to see the desolation that was left. He
brought back a pair of candlesticks, tall heavy brass candlesticks
which must have been in a church. The heat had twisted them
into an extraordinary shape. He hung them on the wall of the
dining-room and I stared at them all through meals, trying to
make sense of the shape.

It was after this that the gossip started. That went on for years
so I can remember it well. St Pierre, they said, was a very wicked
city. It had not only a theatre, but an opera house, which was
probably wickeder still. Companies from Paris performed there.
But worse than this was the behaviour of the women who were
the prettiest in the West Indies. They tied their turbans in a particular way, a sort of language of love that all St Pierre people
understood. Tied in one way it meant 'I am in love, I am not free';
tied another way it meant 'You are welcome, I am free'. Even the

women who were married, or as good as, tied their kerchiefs in the 'I am free' way. And that wasn't all. The last bishop who had visited the city had taken off his shoes and solemnly shaken them over it. After that, of course, you couldn't wonder.

As I grew older I heard of a book by a man called Lafcadio Hearn who had written about St Pierre as it used to be, about Ti Marie and all the others, but I never found the book and stopped looking for it. However, one day I did discover a pile of old newspapers and magazines, some illustrated: the English version of the eruption. They said nothing about the opera house or the theatre which must have seemed to the English the height of frivolity in a Caribbean island, and very little about the city and its inhabitants. It was nearly all about the one man who had survived. He was a convict imprisoned in an underground cell, so he escaped – the only one out of 40,000. He was now travelling round the music-halls of the world being exhibited. They had taught him a little speech. He must be quite a rich man – what did he do with his money? Would he marry again? His wife and children had been killed in the eruption. . . . I read all this, then I thought but it wasn't like that, it wasn't like that at all.

Fishy Waters

The Editor
The Dominica Herald

Dear Sir,   March 3rd 189–

Yesterday I heard a piece of news that appalled me. It seems that a British workman, Mr Longa by name, who arrived a year ago, has been arrested and is being held by the police. Mr Longa is a carpenter. He is also a socialist, and does not disguise his political opinions. It goes without saying that a certain class of person in this island, who seem to imagine that the colour of their skins enables them to behave like gods, disliked and disapproved of him from the first. He was turned out of Miss Lambton's boarding-house after one night and had the greatest difficulty in finding anywhere to live. Eventually he settled in a predominantly negro quarter – another cause for offence. A determined effort was made to induce him to leave the island. When this failed, with their usual hypocrisy they pretended to ignore him, but they were merely biding their time.

He was found joking roughly with one of the many vagabond children who infest the streets of Roseau, and is to be accused of child-molesting and cruelty, if you please. A trumped-up charge, on the face of it. In this way, they plan to be rid of a long-standing nuisance and to be able to boast about their even-handed justice. The hypocrisy of these people, who bitterly resent that they no longer have the power over the bodies and minds of the blacks they once had (the cruelty of West Indian planters was a by-word), making a scape-goat of an honest British workman, is enough to make any decent person's gorge rise. A London barrister, new to this island, has offered to defend Mr Longa without charge. Only one just man among so many?

Yours truly,
Disgusted

The Editor
The Dominica Herald

Dear Sir,   March 10th, 189–

Who is 'Disgusted'? Who is this person (I believe people) who tries to stir up racial hatred whenever possible? Almost invariable with gloating satisfaction, they will drag in the horrors of the slave trade. Who would think, to hear them talk, that slavery was abolished by the English nearly a hundred years ago? They are long on diatribes, but short on facts. The slave trade was an abominable one, but it could not have existed without the help and cooperation of African chiefs. Slavery still exists, and is taken for granted, in Africa, both among Negroes and Arabs. Are these facts ever mentioned? The bad is endlessly repeated and insisted upon; the good is ridiculed, forgotten or denied. Who does this, and why?

Yours truly,
Ian J. MacDonald

The Editor
The Dominica Herald

Dear Sir,   March 17th, 189–

It is sometimes said that African chiefs probably had a good deal to do with the slave trade, but I never heard before that this was proven. In his typical letter I noticed that Mr MacDonald places all the blame on these perhaps mythical Africans and says nothing about the greed of white merchants or the abominable cruelty and indifference of white planters. The treatment meted out to Mr Longa shows that their heirs and successors have not changed all that much.

Yours truly,
P. Kelly
Kelly's Universal Stores

The Editor
The Dominica Herald

Dear Sir,   March 24th, 189–

I hate to interfere with the amusement of your readers, but I must point out that according to English law it is highly improper to discuss a case that has not been tried *(sub judice)*. In this country the custom seems to be more honoured in the breach than in the observance.

Yours truly,
Fiat Justicia

This correspondence is now closed. *Editor.*

On the same day the editor, who was known as Papa Dom, remarked in a leading article: 'These are fishy waters – very fishy waters.'

6 Cork Street
Roseau, Dominica

My dear Caroline,   March 24th, 189–
Your letter rescued me from a mood of great depression. I am answering it at once – it will be such a relief to tell you about something that I don't care to discuss with people here.

You wouldn't remember a man called Jimmy Longa – he arrived soon after you left. Well, Matt found him trying to saw a little girl in two – can you believe it? – and is to be the main witness for the prosecution. The whole place is buzzing with gossip, arguments, letters to the local newspaper and so on. It is most unpleasant. I've begged Matt to have nothing further to do with it, I'm sure there'll be trouble. He says why should there be, Longa's a white man not a black one. I say 'Jimmy Longa will be an honorary black before this is over, you'll see. They'll twist it somehow.' But he won't even talk about it now. I'm not at all happy about Matt. He doesn't look well and is so unlike what he used to be. I begin to wish I'd never persuaded him to settle here when he retired – a visit to escape the winter is one thing, living here is quite another.

The first scandal about Longa was that Miss Lambton turned him out as he got so drunk every night. He's a jobbing carpenter, quite a good one when he's sober, so he soon found a place to live and got plenty of work. His story is that he's on his way to America and stopped off at Dominica to make some money. I wonder who on earth could have advised him to do that! He gave out that he was a socialist, extreme – the new world must be built on the ashes of the old, that sort of thing. He preached fire and slaughter in the rum-shop and everywhere else so you can imagine he wasn't very popular with the white people. Then he got malaria badly and Miss Lambton, who had him on her conscience, went to the hospital to see how he was. She said he looked very ill and told her that his only wish now was to get back to England, but he couldn't raise the money. She started a subscription for him and headed the list with £10, which she certainly couldn't afford. Nearly everyone chipped in and a good deal was raised. But somehow he managed to persuade Miss Lambton to hand the lot over directly. Then disappeared. There was no case against him – he'd been careful not to promise or sign anything – besides, a lot of people thought it comic. They said 'Poor Mamie Lambton, it seems she's very upset. But what a chap! You have to laugh!' Even when he reappeared, more fanatical than ever, nobody took him seriously – he was the Dominica funny story. And now this.

I've got one piece of pleasant news. Because Matt dislikes the town so much we've bought a small estate in the country where he may be happier. It's called Three Rivers – an old place, and as usual the house is falling to bits. It's being fixed up – but lately I've wondered if we'll ever live there.

No one at home would understand why all this is looming over me so much, but you know the kind of atmosphere we get here sometimes, so I think you will.

I'm so glad you are happy and don't feel the cold too much. Perhaps the next time I write it will all be over and I'll be more cheerful.

Meanwhile I send you my love,

Affectionately,

Maggie

The day after Jimmy Longa's trial there was a long report on the front page of the *Dominica Herald*. The reporter, having remarked on the crowded court-room, usually empty for assault and battery cases, went on to say that the prosecuting counsel, M. Didier of Roseau, had seemed so nervous at first that he was almost inaudible. His speech was short. He said that it was fortunate that there had been an eyewitness to the attack on the child, Josephine Mary Dent, known as Jojo, for though Mr Longa's activities were common knowledge in Roseau, no one had dared to come forward to accuse him, a white man. 'There are a certain number of children, abandoned and unprotected, roaming the streets. This child was one of them. The accused is a danger to all children, but these are particularly at risk.' M. Didier asked for a sentence heavy enough to deter possible imitators. He then called his first witness, Mr Matthew Penrice.

Mr Penrice said that on the late afternoon of February 27th he was walking up Jetty Street on the way to the Club when he heard a child screaming in a very distressing way. As he approached the house the screams came from, the sound stopped abruptly – no angry voices, complete silence. The house stood well back from the empty street, and there was a fence round it.

It occurred to him that a child, left alone there, might have met with an accident, and on an impulse he knocked at the wooden gate. There was no answer so he pushed the gate open. As he did so he heard a man say: 'Now I'm going to saw you in two, like they do in English music halls.' The yard of the house was quite a large one; there was a tree in the corner, and under the tree a plank raised up on trestles. A naked little negro girl lay on the plank, her head hanging over the end. She was silent, and her face was almost green with fright. The man's back was to him and the saw in his hand was touching the child's waist. Mr Penrice called out 'What the devil's going on here?' The man turned, dropping the saw, and he recognized Mr Longa, who was not in court. Mr Longa said: 'I wasn't going to hurt her – I was only joking.' He had been holding the child on the plank, and when he turned she rolled off and lay on the ground without moving. Mr Longa repeated that it was a joke. When the witness approached the unconscious child he saw that her body was covered with bruises. He did not speak to Mr Longa again, but wrapped the child in his jacket and took her to the house of Madame Octavia Joseph, which was close by. He then sent for the doctor who fortunately was able to come at once. After the doctor had arrived he went to the police station and reported what he had seen.

Cross-examined by counsel for the defense, Mr Penrice was asked if Jetty Street was his usual way to the Club. He answered that it was not, but he was in a hurry to keep an appointment and Jetty Street was a short cut.

Counsel asked him: 'Would it surprise you to know that information from your household reveals that on that particular day you left for the Club very much earlier than usual? The domestic remembers it clearly, as it was her birthday. As your habits are so regular, she wondered why you had left the house on foot on such a hot day, nearly two hours earlier than usual. Why, then, did you have to take a short cut?'

Mr Penrice replied: 'Two hours is an exaggeration. I left my house earlier than usual to go for a walk – I don't mind the heat

– and I forgot the time, so I was trying to get to the Club as quickly as I could.'

'When you heard the accused say "Like they do in English music halls", was he aware that anyone was listening?'

'No, he didn't know that I was there.'

'So he was speaking to the child?'

'I suppose so.'

'Do you know that there is a popular trick on the English music halls when a girl is supposed to be sawn in two?'

'Yes, I think so.'

'And is anyone ever sawn in two, or hurt in any way?'

'Of course not. It's a trick.'

'Perhaps you were too startled and shocked to realize that when the accused said "As they do in English music halls" he was really declaring that what he was about to do was not to be taken seriously. It was a joke.'

'It was not a joke.'

'And why are you so sure of that?'

'When the man faced me, I knew that it was not a joke at all.'

'I see. But is there not a certain amount of prejudice against Mr Longa in this island? Are you not very ready to believe the worse of him? Has there not been a great deal of gossip about him?'

'I only know Mr Longa by sight. The gossip here does not interest me.'

'So you are not – shall we say – prejudiced?'

'No, not at all. Not in the way you mean.'

'I am glad to hear it. Now, as you say the child was unconscious and badly hurt, would not the normal thing have been either to take or to send her to the hospital?'

'I didn't think of the hospital. Madame Joseph's house was near by and I knew she would be well looked-after so I took her there and sent for the doctor.'

'Mr Penrice, has Madame Joseph ever been in your service?'

'Yes. She was with us for nearly five years, off and on, when we used to winter here before making it our home. That was why

I was so sure that she was not only a kind woman, but a perfectly reliable one.'

'When she left your employment, did you give her a large present of money?'

'Not large, no. Both my wife and myself thought she had given us invaluable service. She was no longer in very good health, so we were happy to give her enough to buy a small house, where she would be comfortable and secure.'

'No doubt she was very grateful?'

'I think she was pleased, yes.'

'As she was so indebted to you, you must have been sure that in an emergency any instructions you gave her would be carried out?'

'In saying that, you only show that you know nothing at all about the people of this island. Madame Joseph is a most independent woman. Even if I – or rather, we – had installed her in a palace instead of a small house, she would not have thought herself bound to follow my instructions. No.'

'And it really seemed to you proper to leave a badly injured child in the care of an ex-servant, however devoted, who had no medical knowledge and no experience of nursing?'

'I did what I thought best for her.'

'And did you tell the doctor that you had taken her there because Madame Joseph was the child's close relative?'

'I did nothing of the sort.'

'But you can imply a thing without actually saying it, can you not?'

'You most certainly can.'

'Thank you, Mr Penrice. You may stand down.'

Mr Penrice was followed in the witness box by Madame Octavia Joseph, a dignified woman who gave her evidence clearly and obviously made a favourable impression on the magistrate, Mr Somers. When she saw the state the little girl was in, she said, she understood why Mr Penrice was going to the police. 'It was a very wicked person did that.' Soon after the doctor came the child recovered consciousness, but at once began to tremble and

scream. Having treated her bruises, the doctor gave her a sedative, said he would call the next day, that she was to see nobody,
and that she was not to be questioned until she was better. Madame Joseph had done her best to follow the doctor's orders and
had taken great care of the child, whose condition was much
improved; 'But she says she does not remember anything about
being attacked. When I told her she ought to try to remember,
she only began to cry and shake, so I thought it better for the
doctor to speak to her.'

The last witness for the prosecution, Dr Trevor, said that on
the evening of February 27th he had been at home when he got
a message to come at once to 11 Hill Street to treat a badly injured
child. When he first saw the child she had fainted and obviously
been savagely beaten. When she recovered consciousness she
was so frightened and hysterical that after treating her he gave
her a sedative. She was probably about eleven or twelve years of
age, but as she was very thin and undernourished, she may have
been a year or two older.

Counsel asked Dr Trevor: 'Have you seen the child since?'

'Yes, on several occasions.'

'When did you see her last?'

'I saw her yesterday.'

'And what did you think of her?'

'I found her condition had greatly improved. She has been
carefully looked after and is well on the way to recovery. Already
she seems quite a different child.'

'When you visited this child, did you ever question her or ask
her who had attacked her?'

'Yes, after I thought she was better I did question her, of course. -
She always behaved in the same way. She says she has forgotten.
I tried two or three times to question her more closely – the only
result is that she becomes frightened, hysterical and quite incoherent.'

'When you questioned the child, was Madame Joseph with
you?'

'She was there the first time, but I have often been alone with the child and this is invariably the way she behaves.'

'Did it strike you at all that because of what has happened, she had been mentally affected?'

'No, I saw no signs of that. She'd probably be quite a bright little thing, given a chance.'

'Did you not think it somewhat strange that although she is so much better, she still refuses to say anything about what happened to her?'

'Perhaps it is not as strange as you think. Some people after a great shock or fright will talk volubly, others "clam up" as they say in parts of England. She'll probably talk eventually, but it's impossible to say when.'

'And you find nothing unusual about this "clamming up", as you call it?'

'I have known cases when, after a frightening and harmful experience, the mind has protected itself by forgetting. If you try to force recollection, the patient becomes agitated and resentful.'

'Do you really think that this interesting but rather complicated theory could apply to a Negro child, completely illiterate, only eleven or twelve years of age? Is it not mere likely that she remains silent because she has either been persuaded or threatened – probably a bit of both – not to talk?'

'I do not believe that the result of illiteracy is an uncomplicated mind – far from it. And I do not know who you are suggesting would have frightened her. My orders were that she should be kept perfectly quiet and see no one except Madame Joseph, whose house is surrounded by inquisitive neighbours. If anyone else had been there I would have been told, believe me. The child certainly isn't at all afraid of Madame Joseph. On the contrary, she seems to trust her, even be attached to her – insofar as a child like that can trust or be attached at all. However, if you are not satisfied with my evidence, why not question the child? In my opinion you will get nothing at all out of her and may do her harm, but you must decide for yourself.'

Here Mr Somers intervened and said that the child must certainly not be questioned by anyone as long as the doctor thought it might be harmful.

Counsel then asked Dr Trevor: 'Were you led to believe that the child had been taken to Madame Joseph's house because she was a close relative?'

'No. I suppose I took it for granted. In any case, I made no suggestion that she should be moved. I thought she was in very good hands.'

Counsel for the Defence, Mr Berkely, said that his client was too ill to appear in Court, but that he would read his statement. This, he submitted, was a complete answer to the charge.

Mr Longa's Statement: 'I had not felt very well that day. It was too hot, so I thought I'd knock off for a bit. But as I might be able to work later on when it was cooler, I left my saw in the yard, with a plank I was working on to make bookshelves. I was very thirsty and had a few drinks, then I fell asleep. I don't know how long I slept before loud screams woke me up, coming from my yard. The noise these children make is very trying and that's putting it mildly. They climb over the fence into the yard to play, and get up to all kinds of mischief. I'd chase them away, but they always came back. They'd follow me in the street, jeering and laughing, and several times I've been stoned. I don't deny I've grown to dislike them very much indeed.

'I got up feeling shaky and in a bad temper, and in my yard I found a little girl lying on the ground, screaming. I asked her what was the matter several times, but she took no notice at all and went on yelling. At last I told her to shut up, get out, and go and scream somewhere else. She wouldn't even look at me, and the noise she was making went through and through my head, so I lost my temper, picked her up and put her on the plank, telling her I was going to saw her in two, but I didn't really mean to hurt her and I told her so. I didn't notice anything wrong with her, or think it strange that she was naked – they very often are, especially on hot days. No, I never meant to hurt her. But I hoped to frighten her a bit, and that she'd tell the others, and then perhaps they'd leave me in peace. These children have made my life a misery, and I wanted to stop them from doing it. I swear that was all I meant – to frighten her. It was just a joke. When Mr

Penrice came and accused me I was too confused to say much. I told him I hadn't meant any harm but he wouldn't listen to me, nor would the policemen when they arrested me. I am sorry for what I did and for frightening her, but I had been drinking. I quite lost my temper and was very angry. That is what happened, and that is the truth.'

To this Mr Berkeley added that Mr Longa was now very willing to leave the island. 'He says that even in England he would not be treated with such injustice. As to the rumours about my client, I am surprised that my learned friend has mentioned them, as he has failed to produce a single witness to substantiate them. Without wishing to impugn Mr Penrice's word, I must point out that there is no evidence at all that Mr Longa was the child's attacker. She may have run into the empty yard to hide, or – more likely – she was thrown there by the real attacker who then made off, feeling certain that Mr Longa would be accused. Mr Penrice admits that he heard Mr Longa saying "As they do in English music halls" before he knew anyone was listening. This seems to me to prove conclusively that Mr Longa's behavior was a joke – a rough, even a cruel joke if you like, but certainly not deserving of several years' imprisonment in a goal not fit for any human being, Englishman or not.'

Mr Berkely ended by saying that Mr Longa was a very intelligent man left terribly alone and isolated – also he was not a well man. It was hardly surprising that he turned to rum for consolation, and easy to believe that, woken suddenly, he felt extremely irritable and behaved in a way that was not normal to him.

The Summing-up. The magistrate, Mr Somers, said that this was a very disturbing case. 'There is no direct evidence that it was Mr Longa who first attacked the child, causing the extensive bruising. He denies it strongly, and the child cannot yet be questioned. I find his statement as read by Counsel for the Defense convincing up to a point. Two things, however, strike me as unlikely. Why should he think that this unfortunate child would know anything about English music halls or the tricks performed there? Why should his mentioning them reassure her? It probably added to her fright. Also, and more important: however drunk he was, could he have picked up a badly injured naked child and carried her to the plank without noticing the marks on her body? According to Mr Longa he noticed nothing, but proceeded with his savage joke. I find this so unlikely as to be almost incredible. He excuses himself by saying that he had been drinking, but he is a man accustomed to strong drink and there is no report of advanced intoxication from the police who arrested him.

'I am not here to speculate and I cannot accept either hearsay evidence or innuendoes supported by no evidence; but I have not been in my post for twenty years without learning that it is extremely difficult to obtain direct evidence here. Often a criminal is quite well-known, but the police find it impossible to produce a single witness against him. There is, unfortunately, in these islands a great distrust both of the police and of the law.'

Here a voice interrupted: 'Can you blame them?' and there was a hubbub in the Court. Several women were in tears. Order was only restored when a threat was made to clear the Court.

Mr Somers continued: 'We can only hope that this perhaps natural distrust will diminish with time. In view of my doubts I am glad to hear that Mr Longa is willing to leave the island. I direct that his passage to Southampton be paid by the Government. Until he sails he must remain in custody of the police, but must be allowed to receive visitors. He must be able to get food or provisions from outside and care must be taken to restore him to health. I am sure that his able Counsel will see that my instructions are carried out.'

The crowd was subdued and less talkative than usual as it left the court-room, but a group of rowdies shouted at Mr Penrice as he came out. He took no notice of this demonstration, but got into his waiting trap and drove off. A few stones were thrown after him, but the rowdies quickly dispersed when a policeman intervened.

'I bet you anything Mamie Lambton's going to start another subscription,' said Matthew Penrice to his wife when he got home. He added: 'Don't look so gloomy, Maggie. I've got one piece of

very good news. Octavia tells me that she's been corresponding
with an old friend in St Lucia with no children of her own who
wishes to adopt Jojo. She's quite sure of this woman and says it'll
be the best thing possible. I think so too. She'd get right away
from all the gossip and questioning here, and start again. I'll see
to it she gets there as soon as she's well enough. I'll take care of
everything, don't worry.'

Maggie Penrice watched the Negro maid Janet pile the coffee
things onto the tray and walk out, silent, bare-footed. When she
said 'What delicious coffee, Janet,' the girl hadn't answered, hadn't
even smiled. But they don't smile here, they laugh, they seldom
smile. Not smilers with a knife. No? Even when they were alone
she didn't speak, but went on folding and unfolding the letter.
She re-read the last paragraph.

'Thank you for the money you sent. I will keep it faithfully
and carefully for her when she grows up and thank you from my
heart for giving her to me. You would be pleased to see her. She
is getting quite fat and pretty and hardly ever wakes up screaming as she used to do. I now close and say no more from my overflowing heart. Wishing you and your amiable lady all health and
prosperity. Anine Dib.'

Maggie said: 'Dib. What a funny name.'

'Syrian, probably,' Matt said. 'Well, that's the last of that, I
hope, and now you mustn't worry any more. Much the best thing
that could have happened. Surely you agree?'

'Perhaps. . . . But Matt, do you think it was wise to send her
away quite so quickly?'

'The sooner the better, I should have thought. Why not?'

The room was at the back of the house, there was no noise
from the street. It was hot and airless and the blinds were half
drawn. She folded the letter carefully and put it back into its
envelope, then pushed it across to him.

'Because it's all over the place that Octavia's in your pay and
that you both sent the child to St Lucia so that there was no
chance of her ever talking. They're saying that you did it and

pushed it off onto Jimmy Longa. The whole thing is utterly ridiculous, of course, but you ought to stop it.'

'Stop it? What do you want me to do? How can I stop it?'

'Surely that wouldn't be too hard. It's so absurd. How could you have done it – how is it even possible?'

'Do you think these damnable hogs care whether it's possible or not, or how or where or when? They've just got hold of something to grunt about, that's all. If you think I'm going to argue with this lot you must be mad. I've had more than enough of this whole damned place. If you really want to know what I feel, I want to clear out. It's not this particular storm in a tea-cup that's decided me. I've wanted to leave for some time, and you must have known it.'

'They'll say you've run away.'

'God, can't you get it into your head that I don't give a damn what they say here? Oh come on, Maggie, don't look like that. I know how you feel, how you dread the cold, how much better you are here, and its beauty and all that – I only wish I felt like you, but to me it's suffocating.'

'Yes, I know. But I hoped you'd feel better when we left Roseau.'

'The hatred would be exactly the same in the country – suppressed, perhaps. If you don't want to leave you needn't. I won't sell Three Rivers or this house, and the money will be all right – surely you know that?'

'But Matt, you find envy, malice, hatred everywhere. You can't escape.'

'Perhaps, but I'm sick of this particular brand.'

'Do you think I'd want to stay here by myself if you went? Do you really think that?'

He didn't answer but smiled and said: 'Then that's settled.' He patted her shoulder lightly, then he went over to an armchair, took up a book; but Maggie, watching him anxiously, cautiously, saw that he never turned a page. Suddenly she screwed up her eyes tightly and shook her head. She was trying to fight the overwhelming certainty that the man she was looking at was a complete stranger.

Overture and Beginners Please

WE WERE SITTING BY the fire in the small dining-room when Camilla said 'I hate my parents, don't you?' Hail was rattling against the curtained windows. I had been told all about snow long before I left the West Indies, hail was a surprise and exciting in its way. I thought I'd be laughed at if I asked what it was.

Another dark yellow curtain hung over the door which led into a passage and beyond that were the empty classrooms, for this was the week after Christmas and the day girls and other seven boarders had gone home for their holidays.

'And what's more,' said Camilla, 'they hate me. They like my younger sister. A lot of that sort of thing goes on in families but it's hushed up of course.'

It was almost dark, I was almost warm, so I said, 'I don't hate mine. They gave a farewell dance for me before I left. We had a band. It's funny, I can remember exactly the face of the man with the shak-shak.'

'How comic,' said Camilla who seemed annoyed.

'They play well. Different music of course.'

'Why did they send you to the old Perse if they were so fond of you?'

'Because my English aunt said it was a good school.'

'That's the one who won't have you with her for Christmas, isn't it?'

'Well she is sick – ill, I mean.'

'*She says!* How do you like it now you are here?'

'I like it all right, but the chilblains on my hands hurt.'

Then she said I would have lots of time to find out if I did like it as she was leaving the next day to stay with friends at Thaxted. 'Miss Born has all of Charlotte M. Yonge's novels lined up for you to read in the evenings.'

'Oh Lord, she hasn't!'

'Just you wait,' said Camilla.

The maid came in to light up and soon it would be time to go upstairs and change for dinner. I thought this woman one of the most fascinating I had ever seen. She had a long thin face, dead white, or powdered dead white. Her hair was black and lively under her cap, her eyes so small that the first time I saw her I thought she was blind. But wide open, they were the most astonishing blue, cornflower blue, no, more like sparks of blue fire. Then she would drop her eyelids and her face would go dead and lifeless again. I never tired of watching this transformation.

After dinner there I was, reading aloud *The Dove in the Eagle's Nest*. Camilla didn't listen, nor did Miss Rode, our headmistress, who was a middle-aged very imposing woman with quantities of black-grey hair arranged like a coronet. She dressed in various shades of brown, purple, puce or mustard and her face was serene and kind.

Miss Born however never took her eyes off me. Miss Born was old, she wore black, she never taught. She represented breeding and culture and was a great asset to the school. 'Drop your voice,' she would say, 'drop it. An octave at least'; or 'That will do, don't go on, I really cannot bear any more tonight.'

We sat around the fire till the clock struck nine. 'Good night Miss Rode.' 'Good night, dear child' said Miss Rode, who was wearing her purple, always a good sign. 'Good night Miss Born.' Miss Born inclined her head very slightly and as I went out remarked, 'Why did you insist on that girl playing Autolycus? Tony Lumpkin in person.'

'Not in person, surely,' said Miss Rode mildly.

'In manner then, in manner,' said Miss Born.

Camilla shut the door and I heard no more.

The staircase was slippery and smelt of floor polish. All the way up to the bedroom floor I thought about Miss Born's black clothes, her small active body. A mouse with a parrot's head. I hadn't even wanted to be in the old *Winter's Tale* and I told them so. However, I said nothing of all this to Camilla for I had been five months in England and was slowly learning to be cautious. Besides the bedrooms were unheated and I had already begun to shiver and shake.

'Don't you think it's frightfully cold, Camilla?'

'No, not particularly. Hop into bed and you'll soon get warm.' She went off to her own room four doors away.

I knew of course that I would not sleep or get warm for on top of everything else an icy wind was blowing through the window, which for some mysterious reason must be left open six inches at the top.

Do not shut your window. This window must not be closed.

I was still awake and shivering, clutching my ankles with my hands, when the maid, who was called Jarvis, knocked. 'I've brought you up a hot water bottle miss.'

'Oh thank you. How awfully kind of you.'

'It is my own hot water bottle,' she said. She asked why I didn't shut my window.

'Well, I thought we weren't supposed to.'

She pushed the sash up without answering. I stretched my legs out and put the bottle where my back hurt and thanked her again. I hoped she'd go away but she lingered.

'I wanted to tell you miss, that I enjoyed the school play this term very much. You were good in that boy's part.'

'Autolycus.'

'Well, I don't remember the name but you quite cheered me up.'

'I'm very glad,' I said. 'Good night Jarvis, don't 'catch cold in this icy little room.'

'I had a great success once in an amateur theatrical performance,' she went on dreamily. 'I played the part of a blind girl.'

'You played a blind girl? How strange, because when I saw you first I thought . . . ' I stopped. 'I thought you might be able to act because you don't look at all wooden.'

'The flowers I had sent me,' she said. 'Roses and that. Of course, it was long ago, when I was a girl, but I still remember my part, every word of it.'

'How very nice' was all I could think of to say. She snapped the light out and shut the door, rather loudly.

She played a blind girl. I thought she was blind. But this sort of thing had happened to me before. I'd stopped trying to make sense of clues that led nowhere.

When, next day after breakfast, Camilla left I got through the morning thinking no bicycle ride anyhow. Patey isn't here.

Miss Patey had been trying to teach me to bicycle. She always skimmed gracefully ahead as though she had nothing to do with me and I followed her, wobbling dangerously from side to side. Once when I'd fallen into a ditch on the way to Newnham, she turned back and asked in a detached way if I'd hurt myself. 'Oh no, Miss Patey, not at all.' I climbed out of the ditch and picked up the bicycle. 'I see your stocking is torn and that is quite a bruise on your knee.' She did not speak again until we got to the Trumpington Road. 'You had better get down and wheel your bicycle here.' 'Yes, Miss Patey.'

Limping along the Trumpington Road . . . past Mrs G's house, a distant relative of my father's. I was allowed to have tea with her every Saturday afternoon. . . . She was called Jeanette and was a very lovely, stately old lady with thick white hair, huge black eyes and a classic profile. She didn't wear spectacles except for reading and her hands were slender and transparent looking. She talked about Cambridge when she was young and the famous men she'd known. 'Poor Darwin. He threaded the labyrinths of creation and lost his Creator.' Or 'Of course Fitzgerald's translation from the Persian was not really accurate . . . '; and the Song of Solomon was an allegory of Christ and His Church.

Another day she told me that she had nearly eloped (tired of her absentminded old husband, I suppose). She was packed and ready to leave but when she was pinning on her hat she saw in the looking-glass the devil grinning over her shoulder. She was so frightened that she changed her mind.

'And what did the devil look like?' I asked, very curious. But she never told me that.

Like so many beautiful old ladies then she had a devoted maid whom I was rather afraid of, she looked at me so sternly, so unsmilingly when she opened the door. Now I come to think of it, Jarvis didn't smile either.

None of the girls could believe that I'd never owned a bicycle before or that there were very few in the island. 'How do you get about then, if there are no trains, buses, cars or bicycles?' they would say. 'Horses, mules, carriages, buggies, traps.' Winks, smiles. 'Is it "honey don't try so hard" or "honey don't cry so hard"?' 'How should I know?' 'Well, it's a coon song, you ought to know.' But when I discovered that though they never believed the truth, they swallowed the most fantastic lies, I amused myself a good deal.

That first afternoon when I had walked along the gravel path which circled the muddy green hockey field, I crossed a flower bed and looked into one of the dim classrooms. It was a grey-yellow day. Not so bad as the white glaring days of the icy wind days. Still, bad enough. The sky was the colour of no hope, but they don't notice it, they are used to it, they expect me to grow used to it.

It was while I was staring at the empty ghostly-looking desks that I felt a lump in my throat. Tears – my heart a heavy jagged weight. Of course premonitions, presentiments had brushed me before, cold and clammy as a bat's wing, but nothing like this. Despair, grey-yellow like their sky. I stayed by the window in the cold thinking 'What is going to become of me? Why am I here at all?'

One hot silent July afternoon I was told that I was to go to England with my Aunt Clare, who had been staying with us for the last six months. I was to go to a school called The Perse in Cambridge.

'It is very good of her to take charge of you.' I noticed that my father was looking at me in a critical, disapproving way. 'I am sure,' he said, 'that it will do you a great deal of good.'

'I sincerely hope so,' said Aunt Clare dubiously.

This interview chilled me and I was silent all that evening. (So, I noticed, was my mother.) I went up to my bedroom early and took out the exercise book that I called 'Secret Poems.'

> *I am going to England*
> *What shall I find there?*
>
> *'No matter what*
> *Not what I sought' said Byron.*
>
> *Not what I sought,*
> *Not what I seek.*

I wrote no more poems for a very long time.

Unfortunately it was a grey lowering August in London, not cold but never bright or fresh. My Aunt Clare, a tireless walker, dragged me round to see all the sights and after a week I went to sleep in the most unlikely places; St Paul's, Westminster Abbey, Madame Tussaud's, the Wallace Collection, the zoo, even a shop or two. She was a swift but absentminded walker and I could easily lag behind and find a chair or bench to droop on.

'She can't help it,' I heard her explain once. 'It's the change of climate, but it can really be very annoying.'

Mistake after mistake.

But I knew the exact day when I lost belief in myself and cold caution took control. It was when she bought me the ugly dress instead of the pretty wine-coloured one.

'It's a perfect fit,' said the saleswoman, 'and the young lady is so pale, she needs colour.'

My aunt looked at the price ticket. 'No, not at all suitable,' she said and chose a drab dress which I disliked. I didn't argue for the big shop and the saleswoman whom I thought very beautiful

bewildered me. But I was heartbroken. I'd have to appear before
a lot of strange girls in this hideous garment. 'They're bound to
dislike me.'

Outside in the hostile street we got into the hateful bus (always
squashed up against perfect strangers – millions of perfect
strangers in this horrible place). The bus wheels said 'And *when*
we say we've *always* won, and *when* they ask us *how* it's done.'
(You wouldn't dare say how you do it, not straight out you wouldn't,
it's too damned mean the way you do it.)

At Cambridge I refused to say anything except 'Oh yes, that's
very nice indeed. This bridge, that building. King's College Chapel.
Oh yes. Very nice.'

'Is that all you can say about King's College Chapel?' said
Miss Born disdainfully.

Privately I thought that a Protestant service was all wrong in
King's College Chapel, that it missed the smell of incense, splendid vestments, Latin prayers. 'You've forgotten that you stole it
from the Catholics but it hasn't forgotten,' I thought. Fortunately
I didn't say this.

'They sang very nicely indeed.'

Well, I walked up and down the hockey field till I'd stopped
crying then went back to the small dining-room where there was
always a blazing fire, I will say. But I could not eat anything and
Miss Rode sent me to bed.

'I hear,' she said, 'that you feel the cold, so you'll find extra
blankets and Jarvis will bring you up a hot water bottle and hot
milk.'

Lying in bed, warm and comfortable, I tried to argue my fears
away. After all, it's only for another eighteen months at the worst
and though I don't particularly want to go back, there it is, solid
and safe, the street, the sandbox tree, the stone steps, the long
gallery with the round table at the top. But I was astonished to
discover how patchy, vague and uncertain my memory had
become. I had forgotten so much so soon.

I remembered the stars, but not the moon. It was a different
moon, but different in what way? I didn't know. I remembered

the shadows of trees more clearly than the trees, the sound of
rain but not the sound of my mother's voice. Not really. I remembered the smell of dust and heat, the coolness of ferns but not
the scent of any of the flowers. As for the mountains, the hills
and the sea, they were not only thousands of miles away, they
were years away.

About three days before the holidays ended, Miss Rode handed
me a letter from Switzerland. 'But I don't know anyone in Switzerland.'

'Open it and find out,' she said.

I put the letter under my pillow for a time, thinking it would
be something to look forward to the next morning, but I was too
curious to wait. I opened it – it was signed Myrtle. I was disappointed. What on earth had Myrtle, a girl I hardly knew, to write
to me about? This was the letter which was to change my life.

Dear West Indies,
I have been thinking about you a lot since I came to Switzerland,
perhaps because my mother is getting divorced. I see now what a silly
lot of fools we were about everything that matters and I don't think you
are. It was all those words in *The Winter's Tale* that Miss Born wanted
to blue pencil, you rolled them out as though you knew what they meant.
My mother said you made the other girls look like waxworks and when
you dropped your cap you picked it up so naturally, like a born actress.
She says that you ought to go on the stage and why don't you? I like
Switzerland all right. There are a lot of English here and my mother
says what a pity! She can be very sarcastic. Let me hear from you soon.
I felt I simply had to write this.
                          Yours ever,
                          Myrtle

I read this letter over and over again, then rolled about from
side to side making up an answer. 'Dear Myrtle, Thanks for letter. I did not know what the words meant, I just liked the sound
of them. I thought your mother very pretty, but yes, a bit sarky.'

Then I stopped writing the imaginary letter to Myrtle for suddenly, like an illumination, I knew exactly what I wanted to do.
Next day I wrote to my father. I told him that I longed to be an
actress and that I wanted to go to the Academy of Dramatic Art
in Gower Street.

'I am *quite* sure. Please think very seriously about it. I don't mind this place and some of the mistresses are quite all right but it's really a waste of money my being here . . . '

When the answer arrived it was yes and I was happier than I'd ever been in my life. Nothing could touch me, not praise, nor blame. Nor incredulous smiles. A new term had started but Myrtle hadn't come back and Camilla was still away in Thaxted.

'There is an entrance examination,' they'd say. 'You won't pass it.'

'Yes I will,' but really I was extremely nervous about this examination and surprised when I did pass. The judges had seemed so very bored. The place was not Royal then and was known colloquially as 'Tree's school'. It wasn't so choosy then perhaps.

My aunt installed me in an Upper Bedford Place boarding-house and left me to it; she strongly disapproved of the whole business. However she soon came back to London and took a small flat near Baker Street to see for herself how I was getting on.

'When you're stabbed in the back you fall like this, and when you're stabbed in the front you fall like this, but if you stab yourself you fall differently. Like this.'

'Is that all you've learnt?'

'No.' I told her about fencing classes, ballet, elocution, gesture. And so on. 'No plays?' she wanted to know. 'Yes of course. I was Celia in *As You Like It* and we did Paolo and Francesca once.' And I was Francesca in the little dark sitting-room.

> ' *"Now I am free and gay,*
> *Light as a dancer when the strings begin*
> *All ties that held me I cast off . . . "* '

'You'll find that very expensive,' my aunt said.

I spent the vacation with relatives in Yorkshire and one morning early my uncle woke me with a cablegram of the news of my father's sudden death. I was quite calm and he seemed surprised, but the truth was that I hadn't taken it in, I didn't believe him.

Harrogate was full of music that late summer. Concertinas, harpists, barrel organs, singers. One afternoon in an unfamiliar street, listening to a man singing 'It may be for years and it may be for ever', I burst into tears and once started I couldn't stop.

Soon I was packed off to responsible Aunt Clare in Wales. 'You cry without reticence,' she told me the day after I arrived. 'And you watch me without reticence,' I thought.

There was a calm slow-moving river called the Afon that flowed at the bottom of my aunt's garden. Walking up and down looking at the water she said that she could understand my grief. My father's death meant that it was impossible to keep me in London at a theatrical school. 'Quite out of the question.' She had heard from my mother who wished me to return home at once. I said that I didn't want to go, 'not yet.' 'But you'll have to.' 'I won't . . . '

Aunt Clare changed the subject. 'What a lovely day. Straight from the lap of the gods' (she talked like that). As her voice went on I was repeating to myself 'Straight from the lap of the gods'.

At last we went up to London to do some shopping for hot weather clothes and one afternoon when she was visiting friends I went to Blackmore's agency in the Strand and after some palaver was engaged as one of the chorus of a touring musical comedy. I was astonished when Aunt Clare told me that I'd behaved deceitfully, outrageously. A heated argument followed.

She said that my contract had no legal value at my age and threatened to stop me. I said that if she stopped me I'd marry a young man at the Academy whom I knew she detested. He'd been to tea at the Marylebone flat. 'He may be a horrid boy but he's got a lot of money.' 'How do you know that?' said my aunt in a different voice, a sharp voice.

'He showed me the letter from his trustees. He's twenty-one. Besides at the Academy everyone knows who has money and who hasn't. That's one thing they do know.'

'If this young man is well-off you ought to think very carefully before you answer him.'

'I have answered him. I said no. But if you interfere with my contract I'll marry him and be miserable. And it will be your fault.'

This went on for a long time. Then Aunt Clare said that it was unfair to expect her to deal with me, that she'd write to my mother. 'Perhaps we'll be rehearsing before she answers,' I said hopefully. But when my mother's letter arrived it was very vague. She didn't approve, neither did she altogether disapprove. It seemed as if what with her grief for my father and her worry about money she was relieved that I'd be earning my own living in England. 'Not much of a living,' said my aunt.

'Some people manage. Why shouldn't I?'

The company was playing a musical comedy called *Our Miss Gibbs*. We rehearsed at the National Sporting Club somewhere in the Leicester Square / Covent Garden area. A large room with a stage up one end. Sometimes boxers would pass through looking rather shy on their way to other rooms, I supposed. It was foggy. First a black fog then a yellow one. I didn't feel well but I never missed a rehearsal. Once my aunt came with me and the girls approved of her so enthusiastically that I saw her in a new light. 'Is that your auntie? Oh, isn't she nice.'

She was a nice woman, I see that now.It was kind of her to take charge of me to please her favourite brother. But she wasn't exactly demonstrative. Even pecks on the cheek were very rare. And I craved for affection and reassurance. By far my nicest Cambridge memory was of the day an undergraduate on a bicycle knocked me flat as I was crossing the road. I wasn't hurt but he picked me up so carefully and apologized so profusely that I thought about him for a long time.

Talking to the other girls I realized that several of them dreaded the tour up North in the winter. We were going to Oldham, Bury, Leeds, Halifax, Huddersfield and so on. As for the boys, one of them showed me a sketch he'd done of a street in a northern town. He'd called it 'Why we drink'. But none of this prevented me from being excited and happy.

The man who engaged me at the agent's was at one rehearsal. He came up to me and said in a low voice: 'Don't tell the other girls that you were at Tree's school. They mightn't like it.' I hadn't any idea what he meant. But 'No, I won't tell anybody,' I promised.

Before the Deluge

WHEN I FIRST MET Daisie she was playing Lily Elsie's part in the English stage version of the *Count of Luxembourg* (Lily was either ill or had gone on holiday). She was a very beautiful girl, perhaps the most beautiful girl I have ever seen. I think sometimes that while there are many more pretty and attractive girls now, there are fewer raving beauties.

There was another beauty in the chorus of the only pantomime I ever played in at the Lyceum Theatre. Her name was Kyrle and I was amused by the reactions of the Lyons waitresses to her. Instead of the sharp, appraising, flouncy glance that they'd give an ordinarily pretty girl, an amazed, humble expression would come into their faces, the way you'd look at Princess Graciosa or Sleeping Beauty just awakened, if you met her out for a walk.

Daisie was taller and more impressive than Kyrle. She had dark red hair, only shoulder length, but very thick and naturally wavy, huge blue eyes and long golden eyelashes which she never made up except for a little vaseline on the tips and on her eyelids. Sometimes she would add a touch of rouge if she thought she looked pale. She had classic features – not aquiline but Greek – a large, sweet mouth and white even teeth. She was rather tall for a musical comedy actress but slim and with a very good figure. I was quite surprised when I gradually learned how spiteful she was, though spiteful, I always felt, in an innocent way.

She gossiped in an ascending scale, exactly as the chorus gossiped. She would start comparatively mildly: 'She's a tart of course,' and end accusing the girl of every known and unknown vice. She seemed to get particularly annoyed if one of her friends married, especially if the man was rich or well-known. 'She's not the sort of woman who ought to get married at all, considering the life she's led, and as for him, well everybody knows he's rotten with it. What a pair! God help their children – if they have any,' she'd end piously. All this didn't prevent her from kissing the friend, when she next met her, and saying quite sincerely, often with tears in her eyes, 'Darling, I hope you'll be so very happy.'

She was really a very generous girl and could be impulsively kind. She was certainly kind to me in a rather patronizing way. Although I was so thin I used to wear long, tight whalebone stays. One expensive pair I had made my waist small and the large satin bow in front supplied the necessary curves, I hoped. Daisie rocked with laughter at this garment and soon persuaded me to throw it away and wear a suspender belt. She didn't approve of my lace and ribboned underclothes either, which were out of fashion she told me. Soon I wore instead very close-fitting directoire knickers. Some of her suggestions were beyond me, I felt the cold too much, but it did sink in that the scantier my underclothes were the better. Then she supervised my buying a suit and thus fitted out I was taken to see George Edwardes, the impresario of the day.

I was rather disappointed in 'The guv'nor', as he was called, for I'd heard many lurid stories about him. He was a quiet man who gave me a cup of tea and some good advice – which of course I didn't take. However, he suggested that I should be in the chorus of his number one touring company visiting all the big towns – Manchester, Dublin, Edinburgh, Liverpool – and if all went well and there were good reports of me he provised that I should be in the next show at Daly's.

I was very pleased. It was decidedly a step up from working for the man who employed me then, who did everything on the cheap, even shipping us to Ireland on a cattle boat. We were all violently sick and as we trooped off at Cork I looked at the other girls and thought what a bedraggled lot we were. And no wonder.

Daisie and I got to know each other quite well and I was often at her flat near Marble Arch, which I chiefly remember for the artificial butterflies on the net at the windows and the curtains of her huge bed. Her battle-axe of a mother disliked me so I can't say that I always enjoyed my visits there, and I felt like a page, walking behind her into smart restaurants holding the flowers that had been given to her after the show. 'I think I'd like a devilled bone,' she would say.

She gave her age as twenty-four and couldn't have been much older, but she had been on the stage for years. She had started before she was ten as a pantomime fairy and gone on from there. She had worked in fit-ups (one night stands). Killing work, she said. She had been a music hall turn billed as the singing star and indeed she had a lovely soprano voice, fresh and true. She worked hard at her singing and still took lessons when I knew her. Her teacher, an Italian, had been a well-known opera singer and was very good, she said.

But it was no use. Her face, her voice, nothing seemed to get over the footlights. In Bond Street people would turn and stare at her admiringly. On stage she was just a very pretty girl among a lot of other pretty girls. Songs that would bring down the house when Lily Elsie sang them were only politely applauded. This puzzled Daisie and she thought about it. Of course she couldn't act. She was always Daisie, the Manchester policeman's daughter and not a Viennese opera star at all, or anything else she was trying to be.

When I first knew her she made fun of temperamental actresses and told me that after Lily Elsie's big scene, she'd faint when she came off. Two of the stage hands were stationed in the wings to catch her when she fell. She – Daisie – thought that this was a fake, all put on and the most utter nonsense.

But gradually she changed her mind. She no longer jeered at temperament. On the contrary, she told me that now she often felt giddy and ill and realized it was a very great strain. One night she too had almost fainted. She said this with a certain amount of pride, as if she'd achieved something.

Soon Daisie's near faints or faints were as much a matter of routine as ever Lily Elsie's had been and unfortunately they weren't confined to the theatre. More and more often if you argued with or even contradicted her she'd sigh, put her hand to her head and flop.

The butterflies vanished (I suppose someone had told her that they were sentimental). They were replaced by huge spiders. I hated these things and looked nervously at them whenever I went into her flat for I was never quite sure that they weren't real. They were too lifelike altogether, crawling up lampshades or wallpaper.

One day she asked me to call and see her about noon. She wanted to speak to me. Something important. I knew that twelve o'clock was very early for Daisie but got there punctually. She opened the door dressed for the street, greeted me shortly and coldly and when we reached the sitting-room began pacing up and down.

At last she said: 'I hear you've been gossiping and telling lies about me all over the place. I think it's rather beastly, after all I've done for you.'

I said I never gossiped and certainly not about her. Gossip didn't interest me. 'And who am I supposed to lie and gossip to?' I spoke angrily because I was surprised and rather hurt. Instead of answering Daisie opened her eyes very wide, gave a little cry, and crashed to the floor bringing down a small table as she fell.

I was horrified. She seemed unconscious and I didn't know what to do. I thought of putting a cushion under her head, then remembered that it wasn't the right thing for every faint. Brandy? But I didn't know where it was kept.

I was still dithering when the door opened and a man came into the room and stared accusingly at me. He must have been waiting to take her out to lunch. Then her mother appeared from the kitchen; one look at her and I knew I was in for a torrent of abuse. I didn't feel that I could stand it and ran out of the flat into the street. As I left I herd him crooning: 'My poor, darling little girl, what have they done to you, my poor little sweetheart.'

Very soon after this my life changed, everything changed and I never saw or heard of Daisie again.

On Not Shooting
Sitting Birds

THERE IS no control over memory. Quite soon you find yourself being vague about an event which seemed so important at the time that you thought you'd never forget it. Or unable to recall the face of someone whom you could have sworn was there for ever. On the other hand, trivial and meaningless memories may stay with you for life. I can still shut my eyes and see Victoria grinding coffee on the pantry steps, the glass bookcase and the books in it, my father's pipe-rack, the leaves of the sandbox tree, the wallpaper of the bedroom in some shabby hotel, the hairdresser in Antibes. It's in this way that I remember buying the pink milanese silk underclothes, the assistant who sold them to me and coming into the street holding the parcel.

I had started out in life trusting everyone and now I trusted no one. So I had few acquaintances and no close friends. It was perhaps in reaction against the inevitable loneliness of my life that I'd find myself doing bold, risky, even outrageous things without hesitation or surprise. I was usually disappointed in these adventures and they didn't have much effect on me, good or bad, but I never quite lost the hope of something better or different.

One day, I've forgotten now where, I met this young man who smiled at me and when we had talked a bit I agreed to have dinner with him in a couple of days' time. I went home excited, for I'd liked him very much and began to plan what I should wear. I had a dress I quite liked, an evening cloak, shoes, stockings, but my underclothes weren't good enough for the occasion, I decided. Next day I went out and bought the milanese silk chemise and drawers.

So there we were seated at a table having dinner with a bedroom very obvious in the background. He was younger than I'd thought and stiffer and I didn't like him much after all. He kept eyeing me in such a wary, puzzled way. When we had finished our soup and the waiter had taken the plates away, he said: 'But you're a lady, aren't you?' exactly as he might have said, 'But you're really a snake or a crocodile, aren't you?'

'Oh no, not that you'd notice,' I said, but this didn't work. We looked glumly at each other across the gulf that had yawned between us.

Before I came to England I'd read many English novels and I imagined I knew all about the thoughts and tastes of various sorts of English people. I quickly decided that to distract or interest this man I must talk about shooting.

I asked him if he knew the West Indies at all. He said no, he didn't and I told him a long story of having been lost in the Dominican forest when I was a child. This wasn't true. I'd often been in the woods but never alone. 'There are no parrots now,' I said, 'or very few. There used to be. There's a Dominican parrot in the zoo – have you ever seen it? – a sulky bird, very old I think. However, there are plenty of other birds and we do have shooting parties. Perdrix are very good to eat, but ramiers are rather bitter.'

Then I began describing a fictitious West Indian shooting party and all the time I talked I was remembering the real thing. An old shotgun leaning up in one corner of the room, the round table in the middle where we would sit to make cartridges, putting the shot in, ramming it down with a wad of paper. Gunpowder? There was that too, for I remember the smell. I suppose the boys were trusted to be careful.

The genuine shooting party consisted of my two brothers, who shared the shotgun, some hangers-on and me at the end of the procession, for then I couldn't bear to be left out of anything. As soon as the shooting was about to start I would stroll away casually and when I was out of sight run as hard as I could, crouch down behind a bush and put my fingers in my ears. It wasn't that I was sorry for the birds, but I hated and feared the noise of the gun. When it was all over I'd quietly join the others. I must have done this unobtrusively or probably my brothers thought me too insignificant to worry about, for no one every remarked on my odd behaviour or teased me about it.

On and on I went, almost believing what I was saying, when he interrupted me. 'Do you mean to say that your brothers shot sitting birds?' His voice was cold and shocked.

I stared at him. How could I convince this man that I hadn't the faintest idea whether my brothers shot sitting birds or not? How could I explain now what really happened? If I did he'd think me a liar. Also a coward and there he'd be right, for I was afraid of many things, not only the sound of gunfire. But by this time I wasn't sure that I liked him at all so I was silent and felt my face growing as stiff and unsmiling as his.

It was a most uncomfortable dinner. We both avoided looking at the bedroom and when the last mouthful was swallowed he announced that he was going to take me home. The way he said this rather puzzled me. Then I told myself that probably he was curious to see where I lived. Neither of us spoke in the taxi except to say, 'Well, good night.' 'Good night.'

I felt regret when it came to taking off my lovely pink chemise, but I could still think: Some other night perhaps, another sort of man.

I slept at once.

Kikimora

THE BELL RANG. When Elsa opened the door a small, fair, plump young man advanced, bowed and said 'Baron Mumtael'.

'Oh yes, please come in,' said Elsa. She was aware that her smile was shy, her manner lacking in poise, for she had found his quick downward and upward glance intimidating. She led the way and asked him to sit down.

'What a very elegant dinner suit you are wearing,' said Baron Mumtael mockingly.

'Yes, isn't it? . . . oh, I don't think it is really,' said Elsa distractedly. 'I hate myself in suits,' she went on, plunging deep into the scorn of his pale blue eyes.

'The large armchair is of course your husband's and the smaller one yours,' said the baron quirking his mouth upwards. 'What a typical interior! Where shall I sit?'

'Sit wherever you like,' said Elsa. 'The interior is all yours. Choose your favourite bit.' But his cold glance quelled her and she added, twittering: 'Will you . . . do have a drink.'

Bottles of whisky, vermouth and soda water stood on a red lacquered tray. 'I'll have vermouth,' said Baron Mumtael firmly. 'No soda, thank you. And you?'

'A whisky I think,' Elsa said, annoyed that her hands had begun to shake with nervousness.

'How nice is ice on a hot afternoon. Are you . . . have you lived in America?'

'No. Oh, no.' She gulped her whisky and soda quickly.

'Charming,' said Baron Mumtael watching her maliciously, 'charming. I'm so glad you're not an American. I think some American women are a menace, don't you? The spoilt female is invariably a menace.'

'And what about the spoilt male?'

'Oh the spoilt male can be charming. No spoiling, no charm.'

'That's what I always say,' said Elsa eagerly. 'No spoiling, no charm.'

'No,' said Baron Mumtael. 'None. None at all. Will your husband be long do you think?'

'I think not, I think here he is.'

After Stephen came in the tension lessened. Baron Mumtael stopped fidgeting and settled down to a serious discussion of the politics of his native land, his love of England and his joy at having at last become a naturalized Englishman.

Elsa went out of the room to put the finishing touches to the meal. It was good, she thought. He would have to appreciate it. And indeed, the first time he addressed her, after they sat down, he said: 'What delicious food! I congratulate you.'

'It all came from various shops in Soho,' Elsa lied.

'Really delicious. And that picture fascinates me. What is it supposed to be?'

'Paradise.'

A naked man was riding into a dark blue sea. There was a sky to match, palm trees, a whale in one corner, and a butterfly in the other. 'Don't you like it?' she asked.

'Well,' said Baron Mumtael, 'I think it's colourful. It was painted by a woman, I feel sure.'

'No, it was painted by a man,' said Elsa. 'He said he put in the whale and the butterfly because everything has its place in Paradise.'

'Really,' said Baron Mumtael, 'I shouldn't have thought so. One can only hope not. Please tell me which shop in Soho supplied the guinea-fowl and really delicious sauté potatoes?'

'I've forgotten,' said Elsa vaguely. 'Somewhere around Wardour Street or Greek Street. I'm so bad at remembering where places are. Of course you have to fry the potatoes up with onions and then you get something like Pommes Lyonnaises.'

But Baron Mumtael had already turned away and was continuing his conversation with Stephen about the next war. He gave it three months (and he wasn't far wrong.)

The black cat, Kikimora, who had been sitting quietly in the corner of the room, sprang onto his lap. The Baron looked surprised, stroked the animal cautiously, then sprang up and said: 'My God! She's scratched me, quite badly.' And indeed there was blood on the finger he was holding up.

'I can't think what's come over him,' Elsa said. 'I've never known him do such a thing before. He's so staid as a rule. You naughty, bad cat.' She snatched him up and flung him outside the door. 'I'm so very sorry.'

'Elsa spoils that cat,' Stephen said.

'I think,' said Baron Mumtael, 'that something ought to be done about my finger. You can't be too careful about the scratches of a she-cat. If you'd be so kind as to let me have some disinfectant?'

'He's not a she-cat, he's a he-cat,' said Elsa.

'Really,' said Baron Mumtael. 'Can you let me have some disinfectant? That is, if you have any,' he added.

'I've got harpic and peroxide of hydrogen,' said Elsa belligerently, repeated whiskies having given her courage. 'Which will you have?'

'My *dear* Elsa . . . ' said Stephen.

She left them and locked herself in the bathroom. When she came back Baron Mumtael was still holding his finger up, talking politics.

'I haven't forgotten the cotton wool,' she said.

At last the finger was disinfected and a spotless white handkerchief wrapped round it. 'One can't be too careful with a she-cat,' Baron Mumtael kept repeating. And Elsa, breathing deeply, would always answer. 'He's not a she-cat, he's a he-cat.'

'Good-bye,' said Baron Mumtael as he left. 'I shall never forget your charming evening's entertainment. Or your so very elegant dinner suit. It's been quite an experience. All so typical.'

As soon as he was out of the door Elsa said: 'What a horrible man!'

'I didn't think so,' Stephen said. 'I thought he was rather a nice chap. It's a relief to meet somebody who doesn't abuse the English.'

'Abuse the English?' said Elsa. 'He'd never abuse the English. It must be comforting to be able to take out naturalization papers when you find your spiritual home.'

'You hardly shone,' Stephen said.

'Of course I shone. He brought out all my sparkle. He was so nice, wasn't he?'

'I didn't notice that he wasn't nice,' said Stephen.

'No. You wouldn't,' Elsa muttered.

She went into the kitchen, caught up the cat and began to kiss it. 'My darling cat. My darling black velvet cat with the sharp claws. My angel, my little gamecock . . . '

Kikimora purred and even licked a tear off her face with his rough tongue. But when he struggled and she put him down he yawned elaborately and walked away.

Elsa went to the bedroom, took off the suit she had been wearing, and with the help of a pair of scissors began to tear it up. Stephen heard the rending noise and called out: 'What on earth are you doing?'

'I'm destroying my feminine charm,' Elsa said. 'I thought I'd make a nice quick clean job of it.'

Night Out 1925

Iᴛ ʜᴀᴅ ʙᴇᴇɴ ʀᴀɪɴɪɴɢ and the green and red reflections of the lights in the wet streets made Suzy think of Francis Carco's books. She was walking with a man called Gilbert, known to his acquaintances in Montparnasse as 'stingy Bertie'.

Gilbert, pointing out that the rain had stopped and that the fresh air would do them good, was taking her to a place which he said was great fun and a bit of a surprise.

They crossed the Seine and went on walking. Suzy was about to tell him that she was getting tired and must have a taxi when he stopped half-way up a quiet side street. They went down a few steps into a long narrow room lined with tall mirrors, and a woman dressed in black came forward.

'Bonsoir Madame,' said Gilbert familiarly. '*Comment allez vous?* I've brought a friend to see you.'

'*Bonsoir Madame, bonsoir Monsieur,*' said the woman showing her teeth.

She doesn't know him from Adam, Suzy was thinking when she lost sight of her and they were surrounded by a crowd of girls in varying stages of nakedness. They arranged themselves in a pattern, the ones in front kneeling, the ones at the back standing. Their spiky eye-lashes stuck out. They opened their mouths and fluttered their tongues at the visitors, not in derision as might be supposed, but in invitation.

I bet they are giving us the bird too, Suzy told herself.

'Choose one,' said Gilbert. Suzy chose a small dark girl who she thought less alarming than the rest. Gilbert chose a much taller girl with red hair and a long chin. Rather like a mare.

The others melted away, presumably to wait for the next clients.

Suzy, Gilbert and their girls went to sit at one of several empty tables at the other end of the room. A very old waiter shuffled up and asked what they'd have to drink.

'What sort of man takes a job as waiter in a place like this?' said Gilbert in English but without lowering his voice. The girls asked for '*deux cerises*', Suzy and Gilbert for Pernod.

'He'll soon be dead,' said Suzy when the waiter had gone. 'You needn't be so virtuous about him. He can hardly walk as it is.'

'A good thing too,' said Gilbert.

The music of a java reached them from some other room. The drinks arrived and the girls began to chat in an animated way but Gilbert answered briefly or not at all and Suzy was silent because she felt shy and couldn't think of anything appropriate to say. After this had gone on for some time the mare began to look sulky but the other girl seemed worried – a hostess who feared the party was going to be dull, trying to imagine a way to liven it up.

Eventually she turned to Suzy, lifted her skirt and kissed her knee.

'*Tu es folle,*' said the mare.

'*Mon amie n'aime pas ça,*' said Gilbert.

'Ah!' said the girl. She was wearing a very short white tunic, white socks and heelless black strap shoes. A brass medal hung round her neck. Her face was quite round. She looked rather stupid but sweet, Suzy thought, smiling and putting her hand on the small plump hand.

'Tut tut,' said Gilbert. 'What am I to make of this?'

'I suppose,' said Suzy looking at him, 'that if she got fed up here she could clear out. Could she?'

'Of course she could.' said Gilbert. 'I'll ask her.'

'*Mais certainement,*' said the girl. '*Naturellement. Pourquoi pas?*' When no one spoke, she added in a low voice, '*seulement, seulement . . .*'

'*Seulement* what?' said Suzy. 'Seulement what?'

'Oh do shut up Suzy,' said Gilbert. 'What's the matter with you? Why these idiotic questions?'

'Come upstairs,' said the mare. 'Come and see us do our "*Cinéma*". You won't be disappointed.'

She also had on a white tunic, white socks and black slippers, but the tunic was open to the waist in front.

'No,' said Gilbert. 'I think not.' He went on speaking to Suzy: 'This place had gone off dreadfully. It really used to be fun, it had an atmosphere. It's not the same thing at all now. Of course we are much too early. But still . . . '

'We might give you a few ideas,' said the mare. 'You look as if you need them.'

'Come along Suzy.' He sounded vexed. 'Finish your drink and we'll try somewhere else.'

'I'm all for that,' said Suzy, 'because I really don't think I'm going down very well here. One of the girls at the other end of the room is going to come across and slap my face any minute.'

'Which one?' said Gilbert turning to look. 'Where?'

'The one with the magnificent breasts,' said Suzy.

A girl with beautiful breasts and a very slim body was staring at her with an extremely angry expression.

'Very bad tempered,' said Gilbert.

'She's getting quite het up,' Suzy said.

'Yes I see,' said Gilbert.

'She thinks I'm here to stare and jeer. You can't blame her.'

The woman who had first met them came up to their table. 'Are any of these girls annoying you?'

'Why no,' said Suzy. 'Absolutely not. We think them charming, don't we Gilbert?'

Gilbert didn't answer.

The woman glanced meaningly at the two girls and walked away.

'*Venez donc,*' said the mare. 'Come upstairs. For you it will be only three hundred francs. And the champagne.'

'No,' said Gilbert, 'I regret but no. Not this evening,' and in

English, 'That's quite enough of that. Let's depart.'

The girls knew that the clients were dissatisfied and intended to leave.

The dark girl was silent. But the mare began a long rapid speech to which Gilbert listened with a wry smile.

'She wants us to stump up, of course,' he said at last. 'I suppose she thinks it a good idea to harp on the difficulties of her profession. Same old miseries. No splendours. Not any more. Sad, isn't it?' He laughed.

The dark girl jumped up and hit the table with her fist so hard that her glass fell over.

'*Et qu'est-ce que tu vuex que ça leur fasse?*' she said loudly. '*Qu'est-ce que tu veux que ça leur fasse?*'

'Drama!' said Gilbert. 'What do you think it matters to them, she said.'

'Yes. Gilbert, we can't walk out and not give these girls a sou.'

'They've had their drinks,' said Gilbert.

'Two cherries in brandy. Not much. Let me give them something, will you?'

'Well,' said Gilbert, 'if I do, will you promise to come on somewhere else? Somewhere where they'll put a bit more pep into it.'

'Yes,' said Suzy, 'if you want me to.'

'All right. Here you are then.' He handed her his wallet. 'Give them each –' He marked 10 on the table with his cigarette. 'That's quite enough.' He turned away to look at the angry girl.

Suzy opened his wallet and took out two notes. She folded them carefully and gave one to each girl. Each smiled and slipped the note into the top of her sock.

'You permit me?' said the dark one. She took off the medal and, giving it to Suzy, kissed her warmly. 'I will be happy to see any friend of yours who visits Paris.'

Dédé was printed on one side of the medal; on the other the address.

'*Alors,*' said the mare briskly. '*Merci bien m'sieur et dame. Au 'voir. A la prochaine.*'

'I wish they'd go away,' Suzy said.

'*Allez-vous-en,*' said Gilbert.

No one took any notice of them as they walked down the long room.

'*Bonsoir Madame. Bonsoir Monsieur,*' said the woman at the door.

They were outside.

'That was rather a fiasco,' Gilbert said. 'Sorry. It won't be difficult to find a more amusing place. I'll get a taxi.'

'Yes,' said Suzy. 'But perhaps I ought to tell you that I gave those girls a fiver each.'

'You did what?' Gilbert said. He opened his wallet and was silent. His silence lasted so long that Suzy couldn't bear it any longer. She said excitedly: 'Why shouldn't they have some money? Why shouldn't they have some money?'

'If you feel like that about it,' said Gilbert, 'why don't you try giving away your own instead of making free with someone else's?'

'Because I haven't got any,' said Suzy. 'That's easy.'

'Of course,' Gilbert said. 'Other people are always expected to pay for your oh-so-beautiful ideas. And all such bloody hypocrisy. You don't care at all really. When you'd given those girls my money you were only too anxious to see the last of them, weren't you?'

'Oh no, it wasn't that,' Suzy said. 'I thought we'd better go before there was any chance of your finding out.'

'What did you imagine I'd do? Make a row? Try to get the money back?'

'I didn't know what you'd do,' Suzy said. 'So it seemed best to get away quickly.'

'Well thanks a lot.' He walked on, to Suzy's relief, still talking in a level voice.

'And it shows how little you know about these things. If those girls had done all their stunts, all their stunts, a hundred francs would have been a royal tip. A royal tip. You've given them ten pounds for nothing at all. I'll be a laughing stock. That bit at the end was a fake. It was the "*cinéma*" for the clients who can't be persuaded upstairs. And you fell for it. I'll be a laughing stock,' he repeated.

'No, I don't think it was a fake,' Suzy said.

But she remembered how confidingly he had handed her his wallet and began to feel guilty.

'Ten quid isn't so very much. And you had a wad of fivers in that wallet. Was what I did so awful? Just think how you'll be received when you go back. The tall handsome Englishman who gives ten quid for nothing at all. You'll be a legend not a laughing stock.'

They'd reached the end of the street.

'A bus that will take you back to Montparnasse stops near here,' said Gilbert stiffly.

They waited. A woman's scarlet hat was lying in the gutter.

'Poor old hat,' said Suzy. 'Poor poor old hat. Someone ought to write a poem about that hat.' She was still holding Dédé's medal.

'Just a word to the wise before we part,' Gilbert said. 'Don't hang onto that medal. I know you, you'll leave it on your night table and whoever brings up your breakfast will see it. Better not.'

'They won't care either,' said Suzy.

'That's what you think. Better not. Believe you me.'

Suzy began to giggle. She arranged the medal carefully under the red hat and holding up her head said solemnly, 'Rest in Peace in the name of Allah the Compassionate, the Merciful.'

'Here comes your bus,' said Gilbert. 'It stops quite near the Dôme and I suppose that you can find your way from there.'

'Yes I'll be all right. *Au 'voir* Gilbert. *A la prochaine.*'

'There's not going to be a next time,' said Gilbert as he walked away.

Suzy got into the bus relieved that it was half empty. She sat down and listened to the voices in her head as she thought about the evening.

'Same old miseries. No more splendour. Not now. *Et qu'est-ce que tu veux que ça leur fasse?*'

The Chevalier of
the Place Blanche[*]

H E WAS intimately acquainted with the police of
three countries, and he sat alone in a small restaurant not far
from the Boulevard Montparnasse sipping an *apéritif* moodily,
for he disliked Montparnasse and detested solitude. He had left
his native Montmartre to dine with a lady and had arrived twenty
minutes late. She was not of those usually kept waiting and she
had already departed.

'*Sacré Floriane*', muttered the Chevalier. He looked at a
Swedish couple at the next table, at the bald American by the
door, and at the hairy Anglo-Saxon novelist in the corner, and
thought that they were a strange-looking lot, and exceedingly
depressing. (*Quelles gueules qu'ils ont,* was how he put it.) The
place was full, but he was certainly the only French client. Then
he felt a draught: someone had come in and left the door open.
He turned to scowl, and, as he did so, the girl who had entered
walked past him and sat down in the chair opposite. She took
possession of his table, as it were, without looking at him and
with only a slight gesture of apology. Evidently another foreigner.
But the presence of a youthful female was soothing, and his ill
humour vanished. She was a tall, blonde girl, not beautiful, not
pretty, not chic; nevertheless, there was something. The Chevalier, who was used to labelling women accurately, decided that

---

[*] This story is a much-adapted translation of one written by Edouard de Nève.

she was of the species *femme du monde*. Then he began to feel
sure that she was an artist, a painter, one of those young people
who come to Paris with the express purpose of making the fortunes of all the hotel and restaurant proprietors of the *quartier*
Montparnasse.

The girl spoke to the waiter. Her accent, though slight, was
unmistakable – English or American. English, he decided, after
carefully observing her hat. At this point an old man, carrying a
concertina, came into the restaurant and asked permission to play.
The proprietor nodded from behind the counter, and he began a
waltz which the Chevalier vaguely remembered having heard
when a small boy. He remarked aloud: *'Tiens!* That makes me
feel young again.'

'It gives me the *cafard*,' said the girl, answering him in French.

'Madame,' said the Chevalier seriously, 'one must kill a *cafard*
at once, cruelly and without scruple.' The girl laughed, but her
eyes were so unhappy that he looked away from her, fearing that
she was about to cry.

He said: 'After all, it is always possible to kill a *cafard*. For
that champagne is best. That costs money naturally, but there
are other ways.' She did not answer, and he went on: 'Do you
know Montmartre well?'

'No,' she said. 'Hardly at all.'

'A pity. I live there. Shall I tell you about it?' He spoke in
English.

She said hastily, 'No, I understand you perfectly. Where did
you learn your English? It doesn't matter, don't tell me. When
you speak to me, will you speak French? I like your voice in French
so much.'

'Is that so?' he asked politely. 'As you wish.'

It was about an hour later that she said, 'Will you take me to
Montmartre tonight?'

'But certainly.' He looked steadily at her with bright, hard eyes.
'Where?'

'I don't mind. Anywhere.'

'*Bon.* We'll go about half past ten to look at Montmartre, and if you are still sad when we come back you are a *neurasthénic.* Hereditary, hopeless.'

'All right,' she said. 'But there's one condition. I pay my share.'

The Chevalier thought this reasonable, acceptable, and in no way contrary to his dignity as a male. He had the habit of pleasing women, but not spending much money on them. Indeed he had organized his life quite otherwise.

They shook hands solemnly. 'Come along,' he said, 'let's go and kill the *cafard.*'

They took the *métro.* 'Place J. B. Clément' she read as they emerged by the light of a street-lamp. 'It sounds like a Deputy.'

The Chevalier, who had seemed preoccupied, told her that J. B. Clément had been, on the contrary, a poet.

'He composed the most beautiful song in the world, the "Temps des Cerises".'

'I don't know it,' she said.

'But you must know it.' He stopped to gesticulate eagerly. 'It begins like this: *"Lorsque reviendra le temps des cerises".*' He sang the line in a voice that was suddenly grave and profound.

She said that she remembered vaguely that it was not a lively song.

'*Comment,* not lively?' He sounded scandalized. 'It is beautiful, and that is enough. It finishes: *"Profitez en bien des temps des cerises . . ."* There's good advice for you.' He began to laugh and walked on.

She glanced sideways at him. Childlike, that's what he was. What could he possibly do to earn his living, she wondered, and ended by asking him.

'I work in an office.'

'You work in an office?' she said astonished.

'Yes. I cheat Americans before they have time to cheat me.'

'You do it first,' she said. 'A good motto.'

He repeated, delighted, 'That's it! I do it first. Look at the grey house opposite. I live there. One evening, will you come to see me and look down on the lights of Paris?'

They were at the end of the old rue Vincent.

'Oh, but it's beautiful here,' she said.

'You must see it from my window,' insisted the Chevalier.

He tried to see the expression of her eyes, for he felt that there was only one logical end to all this, but she neither answered nor looked at him, and her height and what seemed to him the extraordinary austerity of her clothes were rather alarming. He added hastily that that would be for another evening.

They went to a nightclub but after an hour she told him that she wished to go home. 'The *cafard* is dead for the moment.'

In the taxi he asked her name. 'Margaret Lucas. And you? I imagine that a letter addressed to the Chevalier of the Place Blanche won't find you' (for she had heard someone in the night-club hail him by that name – how was she to know with what irony?).

'Ah, you wish to write to me?' he asked eagerly.

'Perhaps. Next time I have a *cafard*.'

He told her ceremoniously: 'Maurice Fernande, 139 rue Vincent. *Pour vous servir*, Mees Margaret.'

'No – just Margaret.'

He said: 'We should drink *Auf Bruderschaft* as the Germans do.'

'Some other evening.'

'Haven't you got any relations here, Margaret? It must be lonely for a young girl by herself in Paris.'

'I'm not a young girl,' she answered indifferently, 'and I've several friends here.'

'Send me a *pneu* when you wish to see me.'

The street was deserted; the last *métro* had gone, and as a taxi willing to climb to the Butte at that hour would be expensive, he decided to walk. As he walked he calculated his chances of escape from a very unfortunate situation. He should not have wasted an evening, evidently.

It was perfectly true that he worked in a Tourist Office. He had waited his opportunity there for three long months. At length the opportunity had come. A cheque for thirty thousand francs had disappeared to be converted, as he knew only too well, into a couple of Impressionist pictures fabricated by a friend of his, and several new suits of clothes.

Things had not gone according to plan. He had not resold the pictures nearly as profitably as he had hoped and he would have to give an account of the cheque much sooner than he had expected. Well, what did it matter, he thought? He could find the money. He could always find the money. There were many women in the world and for what purpose but to aid and comfort in just such an emergency?

There was the Baronne, a doubtfully authentic Baronne, but her money was authentic enough; there was Madame Yda, who had lately set up in business as a *Grande Couturière*. Both these ladies had some affection for him and had never hesitated to prove it in more ways than one. As for the Englishwoman . . . perhaps Fate had sent him the Englishwoman, and he looked anything but childlike as he thought it.

During the following week he got busy, calling several times at the hotel of his friend, the Baronne, always to be told that Madame was unable to receive him. He wrote and his letter was unanswered. She was obviously suspicious or resentful and he concluded, without wasting time on vain regrets, that there was nothing doing. And addressed himself to Madame Yda.

That lady observed him carefully with the eyes of an intelligent monkey; she was thin, elegant and wore pearls, which, if real, were certainly worth having. He spoke lengthily and fluently.

'Sorry *mon vieux*,' she said when he had finished. 'Business is bad just now. Besides, one never sees you except when you want money. That is not clever of you. Thirty thousand francs is a sum.'

'Then it's no?' he demanded.

'For the moment, impossible.'

'Very well, we won't speak of it.'

When she asked him, with a hesitation not without pathos, if he would dine with her that evening – *sans rancune* – 'Impos-

sible' he said, smiling charmingly, and added with his most inso-
lent expression: 'I've something better to do, *ma vieille!*'

He departed without giving her time to answer and went home
deep in thought. In his pocket was a *penumatique* from Margaret
which informed him that she would dine with him that evening
in rue Vincent. They had seen each other several times and the
second time they had met she had confided in him. At least she
had said that she was tired of Paris and wished to go to Austria
or Spain – yes Spain; she had many things to forget, and he had
instantly diagnosed an unhappy love affair. He had not encour-
aged her to give details for all unhappy love affairs are alike and
he had heard the history of so many. He thought that women
were all the same; they complicated things in the most idiotic
fashion. He began to discuss with real interest the details of her
tour in Spain. He calculated rapidly. Yes, this must be her last
night in Paris. He knew the importance of a *mise-en-scène* on
these occasions and he bought crimson roses to place in a yellow
vase, white roses for a black one. He bought things to eat which
he supposed English girls to like. He bought two bottles of Extra
Dry. He tied two pink silk handkerchiefs over the crude electric
light and strewed cushions from his divan (of which he was very
proud) on the floor. Finally he arrayed himself in the garment or
garments which he called his 'smoking' and sat down to wait. He
made no definite plans – he seldom planned things in detail but
her conquest had now become a necessity.

She arrived rather late wearing a dress which, though she
had bought it in a French shop, yet gave the impression of being
completely English. She admired the roses and the view but did
not appear to notice the smoking.

They stood at the window looking down on a glittering silhouette of Paris and he took her hand, kissed it and was instantly
possessed with a real wish to kiss her mouth and an intense curiosity. It was with genuine desire that he tried to take her into his
arms. 'Don't do that. I dislike it very much.' Her voice was calm,
she had not even moved, but his arms dropped to his sides and
he stared at her as if she had flung icy water in his face.

Why then had she come? Was the little fool trying to provoke him? Then he remembered having heard that the English, before becoming animated, must be given something to drink, and without a word he brought her an *apéritif*. But he was a temperamental animal and all his *élan* had departed; he looked gloomy and resentful as they sat down at the carefully decorated little table. She would give him money all the same before she left – *la garce*.

Towards the end of the meal she said: 'Tell me, Maurice, will you come and join me in Madrid?'

'I?' he said. 'I come to Madrid! Ah, if I could – if I had the money. But *voilà*. Remember the office I told you about? I owe thirty thousand francs there and I must give them back tomorrow or I'm *fichu,* done for.'

'Give them back then,' she advised.

'You have good ideas,' he said with a rather embarrassed laugh. 'I to give them back *trente mille balles*? Why, I haven't the first sou of it!'

'I will give you the money,' she said, lighting a cigarette and watching him thoughtfully.

'You will give me thirty thousand francs! *Mon Dieu*, but this is funny.'

'On condition that you come with me to Madrid. We can send the money from there. Is it amusing, Madrid?'

He answered mechanically: 'I think Madrid is ugly – Seville is beautiful.'

She drew a deep breath and thought: 'Seville.'

'What do you find strange in all this? If you knew how unutterably bored I am, how much I disliked my life, you wouldn't find anything I did to get away from it strange. I think it's a very reasonable bargain indeed. I'll give you the money you need – I've got lots of money – you will try to amuse me and make me happier. I'm not asking you to make love to me, I've a horror of that sort of thing. . . . A horror,' she repeated.

He listened with a growing uneasiness as she went on picturing their life together in Spain. 'I think you are a type, Maurice.

You make me see things more vividly and I want to study you. I'm sick of trying to paint,' she said. 'I want to write a book about the modern Apache.'

'The modern Apache!' echoed the Chevalier. And my smoking then, he thought indignantly, hasn't the woman noticed my smoking? Does she think that an Apache . . .

'Well they do exist, don't they?'

He answered with a shrug. 'Oh yes, they existed. And *plus ça change, plus c'est la même chose.*'

'And they're brutal, reckless, all that?' She quoted in a cold amused voice: *'Du sang, de la volupté, de la mort.'*

He did not answer her. He was utterly taken aback.

'In any case, you interest me,' she said. Then, seemingly possessed by a devastating wish to be frank, added: 'As a type – not as a man.'

She considered him in a manner which stung his masculine pride to the quick and turned his uneasiness into definite revolt. He did not know which revolted him more, the idea of trailing about Seville, at the orders of this woman who was neither pretty nor chic, or the idea that she believed him capable – he, the conqueror of women – of playing such a role.

'Non, merde alors! . . .' he thought. He felt hot with rage and resentment and, forgetful of everything but his rage and his desire to triumph over her, he made a superb gesture.

'Don't let's talk about it, Margaret. Tomorrow morning you will be on your way to Spain and I will be here in my bed and that is all. I to come away with you? I? But you would be so unhappy with me as you have never been in your life, my poor girl. Apaches! Apaches. . . . And then? To write books is not what an Apache needs of a woman, I tell you that. You say you have a horror of this and a horror of that. I have a horror of a woman who talks and talks and never feels anything. It's all literature, what you say.'

For the first time she dropped her eyes. 'I've vexed you. I didn't mean to.'

He stared at her sulkily, with dislike.

She stared back, then said, 'I suppose I'd better go. I've enjoyed this evening. It's a pity that . . . oh well, it doesn't matter. Don't come with me on any account. I can find my own way to the *métro*.' She put on her hat without looking in the glass, the unnatural creature.

He longed to do something violent to break down that air of cool friendliness, but the desire to live up to his smoking was too strong. He bowed stiffly and stood listening to the sound of her low heels descending the uncarpeted stairs. Nothing for it now but the midnight train to Brussels and a very thin time indeed.

The Insect World

AUDREY began to read. Her book was called *Nothing So Blue*. It was set in the tropics. She started at the paragraph which described the habits of an insect called the jigger.

Almost any book was better than life, Audrey thought. Or rather, life as she was living it. Of course, life would soon change, open out, become quite different. You couldn't go on if you didn't hope that, could you? But for the time being there was no doubt that it was pleasant to get away from it. And books could take her away.

She could give herself up to the written word as naturally as a good dancer to music or a fine swimmer to water. The only difficulty was that after finishing the last sentence she was left with a feeling at once hollow and uncomfortably full. Exactly like indigestion. It was perhaps for this reason that she never forgot the books were one thing and that life was another.

When it came to life Audrey was practical. She accepted all she was told to accept. And there had been quite a lot of it. She had been in London for the last five years but for one short holiday. There had been the big blitz, then the uneasy lull, then the little blitz, now the fly bombs. But she still accepted all she was told to accept, tried to remember all she was told to remember. The trouble was that she could not always forget all she was told to forget. She could not forget, for instance, that on her next birthday she would be twenty-nine years of age. Not a Girl any longer. Not really. The war had already gobbled up several years and who knew how long it would go on. Audrey dreaded growing old. She disliked and avoided old people and thought with horror of herself as old. She had never told anyone her real and especial reason for loathing the war. She had never spoken of it – even to her friend Monica.

Monica, who was an optimist five years younger than Audrey, was sure that the war would end soon.

'People always think that wars will end soon. But they don't,' said Audrey. 'Why, one lasted for a hundred years. What about that?'

Monica said: 'But that was centuries ago and quite different. Nothing to do with Now.'

But Audrey wasn't at all sure that it was so very different.

'It's as if I'm twins,' she said to Monica one day in an attempt to explain herself. 'Do you ever feel like that?' But it seemed that Monica never did feel like that or if she did she didn't want to talk about it.

Yet there it was. Only one of the twins accepted. The other felt lost, betrayed, forsaken, a wanderer in a very dark wood. The other told her that all she accepted so meekly was quite mad, potty. And here even books let her down, for no book – at least no book that Audrey had ever read – even hinted at this essential wrongness or pottiness.

Only yesterday, for instance, she had come across it in *Nothing So Blue*. *Nothing So Blue* belonged to her, for she often bought books – most of them Penguins, but some from second-hand shops. She always wrote her name on the fly-leaf and tried to blot out any signs of previous ownership. But this book had been very difficult. It had taken her more than an hour to rub out the pencil marks that had been found all through it. They began harmlessly, 'Read and enjoyed by Charles Edwin Roofe in this Year of our Salvation MCMXLII, which being interpreted is Thank You Very Much', continued 'Blue? Rather pink, I think', and, throughout the whole of the book, the word 'blue' – which of course often occurred – was underlined and in the margin there would be a question mark, a note of exclamation, or 'Ha, ha'. 'Nauseating', he had written on the page which began 'I looked her over and decided she would do'. Then came the real love affair with the beautiful English girl who smelt of daffodils and Mr Roofe had relapsed into 'Ha, ha – sez you!' But it was on page 166 that Audrey had a shock. He had written 'Women are an unspeakable abomination' with such force that the pencil had driven through the paper. She had torn the page out and thrown it into the fireplace. Fancy that! There was no fire, of course, so she was able to pick it up, smooth it out and stick it back.

'Why should I spoil my book?' she had thought. All the same she felt terribly down for some reason. And yet, she told herself, 'I bet if you met that man he would be awfully ordinary, just like everybody else.' It was something about his small, neat, precise handwriting that made her think so. But it was always the most ordinary things that suddenly turned round and showed you another face, a terrifying face. That was the hidden horror, the horror everybody pretended did not exist, the horror that was responsible for all the other horrors.

The book was not so cheering, either. It was about damp, moist heat, birds that did not sing, flowers that had no scent. Then there was this horrible girl whom the hero simply had to make love to, though he didn't really want to, and when the lovely, cool English girl heard about it she turned him down.

The natives were surly. They always seemed to be jeering behind your back. And they were stupid. They believed everything they were told, so that they could be easily worked up against somebody. Then they became cruel – so horribly cruel, you wouldn't believe . . .

And the insects. Not only the rats, snakes and poisonous spiders, scorpions, centipedes, millions of termites in their earth-coloured nests from which branched out yards of elaborately built communication lines leading sometimes to a smaller nest, sometimes to an untouched part of the tree on which they were feeding, while sometimes they just petered out, empty. It was no use poking at a nest with a stick. It seemed vulnerable, but the insects would swarm, whitely horrible, to its defence, and would rebuild it in a night. The only thing was to smoke them out. Burn them alive-oh. And even then some would escape and at once start building somewhere else.

Finally, there were the minute crawling unseen things that got at you as you walked along harmlessly. Most horrible of all these was the jigger.

Audrey stopped reading. She had a headache. Perhaps that was because she had not had anything to eat all day; unless you can count a cup of tea at eight in the morning as something to eat. But she did not often get a weekday off and when she did not a moment must be wasted. So from ten to two, regardless of sirens wailing, she went shopping in Oxford Street, and she skipped lunch. She bought stockings, a nightgown and a dress. It was buying the dress that had taken it out of her. The assistant had tried to sell her a print dress a size too big and, when she did not want it, had implied that it was unpatriotic to make so much fuss about what she wore. 'But the colours are so glaring and it doesn't fit. It's much too short,' Audrey said.

'You could easily let it down.'

Audrey said: 'But there's nothing to let down. I'd like to try on that dress over there.'

'It's a very small size.'

'Well, I'm thin enough,' said Audrey defiantly. 'How much thinner d'you want me to be?'

'But that's a dress for a girl,' the assistant said.

And suddenly, what with the pain in her back and everything, Audrey had wanted to cry. She nearly said 'I work just as hard as you,' but she was too dignified.

'The grey one looks a pretty shape,' she said. 'Not so drear. Drear,' she repeated, because that was a good word and if the assistant knew anything she would place her by it. But the woman, not at all impressed, stared over her head.

'The dresses on that rail aren't your size. You can try one on if you like but it wouldn't be any use. You could easily let down the print one,' she repeated maddeningly.

Audrey had felt like a wet rag after her defeat by the shop assistant, for she had ended by buying the print dress. It would not be enough to go and spruce up in the Ladies' Room on the fifth floor – which would be milling full of Old Things – so she had gone home again, back to the flat she shared with Monica. There had not been time to eat anything, but she had put on the new dress and it looked even worse than it had looked in the shop. From the neck to the waist it was enormous, or shapeless. The skirt, on the other hand, was very short and skimpy and two buttons came off in her hand; she had to wait and sew them on again.

It had all made her very tired. And she would be late for tea at Roberta's . . .

'I wish I lived here,' she thought when she came out of the Tube station. But she often thought that when she went to a different part of London. 'It's nicer here,' she'd think, 'I might be happier here.'

Her friend Roberta's house was painted green and had a small garden. Audrey felt envious as she pressed the bell. And still more envious when Roberta came to the door wearing a flowered house coat, led the way into a pretty sitting-room and collapsed onto her sofa in a film-star attitude. Audrey's immediate thought was 'What right has a woman got to be lolling about like that in wartime, even if she is going to have a baby?' But when she noticed Roberta's deep-circled eyes, her huge, pathetic stomach, her spoilt hands, her broken nails, and realized that her house coat had been made out of a pair of old curtains ('not half so pretty as she was. Looks much older') she said the usual things, warmly and sincerely.

But she hoped that, although it was nearly six by the silver clock, Roberta would offer her some tea and cake. Even a plain slice of bread – she could have wolfed that down.

'Why are you so late?' Roberta asked. 'I suppose you've had tea,' and hurried on before Audrey could open her mouth. 'Have a chocolate biscuit.'

So Audrey ate a biscuit slowly. She felt she did not know Roberta well enough to say 'I'm ravenous. I must have something to eat.' Besides that was the funny thing. The more ravenous you grew, the more impossible it became to say 'I'm ravenous!'

'Is that a good book?' Roberta asked.

'I brought it to read on the Tube. It isn't bad.'

Roberta flicked through the pages of *Nothing So Blue* without much interest. And she said 'English people always mix up tropical places. My dear, I met a girl the other day who thought Moscow was the capital of India! Really, I think it's dangerous to be as ignorant as that, don't you?'

Roberta often talked about 'English' people in that way. She had acquired the habit, Audrey thought, when she was out of England for two years before the war. She had lived for six months in New York. Then she had been to Miami, Trinidad, Bermuda – all those places – and no expense spared, or so she said. She had brought back all sorts of big ideas. Much too big. Gadgets for the kitchen. An extensive wardrobe. Expensive makeup. Having her hair and nails looked after every week at the hairdresser's. There was no end to it. Anyway, there was one good thing about the war. It had taken all that right off. Right off.

'Read what he says about jiggers,' Audrey said.

'My dear,' said Roberta, 'he *is* piling it on.'

'Do you mean that there aren't such things as jiggers?'

'Of course there are such things,' Roberta said, 'but they're only sand fleas. It's better not to go barefoot if you're frightened of them.'

She explained about jiggers. They had nasty ways – the man wasn't so far wrong. She talked about tropical insects for some time after that; she seemed to remember them more vividly than anything else. Then she read out bits of *Nothing So Blue*, laughing at it.

'If you must read all the time, you needn't believe everything you read.'

'I don't,' said Audrey. 'If you knew how little I really believe you'd be surprised. Perhaps he doesn't see it the way you do. It all depends on how people see things. If someone wanted to write a horrible book about London, couldn't he write a horrible book? I wish somebody would. I'd buy it.'

'You dope!' said Roberta affectionately.

When the time came to go Audrey walked back to the Tube station in a daze, and in a daze sat in the train until a jerk of the brain warned her that she had passed Leicester Square and now had to change at King's Cross. She felt very bad when she got out, as if she could flop any minute. There were so many people pushing, you got bewildered.

She tried to think about Monica, about the end of the journey, above all about food – warm, lovely food – but something had happened inside her head and she couldn't concentrate. She kept remembering the termites. Termites running along one of the covered ways that peter out and lead to nothing. When she came to the escalator she hesitated, afraid to get on it. The people clinging to the sides looked very like large insects. No, they didn't *look* like large insects: they were insects.

She got onto the escalator and stood staidly on the right-hand side. No running up for her tonight. She pressed her arm against her side and felt the book. That started her thinking about jiggers again. Jiggers got in under your skin when you didn't know it and laid eggs inside you. Just walking along, as you might be walking along the street to a Tube station, you caught a jigger as easily as you bought a newspaper or turned on the radio. And there you were – infected – and not knowing a thing about it.

In front of her stood an elderly woman with dank hair and mean-looking clothes. It was funny how she hated women like that. It was funny how she hated most women anyway. Elderly women ought to stay at home. They oughtn't to walk about. Depressing people! Jutting out, that was what the woman was doing. Standing right in the middle, instead of in line. So that you could hardly blame the service girl, galloping up in a hurry, for giving her a good shove and saying under her breath 'Oh get out of the way!' But she must have shoved too hard for the old thing tottered. She was going to fall. Audrey's heart jumped sickeningly into her mouth as she shut her eyes. She didn't want to see what it would look like, didn't want to hear the scream.

But no scream came and when Audrey opened her eyes she

saw that the old woman had astonishingly saved herself. She had only stumbled down a couple of steps and clutched the rail again. She even managed to laugh and say 'Now I know where all the beef goes to!' Her face, though, was very white. So was Audrey's. Perhaps her heart kept turning over. So did Audrey's.

Even when she got out of the Tube the nightmare was not over. On the way home she had to walk up a little street which she hated and it was getting dark now. It was one of those streets which are nearly always empty. It had been badly blitzed and Audrey was sure that it was haunted. Weeds and wild-looking flowers were growing over the skeleton houses, over the piles of rubble. There were front doorsteps which looked as though they were hanging by a thread, and near one of them lived a black cat with green eyes. She liked cats but not this one, not this one. She was sure it wasn't a cat really.

Supposing the siren went? 'If the siren goes up when I'm in this street it'll mean that it's all U.P. with me.' Supposing a man with a strange blank face and no eyebrows – like that one who got into the Ladies at the cinema the other night and stood there grinning at them and nobody knew what to do so everybody pretended he wasn't there. Perhaps he was *not* there, either – supposing a man like that were to come up softly behind her, touch her shoulder, speak to her, she wouldn't be able to struggle, she would just lie down and die of fright, so much she hated that street. And she had to walk slowly because if she ran she would give whatever it was its opportunity and it would run after her. However, even walking slowly, it came to an end at last. Just round the corner in a placid ordinary street where all the damage had been tidied up was the third floor flat which she shared with Monica, also a typist in a government office.

The radio was on full tilt. The smell of cabbage drifted down the stairs. Monica, for once, was getting the meal ready. They ate out on Mondays, Wednesdays and Fridays, in on Tuesdays, Thursdays, Saturdays and Sundays. Audrey usually did the housework and cooking and Monica took charge of the ration books, stood in long queues to shop and lugged the laundry back and forwards every week because the van didn't call any longer.

'Hullo,' said Monica.

Audrey answered her feebly, 'Hullo.'

Monica, a dark, pretty girl, put the food on the table and remarked at once, 'You're a bit green in the face. Have you been drinking mock gin?'

'Oh, don't be funny. I haven't had much to eat today – that's all.'

After a few minutes Monica said impatiently, 'Well why don't you eat then?'

'I think I've gone past it,' said Audrey, fidgeting with the sausage and cabbage on her plate.

Monica began to read from the morning paper. She spoke loudly above the music on the radio.

'Have you seen this article about being a woman in Germany? It says they can't get any scent or eau-de-cologne or nail polish.'

'Fancy that!' Audrey said. 'Poor things!'

'It says the first thing Hitler stopped was nail polish. He began that way. I wonder why. He must have had a reason, mustn't he?'

'Why must he have had a reason?' said Audrey.

'Because,' said Monica, 'if they've got a girl thinking she isn't pretty, thinking she's shabby, they've got her where they want her, as a rule. And it might start with nail polish, see? And it says: "All the old women and the middle-aged women look most terribly unhappy. They simply *slink* about," it says.'

'You surprise me,' Audrey said. 'Different in the Isle of Dogs, isn't it?'

She was fed up now and she wanted to be rude to somebody. 'Oh *do* shut up,' she said. 'I'm not interested. Why should I have to cope with German women as well as all the women over here? What a nightmare!'

Monica opened her mouth to answer sharply; then shut it again. She was an even-tempered girl. She piled the plates onto a tray, took it into the kitchen and began to wash up.

As soon as she had gone Audrey turned off the radio and the

light. Blissful sleep, lovely sleep, she never got enough of it. . . .
On Sunday mornings, long after Monica was up, she would lie
unconscious. A heavy sleeper, you might call her, except that her
breathing was noiseless and shallow and that she lay so still,
without tossing or turning. And then *She (who?) sent the gentle
sleep from Heaven that slid into my soul. That slid into my soul.
Sleep, Nature's sweet, something-or-the-other. The sleep that knits
up the ravelled.* . . .

It seemed that she had hardly shut her eyes when she was
awake again. Monica was shaking her.

'What's the matter? Is it morning?' Audrey said. 'What is it?
What is it?'

'Oh, nothing at all,' Monica said sarcastically. 'You were only
shrieking the place down.'

'Was I?' Audrey said, interested. 'What was I saying?'

'I don't know what you were saying and I don't care. But if
you're trying to get us turned out, that's the way to do it. You
know perfectly well that the woman downstairs is doing all she
can to get us out because she says we are too noisy. You said
something about jiggers. What *are* jiggers anyway?'

'It's slang for people in the Tube,' Audrey answered glibly to
her great surprise. 'Didn't you know that?'

'Oh is it? No, I never heard that.'

'The name comes from a tropical insect,' Audrey said, 'that
gets in under your skin when you don't know it. It lays eggs and
hatches them out and you don't know it. And there's another sort
of tropical insect that lives in enormous cities. They have rail-
ways, Tubes, bridges, soldiers, wars, everything we have. And
they have big cities, and smaller cities with roads going from one
to another. Most of them are what they call workers. They never
fly because they've lost their wings and never make love either.
They're just workers. Nobody quite knows how this is done, but
they think it's the food. Other people say it's segregation. Don't
you believe me?' she said, her voice rising. 'Do you think I'm
telling lies?'

'Of course I believe you,' said Monica soothingly, 'but I don't see why you should shout about it.'

Audrey drew a deep breath. The corners of her mouth quivered. Then she said 'Look I'm going to bed. I'm awfully tired. I'm going to take six aspirins and then go to bed. If the siren goes don't wake me up. Even if one of those things seems to be coming very close, don't wake me up. I don't want to be woken up whatever happens.'

'Very well,' Monica said. 'All right, old girl.'

Audrey rushed at her with clenched fists and began to shriek again. 'Damn you, don't call me that. Damn your soul to everlasting hell *don't call me that.* . . .'

Rapunzel, Rapunzel

URING the three weeks I had been in the hospital
I would often see a phantom village when I looked out of the
window instead of the London plane trees. It was an Arab village
or my idea of one, small white houses clustered together on a hill.
This hallucination would appear and disappear and I'd watch for
it, feeling lost when a day passed without my seeing it.

One morning I was told that I must get ready to leave as I
was now well enough for a short stay in a convalescent home. I
had to dress and get packed very quickly and what between my
haste and unsteady legs I got into the car waiting outside the
hospital without any idea of where it was going to take me.

We drove for about forty minutes, stopping twice to pick up
other patients. We were still in London but what part of London?
Norwood perhaps? Richmond? Beckenham?

The convalescent home, when we reached it, was an imposing red brick building with a fairly large garden. The other patients
went into a room on the ground floor and I walked up the staircase by myself, clutching the banisters. At the top a pretty but
unsmiling Indian nurse greeted me, showed me into a ward, helped
me unpack and saw me into bed. There was a lot of talking and
laughing going on and a radio was playing; it was confusing after
the comparative quiet of the hospital. I shut my eyes and when I
opened them a young good-looking doctor was standing near me.
He asked a few questions and finally where my home was.

'I live in Devon now.'

'And have you been to any hunt balls lately?'

This was so unexpected that it was a second or two before I managed to smile and say that they must be great fun but that I'd never been to a hunt ball and didn't know what they were like. He lost interest and went over to the next bed.

I couldn't sleep for a long time, the radio and the conversation went on interminably and I was relieved when, early next morning, a nurse told me that I was to be moved into another room.

The new ward was smaller and quieter. There were about fourteen patients but I was still too weary to notice anybody except my immediate neighbour, an elderly woman with piles of glossy magazines at the foot of her bed. She pored over them and played her radio all day. That night we had an argument, she said I ought to put my light out and not keep everybody awake because I wanted to read, I said that it wasn't yet ten o'clock and that her radio had annoyed me all day, but I soon gave in. Perhaps I was keeping the others awake.

Somebody was snoring; just as I thought the noise had stopped it would start up louder than ever and though I had asked for a sleeping pill, it seemed hours before it worked and when I did eventually sleep I had a long disturbing dream which I couldn't remember when I woke up. I only knew that I was extremely glad to be awake.

When I looked at my neighbour her slim back was turned towards me and she was brushing her hair – there was a great deal of it – long, silvery white, silky. She brushed away steadily, rhythmically, for some time. She must have taken great care of it all her life and now there it all was, intact, to comfort and reassure her that she was still herself. Even when she had pinned it up into a loose bun it fell so prettily round her face that it was difficult to think of her as an old lady.

I can't say that we ever became friendly. She told me that she was an Australian, that her name was Peterson, and once she lent me a glossy magazine.

I hadn't been there long when I realized that I didn't like the convalescent home and that the sooner I got out of it the better I'd be pleased. The monotony of the hospital had finally had a

soothing effect. I'd felt weak, out of love with life, but resigned
and passive; here on the contrary I was anxious, restless and yet
it ought to have been a comforting place. The passage outside
the ward was carpeted in dark red, dark red curtains hung over
the tall window at the far end and the staircase had a spacious
look, with its wide shallow steps and broad oak banisters – just
the sort of house to get well in, you would have thought. But I
felt it shut in, brooding, even threatening in its stolid way.

The matron soon insisted on my taking daily exercise in the
garden and another patient usually walked at the same time as I
did. She always carried a paper bag of boiled sweets which she'd
offer to me as we discussed her operation for gall bladder and my
heart attack in detail. But all the time I was thinking that there
too the trees drooped in a heavy, melancholy way and the grass
was a much darker colour than ordinary grass. Something about
the whole place reminded me of a placid citizen, respectable and
respected, who would poison anyone disliked or disapproved of at
the drop of a hat.

No kind ladies came round with trolleys of books, as they had
in the hospital, so one day I asked if it wasn't possible for me to
have something to read. I was told that there was a library on the
ground floor, 'Down the stairs,' said the nurse, 'and to your left.'

When I went in the blinds were drawn and I was in semi-
darkness but I was so certain that I wasn't alone that I stopped
near the door and felt for the light switch. The room was empty
except for a large table in the middle with straightbacked chairs
arranged round it, as if for a meal, and a rickety bookcase at the
far end. There was no one there. No one! 'Oh don't be idiotic,' I
said aloud and walked past the table. The books leant up against
each other disconsolately. They had a forlorn, neglected appearance as though no one had looked at or touched them for years.
They would have been less reproachful piled in a heap to be thrown
away. Most of them were memoirs or African adventures by early
Victorian travellers, in very close print. I didn't look long for I
hated turning my back on that table, those chairs and when I
saw a torn Tauchnitz paperback by a writer I'd heard of I grabbed

it and hurried out as quickly as I could. Nothing would have induced me to go back to that room and I read and re-read the book steadily, never taking in what I was reading, so that now I can't remember the title or what it was about. It was after this that I began counting: 'Only eight days more, only six days more.'

One morning a trim little man looked into the ward and asked 'Does any lady want a shampoo or haircut?'

Silence except for a few firm 'No thank yous'.

Then Mrs Peterson said: 'Yes, I should like my hair trimmed, please, if it could be managed.'

'Okay,' said the man, 'tomorrow morning at eleven.'

When he had gone someone said: 'He's a man's barber, you know.'

'I just want it trimmed. I have to be careful about split ends,' said the Australian.

Next morning the barber appeared with all his paraphernalia, put a chair near a basin – there was no looking glass above it – and smilingly invited her to sit down. She said something to him, he nodded and proceeded while everybody watched covertly. She sat up and he dried her hair gently. Then he picked it up in one hand and produced a large pair of scissors. Snip, snip, and half of it was lying on the floor. One woman gasped.

Mrs Peterson put her hand up uneasily and felt her neck but said nothing. She must have realized that something was wrong but couldn't know the extent of the damage of course, and it all happened very quickly. The rest went and in a few minutes she had disappeared under the dryer while the barber tidied up. When she paid him he said: 'You'll be glad to be rid of the weight of it, won't you dear?' She didn't answer.

'Cheerio ladies.' He went off carrying the hair that he had so carefully collected in a plastic bag.

He hadn't made a very good job of setting what was left and her face looked large, naked and rather plain. She still seemed utterly astonished as she walked back to bed. Then she reached for her handglass and stared at herself for a long time. When I saw how distressed she grew as she looked I whispered: 'Don't worry, you'll be surprised how quickly it'll grow again.'

'No, there isn't time,' she said, turned, pulled the sheet up high and lay so still that I thought she was asleep, but I heard her say, not to me or anybody else, 'Nobody will want me now.'

During the night I was woken to hear her being violently sick. A nurse hurried to her bed. Next morning it started again, she apologized feebly to the matron who came along to look at her. 'I'm so very sorry to trouble you, I'm so very sorry.'

All day at intervals it went on, the vomiting, the chokings, the weak child's voice saying: 'I'm so sorry, I'm so sorry,' and by night they had a screen up round her bed.

I stopped listening to the sounds coming from behind the screen, for one gets used to anything. But when, one morning, I saw that it had been taken away and that the bed was empty and tidy I was annoyed to hear a woman say: 'They always take them away like that. Quietly. In the night.'

'These people are so damned gloomy,' I said to myself. 'She'll probably get perfectly well, her hair will grow again and soon look very pretty.'

I'd be leaving the convalescent home the day after tomorrow. Why wasn't I thinking of that instead of a story read long ago in the Blue or Yellow fairy book (perhaps the Crimson) and the words repeating themselves so unreasonably in my head: 'Rapunzel, Rapunzel, let down your hair?'

Who Knows What's Up
in the Attic?

S HE SAT IN one of a row of deck-chairs with other silent, impassive, elderly people watching the sea. Unlike the sky it was the usual dark grey. But it was calm, the waves making a soothing sound as they rolled in gently.

The beach was empty except for a little boy playing by himself and some way off a man throwing a stick for his dog. Over and over again he threw, over and over again the dog dashed into the water barking, wild with enthusiasm. A cat, now, might get bored even if it could be taught the trick, but dogs must be optimists, thinking every time was the first time. Or perhaps just plain silly.

'I've got the car,' and he was in the next deck-chair.

'That's the Atlantic, isn't it?' she asked.

'Of course. What did you think it was?'

'I thought it might be the Bristol Channel.'

'No, no. Look.' He produced a map. 'Here is the Bristol Channel and here are we. That's the Atlantic.'

'It's very grey,' she said.

But driving along a road by the sea she thought that it was a pleasant little town. Why shouldn't she take one of those flats painted yellow or pink, green or blue? Holiday flats, they called themselves. Spend a week or so here? Then she imagined the town full of people, cars and coaches. Not the same thing at all.

Besides – she made so many plans.

When they turned inland he began to sing. Songs from various operas but not in any language she knew. Every now and again he'd stop and explain what it was all about. 'That he sings when he first sees her. This is when he is dying.'

'They always sing when they are dying. So loud too,' she said.

But he went on singing. He had a good voice. How long was it since she had sat by a man driving fast and singing? Years and years. Or was it perhaps only yesterday and everything that happened since a strange dream?

On the day before this one – which was also yesterday – she'd been sitting in the kitchen of her cottage looking out of the window at the dismal sky and listening to the silence. No farm cart passed. No lorry. When she heard a soft knock, 'That must be Mr Singh' she thought. Everyone else in the village knocked as if they were trying to batter the ramshackle place down. She kept very still and listened. 'Surely he'll think I'm out and go away.'

Mr Singh visited the village at intervals selling blouses, scarves and underclothes; he usually persuaded her to buy something gaudy and useless. It had started one day when she was feeling even more lonely and bored than usual, longing for any distraction; then she saw him fairly often.

'The price is £5 but I will let you have it cheaper. Also I will give you a lucky bead. I am holy man and will pray for you.'

'But I don't want it, Mr Singh.'

'Don't say that. Don't say that. You break my heart, you break my heart. You don't have to buy, only look,' he'd say gently.

How does he get so much into one suitcase, she'd wonder.

'Good-bye mam, thank you mam, God bless you mam.' He always called her mam or mum.

She remembered that the door wasn't bolted. 'He'll walk in and look for me,' she thought. And decided to go into the passage, shake her head at him through the glass top and turn the key.

But instead of the white turban and black beard that she expected, a strange young man in grey was waiting patiently outside.

'I'm Jan –' he said smiling. 'I wrote. Don't you remember? We met last year in London, you gave me your address and said that if ever I was in England again I could call on you. Didn't you get my letter?'

Then she remembered the letter from Holland. It was written in English, three pages of it. She'd pored over the difficult handwriting, the passages of unfamiliar poetry. It said that he would be in London and could he come sometime in the afternoon of Tuesday the – of May? She replied that she'd be pleased to see him and added: 'But this is a rainy place in the spring.'

Tuesday – but this was Monday.

'Of course, of course,' she said, trying to sound welcoming. 'Do come in. You're just in time for a drink.'

But he refused a drink. The sitting-room was dim at this hour and he sat with his back to whatever light there was, talking smoothly and easily about his hotel in Exeter and about the difficulty of finding her place. He was wearing smooth London clothes. He apologized for his English but he had no accent. Every now and then he'd hesitate for a word, that was all.

'You can spend tomorrow with me? Perhaps we could go to the sea. Would you like that?'

'Yes I would. I haven't seen the sea for a long time.'

Next morning he'd arrived wearing country clothes and carrying a large bunch of flowers.

'What lovely carnations'; wondering whether she had anything big enough to put them in.

It was when she was sitting next to him in the car that she noticed he was older than she'd thought yesterday and much more attractive.

'You wrote that it always rained here and look what a beautiful day!'

'Oh, isn't it, isn't it?'

Such a beautiful day. The sky pale blue, the clouds light and white and innocent. It seemed ungrateful to remember icy gales, perpetual drizzle. Now the wind was soft and gentle – almost warm. 'Winds that blow from the south.' Fruit trees covered with flowers were all over the place. As they passed one, she said: 'Cherry, plum, I'm not sure.'

'I don't know. I am not a country man. I am a city man.'

'Yes I can see that.' she said.

She was surprised at the security and happiness she felt. She very seldom felt safe or happy and if it was so for this man whom she'd only met briefly once over a drink and never expected to see again, why pull it to pieces?

All the same his face was so familiar. Then she remembered that life of Modigliani and the photograph on the cover. He was almost exactly like it.

When he asked: 'Are you getting tired?'

'Well – I'll be glad to get home and have a drink.'

'Yes. But do you mind if we go by Exeter so that I can pick up some wine that I think you will like at my hotel?'

When he came out of the hotel he was carrying two bottles of rosé. They drove back home quickly along an empty road, hardly speaking.

'I'll get the glasses? Ice? Or shall I put the bottles in the fridge for a bit?'

'They're still quite cool,' he said. 'Feel.'

She sat facing the light while he opened a bottle, lit two cigarettes and gave her one. Then he took up a book of Dutch poems on the table. 'You read Dutch?'

'No. The English translation's inside. I can't read Dutch or speak it.'

'But you know Amsterdam?'

'A little. Not well. The Hague better. I remember the canals of course and some beautiful old houses. But that was a long time ago. Are the houses still there, I wonder?'

'Yes, some are still there. And in one lives my uncle and his sister.'

'Oh, does he?'

'Yes, and every evening they invite friends and play cards up to all hours. Two, three in the morning you can ring them up and they are still playing.'

She liked his face when he spoke about these people. Amused but pleased and affectionate. It was nice of him to think of them like that.

'Do they play for money or for love?' she said.

'For love. For love. You know,' he said 'I admire my uncle. When I was quite a little boy and my mother died he really brought me up. That was in Indonesia. My father is an artist. I have some pictures of his that I like very much and I like him. But he is too – too soft. That is not a good thing.'

'I suppose not.'

'My uncle is not so.' He took a case from his pocket and handed her a small photograph. 'That is my uncle.'

The uncle looked a bit on the sly side to her.

'I see what you mean,' she said.

'And this is my father.'

'You are like him.'

'Yes I know. And I am fond of him, I feel affection for him but he is not – how do you say – forcible enough.'

'Yes, but if everybody were forcible, what a shambles. Don't you think it's quite bad enough as it is?'

He put the photographs away carefully.

'I am sad that I have to go to London tomorrow.'

'So am I,' she said.

Then, leaning back, he said suddenly: 'Tell me – what do you like best about me?'

She was surprised but answered at once. 'I like your eyebrows best.'

'My eyebrows,' he said. 'My eyebrows?'

He seemed so astonished that she explained. 'You see in a face like yours one expects, or I expect, smooth eyebrows. Black, almost as if they were painted. But yours are shaggy and in the sun they are a good deal lighter than your hair. It's a surprise and I like it very much.'

'No one's ever told me that before.'

They looked steadily at each other for a few seconds then together they began to laugh.

'Oh I must have a photograph of you like that. I'll get my camera, it's in the car.'

'No, don't photograph me. I hate it. I've never liked it all that much, now of course it's a phobia. Please don't.'

'Of course not, if you don't wish it. All the same I'd like to take a few photographs of the cottage if you allow me.'

'Photograph anything you like, but not me.'

At the door he turned. 'We recognized each other, didn't we?'

She didn't answer. She thought: yes, I recognized you almost at once. But I never imagined that you recognized me.

She sat so often in this chair looking at the eternal drizzle, listening to the wind. All night it whistled and whined and moaned, rattled the doors and windows till she had to get up and wedge them with newspapers before she could sleep. All day it tormented the trees. How she'd grown to hate it, the bullying treacherous wind. Even when it wasn't raining, sunshine was just a pale glare.

But today the sun was real sun and the light gold. The grass was yellow, not green. No wonder she felt as if she were in another time, another place, another country. She saw him walking about the field in front of the sitting-room and thought: 'What on earth has he found to photograph there? The cows over the hedge?'

'I'm afraid that field is rough and full of holes. I can't garden much.'

'I like it today but perhaps on a wet dark day it might be sad. But of course you have many friends.'

'Well not exactly. Not in the village anyway. This is a big county, you know.'

'So you are alone here. That should not be.'

'No, no, I'm all right. A very nice woman comes quite often and I've got a telephone. Besides, I like being alone. Not always of course, but one can't have everything.'

'And in the winter, are you alone in the winter?'

'I try to get away for the worst months and then – well it's all a bit chancy.'

'I was thinking, I know a place in Italy that you would like very much. It's quiet and beautiful.'

'It sounds just the thing.'

'And would you think of going there?'

'Why not?' she said. Of course she could think.

Looking worried he said: 'I couldn't be with you all the time. I would be with you as often as I could. But you see there is my job. And there is my wife.'

'Of course.'

'My wife and I don't get on.'

'Oh dear, what a pity.'

'Yes, we have agreed to stay together for the children till they are older. Meanwhile we don't interfere with each other.'

It seemed to her she'd heard that one before, long ago when everything was different. 'It sounds a good arrangement – very fair to everybody –' she said. 'And maybe . . .'

'You don't know my wife.'

'No.'

'She is like this.' Now he was getting excited. 'I was in New York a few months ago. I brought her back a dress – very pretty. I thought to please her but it hangs in her cupboard. She has never once put it on.'

'Perhaps it doesn't fit,' she said.

'Of course it fits her, of course. Such a mistake I would not make. She won't wear it because I bought it and she is like that about everything. She wants to separate as much as I do, believe me, but we have this arrangement because of the children. And so . . .'

'I was only joking.'

'But I am not joking at all. I mean what I say.'

'Yes and it would be lovely, but it's quite impossible, I can't.'

'Why not?'

Of course he must have seen perfectly well why not and if he didn't she was certainly not going to spell it out. That would have depressed her for days, for weeks. How few people understood what a tightrope she walked or what would happen if she slipped. The abyss. Despair. All those things.

She made the first excuse that came into her head. 'Such a fuss. My passport. Besides, I hate packing.'

'I will come and fetch you. I can come in October. I can pack very well. Nothing will be difficult, you will see.'

'You don't know how much I'd like it but really it's just not possible.'

He said nothing for a bit, then: 'Well think about it. If you change your mind will you write to me? You have my address.'

'I'll probably think about it a lot. But I won't change my mind.'

'No one is ever certain of that,' he said and talked of other things. But when he asked her to dine with him she was obliged to excuse herself for suddenly she was very tired, hardly able to move, too tired to say much.

'Thank you for seeing me and for today,' he said at the door, again bowing and kissing her hand. 'I will hope to hear from you. Have nice conversations with the cows in the next field.'

'You never know,' she said.

Before getting into the car he waved and called, 'You will see me again.'

'Yes, yes, that would be splendid. Try to manage it.'

She went back into the kitchen and shut her eyes. 'Why not, why not? Why shouldn't I walk out of this place, so dependent on the weather, so meanly built, for poor people. Just four small rooms and an attic. Like my life.' She put her hand to her head and laughed. 'And who knows what's up in the attic? Not I for one. I wouldn't dare look.'

A small house – it was suffocating. She went to the door and propped it open. Why not? Why not? Hadn't she forgotten her one advantage now? She could do exactly what she liked. She could do something a thousand times sillier than taking a holiday in Italy – that is all it was – no one need know and no one would care. Or rather she could easily arrange that no one knew. And most certainly no one would care.

A voice said: 'I hope I do not disturb you. I saw your door was open and I came in. I have got this specially for you.'

She wiped her eyes hastily. 'You are not disturbing me at all. I was nearly asleep.' She was delighted to see Mr Singh. Any port in a storm. 'What have you brought to show me today? But let me see it in here.'

'This I thought is for you. Beautiful stuff, beautiful. Feel it.'

'Yes. But what's that orange-coloured thing?'

'That is a –' He showed it. 'A short nylon nightgown. Looks a good shape. No lace.'

'Pretty,' she said.

Looking rather surprised, he held it deftly under her chin. 'A very good colour for you,' he said. 'And I have a black one the same.'

When he told her the price of them both she paid him. He didn't try to sell her anything else but shut the suitcase.

She went with him to the door. The wind was getting up and it had turned cold. It won't be fine tomorrow, she thought.

'Good-bye mam, thank you mam, I will pray for you.'

'You do just that,' she said. And locked the door.

Sleep It Off Lady

ONE OCTOBER AFTERNOON Mrs Baker was having tea with Miss Verney and talking about the proposed broiler factory in the middle of the village where they both lived. Miss Verney, who had not been listening attentively said, 'You know Letty, I've been thinking a great deal about death lately. I hardly ever do, strangely enough.'

'No dear,' said Mrs Baker. 'It isn't strange at all. It's quite natural. We old people are rather like children, we live in the present as a rule. A merciful dispensation of providence.'

'Perhaps,' said Miss Verney doubtfully.

Mrs Baker said 'we old people' quite kindly, but could not help knowing that while she herself was only sixty-three and might, with any luck, see many a summer (after many a summer dies the swan, as some man said), Miss Verney, certainly well over seventy, could hardly hope for anything of the sort. Mrs Baker gripped the arms of her chair. 'Many a summer, touch wood and please God,' she thought. Then she remarked that it was getting dark so early now and wasn't it extraordinary how time flew.

Miss Verney listened to the sound of the car driving away, went back to her sitting-room and looked out of the window at the flat fields, the apple trees, the lilac tree that wouldn't flower again, not for ten years they told her, because lilacs won't stand being pruned. In the distance there was a rise in the ground – you could hardly call it a hill – and three trees so exactly shaped and spaced that they looked artificial. 'It would be rather lovely covered in snow,' Miss Verney thought. 'The snow, so white, so smooth and in the end so boring. Even the hateful shed wouldn't look so bad.' But she'd made up her mind to forget the shed.

Miss Verney had decided that it was an eyesore when she came to live in the cottage. Most of the paint had worn off the once-black galvanized iron. Now it was a greenish colour. Part of the roof was loose and flapped noisily in windy weather and a small gate off its hinges leaned up against the entrance. Inside it was astonishingly large, the far end almost dark. 'What a waste of space,' Miss Verney thought. 'That must come down.' Strange that she hadn't noticed it before.

Nails festooned with rags protruded from the only wooden rafter. There was a tin bucket with a hole, a huge dustbin. Nettles flourished in one corner but it was the opposite corner which disturbed her. Here was piled a rusty lawnmower, an old chair with a carpet draped over it, several sacks, and the remains of what had once been a bundle of hay. She found herself imagining that a fierce and dangerous animal lived there and called aloud: 'Come out, come out, Shredni Vashtar, the beautiful.' Then rather alarmed at herself she walked away as quickly as she could.

But she was not unduly worried. The local builder had done several odd jobs for her when she moved in and she would speak to him when she saw him next.

'Want the shed down?' said the builder.

'Yes,' said Miss Verney. 'It's hideous, and it takes up so much space.'

'It's on the large side,' the builder said.

'Enormous. Whatever did they use it for?'

'I expect it was the garden shed.'

'I don't care what it was,' said Miss Verney. 'I want it out of the way.'

The builder said that he couldn't manage the next week, but the Monday after that he'd look in and see what could be done. Monday came and Miss Verney waited but he didn't arrive. When this had happened twice she realized that he didn't mean to come and wrote to a firm in the nearest town.

A few days later a cheerful young man knocked at the door, explained who he was and asked if she would let him know exactly what she wanted. Miss Verney, who wasn't feeling at all well, pointed, 'I want that pulled down. Can you do it?'

The young man inspected the shed, walked round it, then stood looking at it.

'I want it destroyed,' said Miss Verney passionately, 'utterly destroyed and carted away. I hate the sight of it.'

'Quite a job,' he said candidly.

And Miss Verney saw what he meant. Long after she was dead and her cottage had vanished it would survive. The tin bucket and the rusty lawnmower, the pieces of rag fluttering in the wind. All would last for ever.

Eyeing her rather nervously he became businesslike. 'I see what you want, and of course we can let you have an estimate of the cost. But you realize that if you pull the shed down you take away from the value of your cottage?'

'Why?' said Miss Verney.

'Well,' he said, 'very few people would live here without a car. It could be converted into a garage easily or even used as it is. You can decide of course when you have the estimate whether you think it worth the expense and . . . the trouble. Good day.'

Left alone, Miss Verney felt so old, lonely and helpless that she began to cry. No builder would tackle that shed, not for any price she could afford. But crying relieved her and she soon felt quite cheerful again. It was ridiculous to brood, she told herself. She quite liked the cottage. One morning she'd wake up and know what to do about the shed, meanwhile she wouldn't look at the thing. She wouldn't think about it.

But it was astonishing how it haunted her dreams. One night she was standing looking at it changing its shape and becoming a very smart, shiny, dark blue coffin picked out in white. It reminded her of a dress she had once worn. A voice behind her said: 'That's the laundry.'

'Then oughtn't I to put it away?' said Miss Verney in her dream.

'Not just yet. Soon,' said the voice so loudly that she woke up.

She had dragged the large dustbin to the entrance and, because it was too heavy for her to lift, had arranged for it to be carried to the gate every week for the dustmen to collect. Every morning she took a small yellow bin from under the sink and emptied it into the large dustbin, quickly, without lingering or looking around. But on one particular morning the usual cold wind had dropped and she stood wondering if a coat of white paint would improve matters. Paint might look a lot worse, besides who could she get to do it? Then she saw a cat, as she thought, walking slowly across the far end. The sun shone through a chink in the wall. It was a large rat. Horrified, she watched it disappear under the old chair, dropped the yellow bin, walked as fast as she was able up the road and knocked at the door of a shabby thatched cottage.

'Oh Tom. There are rats in my shed. I've just seen a huge one. I'm so desperately afraid of them. What shall I do?'

When she left Tom's cottage she was still shaken, but calmer. Tom had assured her that he had an infallible rat poison, arrangements had been made, his wife had supplied a strong cup of tea.

He came that same day to put down the poison, and when afterwards he rapped loudly on the door and shouted: 'Everything under control?' she answered quite cheerfully, 'Yes, I'm fine and thanks for coming.'

As one sunny day followed another she almost forgot how much the rat had frightened her. 'It's dead or gone away,' she assured herself.

When she saw it again she stood and stared disbelieving. It crossed the shed in the same unhurried way and she watched, not able to move. A huge rat, there was no doubt about it.

This time Miss Verney didn't rush to Tom's cottage to be reassured. She managed to get to the kitchen, still holding the empty yellow pail, slammed the door and locked it. Then she shut and bolted all the windows. This done, she took off her shoes, lay down, pulled the blankets over her head and listened to her hammering heart.

> *I'm the monarch of all I survey.*
> *My right, there is none to dispute.*

That was the way the rat walked.

In the close darkness she must have dozed, for suddenly she was sitting at a desk in the sun copying proverbs into a ruled book: 'Evil Communications corrupt good manners. Look before you leap. Patience is a virtue, good temper a blessing,' all the way up to Z. Z would be something to do with zeal or zealous. But how did they manage about X? What about X?

Thinking this, she slept, then woke, put on the light, took two tuinal tablets and slept again, heavily. When she next opened her eyes it was morning, the unwound bedside clock had stopped, but she guessed the time from the light and hurried into the kitchen waiting for Tom's car to pass. The room was stuffy and airless but she didn't dream of opening the window. When she saw the car approaching she ran out into the road and waved it down. It was as if fear had given her wings and once more she moved lightly and quickly.

'Tom. Tom.'

He stopped.

'Oh Tom, the rat's still there. I saw it last evening.'

He got down stiffly. Not a young man, but surely surely, a kind man? 'I put down enough stuff to kill a dozen rats,' he said. 'Let's 'ave a look.'

He walked across to the shed. She followed, several yards behind, and watched him rattling the old lawnmower, kicking the sacks, trampling the hay and nettles.

'No rat 'ere,' he said at last.

'Well there was one,' she said.

'Not 'ere.'

'It was a huge rat,' she said.

Tom had round brown eyes, honest eyes, she'd thought. But now they were sly, mocking, even hostile.

'Are you sure it wasn't a pink rat?' he said.

She knew that the bottles in her dustbin were counted and discussed in the village. But Tom, who she liked so much?

'No,' she managed to say steadily. 'An ordinary colour but very large. Don't they say that some rats don't care about poison? Super rats.'

Tom laughed. 'Nothing of that sort round 'ere.'

She said: 'I asked Mr Slade, who cuts the grass, to clear out the shed and he said he would but I think he's forgotten.'

'Mr Slade is a very busy man,' said Tom. 'He can't clear out the shed just when you tell him. You've got to wait. Do you expect him to leave his work and waste his time looking for what's not there?'

'No,' she said, 'of course not. But I think it ought to be done.' (She stopped herself from saying: 'I can't because I'm afraid.')

'Now you go and make yourself a nice cup of tea,' Tom said, speaking in a more friendly voice. 'There's no rat in your shed.' And he went back to his car.

Miss Verney slumped heavily into the kitchen armchair. 'He doesn't believe me. I can't stay alone in this place, not with that monster a few yards away. I can't do it.' But another cold voice persisted: 'Where will you go? With what money? Are you really such a coward as all that?'

After a time Miss Verney got up. She dragged what furniture there was away from the walls so that she would know that nothing lurked in the corners and decided to keep the windows looking onto the shed shut and bolted. The others she opened but only at the top. Then she made a large parcel of all the food that the rat could possibly smell – cheese, bacon, ham, cold meat, practically everything . . . she'd give it to Mrs Randolph, the cleaning woman, later.

'But no more confidences.' Mrs Randolph would be as sceptical as Tom had been. A nice woman but a gossip, she wouldn't be able to resist telling her cronies about the giant, almost certainly imaginary, rat terrorizing her employer.

Next morning Mrs Randolph said that a stray dog had upset the large dustbin. She'd had to pick everything up from the floor of the shed. 'It wasn't a dog' thought Miss Verney, but she only suggested that two stones on the lid turned the other way up would keep the dog off.

When she saw the size of the stones she nearly said aloud: 'I defy any rat to get that lid off.'

Miss Verney had always been a careless, not a fussy, woman. Now all that changed. She spend hours every day sweeping, dusting, arranging the cupboards and putting fresh paper into the drawers. She pounced on every speck of dust with a dustpan. She tried to convince herself that as long as she kept her house spotlessly clean the rat would keep to the shed, not to wonder what she would do if after all, she encountered it.

'I'd collapse,' she thought, 'that's what I'd do.'

After this she'd start with fresh energy, again fearfully sweeping under the bed, behind cupboards. Then feeling too tired to eat, she would beat up an egg in cold milk, add a good deal of whisky and sip it slowly. 'I don't need a lot of food now.' But her work in the house grew slower and slower, her daily walks shorter and shorter. Finally the walks stopped. 'Why should I bother?' As she never answered letters, letters ceased to arrive, and when Tom knocked at the door one day to ask how she was: 'Oh I'm quite all right,' she said and smiled.

He seemed ill at ease and didn't speak about rats or clearing the shed out. Nor did she.

'Not seen you about lately,' he said.

'Oh I go the other way now.'

When she shut the door after him she thought: 'And I imagined I liked him. How very strange.'

'No pain?' the doctor asked.

'It's just an odd feeling,' said Miss Verney.

The doctor said nothing. He waited.

'It's as if all my blood was running backwards. It's rather horrible really. And then for a while sometimes I can't move. I mean if I'm holding a cup I have to drop it because there's no life in my arm.'

'And how long does this last?'

'Not long. Only a few minutes I suppose. It just seems a long time.'

'Does it happen often?'

'Twice lately.'

The doctor thought he'd better examine her. Eventually he left the room and came back with a bottle half full of pills. 'Take these three times a day – don't forget, it's important. Long before they're finished I'll come and see you. I'm going to give you some injections that may help, but I'll have to send away for those.'

As Miss Verney was gathering her things together before leaving the surgery he asked in a casual voice: 'Are you on the telephone?'

'No,' said Miss Verney, 'but I have an arrangement with some people.'

'You told me. But those people are some way off, aren't they?'

'I'll get a telephone,' said Miss Verney making up her mind. 'I'll see about it at once.'

'Good. You won't be so lonely.'

'I suppose not.'

'Don't go moving the furniture about, will you? Don't lift heavy weights. Don't . . .' ('Oh Lord,' she thought, 'is he going to say "Don't drink!" – because that's impossible!') . . . 'Don't worry,' he said.

When Miss Verney left his surgery she felt relieved but tired and she walked very slowly home. It was quite a long walk for she lived in the less prosperous part of the village, near the row of council houses. She had never minded that. She was protected by tall thick hedges and a tree or two. Of course it had taken her some time to get used to the children's loud shrieking and the women who stood outside their doors to gossip. At first they stared at her with curiosity and some disapproval, she couldn't help feeling, but they'd soon found out that she was harmless.

The child Deena, however, was a different matter.

Most of the village boys were called Jack, Willie, Stan and so on – the girls' first names were more elaborate. Deena's mother had gone one better than anyone else and christened her daughter Undine.

Deena – as everyone called her – was a tall plump girl of about twelve with a pretty, healthy but rather bovine face. She never joined the shrieking games, she never played football with dustbin lids. She apparently spent all her spare time standing at the gate of her mother's house silently, unsmilingly, staring at everyone who passed.

Miss Verney had long ago given up trying to be friendly. So much did the child's cynical eyes depress her that she would cross over the road to avoid her, and sometimes was guilty of the cowardice of making sure Deena wasn't there before setting out.

Now she looked anxiously along the street and was relieved that it was empty. 'Of course,' she told herself, 'it's getting cold. When winter comes they'll all stay indoors.'

Not that Deena seemed to mind cold. Only a few days ago, looking out of the window, Miss Verney had seen her standing outside – oblivious of the bitter wind – staring at the front door as though, if she looked hard enough, she could see through the wood and find out what went on in the silent house – what Miss Verney did with herself all day.

One morning soon after her visit to the doctor Miss Verney woke feeling very well and very happy. Also she was not at all certain where she was. She lay luxuriating in the feeling of renewed youth, renewed health and slowly recognized the various pieces of furniture.

'Of course,' she thought when she drew the curtains. 'What a funny place to end up in.'

The sky was pale blue. There was no wind. Watching the still trees she sung softly to herself: 'The day of days.' She had always sung 'The day of days' on her birthday. Poised between two years – last year, next year – she never felt any age at all. Birthdays were a pause, a rest.

In the midst of slow dressing she remembered the rat for the first time. But that seemed something that had happened long ago. 'Thank God I didn't tell anybody else how frightened I was. As soon as they give me a telephone I'll ask Letty Baker to tea. She'll know exactly the sensible thing to do.'

Out of habit she ate, swept and dusted but even more slowly than usual and with long pauses, when leaning on the handle of her tall, old-fashioned, carpet sweeper she stared out at the trees. 'Good-bye summer. Good-bye good-bye,' she hummed. But in spite of sad songs she never lost the certainty of health, of youth.

All at once she noticed, to her surprise, that it was getting dark. 'And I haven't emptied the dustbin.'

She got to the shed carrying the small yellow plastic pail and saw that the big dustbin wasn't there. For once Mrs Randolph must have slipped up and left it outside the gate. Indeed it was so.

She first brought in the lid, easy, then turned the heavy bin onto its side and kicked it along. But this was slow. Growing impatient, she picked it up, carried it into the shed and looked for the stones that had defeated the dog, the rat. They too were missing and she realized that Mrs Randolph, a hefty young woman in a hurry, must have taken out the bin, stones and all. They would be in the road where the dustmen had thrown them. She went to look and there they were.

She picked up the first stone and, astonished at its weight, immediately dropped it. But lifted it again and staggered to the shed, then leaned breathless against the cold wall. After a few minutes she breathed more easily, was less exhausted and the determination to prove to herself that she was quite well again drove her into the road to pick up the second stone.

After a few steps she felt that she had been walking for a long time, for years, weighed down by an impossible weight, and now her strength was gone and she couldn't any more. Still, she reached the shed, dropped the stone and said: 'That's all now, that's the lot. Only the yellow plastic pail to tackle.' She'd fix the stones tomorrow. The yellow pail was light, full of paper, eggshells, stale bread. Miss Verney lifted it . . .

She was sitting on the ground with her back against the dustbin and her legs stretched out, surrounded by torn paper and eggshells. Her skirt had ridden up and there was a slice of stale bread on her bare knee. She felt very cold and it was nearly dark.

'What happened,' she thought, 'did I faint or something? I must go back to the house.'

She tried to get up but it was as if she were glued to the ground. 'Wait,' she thought. 'Don't panic. Breathe deeply. Relax.' But when she tried again she was lead. 'This has happened before. I'll be all right soon,' she told herself. But darkness was coming on very quickly.

Some women passed on the road and she called to them. At first: 'Could you please . . . I'm so sorry to trouble you . . .' but the wind had got up and was blowing against her and no one heard. 'Help!' she called. Still no one heard.

Tightly buttoned up, carrying string bags, heads in head-scarves, they passed and the road was empty.

With her back against the dustbin, shivering with cold, she prayed: 'God, don't leave me here. Dear God, let someone come. Let someone come!'

When she opened her eyes she was not at all surprised to see a figure leaning on her gate.

'Deena! Deena!' she called, trying to keep the hysterical relief out of her voice.

Deena advanced cautiously, stood a few yards off and contemplated Miss Verney lying near the dustbin with an expressionless face.

'Listen Deena,' said Miss Verney. 'I'm afraid I'm not very well. Will you please ask your mother – your mum – to telephone to the doctor. He'll come I think. And if only she could help me back into the house. I'm very cold . . .'

Deena said: 'It's no good my asking mum. She doesn't like you and she doesn't want to have anything to do with you. She hates stuck up people. Everybody knows that you shut yourself up to get drunk. People can hear you falling about. "She ought to take more water with it," my mum says. Sleep it off lady,' said this horrible child, skipping away.

Miss Verney didn't try to call her back or argue. She knew that it was useless. A numb weak feeling slowly took possession of her. Stronger than cold. Stronger than fear. It was a great unwillingness to do anything more at all – it was almost resignation. Even if someone else came, would she call again for help. Could she? Fighting the cold numbness she made a last tremendous effort to move, at any rate to jerk the bread off her knee, for now her fear of the rat, forgotten all day, began to torment her.

It was impossible.

She strained her eyes to see into the corner where it would certainly appear – the corner with the old chair and carpet, the corner with the bundle of hay. Would it attack at once or would it wait until it was sure that she couldn't move? Sooner or later it would come. So Miss Verney waited in the darkness for the Super Rat.

It was the postman who found her. He had a parcel of books for her and he left them as usual in the passage. But he couldn't help noticing that all the lights were on and all the doors open. Miss Verney was certainly not in the cottage.

'I suppose she's gone out. But so early and such a cold morning?'

Uneasy, he looked back at the gate and saw the bundle of clothes near the shed.

He managed to lift her and got her into the kitchen armchair. There was an open bottle of whisky on the table and he tried to force her to drink some, but her teeth were tightly clenched and the whisky spilled all over her face.

He remembered that there was a telephone in the house where he was to deliver next. He must hurry.

In less time than you'd think, considering it was a remote village, the doctor appeared and shortly afterwards the ambulance.

Miss Verney died that evening in the nearest hospital without recovering consciousness. The doctor said she died of shock and cold. He was treating her for a heart condition he said.

'Very widespread now – a heart condition.'

I Used to Live Here Once

S HE WAS STANDING BY the river looking at the
stepping stones and remembering each one. There was the round
unsteady stone, the pointed one, the flat one in the middle – the
safe stone where you could stand and look round. The next wasn't
so safe for when the river was full the water flowed over it and
even when it showed dry it was slippery. But after that it was
easy and soon she was standing on the other side.

The road was much wider than it used to be but the work had
been done carelessly. The felled trees had not been cleared away
and the bushes looked trampled. Yet it was the same road and
she walked along feeling extraordinarily happy.

It was a fine day, a blue day. The only thing was that the sky
had a glassy look that she didn't remember. That was the only
word she could think of. Glassy. She turned the corner, saw that
what had been the old *pavé* had been taken up, and there too the
road was much wider, but it had the same unfinished look.

She came to the worn stone steps that led up to the house
and her heart began to beat. The screw pine was gone, so was
the mock summer house called the *ajoupa*, but the clove tree
was still there and at the top of the steps the rough lawn stretched
away, just as she remembered it. She stopped and looked towards
the house that had been added to and painted white. It was strange
to see a car standing in front of it.

There were two children under the big mango tree, a boy and
a little girl, and she waved to them and called 'Hello' but they
didn't answer her or turn their heads. Very fair children, as Euro-

peans born in the West Indies so often are: as if the white blood is asserting itself against all odds.

The grass was yellow in the hot sunlight as she walked towards them. When she was quite close she called again shyly: 'Hello.' Then, 'I used to live here once,' she said.

Still they didn't answer. When she said for the third time 'Hello' she was quite near them. Her arms went out instinctively with the longing to touch them.

It was the boy who turned. His grey eyes looked straight into hers. His expression didn't change. He said: 'Hasn't it gone cold all of a sudden. D'you notice? Let's go in.' 'Yes let's,' said the girl.

Her arms fell to her sides as she watched them running across the grass to the house. That was the first time she knew.

Kismet

O<small>N TOUR THE PRINCIPALS WERE</small> always given the best dressing-rooms while the chorus had to make do with the least convenient and the coldest. As a rule the long interval was the time for dirty stories, singing parodies of popular songs, jokes about an old black sofa in the London office, known, of course, as the casting couch, and shrieks of laughter.

The dresser hovered ready to fetch drinks, usually Guinness; gin and whisky were reserved for birthdays and great occasions, like the time when we all bet on the winner of the Grand National. One of the girls was a great friend of the man who owned the horse. She gave us the tip. 'My little Lambie says he's a dead certainty and it's been kept very quiet. Now's your chance!'

That week the theatre in a North of England town was brand new and we had a warm room with plenty of space. During the interval we could sit round a good fire, something we certainly were not used to, and nearly everyone was busy sewing when a girl called Gaby said: 'Have you heard about China Gordon? She's dead – and you owe me a bob, Billie.'

'Why?' Billie said. 'What for?' Billie was the girl I was sharing rooms with that week.

'Because you bet me a bob that that pink on her cheeks was make-up. Bloom of Roses you said, and I bet that it was natural. She died of consumption and all consumptive people have those round pink spots on their cheekbones. It seems that she got worse suddenly and some man sent her to a sanatorium in Switzerland.

Very expensive. But she died all the same.' Billie handed over the shilling.

'You seem to know all about it.'

'Yes, I heard this morning. I'm not saying China wasn't pretty because she was, but a bit like one of those living on the halls, don't you think? And most men didn't like her so what was the use?'

China was the youngest of the three Gordon sisters. They had been in the chorus with us and all were pretty. But China was a really lovely girl. One of her greatest beauties was her skin, at once transparent and velvety. Someone had called her Dresden China and soon she was always known as China.

The Gordons were often asked by admirers to supper after the show and the other girls were very jealous of them, especially of silent China. So there was great glee when Mollie, the eldest, reading one of her invitations, began to laugh: 'Listen to this man. "P.S. But for God's sake don't bring China!" '

After one tour they had been snatched up by George Edwardes, who was said to have scouts all over the country, on the watch for girls for the Gaiety chorus.

'China was really very stupid,' Gaby said.

'That's enough about her,' Billie said. 'She's dead, poor girl.'

'Why poor girl? Damn lucky girl, if you ask me.' This was Yetta.

Yetta was tall and thin. She always wore a broad black velvet ribbon round her throat and a beauty patch. She must have been very attractive long ago but now she was well over thirty, well over forty, nobody knew. She was the one who drank whisky instead of Guinness, who lived alone and had very little to do with anyone else. She'd been the mistress of a well-known actor-manager and played in the West End – bit parts in straight plays. Everyone understood that after all that, being in the chorus of a touring company must be quite a change. Though aloof, she wasn't unpopular. Even Royce, our stage manager, treated her with a certain amount of respect.

No one had ever seen her anything else but dignified and self-possessed but tonight she hadn't stopped at one whisky; she'd been drinking steadily and, if she was celebrating, she hadn't told us why. 'Yetta, don't drink any more or you won't be able to go down for the finale,' somebody said.

'So I won't be there for the finale, so I won't be there. And who cares? I don't.'

Sure enough, when the callboy shouted and we all got ready to troop down to the stage, she didn't budge. She was crying when we came back, with her head in her arms. Most of the girls, after one embarrassed glance, took no notice of her but Gaby said in a loud whisper: 'Seems we've got one of those ruins that Cromwell knocked about with us. How does she think she's going to get home after all that whisky?'

'Oh, for God's sake, Gaby, shut up!' Billie said. 'We'll take her home.'

'Why don't you shut up yourself, Billie Carly? Always telling people what they must say and what they mustn't say.'

'I could blow you out of the window if I said what I thought about you,' Billie said.

But the quarrel simmered down for everybody wanted to get home and soon they all drifted out and we were left alone with Yetta.

'Come on, ducks,' said Billie. 'Take your make-up off. Here's your dress.'

Yetta sat up. 'If I told you that I used to be one of the prettiest girls on the London stage, you wouldn't believe me, would you?'

'Of course I'd believe you. Thousands wouldn't'

'I don't care if you don't,' Yetta said. 'You can't change what's happened just because you don't believe it. Let me tell you that none of you will be seeing much more of me when this bloody tour is over and it's nobody's business what I do instead.'

'Yetta, we haven't all night to chat,' Billie said.

Between us we got her dressed and down three flights of stone stairs. When she leant heavily on us Billie would say: 'Gawd Norry, what a weight!' But once in the street she shook us off. 'Thanks, but I can manage. Leave me alone is all I ask.' She walked away unsteadily.

We had a key to the house where we lived. It was in darkness, like all the other houses in the street, but the little sitting-room was warm, there was a blue pinpoint of gaslight, two glasses of milk, plates on the table and a covered dish by the fire.

'Lucky I'm not hungry,' said Billie, when she lifted the cover. 'Are you?'

'No.'

It was late but we weren't sleepy either and as the bedroom would be icy we sat sipping milk and talking in low voices so as not to wake the landlady. She wasn't a bad old thing though it was always tepid boiled onions for supper.

Billie said: 'Yetta's silly to drink at her age but she's quite right. I'm not coming back next tour if I can help it. I'm stopping in London. Besides, my husband wants me to have a baby.'

'Oh Billie, are you married, you never told me, do you like him, is he nice?'

'He'd pass in a crowd with a shove,' Billie said. 'But he's not the real reason, it's that I don't get paid enough for the work I do. After all I understudy two of the principals. If they think they can go on being stingy for much longer, they're wrong, I'm off.'

'Well, Billie, you could easily get something else. You look lovely from the front, and your voice is pretty good. I heard Royce say that you were a first-rate dancer. He isn't a man to fling compliments about, is he?'

'But don't you see, that's exactly why they'll try to keep me as a blasted understudy all my life? They know that I could go on any night and not let the show down. I'm useful to them. But when I get like poor old Yetta they'll give me the push pretty damn quick.'

'Why don't you try another management if you don't get on with this one?'

'Because I've signed a contract. I can't walk out without any excuse. If they got annoyed, I mightn't find it very easy to get work, all these people are pals, you know.'

'Billie, they wouldn't do that!'

'Wouldn't they if they felt like it? Oh Norry, you are a sloppy girl, it's pitiful really. *But,*' she said, 'I could have a perfectly good excuse and they couldn't do anything about it. By the time it was all over they'd have forgotten about me.'

'When what was all over?'

'The baby, of course.'

'Billie, don't tell me that you're going to have a baby?'

'Of course not, that's not what I mean, but what's to stop me writing from London, saying I'm going to have a baby? What could they do?' She stared into the fire. 'Remember that fortune teller who got into the dressing-room at Blackburn?'

'Yes I remember. She looked at my hand for a long time and told me that there was going to be a big change in my life.'

'That doesn't mean a thing. They say that when they can't think up anything else. But with me she was serious. She said I'd have two children, a boy and a girl.'

'But Billie, it's not the fortune teller, I've been feeling it all this tour, something *is* going to happen that will change my life. I know it, it's Kismet.'

'Kismet's only a word for good luck or bad luck.'

'No it isn't. It means that you haven't much to do with what happens or what becomes of you. Not really. If it's meant, it'll happen.'

'I never heard such nonsense. People have a hell of a lot to do with what happens to them.'

'They *think* they have. That's the idea.'

'Sounds like one of these fancy religions,' Billie said. 'If I were you I'd keep clear of fancy religions. They're all the same. When they're trying to get hold of you they only tell you the half. When you find out the other half, as of course you do, you wish you had never got mixed up. You don't believe all this, do you?'

'I didn't say I believed in it but sometimes I wonder. I'm sure that what happens to me won't be anything I've planned or even want, but it will happen.'

'Well don't go on about it!' Billie said. Whatever happens to you it will all be the same in a hundred years.'

After the tour I didn't see Billie for over a year. I'd left the company, was living in London, and I hardly thought of her, but she'd given me an address somewhere near Belsize Park, and one day when I was up in that direction I went to see if she was there.

She came to the door when I knocked. Fatter and with a set look about her face and figure that I didn't remember. 'Hello, Norry, where've you sprung from? Come in, what a surprise!'

We went into a sitting-room rather like the ones on tour. From the next room I could hear a baby crying.

'Sit down, I won't be a minute. I've got to see His Majesty.'

There were two candlesticks on the mantelpiece. I was thinking how much I liked them when she called: 'Come and have a look at him now.'

He was an ordinary baby, just like other babies. I said: 'Aren't they sweet when the laugh and gurgle and wave their arms about,' and couldn't think of anything else. She was telling me how marvelous he was when he went to sleep suddenly, but back in the sitting-room she went on about him, how sweet he smelt when he'd just had a bath. 'Then they look at you and clutch at you and your heart turns over.'

'I do like your candlesticks,' I said, to change the subject.

'Yes, Fred made those, he's very clever like that.'

'They're beautiful,' I said. 'I suppose when the baby's older you'll go back to the stage? That's what you planned, isn't it?'

'Oh, I don't know, I haven't time to think about all that now. The fortune teller told me a boy and a girl, didn't she? I wouldn't mind having a little girl. I'd rather like to have a little girl.'

'You seem to be all fixed up,' I said.

'It's all very well but let me tell you there's one thing a baby can do. You stop wondering why you're alive at all. You know how sometimes you get depressed and think what the hell's it all about and why, and so on? With a baby you stop thinking like that. At least I've stopped.'

'Other things can do that, not only babies.'

'Yes, but it's not the same thing, not the same thing at all. Because you're never quite sure. Fred's away a lot and I simply *hate* being alone but a baby's there for quite a long time.'

When she said that I began to think about being alone. Sometimes I wonder whether anybody in the world is as alone as I am now, not even hearing another voice except the landlady's. 'Rain again,' or, 'Perhaps we might have a bit of sun today.'

Unhappy? I've never been so happy in my life. But a day can be long when you're waiting for the night and a week can be for ever. I'm not exactly frightened. There's no reason. None. More of a hollow feeling. Perhaps if I talked about it, even a little, it would be a good thing.

But just as I was thinking this Billie began to yawn. She yawned and yawned and didn't seem able to stop. 'Well, I'm sorry, Norry, but I don't get much sleep, you know. I'll make some tea.'

While we were drinking the tea I stopped wanting to tell her anything. Billie, of all people. For a soppy idea that's a soppy idea if ever there was one.

Soon I said: 'Well, I must be going. Lovely to see you, we must meet some time,' knowing, as I said it, that I didn't want ever to see her again.

Walking down Haverstock Hill I thought how changed she was. Then I forgot all about her as I began wondering, as usual, if there'd be a telegram or letter waiting for me. 'My darling kitten,' the letter would start. 'My darling kitten.' Perhaps I'd see him tonight. Perhaps tomorrow. I began to plan what dress I'd wear for I had plenty to choose from now.

The Whistling Bird

I FIRST SAW LILIANE, my cousin, at one of the few
old estate houses left in Dominica – a baby a few weeks old. She
was dark, small, and silent, except that every now and again she
would wail, a thin, strange cry, as if she were protesting being
born. I was told that she was very delicate and not expected to
live, and I remember my grandmother saying something about
the sins of the fathers being visited on the children. My grandmother was full of these threatening Biblical quotations, though
I don't think that she was at all a religious woman. Soon after
this I left the island for England and school.

I met Liliane again in a St Lucia hotel during my first visit to
the West Indies for many years. She was then in her twenties –
a tall, energetic girl in spite of my grandmother's prophecies. I
had lost touch with many of my West Indian relatives, and I heard
for the first time of her family's changed circumstances. Her
father had died suddenly, leaving very little money, and his widow
and three children were obliged to give up the estate. The son,
who was called Don, joined very composedly in talk about their
future plans. Then one day he got up from the table at the end of
a meal, went into the bedroom, and shot himself. There were
various explanations of this. When in England, he'd been anxious to join the Navy. Perhaps he had failed an exam and was
unable to forget it. Perhaps he suddenly saw what his future life
would be and couldn't face it. Anyway, that was the end of Don.
He was eighteen. His mother, whom I remembered so well as
pretty Evelina, went back to St Lucia, the island where she was

born, with her two daughters. There she met an English woman who, planning to start a hotel outside Castries, befriended, or perhaps made use of, the entire family. Intelligent Liliane was the cashier, pretty Monica the receptionist, Evelina the manageress, who dealt with the staff and the food, for she knew a lot about real French Creole cooking, which can be delicious.

We stayed several weeks at this hotel, and I found it very attractive. I was happy there. One afternoon when I asked for tea, the tray was brought up to my room by a woman dressed in the old fashion, in what used to be called the *grande robe* – a long, gaily colored high-waisted dress, a turban, and heavy gold earrings. It was the past majestically walking in.

I did not see very much of Liliane. It was Monica who told me about her long, lonely walks at night – she often didn't come back till dawn, though she was at work early – and that she edited a magazine, writing all the stories, calling herself by different names: 'Lady Amelia', 'Onlooker', and so on. But there was usually a short poem, which she signed with her initials, L. L. I remember one about English Harbour in Antigua, once Nelson's headquarters but then in ruins, not yet dolled up for tourists, and supposed to be haunted by a Lieutenant Peterson: a long romance about Lieutenant Peterson, wicked Lord Camelford, Captain Best, and a masked ball, belonging more to the old West Indies than to the West Indies as it is now. I was back in London when I had a letter from Liliane, telling me of Monica's death: the old story – a young Englishman to whom she was engaged had left the island without explanation. When it became obvious that he wasn't going to write or return, she went to bed and was dead in a couple of weeks. For Evelina this was one misfortune too many, and she gave up and died soon afterward. Liliane, the survivor, wrote that she was coming to London, and it was there that I met her and got to know more of her.

She was a strange girl, shying away from any attempt to help her, insisting that what she did was her own business and no one else's. I have never known anyone who kept her contacts with other people so formal. She never said 'I'll come tomorrow after-noon' but 'I'll be with you tomorrow at a quarter to four and I'll leave at half past five.' So it would be. She had found a job, she told me, and something about her voice made me sure it wasn't a well-paid job, or one she liked or wished to talk about.

She lived in a small bed-sitting-room beyond Hampstead. In one corner was a silver tea service brought from the West Indies. Also to my surprise, she had the portrait of Old Lockhart, her great-grandfather and mine, who had arrived in the West Indies at the end of the eighteenth century. He stared as blankly as ever. It was impossible to know whether he was a bad man or a good man lied about, or someone who just did what everyone else did without thinking too much about it. The Spanish great-grandmother, whom I'd always been so curious about, wasn't there. Liliane didn't talk much about her past or the West Indies but did talk a good deal about her love for England, London, and the Royal Family. Someone once said of her, 'I can't keep my face straight when I'm talking to that old Rip Van Winkle.'

'Be patient with her – she's an anachronism,' I said.

'But such a damn bore.'

Underneath all this she could be gay and full of life, and almost crazily generous with the little money she had. After I went to live in the country, she would say that she was the Lon-doner now, I a visitor and her guest. She as hostess must pay for all our outings. It needed a lot of arguing to convince her that that wasn't how I saw it at all. One day she told me that she had sold one of her poems. 'Dorinda isn't mine anymore' is how she put it. 'I've sold Dorinda.' So she still writes poetry, I thought. She gave me a copy of the poem.

> My name is Dorinda and I live so gay
> In a little hut with flowers on a shilling a day.
> The white man made me but he cannot tell
> The secret of my laughter like a golden bell.
>
> My name is Dorinda and I live so gay
> In a little hut with flowers on a shilling a day.

The black man made me but he'll never know
The secret of my dark heart which he made so.

As we got to know each other better, she showed me other poems. I often wondered when she wrote them. After she came back tired from the office to her little bed-sitting-room? Or on Sundays – did she walk about Hampstead Heath to the tune of 'Trinidad Selina'?

Watch her walkin' and stop your talkin'
See her dancin' – she dances on air.

I was certain that some of her songs were salable, and I knew how badly she needed the money, but I didn't know how to set about selling them. Even if by some miracle someone liked the words, wouldn't they be set to the wrong music and spoiled? Also, Liliane wasn't encouraging. She seemed not to have the slightest wish to make money out of poems – even to be somewhat hostile to the idea. It was as if she meant to keep them to herself, to protect them, and I understood this far too well to argue with her.

I didn't go to London for some time after that. Then I heard from a friend that she wasn't at all well. I'd noticed it the last time I'd seen her. All the spring and pride had gone out of her walk – she had walked beautifully when she first came to London – and she rarely smiled, which was a pity, because her white, even teeth were her greatest beauty.

The last time I saw her, she showed me a poem. 'This is different,' she said. Unlike the others, it was a sad song, about a man who kills his sweetheart, hides her body in the Dominica forest, and escapes to England before she is missed. But he cannot forget her.

Devil made me lash her down, devil made me kill.
Sorrow made me leave her
Now she's dark in Dominica
And I'm lonely in the snow. . . .

*I wish I were beside her, where the mountains hide
  her.*
For the whistling bird is calling me.

She said, 'The whistling bird – you remember. The mountain
whistler?'

'Of course.'

'My mother called it the *siffleur de montagne, le solitaire.* I
expect there aren't any left now.'

'Perhaps a few.'

'What about the parrots? Long ago the forest was full of parrots, green and grey. There isn't one now.'

'Parrots,' I said, 'are different. There's money in parrots. Who'd
buy a mountain whistler? If it were caught, it would probably
die.'

'Not at once' said Liliane.

After thinking a lot about her, I wrote and begged her to take
a holiday, enclosing some money to help. She wrote back coldly,
returning the money and adding that I must know that she didn't
want to leave London and didn't need a holiday. I decided that
when I saw her next I would argue her into taking one all the
same. Then I heard that one morning she'd got up, had her usual
obligatory tepid bath, and was dressing to go to her horrible job,
when she fell. The landlady heard the noise and rushed to her
bedroom. She was dead.

After all, I saw comparatively little of Liliane. She may have
had other friends, another life that I didn't know about. But I
never caught a glimpse of it.

'Woe to the vanquished', they say. Need it be so much woe
and last such a long time? Anyhow, not Don, not Monica, not
Evelina, not Liliane will join in that complicated argument. For
it is complicated, whatever the know-alls say.

Invitation to the Dance

HERE WEREN'T very many white families in Roseau but nearly all had their fair share of children, some as many as twelve. So, every fine afternoon a certain number of little girls and boys would be taken to the Botanical Gardens to play. I was one of them but, unlike the others, I was alone. Both my brothers and my elder sister had left the island. My younger sister was still a baby.

The nurses would sit on a bench and chatter. We would play, at first nearby, gradually getting farther and farther away until we were out of sight. The game I liked best was Looby Looby Li. I thought it better than Tug of War or any of the 'I-pick-you, I-pick-you' games which always ended in a quarrel, much more exciting than Kiss once, kiss twice, all fall down, which grew monotonous and didn't seem to lead anywhere.

Looby Li was a very energetic game, not to be played on hot afternoons. First, joining hands, we danced round in a ring, singing:

> *Will you dance Looby Looby Li*
> *Will you dance Looby Looby Li*
> *Will you dance Looby Looby Li*
> *As you did last night?*

Then we sang the verses. For Looby Li was about the game of love and chance. Each verse described some variation of the game and after each we'd try to act out the enigmatic, scarcely understood words we'd sung. Then we'd join hands again for the chorus:

'Will you dance Looby Looby Li, etc. . . . *As* you did last night?'

I for one pranced about in all innocence. So, I think, did most of the others, and I was very surprised when one day my mother asked me: 'Do you ever play a game called Looby Li?' I said yes, we did, and that it was a good game and that I liked it.

She asked: 'Who started it? Who taught you the words?' I answered truthfully that I didn't remember, I didn't know; but immediately added: 'Perhaps it was Willie.'

She said: 'Willie? Well, I'm surprised at Willie, I'm astonished at Willie. Where did he pick it up?' But I was miserably wondering why I had told such a lie. For it wasn't Willie and I liked him the best. I didn't want to get him into any sort of trouble. Why had I said it was Willie when it wasn't Willie? I don't remember the rest of the conversation but it ended by her saying that whoever had started it, I must never play it again. Never. It was the reverse of a good game. It was a wicked game and I must forget all about it. 'Now promise me,' she said, then went off forgetting apparently that I hadn't promised anything at all.

Very soon after this, it may have been the next day, when afternoon came at the Botanical Gardens, some suggested playing Looby Looby Li. But the older girls and boys gathered in a group whispering and giggling. Finally one of them announced that he was sick of Looby Li, that it was a silly game, a baby's game, a lot of rubbish. 'Let's play something else. Let's play Tug of War.' But in spite of all this camouflage, everyone soon knew what had happened. Some man or some woman – impossible to know – had watched us playing, then gone away to report that we played disgusting games, sang disgusting songs, that the nurses were lazy brutes, sprawled on the benches gossiping, and didn't care what we did or even know where we went. Most of the children had been spoken to and the older ones decided that Looby Li wasn't worth the trouble and we wouldn't play it any more.

But even when I grew older I remembered and thought about it. Was it a negro song? Was it a negro version of a French song? I didn't think so. At the time I'm writing of, West Indian music had far more of a Spanish rhythm than it has now. But Spanish,

American, or African, it was always sad. Looby Li was a quick dancing tune, full of gaiety and light-heartedness. I know it wasn't any sort of a negro sound. Later, when I was fascinated by novels of the Middle Ages, I decided that it was an English song of very long ago, before Cromwell and the Puritans, before Henry VIII and the Reformation. Sung in the remote country, it had trickled down the centuries, trickled out to the West Indies, there at last to die, or to be changed out of all knowledge like so many other things. Try as I may I can't remember who taught us the words and the music or why I said 'Willie' when it wasn't Willie.

INTERFACIAL SUPRAMOLECULAR ASSEMBLIES